London HOLIDAY

A Pride and Prejudice Romantic Comedy

Nicole Clarkston

ISBN-13: 978-1717521095
ISBN-10: 1717521096

DEDICATION

To my best friend, my love, my partner in crime;
the one who keeps me grounded and gives me wings.

CONTENTS

ACKNOWLEDGEMENTS

This has been, in all probability, the most fun I have ever had writing a book. *London Holiday* is an idea that was buzzing around for almost two years, but I never allowed myself to touch it, nor even talk much about it. I very firmly told myself that it would have to wait a touch longer, at least until *Nowhere But North* was in the final editing stages, but it absolutely refused. After writing *These Dreams* and some of the scenes from *Nowhere But North*, my muse needed therapy, and this was it.

My dear friends, Janet Taylor and Joy King have been my sounding board from the very beginning. I owe a great deal to them both for egging me on—to Janet, for her creative imagery and inspiration, and to Joy for waking me up before dawn to get back to work. On so many occasions, Joy helped me to think through plot issues and find new ways to embarrass our dear Darcy.

Janet, once again, has outdone herself on the cover. She never fails to astound me with her gifts, but this time, the cover is very personal. Her grandson Chayseland Taylor and Chayseland's friend Kennedy Smith are featured as our beloved couple, and they look absolutely perfect!

I must also thank Don Jacobsen. Recovering from surgery, Don read most of this book while lying flat on his back and holding his laptop above his head! His word suggestions were invaluable, particularly for that tricky first chapter of any book. He saved me from some period inaccuracies and several cases of the dreaded "writer's blindness."

Rita Deodato chimed in with some very helpful plot feedback, clarifying certain issues. I am always thrilled by her thoughts and suggestions.

Debbie Fortin was battling a 101-degree fever and a lost voice when she was proofing this book, but she soldiered on! I am sincerely indebted to her for her sharp eye and good catches.

Lastly, I must thank Betty Madden for giving the book a final sweep before publication. She took me back to punctuation school, and I am grateful on your behalf for her exacting precision.

-*NC*

One

F itzwilliam Darcy crossed his arms and stared. "I will not marry Anne, Aunt Catherine. It is a matter of prudence—I will require an heir, and Anne is not healthy enough to bear one. Considering her frail constitution, it appears unwise to continue the family history of wedding cousins to one another."

Lady Catherine whirled from the fire. "Fitzwilliam Darcy, I mean to see that you do your duty. Do you not recall that this was your mother's favourite wish? Have you forgotten that even your lamented father sanctioned the match, and the earl also speaks in support of it? Have you so little respect for your mother's family that you would reject the unified voices of all? The announcement shall print on the morrow, and you are an engaged man whether you like it or no."

"I shall have it repudiated!" Darcy objected. "You will not force my hand, Aunt Catherine. I will not have Anne, and that is the end of it."

"If you do not marry her, she will be ruined! Everyone has been expecting the engagement for two years now."

"That is because you have been broadcasting it as a fact. I have never viewed my cousin as a potential wife. I do not wish to see her ruined, but that would be your own doing, not mine."

"Fitzwilliam Darcy, I am ashamed of you! You would deny the claims of duty and your family?"

"My duty to my family requires that I produce a healthy heir. It would be better if my wife did not expire in the process."

"Anne is perfectly strong and quite capable of bearing a child."

"Anne would break if I were to touch her with more than a cousinly embrace. The marriage bed itself might be the death of her."

"Fitzwilliam Darcy! That you should speak to an old woman with such callous indecency!"

"If it is what is needed to persuade you that Anne is not a suitable match for me, I would take up the speech of a sailor. I will not marry Anne, and that is my final word on the matter." Darcy enforced this remark with a firm jerk of his head and turned to go. "I expect you and Anne will be returning to Kent on the morrow?"

Lady Catherine's mouth clamped in rage. "I shall leave London only when I have received assurance that you will fulfil your obligations to Anne!"

"That, I shall never do, for no such obligation exists. You must make yourself comfortable for an extended stay, I am afraid."

Lady Catherine stamped her cane on the ground in a fury. "Very well! Then I shall know how to act."

Darcy stifled a sigh and retired to his chambers where his valet, Wilson, appeared to help him out of his coat and cravat.

"Did you wish for a nightcap, sir?" sagely enquired his long-time body man.

It was not Darcy's way to drink himself into his bed, but his mind was still roiling with anger at his relation. Perhaps a drink would help soothe him to slumber. "Yes, thank you, Wilson. A brandy, if you please. And would you be so good to have a book sent up from the library?"

"Do you have a preference, sir?"

"No. Anything will do—your choice. The duller, the better."

"Very good, sir." Wilson gathered his master's clothing and disappeared to procure the requested items.

Darcy sank wearily into the chair at his writing desk and frowned out of the darkened window. The surest solution to this predicament with his aunt and cousin was to find another wife. A *suitable* wife. The only trouble was that every eligible lady he had encountered was either as offensive as his aunt or as insipid as his cousin. There was not one with whom he would wish to share his house, to say nothing of his bed, for the remainder of his days. He was yet unwilling to condemn himself to such a sentence, and with Georgiana's recent heartbreak at Ramsgate, he had enough domestic trials without adding *another* woman to his house.

In short order, Wilson had returned with a hefty treatise on different varieties of wheat and agricultural planting seasons. Apparently, he had taken his master at his word and found a book guaranteed to render him comatose, from either reading it or being struck over the head by it. He also presented a tray with a snifter of brandy, generously measured even for a man of the master's height. "Is there anything else I can do for you, sir?"

"No, thank you, Wilson. You may retire, and I shall speak with you in the morning."

"Very good, sir." Wilson bowed and retreated.

Darcy stretched in his chair and reached for his drink, sighing in at least partial satisfaction. Not many valets would be content to perform the tasks of a common footman. He was a good man, Wilson was. All his people were—at least the ones he knew. There were too many to know them all well, and therein lay part of his troubles this night. If only he could go about with fewer hangers-on, fewer who depended upon their connection to him, and fewer who took an interest in his affairs. Occasionally, he even wished to remove to the hunting lodge at Pemberley, with only Georgiana and perhaps Richard for company. He would dress himself, cook as his tenants did, and carry on with a simple existence, leaving the greater part of his worries here in London.

That was all twaddle, and he chided himself harshly whenever the irresponsible fancies came to him. He was *the* Darcy, presently the last male of a proud line, and there was a certain honour in carrying that torch on behalf of his forefathers. There were times, however, when he confessed even to himself that the trappings of his station were not all pleasant. This business about marriage was but one of any number of restrictions clouding his path.

Marriage. To Anne! His aunt must be daft if she thought he would yield. It would be a miserable time of it in his house until she gave in and returned to Kent, and he calculated that he was set for at least a month this time. Darcy held up the rich, dark brandy to the firelight, wishing it would wash away all his troubles. That being a futile hope, he lifted it and drained the entire contents at once.

Ten minutes later, he was in his bed, still half-dressed and reading his exceedingly dull book. The brandy must have been of a remarkably potent vintage, or the book even less interesting than he had persuaded himself to believe, for within a very few minutes his eyelids were already beginning to feel rather heavy. They startled open, however, at a commotion at the door. There was a frenzied knock, and he bade entry more out of curiosity than a desire to see anyone.

Wilson stumbled into his room, his expression wild with alarm. "Sir! You have not already taken your drink?"

Darcy cast his glance to the empty glass on his writing desk. "Was I meant to admire it from afar?"

"Sir, I have good reason to believe it has been tampered with."

"Tampered with? Who would do such a thing in my own house?"

"Lady Catherine, sir!"

"Wilson," Darcy tossed his book aside and peered cautiously at his loyal manservant—a man he had been accustomed to think of as rational. "Do you mean to suggest that my aunt would break into my cellars, pull the stoppers, and somehow adulterate the drink?"

"Sir, it was one of the footmen, on Lady Catherine's orders. I overheard a few of the maids talking, and it sounded as if Lady Catherine had intended for you to take your drink and fall so soundly asleep that she could bring Miss de Bourgh into your bed later so that they might force a marriage."

"What? Even my aunt could not suggest something so ludicrous. Have you been drinking yourself, Wilson?"

"Well… sir, the same footman invited me back behind the kitchens, as he had a little left of his evening drink and wished for a companion. I thought nothing of it, as the same chap has occasionally offered me a drink on previous visits to Town. He was off his duty, sir, and I thought there would be no harm."

"Wilson," Darcy heaved patiently, "please come to the point. I am rather fatigued, but I believe I heard you make unfounded accusations against my relative. As I know that could not be the case, I would prefer that you cleared up the matter."

"Sir, it was after the drink with the footman when I overheard Lady Catherine's maid making the arrangements. Clearly, I was not meant to hear that, sir, but several others were enlisted to help her. It was no secret."

"Do you mean my own staff would conspire against me? Wilson, that is quite impossible. Every member of this household has been with the family for at least a generation."

"Sir," Wilson suggested uncomfortably, "they were with Mr George Darcy, who was sympathetic to Lady Catherine's cause, and some of them were even recommended for their positions by Lady Catherine herself. I have it on good authority that a number of them are quite on her side of matters. I also fear that those individuals she found beneficial to her purposes may have thought it no harm to take some additional pay from Lady Catherine. I am sorry, sir, but I am quite uncertain who may be trusted. I have a strong suspicion about that drink you took, sir, as it was given into my hand by the same footman who poured my own drink. Are you feeling well, sir?"

"As a matter of fact," Darcy rubbed his jaw, "I am feeling rather unnaturally drowsy."

"Then it is as I feared, sir! I believe we have both been drugged. I expect within an hour, we shall be beyond consciousness."

"Wilson, that is a rather malicious accusation. Can you be certain of any of this?"

"Sir, I have seen evidence with my own eyes. Lady Catherine always brings several of her own staff, and you brought only myself and a pair of stable lads from Pemberley. I fear there is more to this than mere suspicion, sir. We must think how to act for your protection."

"Protection from my own household! You must have imbibed too much, Wilson."

"Sir," the strain of fear began to bead as sweat upon the valet's brow, "I heard it myself. A maid was sent to tell Miss de Bourgh that all was in readiness and waited only upon you to retire!"

Darcy stared in astonishment. "Is there no reason or sense left among my staff? How many of the household have been disloyal?"

"I have no way of knowing that, sir, and I would not unjustly accuse the innocent. I only know that many of the downstairs staff have likely thrown in their lot with Lady Catherine, seeing as that's the way the wind is blowing—begging your pardon, sir, but that is what is said below stairs. She makes promises, sir, and I have heard of it myself."

"Such as? What could she possibly say that could make my own household risk being turned out with no character? And why would any wish to betray me for my aunt's good favour? Have I not always been a generous master?"

"Yes sir, it is only that they wish to be found amenable in the eyes of the future mistress as well. It is accounted as inevitable that you shall marry Miss de Bourgh, who will then spend more of her time here than yourself. Lady Catherine has done a substantial bit to enforce that opinion. She always leaves generous gratuities where they are not required, and she speaks with great sentiment of your father. Many of the older staff and those of the younger set who prefer an extra drink now and then are much disposed in her favour. I have no reason to believe it is like that at Pemberley, sir, but you are here less often. Perhaps your character when in Town is…."

"Is what?" demanded Darcy.

"Well, sir, though I must beg your pardon…"

"Speak frankly, Wilson. You are quite safe," assured Darcy wearily.

Wilson drew a breath and nodded. "It is only that you are thought to be less approachable here in Town than you are at Pemberley. I quite understand, sir, for when you are here you have business to be about and social functions which weigh more upon your time. Few are privileged with a more personal acquaintance with you, such as am I. Unfortunately, sir, the effect has been that few know you well enough to disbelieve Lady Catherine's assertions. I believe it is commonly thought that Miss de Bourgh and Lady Catherine would do the house good, and that matters only want a little assistance to move forward."

"My aunt has corrupted my household!" Darcy breathed, his mind reeling and numb. "I would not have thought it possible! What is to be done? I will not permit my aunt to force my hand into marriage."

"Sir, I could lock your door, but the housekeeper and the butler both have the key. I do not know if they are to be trusted, but the butler is the one who unlocked the brandy cabinet."

"What drug was used? How incapacitated shall we be?"

"I do not know, sir, only that I heard talk of one hour, and that was considering a man of your height."

"That is little time," mused Darcy. "Are you certain there is no one else in the house we can trust?"

"There probably is, sir, but I do not know who they are. I fear that we may not be conscious long enough to stage an inquisition."

"Then I must go elsewhere, for it is not safe here until I am no longer incapacitated," decided Darcy. "I believe Colonel Fitzwilliam is in Town, and his apartment is not far."

"Very good, sir, I shall summon the carriage."

"No, no carriage. If I am to escape my household in the dead of night, I must do it discreetly. Fitzwilliam's apartment is easily within walking distance, and my aunt will be none the wiser until I am beyond reach."

"But, sir!" protested Wilson. "You cannot walk that distance safely. What if you were to fall unconscious? What if the drug overpowers you?"

"The cool air will help me to remain alert some while longer. You said I had an hour. It will take me only a quarter of that to walk the distance."

"And it has already been more than that, sir."

"Then I had better make haste." Darcy rose from his bed, feeling a slight wave of dizziness shake him. Whatever he did, he must do it quickly!

"Sir, with all due respect, a man of your station walking out at night is rather vulnerable. Had you not better take a carriage? At least take a footman with you, sir."

"You have said yourself that we do not know whom to trust."

"Then I shall attend you, sir," Wilson declared.

"No, I will ask you to remain here and be my eyes and ears. You can be of far greater use to me if you feign ignorance and convey to me how the matter lies tomorrow. I would know who has been honest, and who must be turned out. I expect we will both experience raging headaches upon awakening and must seek some chance to gather our wits."

"And what of you, sir? Would it not be difficult to explain your disappearance?"

"I declined the drink you brought me and went out without apprising my aunt," suggested Darcy. "Of course, as my valet, you would naturally know of my destination, but the entire household need not be alerted. I do not normally rouse everyone when I wish to go out late."

"You do not normally attend your club in the evenings at all, sir."

"My aunt would not know that. You can tell them that I had a note from an old friend who was in Town and wished to see me. That much is not untrue, for I have had such a note, but I declined the request earlier this evening. Still, it will give her pause enough, if she understands that others will know of my whereabouts and can provide an alibi if need be. Meanwhile, I shall be recovering my faculties at Colonel Fitzwilliam's apartment."

"Sir, I must protest. It is not safe for you to walk out alone. You would be a target for footpads!"

"As myself, perhaps, but dressed as a manservant, I would not. Quickly, find me a set of clothes. Is there not a footman about my height? It will be well, Wilson. The sooner I am dressed and safely away from here, the less chance my aunt has of succeeding in her scheme."

Two

"Oh, Lizzy, was this not simply a divine evening?" Kitty Bennet, aged sixteen, leaned back against the seat of the carriage and gushed her delight. "The music, the lights—I have never seen so many candles. And that soprano! Would Mama not simply swoon over her gown?"

"It was all stunning," her older sister Elizabeth agreed. "The new Pantheon Theatre is not so lovely as the old, they say, but it is quite beautiful enough to suit my fancies. Aunt Gardiner," she turned sincerely to that lady, "thank you so much for bringing us. Your generosity to us takes my breath away."

"You are most graciously welcome, Lizzy. I confess, I had been longing to see the new hall myself, and you provided just the excuse I sought."

"It is a pity that our uncle could not come this evening, for he would have enjoyed it greatly, I think."

"Yes, he would have," Mrs Gardiner agreed, "but I expect he will have accomplished a great deal of business this evening, and he will now be able to enjoy the park with us tomorrow. I believe your uncle really prefers the park to the opera."

"As does Lizzy," snorted Kitty. "But even you must admit, Lizzy, that was an evening to remember. What a pleasure it was to meet that lovely Mrs Jennings—she liked you very much, Lizzy, and that is something grand, I think. Did you see the gowns on some of the ladies above us in the private boxes? And each of the gentlemen looked so fine and handsome! There was that one fair-haired fellow who looked our way twice, and I am sure he liked me. Oh, Lizzy, you needn't scoff at all the gentlemen! Do not forget, Mama has given you specific instructions to catch a husband while you are in Town, or you shall be stuck with that odious Mr Collins."

"If only the catching of a husband were as simple as catching a fish, perhaps I should succeed."

"Lizzy, you must not speak of such things in Town. What would Mama say? No one here knows that you are not a proper lady, so it is best to let them believe otherwise as long as they may."

"Now, Kitty," Mrs Gardiner chided, "Lizzy is perfectly ladylike, even when she is indulging in sport. Although, Lizzy, perhaps it is best not to reveal at first that your father and uncle have taken you out in their fishing boats, but there can be no harm in speaking of the outdoors in general. Flower gardens are quite safe to talk of. And who knows? We may meet with a gentleman who truly prefers remaining at his estate to life in Town. Many men retire happily from Town again after they have secured a wife, and such a man might be attracted to a woman knows something of the country."

"La, that is not what Mama says. She says even country gentlemen prefer a refined lady. That is why Jane will marry first. Mama says that a gentleman is coming soon to let Netherfield Park and that he is sure to save us all by falling violently in love with Jane, as she is the most beautiful of us all, or so Mama claims." Kitty emitted a little snort, which spoke as much of her reluctant agreement with her mother's assessment as it did for her own mild sense of jealousy.

"He will be a fortunate man then, if his taste is so exquisite," soothed Elizabeth. "Jane would be valued and admired by any sensible gentleman, no matter where he lived."

"And so shall you, Lizzy," her aunt interjected. "Do not allow your mother, or your most *helpful* sister here, lead you to believe otherwise. You are a perfectly lovely young lady, and even that sorry business with Lydia and Mary may be overlooked by the right sort of gentleman. Any man to catch your eye should call himself blessed."

"It is not the gentleman who must catch the lady's eye, but the reverse," chuckled Elizabeth. "I know very well into what straits my sisters and I have fallen, though you are kind enough to spare me the full measure of the world's disdain, Aunt. I have no desire to remain a spinster as Mama has accused, but I find it highly unlikely that I could go home next week an engaged woman. I mean simply to enjoy my visit."

"Then indeed, enjoy it we shall. What else did you wish to do while you are staying with us?"

"Perhaps Kitty had other notions, but I have always wished to see one of London's pleasure gardens. Do you think Uncle would object?"

"Oh! I have not been since before Maddy was born, Lizzy, but that sounds delightful. Perhaps we will speak to your uncle and see if he will take us tomorrow."

Elizabeth was smiling her delight at her aunt's easy agreement and gazing out the window of the carriage when a figure in apparent distress caught her eye. She saw only a hunched-over flash of dark clothing; then he disappeared. An instant later, the carriage lurched as the driver pulled up the horses in alarm.

Mrs Gardiner caught at the hand loop, then put her head near the window to listen as the driver addressed someone outside. "Clear off, my good man," he was ordering. "You have upset the ladies!"

They heard a slurred apology, and Elizabeth, who sat on the proper side to see, gestured to her aunt as the figure came back into view. "Aunt, look. That man there, do you see him? He looks as though he has been injured. See how he holds his head? Perhaps he needs help."

Mrs Gardiner did look, and to her dismay saw a tallish fellow, dressed respectably as an employee of a good household, staggering to the curb. "More than likely he is intoxicated. Look away, Elizabeth. Do not let him see you."

"He does not have the appearance of a drunkard or a criminal, Aunt. Is that not livery he is wearing? Surely no master would countenance such behaviour, and particularly not in public."

Mrs Gardiner reluctantly turned her eyes back to the man on the walk. He was clinging lethargically to a street lantern, his face pressed against the cool metal of the post. What they could see of his expression revealed that he was nearly asleep where he stood and only wanted a horizontal posture to make it a reality. His clothing bespoke some connection to gentility, as Elizabeth had asserted, else she would not have dared give a stranger on a dark street a second glance.

"Lizzy, this is not Meryton," Mrs Gardiner decided. "You cannot believe appearances. I have heard of ladies' carriages being set upon by ruffians after they have stopped to help someone who appeared to be hurt. I am very sorry for the poor fellow, if indeed he is in distress, but it is not our place to look to him."

"Aye, I've heard the same thing, Lizzy," seconded Kitty. "Remember that story Lydia told us?"

"That was on a deserted road near a seaport. We are still in Mayfair. You cannot believe that criminals could set up such a ruse in this neighbourhood, do you? There are too many about, and the houses nearby too well secured for such activity to succeed. Can you not at least ask the driver to see to him?"

Mrs Gardiner's brow puckered in concern, but she obliged her niece. "Jones, please step down and see if the man is injured."

The carriage rocked as the driver obeyed, and the ladies watched him approach the man on the walk. "My good man, are you well?" they heard Jones enquire.

There was a moan, and some muttered reference to a cousin, then the man's head drooped against the post. Jones leaned close, and the ladies could see their driver sniffing the other man's person. He returned directly.

"I do not think he is intoxicated, ma'am, but neither does he appear to have any sort of head injury. I can think of no reasonable explanation for his condition."

"We cannot leave him here on the street," Elizabeth insisted. "He truly will become a victim of some crime if we do. Look at him, his knees are buckling."

"Perhaps he works in the nearest house," Jones suggested. "Do you wish me to ask?"

"Please do," Mrs Gardiner agreed. "We shall be safe enough in the carriage for a moment." She glanced at her niece, a nervous hope written across her features.

There was only one large house on this corner, and there was no knocker on the door, so Jones apparently decided to try the one across the street. The man had, after all, been crossing when they had nearly run him down. The ladies waited in silence for his return, watching all the while as the man on the walk began to sag lower and lower to the ground. Finally, just before Jones' return, he crumpled, and his head struck the pavement. Elizabeth cried out in dismay, and it was only her aunt's staying hand which kept her in the carriage.

"They claim that none of their footmen could have made such a spectacle," Jones reported. "I doubt they would acknowledge him, even if he did belong to that house, for it would be too much of an embarrassment."

"You said he does not appear to be intoxicated?" Mrs Gardiner glanced back at the man.

"There is no odour of drink, ma'am, but I cannot be certain."

"Aunt, is it not our duty to look to those in distress?" Elizabeth reminded her.

"I do not consider that a mandate when the man is a rather tall stranger and we number but three ladies."

"And one driver!" Kitty helpfully pointed out. "It would not be so very hard to have Mr Jones set him on the box. He could stay below stairs this evening and go on his way on the morrow. I can see Lizzy has got this in her head, Aunt, and we shall have no peace until she sees that ridiculous fellow safely put up for the night."

Mrs Gardiner sighed and frowned at her nieces. Elizabeth was watching her intently, with a small quirk of her brow. As her younger sister had surmised, she had indeed taken the man's welfare to heart, but she was not petulant. Instead, she employed a measure of playfulness to achieve her ends.

"He is too well-dressed to be a vagabond, Aunt. Perhaps he is a highly valued employee of some handsome and rich single gentleman, and some ailment has befallen him. After he is recovered, both he and his employer will be so grateful for our assistance that his master may thank us in person. I may then have the pleasure of informing my mother that I obeyed her wishes to find a husband!"

Kitty laughed and declared it a good joke, but Mrs Gardiner was still reluctant. "We have no way of knowing anything about the man. He is not a gentleman, clearly, and he could have come from anywhere."

"Aunt, I am confident we shall be quite safe. Look at the man! I do believe he is drooling. Can anyone be more harmless?"

Mrs Gardiner rolled her eyes and summoned Mr Jones. "Do you think he can ride on the box with you?"

"If I can wake him, ma'am." He went, therefore, and nudged the man on the pavement. When that did not yield the desired result, he shook the man's shoulder, earning only a groan in protest for his efforts. Jones, at last, picked the man up by his lapels—a considerable feat, as he was a rather large man—and rattled him to and fro. The dark head only rolled back, mouth slightly agape, and a throaty rasp escaped him. Jones shook his head. "I cannot lift him if he is not to be gotten to his feet, ma'am."

"Right, then," Elizabeth muttered, and handed her muff and bonnet into her sister's keeping. Before her aunt could object, she was out the door of the carriage and staring down at the man on the ground. "Can you lift his shoulders, Jones? I think I can help you drag his feet."

"Lizzy!" Mrs Gardiner cried from the coach. "What in heaven's name?"

"He can ride on the rear-facing seat, Aunt. We will all have to squeeze together. It is perhaps only twenty minutes to your house; we shall manage."

Mrs Gardiner, lacking the powers to resist, put two slim fingers to her aching head as Kitty sniggered beside her. She left unspoken her horror at Elizabeth being seen engaged in hauling a dirty man off the streets and into her uncle's private carriage. How would she ever explain this?

Elizabeth grasped the man's silver-buckled shoes, which seemed to curl his large feet in a way which must have been uncomfortable, and tugged at their weight as Jones stumbled with his torso. The sleeping man snorted once or twice at the insult of being dragged, groaned an indignant protest directed toward someone named Wilson, and tried to roll over in Jones' grasp.

By the time they reached the carriage, Kitty was on the pavement as well. Her intentions were helpful, but her efforts were less so. It was Mrs Gardiner, the sensible one who still objected to this madness, whose assistance was the most valuable in lifting the inert form of their unwitting guest. She braced her feet and bent to raise him from above while Jones hefted from below. If the man were conscious, he would rightly have just cause for deepest mortification at the way the strange lady was forced to grasp his person. It was just as well he was not. The task completed, Mrs Gardiner straightened her bonnet and shot her nieces a glare which swore them forever to secrecy.

The man did not fit well, inert and crammed into the small carriage bench. The girls crowded on either side of their aunt and stared at the broad shoulders, nearly bursting the seams of the coat, and the long, white-stockinged legs that threatened at any moment to drag his entire frame down to the floor of the carriage. As Jones mounted the box and the carriage dipped slightly, Mrs Gardiner breathed a prayer that he—whoever he was—would remain where they had stowed him.

It was not to be. The horses moved off, and the body rolled with a heavy thud to their feet. The ladies drew back, each cringing and fearing that their assistance may have injured the man even further. The stranger, however, only stirred with a grunt and proceeded to nestle his large frame more comfortably in the small space. His forearm thrashed about as he sought some place for his head, and at last, he was satisfied by wrapping it around Elizabeth's legs and pillowing his face upon her satin shoes.

Elizabeth tugged uncomfortably at her feet but could not extricate them without engaging in a wrestling match with a very strong and very unconscious man. She grimaced at her aunt. Mrs Gardiner rested her head back against the carriage squabs and exhaled, trembling. "We tell no one of this," she commanded.

Three

His eyes were leaden weights, throbbing and aching with each queasy pound of his chest. What had he done last night? Even a fall from his horse typically did not cost him so dearly the next day.

Darcy groaned and cast a hand over his face, a deed which instantly earned him another stab through his brain. He moaned again. Where the devil was Wilson? The man ought to be there with a cool cloth to salve these burning sockets in his face.

He tried to call out for his man but forming the word in his mouth made his head spin and writhe again. Instead, he managed only a garbled moan and rolled to his side. There was some sort of feminine disturbance nearby, and it sounded a great deal like a noisy ballroom. Surely, he was not in one of those, for he was quite certain that one was not permitted to assume a supine posture in such a venue. More was the pity.

One pulsing eye slit a fraction. The image he perceived was blurred—a pale shape, with dark edges… and a loud voice. A decidedly *female* voice.

His stomach gave one great flip as his body spasmed in panic. Good heavens, it had finally happened! Someone had gotten the better of him and staged a compromise, and the giggling miss who was watching him rouse from his helpless stupor was to be his bane for life.

He wheeled to the opposite side of… he supposed it was a bed, but the crackling straw mattress felt unlike any bed he had known. He remained there, ignoring the petulant dismay in that wretched seductress's tones, while he rubbed his eyes and cradled his head.

"Lizzy!" the malefactress cried out. "He's awake!"

Darcy clutched the searing orbs in his eye sockets. "Have a care, madam," he growled. "The deuce is driving the very steeds of Hades in my head, and I suppose I have you to thank for it. Very well, you have ensnared me squarely, but have the decency to gloat in silence while I try to reconcile myself to my fate."

"Whatever *that* means," scoffed a girl's voice. "Lizzy! Are you coming back with the powders?" she called. *Loudly.*

Darcy winced and hissed his displeasure. He pinched his nose, hoping his brain would remain within his skull, then cautiously lowered his fingers to survey his captor. Oh, devil take it, she could be no older than Georgiana! At least he could have been trapped by a woman of some maturity, but no! He was to be the prey of a child barely out of the schoolroom!

He was snarling in silence at his misfortune when another woman rounded the door. Ah! So, this must be the accomplice. His lip curled.

"Good morning!" the dashed minx beamed in pleasure—and well she might, for they had achieved their ends. "I am glad to see you recovered. You were in quite a shocking state when we found you. We feared we would have to send for the apothecary. How is your head?"

Darcy stared at her. *She* was clearly no child. In fact, though he would be hard-pressed to call her a beauty, there was a remarkably fine look of intelligence—or perhaps cunning—about her eyes and a convincingly earnest concern in her voice. A fine actress! Her features were not fashionable, but striking, even so. She might even be declared tolerable, under different circumstances. A pity she was culpable in a scheme to ruin him! He rubbed his forehead, hoping the hellish nightmare would simply vanish.

"Oh, I am sorry," the second Jezebel whispered. "I have spoken too loudly for your comfort. Here, a nice cup of coffee might set you right, and I brought you some headache powders. My uncle had some at hand for sickness."

Darcy propped one bleary eye open. A maid was setting up a tray in the small chamber… oh, what a jolly fudge, he appeared to be installed in the servant's quarters! Had they not even the decency to compromise him properly?

"Lizzy, you had best send for Aunt," the younger noted. "He is looking rather green. I think he must have struck his head! Ask who he is."

"Do you not know?" he snorted bitterly. "I rather expect you and your ilk know more of my name and my prospects than my own mother could have! How dare you play the innocent after all that has transpired?"

The women traded curious glances. The younger circled her finger insultingly round her ear, while the elder shrugged her shoulders and ventured, "Sir, can you give us the name of your employer, so we may send word of your welfare? My aunt's coachman can drive you if you are too ill to walk. Where were you bound last evening?"

Darcy glanced over his shoulder and found no one sitting behind him whom she might be addressing. "My... employer?"

"Why, yes, of course," she answered patiently. "You are still wearing the livery, so I surmised that you have not been turned out or anything half so dreadful. Had you met with some accident? I am certain that someone must be concerned that you did not return. If you can tell me your employer's name, I shall pass it on to my uncle's manservant so that he can assist you."

Darcy glanced down at his person. He was, indeed, clad in the livery of his own house, with a pair of shoes half an inch too small tucked neatly beside his cot... a footman's cot. A dizzying horror knitted in his stomach and a hundred realisations struck him at once. His aunt! Wilson! And how in blazes had he ended up....

"I beg your pardon," he pressed his fingers to his forehead again, "but, where am I? Are you perchance Colonel Fitzwilliam's... er... hostess?"

Twin chocolate brows arched. "I am not familiar with that name. You are at the home of my uncle, Mr Edward Gardiner, of Gracechurch Street. We—my aunt and my sister and I—discovered you nearly unconscious in the street. We brought you here last night as a matter of charity. Are you in need of help? If you are, after all, searching for new employment and can provide a character, perhaps my uncle might consider—"

"Employment!" he nearly laughed. "Do not insult me."

The lady narrowed her eyes. "We have gone to considerable trouble for a fellow creature, and a stranger at that. The least you can do is to show a little gratitude." She rose in a swirl of pale skirts and made a shooing motion toward the younger girl. "You deserve no further notice from us, but if you are inclined to accept the house's assistance, you may apply to the housekeeper."

Chastised more by his own conscience than her words, Darcy put out a hand in entreaty. "Wait, please!"

She turned back in open scepticism, one eyebrow lifted as she apparently waited for him to further prove his maleficence.

"Forgive me, madam. It would seem I am obliged to you for caring for me. I am not accustomed to depending upon others, and I have almost no memory of last evening's events."

She appeared to soften somewhat. "Do you know how you came to be in such a state?"

He furrowed his brow in thought, then realised that he still sat on the servant's cot while one of the ladies of the house was standing in attendance over his "sick bed." He scrambled abruptly to his feet, grateful that none had thought to relieve him of the ill-fitting clothing. "There was something in my evening drink, I believe. One of the... the footmen... perhaps it was thought to be amusing."

He began, for the first time, to release some of his initial annoyance at finding himself set upon by these strange ladies. Clearly, they had not staged a compromise, for they did not even think him a gentleman, let alone Fitzwilliam Darcy of Pemberley. If he were prudent, they might never know his name, and he could be yet a free man.

A fresh smile—and an enchanting smile it was, if he permitted himself to confess so much—warmed her lively features. "You must be mindful of whom you share a drink with in the future. Your friend's prank nearly got you run down by our carriage."

"I thank you for the advice, madam, and for removing me from the streets."

"It was only our duty, or such is the prevailing sentiment in Hertfordshire when one happens upon another in your condition. I understand most Londoners do not concur, so it is fortunate for you that my uncle, and, most particularly, my aunt, are of more generous inclinations than many in Mayfair. It is she, as the mistress of the house, to whom you are truly indebted. She is detained at present, but she will be pleased to know that you are human, after all, and display something akin to appreciation for her interest in you."

She stepped back, scolding him for his prior insolence with a compelling thinning of her pink lips. She gestured to a maid to finish setting a crude coffee and biscuit before him and continued, "I shall return now to my cousins. The staff have been instructed to see you have what you need to make a safe return to your employer."

She left him then, seeming to drag her unwilling sister by stern gestures and unseen facial expressions. Darcy loosed a shaky breath. He glanced at one of the nearby household servants, who looked on with less goodwill than the ladies had, and decided to address himself to the humble repast. Perhaps it might help his throbbing head, so he could see and think clearly enough to make his way to his cousin's lodgings.

Another look at the footman informed him that his typical etiquette when eating had been noted as suspicious. His face and inflexions, too, would eventually alert someone to his identity, if they knew anything at all about London's society. Hurriedly, he forced himself to bolt the remainder of the meal. The sooner he was out from under scrutiny, the safer he was from the rector's noose.

～

"Has your good deed gone on his way, then?" Mrs Gardiner looked up from her seven-year-old daughter's latest doll dress as Elizabeth and Kitty entered the nursery. "Gracious, I might have thought he would sleep another hour or two, after his condition last evening."

"He could not have slept another moment, even if he were dead, with Kitty shouting in his ear," Elizabeth reported.

"I did not shout, and anyway, he was already awake when I started calling for you," Kitty grumbled. "Why you made me come take your place and watch over that stranger like a sick baby, I shall never comprehend."

"I told you, I went to ask for the headache powders. As for watching over him, we took him in, after all, so it is our duty to see that he is looked after."

"Lizzy, you did not watch over a sleeping footman!" protested Mrs Gardiner. "What ever shall I tell your father?"

"Only from the doorway, Aunt. Mrs Barker kept one of the maids with me at all times—there was nothing improper. It is not as if he is a gentleman, whose presence could compromise me in the wrong situation. He is someone else's servant, and he was not only unconscious but also fully clothed. Everything was done properly. How can there be any harm in that?"

Mrs Gardiner shook her head. "It just sounds questionable. Please, Lizzy, you must keep this quiet, and speak with me next time, before you decide to adopt any more strange men off the streets."

"I wish I had not taken in this one! You should have heard him when he awoke, Aunt. A more disagreeable, prideful man never existed!"

"Then why did you offer him employment?" charged Kitty.

"Oh, Lizzy, you did not!"

"No," Elizabeth glared at her sister. "I merely asked… oh, never mind. It does not matter, for he scoffed at the very notion of work. As if he were some son of nobility! Perhaps a footman of his impressive height and features can afford to be more selective, but I declare, Aunt, I would not recommend taking him on if he were the last footman in Town."

"He just might be the most *handsome* footman in Town," giggled Kitty. "Admit it, Lizzy, you are not blind. I saw how you admired his figure."

"You mistake frustration for fascination. I assure you, it was the former I felt for him. Anyway, he ought to be well on his way by now, wherever he means to go—I am sure I don't care where. We have wasted enough breath on him, so let us speak of pleasanter things. Aunt, did our uncle agree to a tour of one of the gardens?"

"I believe so, yes. He has some work to finish first, and of course, the best sights are to be had later in the day. He recommended Vauxhall if his business today goes smoothly and he can return home soon. It is a bit of a drive, but I think you will find it worth the journey. Shall we depart after tea time?"

Elizabeth barely restrained a squeal of delight. A long-time fantasy was to be realised for her, and it was a cheerful diversion from her disappointment in the recipient of her goodwill. Such a waste of a handsome face and perfectly good livery! But she was determined to think of him no more.

She hurried from the room to change into a fresh gown and take her own breakfast. It would be some hours before they were to go, and a brisk walk in the park might revive her spirits while she waited. She prepared herself, therefore, to go out, perfectly untroubled by any suspicions that she might, upon quitting the house, accidentally encounter that wayward domestic.

Four

"Where is that manservant? I will see him immediately!" Lady Catherine rapped on the door of Darcy's dressing room with the silver knob of her cane—less out of a servile tendency to request admission to a room than impatience at finding the way blocked. The lady had already made an inspection of the master's chambers, most particularly the rumpled bed. She had been informed that Darcy was not in residence at the moment, but that did not prevent her from again demanding entry to his quarters.

"Yes, My Lady, right away!" Dawson, the head butler, was a man of six and fifty and would never dream of defying her ladyship's wishes. She had spoken of generous pensions, and she was the mother of the future mistress of the house, he had naturally tendered her his loyalties—divided equally, of course, with his fidelity to the master. It might have been reasonable to object to her request, had his master been present, but that was not the case, and he could find no plausible excuse to deny her ladyship's demand. That it was irregular was a matter of course, but then, irregularity was often the order of the day when her ladyship was a guest at Darcy House.

The butler produced the key, held the door for the great lady to pass through, then preceded her into the recesses of the chamber, so that he might serve his office. Undoubtedly, he was also motivated by a desire to shield the lady's feminine sensibilities, for a lady entering a man's sleeping quarters unexpectedly might encounter something she would not wish to see.

In this case, it was Wilson, groggily stretched out on his typical pallet in Mr Darcy's dressing room. The butler stuttered in horror upon beholding the untucked shirt, the slovenly hair, the half-unbuttoned fall of the man's breeches. He looked to have arisen from his drunken stupor only long enough to relieve himself, then stumble back to his bed.

"Sir! Have a care for your presentation!" the butler admonished the drowsing man.

Wilson lifted his head, his features slack and his eyes hazy. "Dawson, ish that you, old chap? Closhe that dratted shutter, the light ish burning a hole in the back of my shkull."

"Mr Wilson! There is a lady present!"

Wilson rubbed his eyes and squinted. "Perhaps she can eashe my headache. Shend her in, man, and be quick about it!"

If the staid and proper valet of Fitzwilliam Darcy were intentionally irreverent and facetious to better serve his master's interests, it would have been difficult to determine. It was clear that the butler merely considered him still intoxicated; an opinion that was reinforced when Wilson made an attempt to rise, then stumbled to his backside again. In truth, he had faltered more out of astonishment than lingering dizziness, for at that moment the "lady" commenced a diatribe which, in any other circle but London's *ton*, would have proved her to be less a lady and more a harridan.

"Mr Wilson! I am ashamed of you; a gentleman's valet, comporting himself as a slovenly drunkard while in the very chambers of his master? I shall have you turned out at once! What has Pemberley come to, that a sluggard could have risen to such a rank within its halls?"

Wilson staggered to his feet and swept the lady a respectful bow—a motion which discomposed him to such a degree that he found it necessary to grasp a nearby table for stability. "I meant no dishreshpect, My Lady," he slurred. "I'm afraid I'm not quite myshelf thish morning. My mashter offered me a drink lasht evening that he had not intended to take, after ordering it. I am afraid the mashter's vintage is finer than I am accustomed to. My humblesht apologies if I have caushed offenshe."

Lady Catherine's eyes narrowed. "He offered a drink to his manservant? Which drink, and why?"

"Yesh, My Lady," Wilson answered promptly. "The brandy Mr Dawshon shent up. Mr Darshy shaid he would have a drink at hish club, and that he might ash well wait."

"His club! Why was I not informed that he had gone out last evening?" She turned to the butler in an outrage. "I was to be told of all my nephew's activities! It is only my due, as his nearest relation and his future mother-in-law, to be given the respect of foreknowledge!"

"I am sorry, My Lady," the butler bowed in abject submission. "This is the first I have heard of it myself. It is not Mr Darcy's habit to attend his club of an evening, particularly with no notice given for his carriage."

Wilson was standing—somewhat crookedly—as his head tilted to follow the conversation. The dazed look in his eyes cleared in some measure when he perceived himself the object of scrutiny again, and he seemed to come to his senses. His speech, this time, had improved marginally, though he still dragged his 'r's. "Mr Darcy received word from a friend just before he retired, asking for his company, My Lady."

"At night! What can you mean, did this man drive to the house and carry off my nephew in a curricle, with no one to witness? Impossible!"

Wilson caught himself as his body was beginning to list in the other direction. "He… he walked, My Lady."

"Walked! Now I am certain of it. Dawson, you must have this man set out of the house at once, for he is neither fit to be seen nor suitable for service. His tongue drips lies, and his person is offensive!"

Wilson had busied himself tucking the tail of his shirt into his breeches, but he dared do nothing about the two loosened buttons of his fall. He left that part of his shirt hanging to provide for some degree of modesty, glancing down with conscious discomfort at his shameful appearance.

"It shall be done, My Lady," Dawson bowed, then levelled a stern look toward Wilson. "Your ladyship may rest assured that intoxication while on duty is never tolerated in this house."

Lady Catherine stepped nearer the footman, untroubled by his dishevelled attire, and sniffed his breath. Wilson stood erect, his pupils dilated and staring directly ahead as she examined his eyes, contrasting them with the lack of redness and perspiration upon his complexion one might expect of a drunkard. She stepped back, after an invasive examination of his person, and declared, "You were unconscious all night."

Wilson shifted uncomfortably. "I… slept rather soundly," he confessed.

She smiled faintly. "Then you could easily have been mistaken about Mr Darcy's activities."

Wilson made no answer. It was not necessary, for Lady Catherine had accurately surmised his state, and there was no possible way to deny it.

"Darcy went to no club," she informed the butler. "He was here long enough for the damage to be done last night and has gone to another's house in an attempt to hide his disgrace. Club, indeed!" she scoffed, shooting a dismissive glance toward the valet.

"My Lady, I only report what I was told," protested Wilson. "I assisted his preparations for departure myself, and he left at once."

The butler, upon receiving permission to speak from the lady's demanding expression, answered, "Mr Wilson has always been known to be honest, My Lady. He may be in disgrace at present, but I think there is no duplicity in him."

She looked back to the shamed valet, her eyes crinkled. "In his condition, his memory of last evening's events cannot help but be faulty. No one could credit his words. Now, Mr Wilson, where is that tradesman friend of your master's? Is he in Town?"

"My Lady, Mr Bingley is presently in the North, but I believe he is expected in Hertfordshire next week. Mr Darcy had intended to join him there, to advise him on an estate he has just leased."

Lady Catherine frowned. "Then I shall speak with Colonel Fitzwilliam. Dawson, have this man removed from the house!"

"With all due respect," Wilson objected, "if your ladyship wishes to advise and counsel my master, I might be able to persuade him to listen. I have been Mr Darcy's valet since he was a boy, and Mr George Darcy himself commissioned me to look faithfully to his best interests."

This seemed to give her pause. She glanced back to the butler, one eyebrow lifted. "Think not that your continued employment is conceivable, after the figure you have cut here this morning. However, if you wish to be of one last service to your master, I shall retain you at my leisure until his future is secured."

Wilson bowed, his face awash with apparent relief. "Thank you, My Lady."

~

Darcy quitted the mortifying address in Cheapside as discreetly as possible. That anyone might see him in residence at a tradesman's house was a dreadful enough thought. That they might note him clad in livery and exiting through the servant's entrance was unthinkable. Why, an entire month of ablutions would be insufficient to restore his dignity after passing the night in such a neighbourhood, and on a footman's cot!

The deplorable circumstances which had placed him in this ridiculous costume and under the power of others half his rank could have been resolved by a simple explanation, and a bit of transparent honesty. However, nothing was simple when Lady Catherine was involved, and nothing could be permitted to remain transparent when single young ladies sniffed out an eligible bachelor.

The shoes hurt. Darcy paused for a moment to flex his aching foot, already blistered from the previous evening's short walk. What a farce! He still could not fathom what he had been thinking, venturing out on his own in such attire, all while knowingly drugged. The coach and four rattling round inside his head did little to assist him in ordering his thoughts. He pounded a fist to his forehead as a particularly brilliant ray of sunshine stabbed his brain.

He felt conspicuous. His attire, while not a formal serving costume, clearly marked him as a footman belonging to a fine house—much finer than could be found upon Tradesmen's Row! He suppressed a curl to his lip and tried to lengthen his strides to avoid more curious gazes, but his toes protested. Unable to resist seeking relief and wishing to arrive at Colonel Fitzwilliam's abode before crippling himself, he sought out a small alley which stood between two houses. A pitiful attempt at a tree had been planted there, likely with more hope than skill, and it provided just enough leaf to conceal his face. He glanced about to see that none might notice him, then slipped into the dark corner and instantly tore off the offending footwear.

As he leaned back against the trunk of the spindly maple, ruining the silk stockings in the dirt and massaging his throbbing toes, he heard ladies' voices approaching. He groaned. *Precisely* what he needed. He drew as far into the shadows as his tall frame permitted and only hoped they were no more observant than most ridiculous ladies.

Fate had determined to be cruel today, for it was the tradesman's two nieces. The silly one seemed inclined to gad about, oblivious to her surroundings save for one red-coated officer on the far side of the street, but the other... he clenched his teeth and growled when those expressive eyes lit directly on him. One eyebrow curved, her lips did likewise, and she clutched at her sister's hand to draw the other back to where she stood. Laughing.

Oh, she may not have made a show of it. Surely, she did not chortle or snicker aloud, nor did she point or otherwise call attention to his presence. But there was laughter in her eyes and unrestrained amusement in that enigmatic smile. Devil take it, but she did have a charming smile.

"Have you already lost your way, sir?" she asked when it was too obvious that they had acknowledged one another. "Or is your employer a wood nymph?"

He repressed a scowl. A footman would never scowl at a lady, and he was a *footman* if he wished to avoid being served up as a husband for the vexing creature. Heaven help him if her relations ever discovered exactly whom they had sheltered for the night! What further lies might be spun to force his hand? He cringed as he tried to wedge his feet back into the shoes and stepped from the branches. "I have no proper explanation, madam."

"Perhaps you merely enjoy what there is of nature to be found in this neighbourhood. Shall I imagine a tragic boyhood for you, where you sought refuge and seclusion in the peace of the woods from your unfortunate home? Or shall I content myself with the explanation that you truly are... peculiar?"

Darcy stepped fully clear of the alley now, manfully stifling whatever protests his body would make to his attire, but she saw through the tight expression on his face and the foreshortened steps as he minced toward her.

"Oh! Oh, your shoes must pain you. I noted last night that they fitted you ill. You should apply to your master for a better pair, for surely he would not deny you such."

"I beg your pardon, madam, but did you say you noted the fit of my shoes?"

At that moment, the sister, at last, deigned to speak. "Well, of course, she did. Lizzy notices everything, and she could hardly help it when she was assisting Jones to drag you into the carriage."

His eyes widened. *She?* Had helped *drag* him? He may not have been acquainted with many tradesmen's daughters, but he did not think them generally inclined to personally cart unconscious men—footmen, no less!—off the streets at night. And she had the audacity to call *him* peculiar!

The lady was attempting to hide her chagrin. She made a sideways shushing noise, and her elbow twitched into the younger girl. "My sister speaks out of turn," she pardoned herself, sending another firm look to her left. "I hope you have not far to walk. Good day."

The younger lady was compelled to walk on by the impatient elder, and for a mercy, neither offered a backward glance. Darcy sagged… only a little. Few folk were yet out upon the streets, but their number would only increase—and with it, his chances of being recognised.

He considered hiring a chair to take him to his cousin's residence, for it would take him the better part of an hour at his gimping pace. He dismissed it on the grounds that it would only encourage speculation about him. No, a footman out on an errand for his master either walked or was given a mount. Since he had no mount and could not countenance the gossip if it were reported that a driver had picked him up in Cheapside dressed as a domestic, he would walk. Curling his toes under the balls of his feet and limping evenly on both, he did just that.

Five

Colonel Fitzwilliam was, indeed, at home. He was in the habit of rising early from his long days in the army, and even when off duty, he could scarcely remain abed after seven of the clock. He was already up and enjoying a cup of coffee—no tea for him in the mornings—when his batman informed him that he had a visitor.

"So early! Perhaps a friend ran aground at the gambling tables last night, eh? Well, show him in, Jenkins, show him in."

"Colonel, it is Lady Catherine de Bourgh who wishes to speak with you."

Fitzwilliam nearly spit his coffee. He managed to salvage his dignity in that regard but could not avoid spilling a few drops as he set it on the saucer. "My aunt! What in blazes could she want? Never mind, Jenkins, of course, you could not formulate the answer to that. That would imply reason on my aunt's part, and I suffer under no illusions that she has submitted to such an authority. Well, show her in, and I shall make myself presentable."

He stood, inspecting his coat to be certain that no crumbs besmirched it. Lady Catherine descended upon the apartment like a thunderstorm, cracking and pouring down the force of her displeasure. What he had done to merit this personal call at his humble abode, he could not say, but likely enough, it had something to do with Darcy.

He was right.

"Fitzwilliam, where are you keeping him?" she demanded at once.

"Him... forgive me, Aunt, but I have not the pleasure of understanding you. Good morning to you as well, by the by. There is no one here, save Jenkins and myself. And my housekeeper, of course, but...."

"Fitzwilliam Darcy! He has come here, has he not?"

"Darcy? I beg your pardon, Aunt, but I last saw Darcy a fortnight ago. I have only just gone on a short leave, do you see, but I intended to call upon him this morning."

She stalked nearer. "Do not play coy with me, Richard Fitzwilliam. What has he arranged? I must know all his plans."

"I would certainly reveal what I knew, Aunt, but Darcy is not here, nor have I had word from him. Perhaps he is paying a call on some friend or other."

"You and I both know that Darcy never pays social calls at such an hour, and apart from yourself, there is only that tradesman to whom he might have gone for an informal visitation."

"Bingley? He is not in Town at present. Have you truly not seen Darcy since last night?"

She drew herself up. "Of course, I have not, and that is the subject of my desired conversation with him." Lady Catherine seemed to pause. "You will swear that he did not come here… perhaps this morning?"

"Unless I was still abed, Aunt, which is unlikely. May I ask, why the urgency? If I am not mistaken, you are his guest at present, and he will only naturally return to the house when his errands are complete. Has something happened?"

She pursed her lips. "Indeed, something has happened. He has ruined my daughter. Compromised her, beyond hope of recovery, and practically before my very eyes!"

"No! I cannot believe this, Aunt. Darcy would never… and Anne! I find it difficult to credit, Aunt."

"She was in his bed this morning," asserted the lady. "I would have him found at once so that the settlement can be drawn up and the wedding might be arranged. As you cannot testify to his whereabouts," here, she smiled faintly, "I shall speak with him once he has returned to the house. I shall depend upon your support to ensure he behaves the gentleman toward his cousin hereafter. I shall call next upon the earl to discuss the matter with him. Good day, Fitzwilliam."

Colonel Fitzwilliam stood aghast as his aunt departed in a sweep of black and an irregular tapping of her cane—a means of expression, rather than a necessity for mobility.

Darcy and Anne! If his aunt had not sworn to it, he could never have believed it. Darcy could have any woman he wanted, as a wife or even a mistress, but Anne? Apart from a sickly, unappealing person, there was the matter of her mother. No man in his senses would touch her, least of all Darcy! The man must have been desperate… or intoxicated. After seven and twenty years of celibacy—as far as he knew—perhaps it was a little of both. Besides, any man would be driven to drink with their Aunt Catherine as a guest.

Fitzwilliam shook his head and sighed. Well, Darcy could step into the hornet's nest if he wished. He wanted no part of it for himself.

~

"Kitty," Elizabeth sighed in exasperation, "I do wish you would let the matter rest. Of *course*, he was handsome. It might be said that a footman's only duty in the finer houses is to be handsome. They are chosen in matched sets like bookends, fitted with gloves and a powdered wig, and displayed as prize Adonises to serve their masters at table. What else would you expect, but that the one we encountered would be a prime specimen?"

"Prime, yes, but not at all nice. He was hardly deferential, and he only showed a bit of gratitude for our pains after you made him feel guilty."

"That probably accounts for how we came upon him. His employer must have dismissed him for insolence. It is strange, however, for he seemed more cultured than I would have expected. Did you notice how he always said 'madam,' rather than 'ma'am,' as all the others do?"

"I think he admired you, Lizzy. Why else would he lie in wait for us to pass by?"

"He had taken his shoes off! That is not what I would call lying in wait, and besides, we have no business troubling ourselves over one barmy footman. You really must learn to think of other matters besides the male sex."

"I think a great deal of other matters. Bonnets, for example. Did we not pass that milliner in Newgate? Or was it Skinner Street?"

"I thought it was Holburn Street. Almost to Bloomsbury Square, I believe."

"We simply must go back! Their display was so delicious, I have scarce thought of anything else. Let us ask for Uncle's carriage and go?"

"I wish to walk, Kitty. That was the entire purpose of our outing, but it would not take more than half an hour to walk there if you insist."

"Laws, you are peculiar, Lizzy! Mama would be horrified to hear of us walking all about Town."

"She is not here, and it is not as though we have anyone to impress or even any who would know us."

"Oh, very well. I will agree to your abominably long walk if we go to the milliner's rather than the park."

"I doubt they are even open for business at this hour."

"Surely they will be by the time we arrive. I intend to buy a new bonnet, and you should buy one too, Lizzy. That way, you shall have some remembrance of our little holiday with Aunt and Uncle."

Elizabeth reluctantly agreed—not because she wished for a bonnet, but because she desired a few moments of peace and to distract her sister from teasing about that ridiculous footman. Heaven help her if Mama ever found out!

~

Colonel Fitzwilliam's sides hurt. His cheeks hurt, his eyes were streaming tears, and he could scarcely breathe. Fitzwilliam Darcy, one of the enigmas of the *ton* and among the wealthiest men in Britain, stood in the midst of Fitzwilliam's rooms at just past nine in the morning, unshod and clad as one of his own footman. Had not Lady Catherine already shocked him into sobriety once this morning, he would have suspected himself of too much to drink.

But really… barefoot? Fitzwilliam Darcy! So diverted was the colonel, in fact, that he could no longer stand. Rather than exhibit the worst sort of rudeness—after all, laughing at a man was one thing, but sitting before one's guest was seated was quite another—he offered Darcy a chair and fell into an opposite one himself.

"Do repeat that. You said that you had been drugged? Who poured that down your gullet?"

Darcy appeared to clench his teeth. "Our aunt has acted out of desperation. She intended to force a compromise by secreting something in my drink, but I have forestalled that."

"How? Have you found a way to divert our aunt from her plans to wed Anne to you?"

"I was simply not there when the compromise was intended to take place." Darcy turned to glance at the sleeve of his jacket and flick off what appeared to be a small bit of bark.

"Really? Where did you go?"

"Here." Darcy frowned at something, and if Fitzwilliam was not mistaken, the man's knee was twitching as he sat in the chair.

"Here? Have you been a ghost that I did not see you?"

"I had set out for this destination last night, but I did not arrive as intended," Darcy gritted between his teeth. "However, I am here now. Should our aunt send her emissary to verify my whereabouts, they will see that I am presently a guest in your house."

"I'm afraid it's a bit too late for that, old chap. Aunt was here herself, not quarter of an hour ago."

"What?" Darcy shot to his feet, then winced.

"Something the matter with your foot, old man?"

"Never mind that. You said that Lady Catherine had come here? Herself?"

"Yes, came all in state to search you out. I told her I'd not seen you. She seemed content with that and went on her way."

Darcy sank back into the seat. "You told her you had not seen me?"

"It was only the truth. A soldier in His Majesty's Army does not lie, you know."

"Nor would I ask it of you, but if she knows I was not here, then she knows you cannot vouch that I was not in my own bed."

Fitzwilliam frowned. "That may prove awkward. Where were you, precisely?"

"It does not matter."

"I should say that it does, unless you were somewhere even more embarrassing than in our cousin's arms. Personally, I would confess to an evening at Covent Gardens and openly set the... uh... lady up with her own establishment, so everyone knows about it all. Unless she was married, of course."

Darcy massaged the bridge of his nose. "If my head pained me any less and I thought I could walk the distance to your chair, I would cut out your tongue for such a speech."

The colonel laughed. "I'd like to see that. What do you intend to do now? You cannot very well go back home, or Aunt's claims will be unassailable. She has already gone to my father."

"She has!"

"Unless, of course, there is someone at your house who can vouch for you. You have a veritable army of servants. Surely at least a few knew of your activities last evening."

"That is precisely the problem. It has come to my attention that not all my servants believe a variance exists between my interests and my aunt's—or worse, some have tendered her their loyalty. The only one I know I can depend on for a certainty is my valet, Wilson."

"Well, then, there you have it. Your valet sleeps in your dressing room. He would surely have noted if a lady were in the chambers."

"Not if he were drugged as well, as I believe he was. Even if he could provide a reliable account, who would believe him against Lady Catherine de Bourgh, particularly if several others of the household dispute his testimony?"

"Ah! Then you do have a problem. Well, I offer you my congratulations on your recent engagement, Cousin."

"Engaged! You must be mad. Have you ever thought about what a man's life would be with our aunt as his mother-in-law? I think I would sooner join the Navy and die under Nelson's flag."

"They say the sea is as good as a mistress to a man," the colonel chortled. "But seriously, what will you do, Darcy? Our aunt has you neatly trapped. You cannot very well go home until you have a convincing alibi, and you can do nothing about that from here."

"I must contact my valet. He was to report all he learned this morning while giving the appearance of cooperation with Lady Catherine. Will you have your batman carry a message to him?"

"Strategic error, cousin. Aunt saw my batman just this morning, as did her own manservant. If they discover secretive messages passing between the two, your valet becomes suspect."

Darcy growled in frustration. "At least lend me a respectable suit of clothing. I cannot bear to be seen as a footman any longer."

"The livery becomes you rather handsomely, but I shall see what I have to suit the great Fitzwilliam Darcy. On second thought, you may want to consider keeping that livery. Did anyone look at you and speak to you by name as you were walking here?"

"Well…" Darcy shifted uncomfortably in his seat. "No."

"Something to consider, if you have need to return to wherever you were last night without being noticed. Or," he grinned at the expression of horror upon his cousin's face, "you can take a suit of my clothing and hire a chair back to your own house, where you will be served with marriage articles by my father and our aunt. I leave it to you."

Darcy's frown deepened further, and Colonel Fitzwilliam, if forced to confess, might have liked to make some comments about enjoying Fitzwilliam Darcy's great dilemma rather enormously.

Six

At least the shoes were an improvement.

Darcy had also traded his hat for one belonging to Fitzwilliam's batman, hoping that the nondescript chapeau would lend him a bit more anonymity. He had no notion where he was to go or what he was to do, and Fitzwilliam had been blasted little help. Somehow, he must find a way of speaking to Wilson, and learn what could be said in his own defence. Surely there was some other who could testify to the conspiracy his aunt had brought to his own household.

But how to prove his location last evening? The only persons capable of vouching for him would be those who did not even know his name. Darcy shuddered. There were a great many things he would rather do than go back to that tradesman's house, announce his identity, then beg for a witness to his presence. There were two single ladies living in that house, and he did not wish to become their prey any more than he wished to be shackled to his cousin.

He marched aimlessly down the pavement, his mind focused on his walk only enough to be certain that he was not noticed by anyone who might recognise him, when a flash of inspiration dawned. Hertfordshire was only half a day's ride, and he had more than enough pocket money with him to hire a mount. He could ride fast and hard to Bingley's newly leased estate and establish himself as a guest there. He had been intending to journey there the following week anyway, and Bingley would be only too happy to have the house opened to him early.

However… the notion passed when he realised that in the eyes of the *ton*, fleeing Town at this precise juncture would be as good as an admission of guilt. No, he must face his aunt to contradict her falsehoods, and he needed information. He dared not count upon his uncle's assistance, either.

He rounded a corner and paused upon noting a familiar carriage just setting down its passenger on to the same street. Heaven forbid, it was Lord Wexley's execrable wife! Darcy glanced about for a doorway into which he might slip, but every one of those would lead him into a shop where people could see his face even more closely.

He turned about, glancing only once over his shoulder to see where the lady had moved after her carriage had set her down. Before he had fully turned back to his path, he collided headlong into a wall of parcels, seemingly all shrouded in a frothy array of cream satin and lace.

"I beg your pardon!" cried a sickeningly familiar voice.

His apology was automatic, and he was already reaching to pick up the boxes he had crashed into when he looked up at the faces of the young shoppers. If Fitzwilliam Darcy had ever wished to be swallowed up by the pavement or disappear into a nearby shrubbery, this was the moment.

Dark brown eyes sparkled, and rosy lips twitched. "I see we are destined to encounter one another repeatedly today! Tell me, sir, shall I assume that you have caught up with us to enquire after a new position? I am afraid my uncle has no present need for a jester."

Confound the woman! Did she have to be so bleeding glib at every encounter? Darcy tipped his hat, biting firmly down on his tongue. "I beg your pardon, madam. It was quite accidental, I assure you." He bent to collect the dented hat box and dusted a bit of imaginary dirt off the top. "I hope I have not damaged your purchase."

"If you have," the lady returned, "I would think it a poor performance on the part of the hat box. I am certain it has managed to serve its office." She sighed very lightly, an expression of teasing exasperation, and held out her hand to receive the box.

"Make way!" grumbled a sour voice behind him. Darcy started. He turned about and looked full into the face of Lady Wexley, who had apparently destined that very same millinery shop for her own custom.

Darcy felt his stomach lurch, and his toes curled in dread. She could never fail to recognise him, particularly not after the way she had repeatedly thrown herself into his path last season before Lord Wexley had claimed her hand. He closed his eyes and prepared the explanation he knew would be demanded, but she only groused in the direction of the two young ladies.

"Have your footman stand back!" she hissed at them. The rest of her words were offered to the benefit of no one in particular, and everyone in general, so that all might appreciate her lament. "Abominably rude, these tradesmen's daughters. Walking about town with a strapping footman in counterfeit colours and putting on airs as if they were gentlemen's daughters! It seems that simply *anyone* may now shop in this part of town," she sniffed.

She passed on by Darcy as if she had not even noticed him, and he began to breathe… only very faintly. She had not recognised him! She would not even look at him, clad as he was! His heart began to beat a little more quickly. Oh, the possibilities!

The dark-haired minx before him did not seem at all put out by her abuse at the hands of Lady Wexley. She appeared, rather, to be struggling mightily against an outburst of laughter. Her eyes danced, and she was obliged to tip her face slightly away as a distinct snicker escaped her.

The younger girl, the one with the lighter hair, still seemed vexed. Hand on hip, she glared after the closing door. "Lizzy, did you hear what that odious woman said about us? I should tell our aunt, if it would not grieve her."

"Indeed, few could not have heard, Kitty," chuckled the elder sister. She composed herself and extended her hand once more to Darcy. "May I have my bonnet? It seems my presence in this neighbourhood has distressed some of its residents, so I shall take my leave."

He gave her the parcel, realising only after she had taken it that he was puzzling curiously over her face. Was it the pert little nose, so unfashionable in the finer circles, or the faint crease in her fair skin where a wider smile lurked behind the demure one? Perhaps it was simply the shape of her cheekbones—high yet soft—contrasted with the sharp intensity of her dark eyes, which was so interesting to look upon.

"Is something amiss with my appearance?"

"No!" He cleared his throat and bowed. "Forgive me, madam."

One side of her mouth tipped upward. "I take it by your presence here that you are out upon another errand for your master or, perhaps, your mistress?"

He opened his mouth to make a reply but could think of absolutely nothing to say. He abhorred disguise, and her presumptions, if he were to verify them, would be the worst trail of lies imaginable. But the truth—the truth was even more wretched! He settled instead for diversion.

"I have not yet made my way back. I… do not think I am expected."

"In that case," the young lady smiled, "you have a holiday. I suggest you use it to best advantage, rather than lurking outside of milliners' shops."

"Indeed. If I may be so bold," he looked about, "I cannot help but note that you are unescorted. Do you often walk out without protection?"

"Gracious, but you are impertinent! Perhaps I have been permitted too much freedom, but I am not alone. My sister is with me, as you see."

Darcy glanced at the other girl, who was tapping her toe and pouting her impatience. "Of course. May I call for a chaise to take you back to your dwelling?"

"That will not be necessary, but I thank you. We are rather accustomed to walking and most fond of our liberties."

"As far as Gracechurch Street? Your... your uncle permits such?"

She stared at him with some incredulity, her brow furrowed and her head shaking faintly at his audacity.

Footman, you are a footman! "Forgive me, madam, I spoke out of turn. Your uncle seems a... a generous man."

"My uncle is among the kindest and most noble men alive," she vowed, those eyes sparking in defence of her relation. "I will not have it said that he is remiss in his duties. Certainly, he would have insisted upon a carriage, had we informed him when we set out that our walk would become such an outing. And if you are, after all, seeking employment, you could do far worse than applying to Mr Edward Gardiner."

A thought pricked Darcy. "He is an... honest... employer?"

The lady tipped her shoulders lightly. "I am perhaps biased, but I can testify that his staff are all exceedingly loyal and speak well of him."

Darcy winced. That remark stung more than he cared to admit. He stifled the feeling, intending to dissect it later, and swept them a gracious bow. "In that case, madam, may I offer my escort to the ladies as they return to their residence? I would count it an honour to carry their parcels."

"Well," the younger girl spoke up for the first time in some while, "he certainly knows how to be chivalrous when he wants to be, Lizzy." To this, she added some mischievous grin, which remained a mystery to Darcy, but 'Lizzy' seemed to understand perfectly.

~

"I am sorry, Lizzy, but your uncle has gone out. I understand there was some urgent message from the warehouse. I am in hopes that he shall have returned within the hour so that we might still take our outing, but perhaps it might be more serious than that. I do apologise, Lizzy!"

Elizabeth tried not to show her disappointment. Her aunt and uncle were the most gracious hosts, and she would not wish to seem ungrateful. "Thank you, Aunt, but it is no matter. I will wait to speak with him when he returns." She stepped back toward the door, but her aunt's voice stopped her.

"Was there something of import? Perhaps I might be able to advise you."

"No, Aunt, it was nothing quite like that. I only wondered if Uncle might be seeking another household servant. I shall ask when he returns."

Mrs Gardiner peered over her sewing with a knowing look. "You are not still bothering with that footman, are you? Lizzy, why ever should you trouble yourself? He was quite obviously intoxicated and probably justifiably turned out."

"I take no interest beyond the word I have given, which was merely to offer my opinion of my uncle's generosity and fairness as an employer. If the man should choose to apply, and if my uncle should choose to receive him, it is certainly no business of mine."

Mrs Gardner thinned her lips sceptically, and she raised an eyebrow at her niece. "Lizzy, I have some duties to be about this morning. Would you mind very much taking your cousins out for air with their nurse? They may go alone, of course, but it is best if someone attends them, and I think you could do with the diversion."

"Of course, Aunt." Elizabeth reached down to give her youngest cousin a playful embrace and watched wistfully as her aunt rose to go speak with the nurse.

She sighed. Now, what was she to do with that footman who was waiting below stairs? And why was it that he had considered it such an insult when she had asked him to wait in the kitchens? He should have counted it a hopeful sign, but instead, had clearly struggled against a vocal protest that he was not invited to the drawing room.

Perhaps she was, indeed, wasting her time with him. After all, how often did a servant expect to speak directly with the master when he applied for employment, yet had she not attempted to secure him such an interview? He had not even a written character by his former employer! She was doing him a favour, offering to speak on his behalf on so little inducement. After all, what had he done for her, apart from knocking down her parcels?

Well... he had picked them up again. And carried them—badly, but his only complaint had been an entertaining assortment of grimaces and scowls. She tried to forget how gallantly he had shielded her from the dirtier parts of the street, or how he had suggested a safer route for her to walk home. He was only trying to impress her in hopes of employment, surely, but there had been about him an air of command which would suit his prospective post ill. He ought to be inquiring at the Army instead of a household, but perhaps he would like taking an officer's orders even less than an employer's.

Elizabeth determined—again—to dismiss him from her thoughts and released her cousin back into the care of her nurse to make ready for her outing. "Kitty?" she called into the next room. She rounded the corner and found her sister seated near the fire. "Would you like to come for another walk? I am going out with our cousins."

Kitty, who had been fussing with her new bonnet, looked up to Elizabeth with a sneer of disdain. "You have already tired me sufficiently for one morning, Lizzy. If you do indeed insist on attending the Gardens this evening, I require some rest, or I shall begin to cough, and you know how that drives Uncle to distraction."

"If we go, it will not be for many hours yet."

"Nevertheless, I am quite happy here for now. If only Aunt had some darker ribbon!"

"Very well. Aunt has asked me to accompany the children, so I shall see you when I return."

"Lizzy, what do you intend to do about your dashing new footman? Did Uncle speak with him?"

Elizabeth shook her head nonchalantly. "Nothing at all, for he is not *my* footman. Uncle is away at present, and I have already exerted enough effort for that man. I am in no humour to give consequence to footmen who have been dismissed by other masters, and despite your teasing, he is not fine enough that I should be tempted to bother with him further."

Kitty cleared her throat and coughed, smirking all the while.

Elizabeth, filled with a sudden sense of foreboding, turned around. Her mysterious stranger had apparently broken the injunction to remain in the kitchens and had not only found her out but had heard every word.

He looked to be darkly displeased, eyes piercing, and cultured tones clipped as he glared back at her. "You have long been wishing for my absence, I see. Very well, I shall trouble you no further. Good day, madam."

Elizabeth blanched in mortification as he turned and marched away. Then, a sense of indignation welled up within her. "What was he thinking of, coming upstairs and surprising us like that?" she demanded of Kitty. "No one of decency would have done so, and least of all one who wishes to be employed at the house!"

Kitty offered no answer but a giggling snort, as she held her hand over her broadening grin and laughed riotously. "I don't know Lizzy, but I have never seen anyone so thoroughly mortify you! He caught you fairly, whether you confess it or no."

Elizabeth made a sour face and took up the reticule that she had set aside but minutes before. "Enjoy my moment of humiliation to its fullest, if you will, for it shall be the last. Never again will I exert myself for someone such as that!"

"You would not have been so embarrassed if you had not spoken so ill," Kitty pointed out—perhaps the most sensible observation she had uttered in the past six months.

This did nothing to improve her sister's humour. "I will return in an hour or two, Kitty," she grumbled. "Do try to finish laughing at my expense before I come back."

Seven

Not *fine enough to tempt her! Fine enough, indeed!* He ought to have announced his identity to that strumpet's face. Let her then pronounce again that he was not fine enough for her! A daughter of trade! He would have laughed aloud, had he not been so irate.

If the scion of Pemberley could be said to stomp, he was most decidedly stomping now. Very few other descriptors of his ambulatory attitude could quite capture his mood as he stormed away from the tradesman's house in Cheapside. He had not even had an opportunity to speak with the master, but no uncle could possibly be reasonable enough to atone for that sabre-tongued miss!

No, even if she were the last alibi in the city, he would have nothing to do with that household. She would be just the sort to learn of his true identity and try to ensnare him. She, who had not even the decency to see through his present trappings and recognise the distinguished gentleman at first glance! She, yes, she would be just the sort to put on a sweet face for a wealthy man when she would do nothing of the kind for a... he hissed in aggravation.

Unfortunately, she *had* exerted herself for his benefit, while asking nothing in return. Thus, he had not even the pleasure of denouncing her as a heartless wench. She was merely... baffling.

But he would think no more of her. Something else could surely be found to solve this dilemma. Perhaps... perhaps his uncle would not be so unreasonable after all.

~

"Compromised Anne? Darcy? Well now, his blood is red after all. I could hardly believe it if you had not sworn to it, but this is fortuitous. It seems one way or another, we shall have the boy settled." The Earl of Matlock laced his fingers over his abdomen as he lounged in his favourite chair, his sister pacing like a caged tiger before him. "Has he made the engagement official?"

"No! He is not even to be found. He disappeared in disgrace after ruining my daughter, and I must see him brought to rectitude!"

"He may have acted on impulse, Catherine, but I would not expect Darcy to allow his cousin's disgrace to fall only upon her. Certainly, he has only gone to draw up a settlement."

"He has been away some hours. I have it from the staff that he was not seen after the middle of the night. He compromised my daughter, and then he fled!"

"It is his own house," the earl reasoned. "He must come back some time or another. Where else could he go?"

"In search of one to vouch for him. I think he went to some friend so that it might be falsely sworn that he was not at home when my daughter was found in his bed."

"Well, was he?"

Lady Catherine made no answer but for a deep scowl and an almost guttural noise.

"Well," the earl shook his head in dismissal. "No matter. It is his bed, in his house, and if Anne was… disgraced… then he must do the proper thing."

"I shall depend on you to ensure that he does. I know what he is about, and I will not see him evade his responsibilities to Anne. He has attempted it for far too long!"

"The surest way to ensure that he does is to have the betrothal announced publicly."

"That I have already done," she smiled, and moved to his desk where a footman had already placed the morning paper. She searched up the appropriate entry and displayed it before him in triumph.

The earl laughed quietly. "Then it sounds as if there is nothing left to do. He must marry her, or he will be as disgraced as she."

"Indeed, he shall."

~

It was humiliating, lurking outside the servants' entrance of his own house as if spying on his staff. He was hoping that at any moment, Wilson might be seen stepping out for a bit of fresh air. However, nearly half an hour had passed with no sign of the man, and there was no reasonable expectation that he would emerge. Darcy had been praying for good fortune, rather than depending with any certainty on Wilson's activities, and it appeared that he would be disappointed.

He began instead to search for other faces as they would trickle out on some errand or another, and to weigh each one in the light of his new suspicions. Upon whom could he depend for discretion and a truthful account?

Nelly, the cook's assistant? No, far too flighty. She would talk to everyone, telling all and sundry that the master had arrived at the servant's entrance wearing a footman's costume. Insupportable!

Ned, the butcher's boy? No, too simple to orchestrate the request. He would sooner depend upon his hounds.

Two or three maids came and went, their irreverent chattering putting him off any hope of speaking with them. Next was a pair of footmen walking together, speaking in low voices. *Certainly not.* He could trust no one who would speak in a voice not meant for others' ears. It may have all been innocent enough, but he needed someone in whom he could be confident.

He had been ready to surrender and walk into the house himself in search of his manservant, embarrassment be hanged, when the carriage pulled into the mews. Darcy stepped back into the shadows, watching it cautiously. Its passenger had naturally been sent down at the front of the house, and now the coachman returned the horses to the stable. The coachman! He would have little to do with any gossip surrounding the house but could easily arrange a meeting with Wilson.

Darcy watched for his opportunity. It seemed an hour dragged by before the coachman had seen the horses put up properly by the stable boys and had stepped away from his duties to smoke a pipe. At last, Darcy dared to step up to the man. "Mr Smith, may I have a word with you, please?"

The coachman jerked and sputtered, singeing his fingers and shaking them to relieve the pain. "Mr.... Mr Darcy, sir? Sir... Yes, sir!" The coachman was well schooled in proper etiquette for his station, but even he could not help staring up and down at Darcy's vestment.

"Smith, I desire to have a message sent to the house. Will you please see Mr Wilson brought out for a private word?"

The coachman touched his hat smartly but then appeared at a loss. There was no procedure in place for the master requesting the coachman to send a message to one of his own servants. It was always a servant who carried the message to him from the master unless some emergency in the stables required that the master be notified—but never by the coachman himself!

"Smith, if you please, I have not all day to wait. Tell him I shall meet him in the mews."

"But... sir, begging your pardon sir, how shall I send the message?"

Darcy nearly rolled his eyes. "One of your errand boys should be sufficient to the task. Have you not a boy who carries orders for the stables? Better yet, do it yourself. I require Wilson's presence at once, and it is a matter of discretion."

Smith was still shaking his hand vaguely, his face a study in bewilderment. "Yes, sir." He put out the pipe, which had been smouldering in his far hand the entire time, and touched his hat again to the master.

Darcy watched him go, feeling somewhat less than hopeful that the message would be conveyed quickly. He then took himself to a bit of an alcove near the back of the mews to await Wilson. Half an hour passed. Darcy removed the shoes again, rubbing his swollen toes. Fitzwilliam's shoes were an improvement, but they did not answer for the insult already done.

Another quarter of an hour drained away, during which he had ample opportunity to once again appreciate the ridiculous irony of his circumstances. At last, there was a scuffling of small feet on the paving stones, and presently before him stood a boy of perhaps nine years old. The lad stared up at him respectfully, with no trace of intimidation as he waited for the master to address him.

Darcy stared at the boy. "And what is your name?"

"Nick, sir. Cook's son. I was sent with a message for you, sir."

This boded ill. Wilson could not meet him in person? "Give me the message, please," he answered tightly.

The boy extended a white piece of paper to him. "I'm to await a reply, sir."

"Yes, of course." Darcy scanned Wilson's note quickly.

Sir,

Lady Catherine has taken me into her trust in one matter, at least. She has asked for your schedule while here in town, to see if my information matched that of the butler. I told her that I was privy only to a small amount of information, but I was able to assure her that I knew more of your personal habits than the butler and that my information was accurate. I believe she has some confidence in me now and will be willing to be led by my advice.

She has just returned from speaking with the Earl of Matlock, and I was told to alert her at once when you returned to the house. It is a pity, sir, that you have not returned to the house, for I shall be unable to oblige her in this matter until informed otherwise.

I have not yet been able to determine the loyalty of all the household staff. The butler, housekeeper, and at least three of the upstairs maids are colluding with Lady Catherine, but I have yet to find a dissenting opinion on the matter of last evening's events. I await your orders, sir, but I dare not depart from the house while under scrutiny unless you request otherwise. Please advise me of your wishes.

Wilson

Darcy crumpled the note. Reply, indeed! It was nonsensical that he should hide from his own employees. Better that he should enter at once through the front door to confront this evil, dismissing all who would speak untruths against him and demand a capitulation from his aunt!

"Take a reply back to Mr Wilson," he commanded the boy. "Tell him that I desire my own clothing and that I will arrive presently."

To Darcy's disappointment, when the boy returned he brought only one other boy to help carry his clothing. Wilson was conspicuously absent, and Darcy would not disrobe before two lads. He moved to dismiss them, but the first boy, after holding out his hat to him, then offered a copy of the morning paper.

Darcy took it. "What is this?"

"Mr Wilson said I should bring it, sir. Good day, sir."

Darcy glanced it over in puzzlement. Why would Wilson think the paper so important that it could not wait? No explanation was forthcoming, as the boys had already vanished. He turned it over, glancing at the mundane entries. Then, near the bottom and printed in bold letters, one particular entry circled in thick black ink stared out to him.

Good heavens, he breathed. *It is worse than I feared!*

Eight

Darcy arrived at his uncle's house at nearly the same moment as Richard, who was calling upon his mother. They were shown into the drawing room within minutes of one another and were left to await the earl and countess.

"Well?" Richard snickered, "I see you have found new clothing. What was the matter with the footman's costume? Too tight across the shoulders?"

Darcy glared at the floor, too infuriated to speak a word.

"I say, did you read the paper this morning?" Richard goaded. "Word has it that Lord Wharton plans to take a new wife. But I expect you have not seen the paper yet today."

Darcy brooded more darkly, if that were indeed possible.

"A proper heiress, of course. No title of her own, but the daughter of a peeress, just the same. Money and connections do a fine job of purchasing beauty, but for all that, I would declare the lady merely tolerable. Still, I should offer my own arm as well, if the lady taking it could place such wealth into my hand. Ah, well, no use fantasising, is there? There was another entry in the same section which I found rather more intriguing than Wharton's announcement. I wonder if there is any truth to it? But I suppose it would be of no interest to you."

"I have seen it, Richard!" Darcy erupted.

"Temper, temper, Darcy. I thought you would be honoured to see your name in the paper beside someone as distinguished as Lord Wharton. Tell me, is Anne pleased?"

Darcy lurched from his chair and began pacing the room. "What am I to do, Richard? I have no wish to ruin her, but our aunt has made it impossible to do otherwise!"

Richard offered a laconic shrug, a lazy smile, and suggested, "Perhaps you could disappear for a while, just after the wedding. Think what freedom! No estate worries to trouble you, no burdensome wives or in-laws hanging round your neck. Yes, it is just the thing. I might have chosen India, but a crusty former bachelor like yourself might find the wilds of Scotland more to his liking. Shall you be boasting a beard and kilt when next we meet?"

"Richard, do not be preposterous."

His cousin laughed jovially. "I was only trying to help. If you do find it so distasteful to marry a wealthy heiress, I can think of a chap or two who might step into your place."

"Impossible. Nothing of good can come of this."

"Nothing? Surely it is not so dire as that. You do take things far too seriously, Darcy."

"Marriage is one of those things which should be taken seriously, as are deceitful relations. I will not suffer my aunt to dictate to me in this matter."

"And you need not do so. Any luck with that alibi?"

Darcy had paced to the window and was now staring out of it. "No," was the flat answer.

Richard gave a little whistle. "Well then, wedding bells it shall be. Unless, of course, you pay Anne off with a handsome settlement, making yourself look the guilty party in the matter—assuming she would accept a settlement. She will still be ruined, and you will still be considered a scoundrel, but you will be free."

"There must be some better solution than that. I have done nothing to legally obligate myself—" Darcy was interrupted when the door opened to admit his lordship. Darcy bowed slightly to his uncle, who approached with a congratulatory smirk.

"Well, Darcy, it is about time I was able to say this to you. May I wish you joy?"

"I wish you would not, Uncle. I had nothing to do with these engagement rumours. They were falsified by my aunt to force my hand."

"Falsified? Darcy, that is a vile bit of slander against your aunt. You would not dare speak such without proof."

"I have proof, Uncle. I was not at home last night when my aunt claims my cousin was found in my bed. I do not even know if she was truly in my bed, but I was certainly not there with her."

"Then your servants could naturally verify this fact. Why have you not confronted your aunt, if what she speaks is not true?"

Richard coughed. Darcy's fingers twitched.

"I am afraid it is not so straightforward, Uncle. My aunt has seen fit to cultivate the loyalties of my servants. It was done, and done well, before I knew a moment's suspicion."

"Really, Darcy, I had looked for better from you. Do you expect me to credit such an account? That you, the master, have so badly managed your affairs that your elderly, widowed aunt could have defrauded you beneath your very nose? If it were not so laughable, I would say such a man deserved to reap the fruits of his failings."

Darcy's teeth clenched. "My aunt is far from a helpless widow."

"Catherine? No, indeed. I believe if we had a dozen of her, we should set them loose in the Tyrant's household and this war with France would be over within a se'nnight. But that does not answer for these claims of yours. Am I to believe that Catherine would conspire against you and risk ruining her own daughter, simply to force a marriage?"

"Believe what you will. That is what has occurred, and I am determined that she shall not succeed."

"I suppose you have some explanation as to where you were last night, if not in your bed?"

Darcy frowned. "I have."

"Well? Was it some other fair creature in your arms? Is it rather some greater disgrace which prevents you from speaking?"

Darcy drew a steadying breath. "It may not seem a plausible excuse, but my valet alerted to me to a substance in my drink which was intended to render me unconscious. I had already consumed the drink when I learned of it. I left the house at once to prevent the very sort of compromise my aunt claims took place."

"You left? At what time? Where did you go?"

He glanced at his cousin. "It was shortly after eleven when I departed. I intended to go to Richard, but I was… detained. I did not arrive at his apartment until morning."

The earl crossed his arms and raised his bushy brow. "The last time I examined my clock, there was a handspan of time between eleven and my breakfast hour. How do you account for it?"

Darcy stared at the carpet, his jaw working. "As I described to you, I had been given a substance in my drink…."

"So, what you mean to say is that you have no memory of last night's events? How, then, am I to believe a word of your defence?"

"I do recall leaving the house and walking. That much I remember with clarity."

"Perhaps you do not remember coming back in? Staggering to your room with Anne for company? Forgive me, Darcy, but I am afraid I must take up your aunt's cause. You offer no proof of your claims, but Catherine does. You must marry Anne after such a debacle. If you do not, the disgrace to the family does not bear thinking of."

Darcy bristled. "I am innocent of any wrongdoing!"

"If you have evidence of your innocence, I suggest you produce it, and rapidly. And Darcy, do not act rashly—an angry confrontation with your aunt will serve you ill. I will not tolerate a public row within the family!"

~

Darcy took his leave but a few moments later, now nearly shaking with unsatisfied indignation. Richard followed closely at his heels, apparently too diverted by his cousin's woes to wait upon his mother. He would not miss a moment of his entertainment.

Darcy turned back in annoyance. "Have you not something more useful to be about?"

"Not at present."

Darcy stepped into his carriage and found, to his great irritation, that Richard had not awaited an invitation to join him. He took the opposite seat, casting his arm over the cushion in satisfaction.

"So, where to? Back to the house, where you will naturally ignore my father's edict and toss our aunt from your property, creating a scene to embellish every drawing room from here to Derbyshire for the next nine months? Or do we go in search of this proof of yours, which no doubt rests in the charming hands of a lady of uncertain age, who—"

"I did not ask for your company," Darcy interrupted sourly. "Nor are your suggestions helpful."

"Come now, Darcy, I would never abandon a wounded comrade. I always stay to drag him off the field, or at the very least, keep the surgeons away from him until they can inflict no more harm."

Darcy turned away, scowling through the window.

"What of Anne?" Richard suggested. "She knows the truth of what happened last night. Cannot you simply speak with her and sort this nonsense out?"

"Anne has made no objections to her mother's ambitions these four and twenty years. I presume she must have been complicit in the affair, as it was predicated on her willingness to be found in my bed in a shocking state of undress."

"Yes, but is any of that true?"

"It does not matter if it is or not. She submitted to the plan and consented to have the report made that there had been a liaison. That is sufficient evidence of her intentions. There is no benefit in speaking to her, and potentially even greater harm if we are seen speaking privately."

"You are assuming our aunt had given her a choice in the matter."

"You were present at each of my last visits to Rosings. Indeed, she was the very reason I insisted upon your company! Has she ever shown any reluctance toward marriage to me?"

"No, but neither has she hopped between your sheets. Quite seriously, if I did not know you so well as I do, I would account you mad. Why would they wait to stage a compromise in London when it would have been so much easier last spring in Kent, at their own house? Or again this coming April? I hear Aunt even has a new rector eating out of her hand, so a wedding could have been got up in short order. Surely Rosings would have been her choice."

"Unless Anne has suddenly grown desperate for some reason."

"Yes, but even at that, we should have seen them at Christmas. Unless of course…. Oh, by thunder, *that* is what you suspect, is it not?"

Darcy merely arched a brow and said nothing.

Richard nodded and steepled his white fingers, biting his lips. "Tell me you have proof of where you were last night, Darcy."

"As you say, the truth can be equally troublesome."

"You do not mean you were with some other young lady? I was only teasing, you know, but did you…?"

"Not intentionally, but yes. I was found in Mayfair and apparently not in possession of my faculties. The party who looked to my well-being was a tradesman's niece from Cheapside."

"Was she amiable?

"I did not stay to find out."

"Pretty?"

"That is hardly the point. Even if she were—which she is not—I will not suffer her tender mercies. What does it profit me to escape one forced marriage to a lady who is at least from the proper circles only to be ensnared by an ill-mannered, impertinent, unsophisticated and completely unsuitable tradesman's niece?"

"Unsuitable or not, you must have spent a deal of time in her company, to have learnt so well how much you dislike her."

"I was forced back into her company in hopes that she might be trusted with the truth. I was disappointed."

"Well, I know that if my choices were between an impertinent tradesman's niece—who seems to have touched a larger nerve than I have known you to possess—and our sickly and possibly gravid cousin, I would choose… oh, dash it all, Darcy, but is there not a harlot or some lascivious widow you can pay off to vouch for you?"

"I would prefer if you did not try to advise me."

"Come, can it really be so bad to go back to that… what was it? Unmannerly, ill-favoured—"

"I never said she was ill-favoured."

"In fact, you did. You cannot even keep that bit of the tale straight!"

"I said she was not amiable and that she lacked culture."

"You said you did not stay to find out if she was amiable."

"It does not signify! She is wholly unsuitable, whatever your intimations, and hardly a gentlewoman."

"But she took you in off the streets, and even dressed as a footman, rather than a gentleman."

"What does that matter?"

"Naturally she did not make you sleep in the stable, nor force you out on your own while still incapacitated. I would wager she even saw to it that you were fed before you naturally insulted her on your way out the door. Indeed, she must be an utter heathen."

"Many a woman can play at the Good Samaritan. That is hardly a proper qualification for a wife."

"It is not a bad place to start. So, which is it to be? Anne or this… what was her name?"

"Miss Elizabeth… something. Her uncle's name was Gardiner."

"You were not even properly introduced?"

"She thinks I am a footman!"

Richard stared for a moment, then his face broke into a wide grin. In another moment, he was holding his belly and wiping tears of laughter from his cheeks. "Oh! Forgive me, Darcy, but this really is the most entertaining story I have heard in months. Did she set you up in the servants' quarters and all?"

Darcy folded his arms and looked away.

Richard was still hooting in merriment when the carriage rolled past Darcy House and onward toward his own dwelling. When he recognised their surroundings, he looked to his cousin in confusion. "You are not going to your own house?"

"No. And neither are you."

"Ah," Richard nodded in understanding. "Off in search of your impertinent daughter of trade?"

"My solicitor, if you must know."

"You intend to post a retraction? You cannot do that without some valid cause, you know. Rumour is only rumour in the papers, but an official statement…."

"And when the more salacious bits reach the gentlemen's clubs? Almack's? Far more than rumours of an engagement will be spread. Anne's reputation will be irredeemable, and my own, in tatters. If I act immediately to prove there is nothing to the reports of an engagement, perhaps my innocence will also be believed."

"I think you are being a little too optimistic. Everyone prefers a juicy bit of tittle-tattle to the truth, even if it is disproved later."

"Then I shall simply have to disprove it sooner than that."

"May I wish you the very best of luck with your 'proof,' then. Of course, if your Miss Elizabeth did not know who you were and is of any sort of a generous nature, she and her family might well vouch for you without making any demands of your honour. She may never even need to know your name! A letter from a good house should suffice. Had you thought of that?"

"If she gives such assurance, the result may be a very public 'broken engagement.' With another lady in disgrace over the affair, can you believe that her name would also remain anonymous? The *ton* would search her out mercilessly, and she would be presumed to be my mistress. Tradesman or no, what uncle would not then demand satisfaction of me? After one embarrassment, I could do nothing to avoid a second."

Richard pursed his lips and sat in contemplation for a moment. "Right, then. May I stand up at your wedding?"

Nine

"I think the colonel's advice to be sound, Mr Darcy." The bespectacled little man of business gave the paper back into Darcy's hands with a melancholy shake of his head. "I will, of course, issue any statement you please, but in my experience with these matters, I often find that the innocent party is harmed more greatly than his accuser. It is supposed that he speaks untruths in a vain attempt to ward off public scorn. Have you any proof at all, sir?"

Darcy emitted a long, silent growl, and shot his cousin a look which clearly swore *damn you for being right*. "The evidence you speak of does exist, but it may be difficult to procure. I intend rather to coerce a confession from my aunt, thereby clearing my character."

The solicitor's expression remained carefully neutral, but in his eyes flashed a condescending sympathy, almost pity, for Darcy's obstinate simplicity. He risked a swift glance toward Fitzwilliam, then bent his greying head to scribble down some note. For his part, Fitzwilliam's face was one of composed innocence, and he was studying the ceiling, the bookshelves, the casement—in short, everything but Darcy.

"Have you some different advice to offer?" Darcy asked, caring little who would answer.

Fitzwilliam held his hand toward the solicitor, who cleared his throat before speaking. "Mr Darcy, certainly you are aware of the repercussions...."

"The wording must be printed with care. I suggest only that we print a contradictory rumour, declaring the previous a mistake. I need not directly accuse my aunt of falsehood."

"Come, Darcy, she will bring the matter to a point herself. You know our aunt—she will raise such pandemonium that you will be forced to either make your accusation public or withdraw your protest and capitulate. There is no saving face in this matter."

"With all due respect, Mr Darcy, may I recommend preparing for just such an outcome?" the solicitor added his opinion. "It may not go as poorly as the colonel predicts…."

"And yet, it may," sighed Darcy. "Very well. Have this sent to the papers to run in the morrow's press, and I shall make what arrangements I am able. And post a letter to Mr Hodges and Mrs Reynolds at Pemberley, asking them to come to the London house at once to oversee the hiring of new staff."

The solicitor bowed. "Of course, Mr Darcy."

They departed the office together, Fitzwilliam whistling some crude battlefield tune and Darcy wishing his cousin on another continent. "Well, Darcy, are you for the house now to stare down the canon? I shall happily serve as your second if she chooses swords or pistols, but if it is to be a tongue lashing, I pray to beg off."

Darcy sank into the cushion of his carriage with a sigh. "It must be done."

"Aye, but only a fool arrives on the field without a weapon. Have you anything in your scabbard but your own sour temper?"

"You make me sound rather like an ogre. Do I not have every right to be offended by her actions? Shall I not insist on justice?"

Fitzwilliam stretched his Hessians across the carriage and lounged more comfortably in his seat. "In the First, we have a way of sorting the new recruits who will be shot first. It is always the rash, headstrong ones, indignant and fully assured of their right to justice. The clear-headed ones with a plan and some preparation tend to survive."

"I am not searching out the 'plan' of which you speak. I have already told you why that is impossible."

"Well, I suppose it is your neck in the noose, after all."

Darcy scowled in frustration and fell silent, staring out the window but still sensing Fitzwilliam's laughing attentions on him. They rode on for several moments, with Darcy's fingers drumming the cushion and Fitzwilliam's toes tapping away to some cheerful tune of his own making.

At last, Darcy conceded. "Perhaps I shall search out this Mr Gardiner once more and learn what I can of his character."

~

It seemed an eternity before the children's nurse had all three of them properly bundled to set out for their airing. Had Elizabeth not already taken her constitutional, she might have begun to fret at the delay. The nurse appeared to consider it a slight against her abilities when Elizabeth offered to help, so she withdrew and bided her time with her sister. At last, she was informed that everyone was ready—the youngest in his pram and pushed by his nurse, the middle taking one of Elizabeth's hands, and the eldest gaily twirling Cousin Elizabeth's parasol.

"Where shall we go today?" she asked of them, ducking swiftly to avoid a terrible accident between the parasol and her bonnet. She hated the contraption and never used it at home, but in London, her aunt insisted, and she remembered it approximately half the time. It was but a small price to pay for the freedom of walking out, save when one of the children took charge of it.

Elizabeth gently reclaimed the item and asked her question again. "Do you prefer the fountain or the pond?"

Jenny, the younger, voiced her enthusiasm for the pond, but her elder sister Maddy had a special coin she wished to toss into the fountain. Thus, it was decided.

The children's morning outing, it must be confessed, tended to be a far grander adventure when Cousin Elizabeth visited. This day being no exception, it was nearly two hours before the small party reversed their steps. The cranky toddler harassed his exhausted nurse in the fore, while Elizabeth with the two girls brought up the tail of their little procession. She was sauntering along merrily, humming a silly song to them, when one of them called her attention to something.

"'Lisbeth, that man is staring at you."

"I beg your pardon?" She turned about to identify the source of her cousin's accusation. It was *he*, on the opposite side of the street, and looking as if he wished to cross over to her. "Oh! Not him again. Look away Maddy, he is not worth your trouble."

"'Lisbeth, he's walking this way. I think he wants to talk to you." Elizabeth ignored her cousin's advice and walked on, head held high as if she had not heard.

He was not willing to permit such an easy escape. "Madam, a word, please, I beg you."

Elizabeth sighed, drew a bracing breath, then turned to face him with her cousins' small hands clasped within her own. Indeed, it was that same footman again, but this time he was attired rather lavishly, in a suit of clothes which might have accounted for half her father's annual income. She arched an eyebrow. "I see that your circumstances have improved somewhat over the course of the morning."

"Would that that were true," he frowned. "I came to ask one more service of you, madam."

There was a stirring to his left, and Elizabeth noted for the first time another man standing nearby. He also seemed to be dressed as a gentleman, though slightly more modestly. He may not have been so handsome as the footman, but he seemed to be surveying her with an open cheer which more than made up for any lack of symmetry to his features. Elizabeth gave a small curtsy in his direction, but as she was not properly introduced to the gentleman, it would be unladylike to speak to him. Somehow, it was less improper to speak to the 'harmless' footman whose bare feet she had seen, than to the pleasant-looking gentleman in his company.

She surveyed her 'footman' once more, wondering whom he had swindled and plundered to obtain such a vestment. "You do not appear to be in search of work any longer, and I presume you have been reunited with your…" she swept a significant glance toward the other man, "…*employer*. I am left to wonder what service I could possibly render you."

He looked uncomfortable, fumbled with the silver handle of an extravagant walking stick in his hand, and spoke. "It is a simple matter of fact verification, madam. I have found it necessary to speak to the master of the house where I lodged last evening so that my whereabouts might be ascertained by one who holds an interest in the matter."

Elizabeth glanced to the other gentleman again, but his carefully neutral expression revealed nothing. The taller man continued.

"Unfortunately, I have just learned that the master of the house is not at home, nor would any inform me of his whereabouts."

"And therefore," she supplemented, "you find it preferable to accost a lady and two children on the street in your search for information regarding him?"

"That is not precisely… I intend no offence, madam. But as you have placed it so bluntly; yes, I would wish to speak to Mr Gardiner, and I must do so urgently. May I trouble you for the information as to where he is to be found?"

Elizabeth began to grow suspicious. "If you will answer the question for me."

He looked baffled. "Which question?"

"Why you are so determined to seek him instantly that you could not wait an hour or two, as an honest man would. And why a discharged footman—if you are indeed of such an honourable profession—should dare to continue asking after a man of good standing when he has no justifiable cause to be favourably received."

At the word "footman," the other gentleman appeared to snicker. Elizabeth shifted her eyes to him curiously, and he seemed to recover himself. "I beg your pardon, madam, for we have not been introduced."

"I fear we are destined to remain strangers, then," Elizabeth dipped her head courteously. "For there is none present to perform the office, and I am in the company of my young cousins. I am afraid, sirs, I must bid you a good day." She turned her back with a serene smile, but all the while she could virtually feel that insolent glare following after her. It was the most satisfying thrill she had known all day.

He permitted her to escape for but a moment, and Elizabeth heard what sounded like muffled whispers exchanged between the two men. A throat cleared, and long heavy steps sounded behind her.

She turned again, causing him to draw up prematurely when he found himself almost upon her without warning. "May I ask what is so urgent? Your persistent reappearances and your sudden alteration in wardrobe do, you must know, seem suspicious. Are you a man to be trusted?"

"I am among the most trustworthy, I assure you."

"Are you? I first encounter you under the influence of some intoxicant, staggering alone on the streets at night. In the morning you insult me, take off your shoes in public, and follow me everywhere I turn. Now I see that you are dressed in... excuse me... *borrowed* clothing, and have accumulated a sort of hanger-on. I am left to presume that you are some manner of fraud."

His eyes widened in indignation. "Fraud! Madam, do you know to whom you speak?"

"That is precisely the problem, is it not? Perhaps I shall assume that you are in the company of your employer, who for some reason permits you to callously insult a lady on a public street. In that case, I do not wish to be introduced to him any more than I wish to know by which address one should call his hired man. Good day." Elizabeth turned to walk away again, but this time she was stopped by a loud roar of laughter from the second gentleman.

"Oh! I must breach all rules of etiquette, madam, for you are a marvel, and well worth knowing better. I beg to be permitted to introduce myself to you. Colonel Fitzwilliam, at your service, and this rather gruff fellow here means no offence, I am sure."

Elizabeth dipped her head. "Colonel Fitzwilliam. I have heard your name before." She shifted a knowing smile to the other, then turned to her young cousin. "Now, Jenny, you must listen very carefully to me. Maddy, you as well. This gentleman here has quite seriously broken all protocol and brazenly introduced himself to me, without a proper escort or friend at hand to make the introduction as it should be done. A well-bred lady never listens, nor responds to such an audacious gentleman.

"It would be most discourteous of me to respond in kind with my name, which, as you know, is Elizabeth Bennet. It would be even more foolish and uncouth to remain standing here and accidentally continue the conversation with such a careless gentleman. He will no doubt ask my destination upon this walk, which is not my uncle's warehouse on High Street, but your house on Gracechurch, for so long as I remain before returning to Hertfordshire, I desire to visit with my aunt and with you.

"And girls, there is one thing more which I must most seriously implore you to heed. No lady in her right mind would concede to the wishes of such a bold and foolish gentleman if he were to ask where her uncle was to be found later in the day, which I hope shall be escorting his family on a leisure outing to Vauxhall Gardens. He will, of course, bring his own manservant to accompany his family, so that we shall not be troubled by others seeking to take advantage of us.

"Such men do exist, you know. They may parade about in stolen finery and brandish their tin walking sticks so that a lady's head is turned, but they are little more than snakes, my dear. A proper lady must learn the difference. There, now that we have spoken of etiquette for today, what do you think of seeing to some nice refreshment with Nurse? I see that she has already gone far ahead of us, and your brother is likely to have all the scones for himself if we do not make haste."

The footman's face had altered from mere impatience to affronted incredulity. His mouth had opened, his eyes had begun to spark, and that ridiculous fake walking stick twisted in his grip. Elizabeth graced him with one last little smile of victory and turned away.

Ten

"Follow her! Whatever for?" Darcy almost snarled in contempt at his cousin. "I will have nothing more to do with her! Why should I harass myself further by ingratiating myself to such a minx?"

"I can think of a couple of reasons, the least of which being your desire to escape an unfavourable match with our cousin. Darcy, if you do not catch her up, I will!"

"And do what? Invite her back to take tea with your mother? Or had you less noble intentions?"

"Darcy, you dunderhead! Anyone can see that she is no shopkeeper's girl or strumpet. If I had to guess from her manner and what she said, I would wager my brass buttons that she is a country gentleman's daughter who merely happens to have an uncle in trade. I *do* have a passing familiarity with ladies, after all. By the by, you were somewhat less than forthcoming when you described her appearance as 'unremarkable.'"

"I said no such thing. I said she was unsuitable and impertinent. I find now that her manners were at their *best* when I *first* encountered her, and I have no hope of their improvement." Darcy turned sharply away, thinking to thump his walking stick on the pavement in aggravation, but it would only remind him of his aunt's ways. Instead, he gave it a swift toss, caught it, and tried to march away, but Fitzwilliam was by now dragging at his shoulder.

"Impertinent she most certainly is, but unsuitable? I think I have never seen a woman better suited to you. Come, you must marry *someone*, and at least this one would be entertaining for me."

"Marry her! I only intended to speak with this Mr Gardiner, not make an offer to that impossible woman."

"You could do far worse," Fitzwilliam reasoned. "If you ask me, it is you who are being impossible, not she. She did, after all, give you the information you sought, and she was perfectly in the right about speaking to strange gentlemen on the street. You must confess, she is not unpleasant to look at, she is most interesting to talk to, and she holds the key to your independence from Anne."

"A fine sort of independence you speak of. You would have me bound to a nobody from Hertfordshire. Have you any idea the mockery such a union would be in the sight of the *ton*?"

"When have you ever cared about offending the *ton*? You despise most of them. I think rather that you delight in frustrating them by doing precisely as you please and watching them fall over themselves to placate you anyway."

"That is only because I have remained a bachelor. They will be less forbearing when that circumstance changes. Do not forget, Richard, that I have Georgiana's future to secure as well."

"Darcy," Fitzwilliam caught his arm again, looking over his shoulder, "she is nearly gone! By thunder, man, if you do not do an about-face this instant, I shall drag you by your lapels!"

"Do not change the subject! I spoke of Georgiana—"

"Who needs a sister more than she needs a husband at the moment. You happen to have stumbled upon a pretty one who willingly spends time with young children and has a sense of humour, though you are too daft to see it. What more do you require?"

"Do not be such a simpleton. You know my requirements perfectly well."

"I know that if you go back to your house just now, you will be given a bride whether she meets your requirements or no. At least take the lady's hint and seek out her uncle on High Street. *I* would like an introduction to him, even if you do not."

Darcy glared at his cousin but was not afforded an opportunity to make the indignant reply he would have liked.

"Darcy? Darcy, it *is* you!" a passer-by stopped and offered them a short bow. "And Colonel Fitzwilliam, it is a pleasure."

Darcy's eyes widened to a panicked glare at his cousin. *Damnation!* He turned slowly, swallowing his frustration, to make a polite response. "Mr Dalrymple. How do you do, sir?"

"Capital! Darcy, I understand congratulations are in order. I imagine Lady Catherine de Bourgh and Lord Matlock must be pleased. May I extend my well wishes to you and Miss de Bourgh?"

"There has been some mistake, sir," Darcy spoke quickly. "I am not betrothed. It is a rumour, sir, nothing more."

"A rumour! That is unfortunate. Why, I have just come from my club, and it is commonly spoken of as a fact."

"It is!" Darcy paled slightly. "Mr Dalrymple, there is no truth in it. The gossip is in exceedingly poor taste. And you say it is commonly accepted?"

"Indeed, it is the talk of the club this morning, even more so than Lord Wharton's betrothal. That much has been long overdue for months, if you take my meaning." Dalrymple grinned suggestively, nudging Fitzwilliam with a low chuckle which he must have imagined to be discreet.

"The rumour in the paper," Darcy insisted, "does no one doubt its veracity?"

"*Papers*, my good man, for I have seen it in at least two publications, and certainly there are more. Let me see…" Dalrymple scratched his cheek in thought, then shook his head. "None that I recall. There were not a few comments that you buckled to your aunt's wishes at last—"

"I did no such thing! It is a sham, I tell you. I am not betrothed to my cousin. It is a shameful falsehood, and I shall depend upon you to set right anyone who repeats it in your hearing!"

Dalrymple rolled his eyes uncertainly to Fitzwilliam and pursed his lips in the way of a man who wishes to affect surrender, merely to escape. "Naturally, Darcy, naturally. Oh, dear!" He tugged the pocket watch from his waistcoat, scarcely glancing at it but professing full knowledge of its information. "I am expected! Pardon me, Darcy, Fitzwilliam, but I really must go. Good day!" Dalrymple sped away, seemingly sorry that he had stopped.

"There, you have gone and done it, Darcy. Now, Dalrymple and anyone he comes upon will think you touched in the head. I understand your frustration, old boy, but you harm yourself by this obstinacy. Are you certain you cannot swallow your pride and go after your rescuer?"

Darcy leaned heavily on his walking stick, flexing his fingers over the silver knob and muttering his thoughts. Fitzwilliam could not make out his words, but he suspected they ought not to be repeated in polite company.

~

The manservant glanced over Darcy's apparel, obviously recognising him from the kitchens that morning and still slightly miffed at their last conversation a quarter of an hour earlier. It was clearly written in his eyes that he wondered the same of Darcy that would have puzzled anyone else of sense, but he answered the question willingly enough. "Sir, the lady has not yet returned to the house."

"That is impossible. I spoke with her not a moment ago on the street, and she was walking this way. Is she disinclined to speak with me again?" Darcy felt the annoyance rising in his chest again. Blast the woman! Why must she be so bleeding difficult?

"I saw her as well, sir, approaching up the street with the children. She did not care to enter with them. As another caller had just arrived at the house, it was not possible for me to make inquiries of her. I believe she has gone walking."

Darcy's eyes widened incredulously. *Again?* Never had he known a lady who did not stay at home for even an hour in the morning. "Do you know where she might have gone?"

The manservant blinked and refused to answer.

"I mean the lady no harm," Darcy insisted. "But it is of the utmost importance that I speak with her. Or… with any lady of the house, if the master is not at home. I understand they would all recognise me."

"Mrs Gardiner is indisposed at present sir, but Miss Catherine might be willing to receive you."

"Wait…" Darcy flinched, remembering that vacuous simpleton of a girl whose face had been the first thing he had seen upon awakening. "No, I would prefer to speak with Mrs Gardiner or Miss Elizabeth."

"Mrs Gardiner is not expected to be down for some time. I am afraid you will have to wait, sir," the manservant answered stiffly.

Darcy suppressed a sigh. "May I wait within for Miss Elizabeth's return?"

The manservant swept his eyes up and down Darcy's person. It was clear that he, too, wondered at the sudden change in attire and circumstances and found little to trust in the strange gentleman. "I am afraid that is not possible, sir."

Darcy felt a scowl beginning to settle over his features and tried to school it away. "Very well. I shall return in an hour." He turned and marched down the steps, Richard doggedly laughing at his heels.

"Why would you not speak to the other young lady? Could she not serve as a witness as well? Or do you, in fact, already nurse something of a *tendresse* for—"

"She is even sillier than the other," Darcy grumbled. "It may yet be that I shall find my name entangled in gossip with one or the other of those ladies, and I would rather that it not be with one of Georgiana's age. I may be seen as ungentlemanly, but I am no bounder who preys on mere children."

"I see," Richard grinned. "And I suppose it does not hurt that Miss Elizabeth has a pleasing figure…"

"I am not thinking of her figure, Richard."

"Oh come, admit it, man! One of Venus' daughters, she was. There is no use in denying it, for I saw the way you looked at her. I began to wonder if you truly were such a monk as I had always thought you to be!"

"She does have remarkably fine eyes," Darcy confessed, rather softly.

"And she is clever," suggested Richard hopefully.

"I wish you would not extol the lady's virtues to me at present. I merely desire her word and an introduction, nothing more and nothing less."

"And where do you seek it? For with those long strides of yours, I can hardly keep up. You must have some direction in mind."

"My carriage. It waits for us in the mews. I regret that I have found it necessary to change my garments once more, for I prefer not to be recognised as I walk the street. I cannot afford the diversions my face and appearance inevitably inspire. I brought the footman's garments with me, as I had no other place to dispose of them, and unfortunately, I again have need of them."

"You always said 'disguise of every sort is my abhorrence,'" chuckled Richard. "And now you wish to disguise yourself?"

"Until this matter is settled, I merely wish to avoid certain conversations with those who might recognise me, and fortunately for me, that also means I must bid you a good morning. Once secured of the statements I require, I shall meet you again at your apartment—two hours at most."

"Aunt is bound to have someone watching my building. The longer you stay away from home, the more desperate she will become."

Darcy stopped, growling under his breath. "Of course. Is there not a public park on Elm?"

"Indeed, there is. Tell you what, old boy. I shall poke about innocently myself, so what do you say we meet a bit later—perhaps by two? That should permit me ample time to appear casual, and you can go about harassing this Mr Gardiner. How do you intend to find him? Will you lie in wait at the lady's door?"

"There is a neighbourhood fountain, not eight streets over to the west. It is worth searching there, for the situation is small, and it will require but a few moments. If she is not to be found there, I shall return to the house in an hour."

"Such a bother! Would it not be simpler to marry Anne and be done with it?"

Darcy shot his cousin a nasty glare, earning only a laugh in return, and stepped into his carriage with renewed purpose. He changed only the cravat, coat, and hat, thinking those items sufficient to mark him as "Not Fitzwilliam Darcy of Pemberley," and emerged again.

"Your boots," Richard pointed.

Darcy groaned. Indeed, his boots.

A few moments later, he was standing on the curb in too-short breeches and the scuffed, uncomfortable shoes borrowed from Richard's batman, and the carriage had pulled away. At least Richard and his infernal laugher had gone with it. "Give the future Mrs Darcy my regards," had been his adieu from the safety of the coach. Darcy bit down on his tongue and set out.

The fountain was indeed near and was surrounded by a small bit of nature. It was little more than a rotunda of trees, situated upon a small grassy knoll and suited with a bench. Upon that bench rested... to Darcy's dismay, either his heart performed an acrobatic feat, or he suffered a moment of indigestion. He paused to assure himself that it was *not*, surely, the effect of the idyllic scene he had happened upon.

She was surrounded by the leafy golds of early autumn, her down-turned face softly reflecting the earthy warmth of the scenery. A shaft of light broke through the shedding branches and poured over her shoulder, bathing her figure in a heavenly sort of innocence. She was reading a book, and it must have been a highly engrossing one, for she did not look up at his approach. She continued lovingly turning the pages, her expressive eyes lighting whenever they found a passage of interest. Little smiles would pass over her features, but she seemed deaf and blind to her surroundings.

Darcy drew approximately ten paces from her and stopped, his hands clenched as he tried to decide what to do with himself. He had never before advanced toward a lady who did not hungrily watch his approach and long for an introduction. This one was utterly indifferent… which was just as well, for she was not of his sphere. He must take care to remember that!

She serenely turned another page, long dainty fingers seeming to relish their task. He could count the lines she read in the number of times her eyes flipped from left to right. Eighteen.

She then sighed, as one who savoured and took to heart every word of the prose, and began to close the book without looking up. "What more would you have of me, sir?" She slipped the little book into her reticule, and then, at last, lifted her chin and met his eyes. "Whatever it is, you are certainly a persistent fellow."

"I have reason to be, madam. May I sit?" He gestured to the other side of the stone bench.

She raised her brows in acquiescence but spoke not a word.

"Thank you." Darcy lifted his coattails and took the seat beside her, his back straight and his feet square upon the ground. He felt those mirthful eyes once more sweeping over his change in apparel, but she said nothing. "Madam, I believe I owe you something of an explanation."

"That is the usual way of obtaining what one desires."

Darcy glanced down at her, catching himself when he realised that looking into her eyes seemed to have a hypnotic effect on his mind. Perhaps it was only the lingering effects of the tainted brandy, but his vision seemed to swim. Thoughts fled, and his tongue was useless. He cleared his throat and looked away.

"I… I understand I have given you sufficient cause to doubt my character. Please allow me to assure you, madam, that you find me in extraordinary circumstances. I have not a deceitful nature, and I deplore all manner of artifice. I do not intend to profit by imposing myself upon you as someone I am not. Rather, I have reason to protect myself from those near to me whose intentions are less than honourable."

"So, which is the true man? The insolent footman or the arrogant gentleman?"

Darcy felt himself bristling. "You think me arrogant?"

"Sir, my precise impression was that if we had met upon equal terms, you would have found me, and any other persons with whom I associate, beneath your notice. The guise of a footman is a poor one for you, sir, because you have not the least measure of deference."

Darcy stared at the ground as if stung by a physical lash. *If she knew my name, she would not dare!* But she did not… and if she had no reason to flatter him, she also had no cause to abuse him without reason. "Have I been disdainful to you, madam?"

Her only answer was a sweetly arched brow and a pointed search through her reticule to retrieve her book. Darcy seethed. What right had she, this queer woman who wandered the streets and parks alone all day rather than conducting herself as a lady ought, to accuse him of any impropriety of manner and address?

"Madam, I have trials enough without bandying useless words regarding my recent actions and attitudes. I suffer cruelly in my own conscience already, for I do not take lightly the course upon which I am set. If it is in your mind to improve my character by your reproofs, I assure you that one moral dilemma is sufficient to the day."

She had returned her attention to her book, ignoring him completely. His hands fell to his knees in disgust, and he prepared to rise when a gentle laugh from her halted him. Unable to resist, he looked to her. Such a peculiar creature!

"So disguise shall, by the disguised,
Pay with falsehood false exacting,
And perform an odd contracting.[1]"

Her ruby lips curved in obvious enjoyment and her eyes lingered on the page for a few seconds more. Then, as if she were one of his masters waiting upon him to answer his examinations, she lifted those dark lashes and held him in her grasp… the very image of perfect composure.

Darcy smiled. He could not help it. She was probing him; measuring his breeding and education, testing his willingness to prove himself, and perhaps— if that twinkle about her expression offered any insight into her own thoughts—even weighing his good humour. Never one to allow a lady to think the less of him, Darcy rose to her challenge.

"Only in this disguise I think't no sin
To cosen him that would unjustly win.[2]" he quoted.

Her own smile blossomed, and she appeared satisfied. "There, sir, you have answered your dilemma. Where one has been dealt with ill, and the intent is

---

[1] William Shakespeare, Measure for Measure (ed. W. G. Clark, W. Aldis Wright) Act 3, Scene 2
[2] William Shakespeare, All's Well That Ends Well
W. G. Clark, W. Aldis Wright, Ed) Act 4, Scene 2

pure, perhaps it is necessary to resort to… shall we say *less public* means of just compensation."

Darcy's spine relaxed, abandoning any notion of quitting the bench and her company. She was a curiosity! "I have done badly in not introducing myself to you," he confessed.

"Oh! Pray, do not, for if you seek discretion, you must not depend upon even my confidence. You shall remain to me a footman, and I simply 'madam' to you."

Darcy's brow furrowed in amusement. "Then, madam, I may I ask you a question?"

"That seems a harmless enough request."

He drew breath, then forged boldly ahead and prayed that she would not misunderstand. "Do you consider that marriage ought to be between willing partners?"

The trace of a line appeared at the corner of her mouth. "Sir, may I remind you that you are speaking to a lady?"

"My words were not intended as a proposal, madam," he corrected quickly.

"Nor did I take them as such. I merely wonder if you recognise that it is more often ladies who are faced with an unappealing and undesired marriage partner. We have not the liberty of choosing; only of accepting or rejecting."

His face softened. "Then may I submit to you that you are incorrect in one regard? For often, the gentlemen have equally small choice in the matter. Family interests can, and often do, take precedence over the gentleman's desires."

"I am perfectly aware of that. Are you, then, the unwitting victim of such an attempt upon your affections?"

"Not my affections, but my honour. Without burdening your conscience by naming those who have compromised their own characters, I may tell you that time is of the essence and the consequences do not bear thinking of, should I fail in proving my innocence. Pray tell me, would my host and hostess of last evening be willing to testify to my presence in their home?"

A faint shadow crossed her features, and her gaze became distant for a moment. "I believe I can safely introduce you to my aunt. Surely… yes, I believe her caller will have gone by now, and she will happily receive you. I think she will be pleased to send their manservant to show you to my uncle."

Darcy stood and offered her his assistance to rise. "I thank you, madam."

Eleven

"Oh, Lizzy, you have a caller," came Kitty's sing-song voice from the parlour.

Elizabeth froze, her neck prickling with dread. "Tell me it is not..."

Kitty merely smirked suggestively over the edge of the book she held... a hand-embossed copy of Fordyce's sermons. "He has proven most entertaining and considerate," Kitty sniggered. "He thought that I would profit from borrowing one of his books, as apparently 'the young ladies of our family must want instruction in all matters moral.' It was easier than listening to him speak, and so I have been reading for the last half hour. What do you think, Lizzy? Are you not proud of me?"

"He does not intend to remain as a guest, does he? Why, he and my uncle were scarcely introduced. He could not dare impose!"

"I believe his room is two doors down from yours."

Elizabeth groaned. "And I thought I would be safe here in London from him! I never imagined he would follow us here."

"He did not follow *me*," corrected Kitty. "I am only here as your 'companion,' and a laughable employment that is, since I never know where you are. Lizzy, where have you been? The children said you came back with them earlier and disappeared before even entering the house."

"I saw our cousin just coming up the steps as I was far down the street, and so I brought the girls to the door and left again before he saw me approaching the house. I imagined that he would learn I was out and go away, but I see his intentions were more determined than that. How ever am I to be rid of him?"

"Mama says the simplest way to manage a man you cannot abide is to marry him, then you may direct his life and send him wherever you wish."

Elizabeth shuddered. "Good heavens, no. Kitty, if anyone asks, I have taken violently ill and am retiring to my room."

"That is no good. He will insist on ministering to you, and perhaps reading you your rites if you act convincingly ill. Then you shall be obliged to die or risk the disappointment of Mr Collins and that silly patroness of his."

Elizabeth felt herself pouting. "Yes, I suppose you are right. I will simply have to be out all day… every day…. Oh, how could he imagine staying here? Surely his acquaintance with our uncle is so slight that he will not dare impose more than a day or two."

"I believe he mentioned as long as a fortnight, depending upon some other business he claimed while here in Town," Kitty turned the page neutrally. "Our aunt was at once taken ill with a coughing fit, and I have not seen her since. I wish I had thought of that!"

"And Mr Collins himself?"

No reply was necessary, for that moment a man's voice was heard in the upper passage, and some ponderous shape moving about upstairs caused the floorboards to squeak.

"It is no good hiding behind the drapes," Kitty observed, after noting the sudden direction of Elizabeth's frantic gaze. "He is bound to look out the windows while he waits for you to return."

"Then I must away at once! Kitty, you have not seen me."

Kitty flipped another page. "Mmm-hmm… what was your name again?"

Elizabeth gasped with feverish relief. "Thank you, Kitty! I will be at our uncle's warehouse if Aunt should be concerned." She lashed her bonnet once again under her chin, just as she heard the first footsteps creaking on the stair. In another half a moment, he would be down, and her attempt at escape all for nought. The main passage, therefore, was no use, so she hastened to complete her preparations in the front foyer.

Her footman was awaiting her… or gentleman… whatever he was. He opened his mouth to speak something of indebtedness or gratitude for her troubles to introduce him, but she firmly grasped him by the elbow. "Come quickly!" she hissed. "Now, not an instant to lose!"

He gaped slightly, his mouth still open as if he wished to speak but could not find any words.

"Come away at once, or I shall abandon you in this house in the company of the most insufferable man you have ever encountered!"

"Forgive me for asking, but was I not a candidate for that title not half an hour ago?"

She turned to survey him with a new appreciation and would have laughed outright, had she not been in such a hurry. "You have lost the contest. Now, come quickly if you will, or you shall be forced to spend your day listening to a fool raving about boiled potatoes and chimney pieces!"

This provided the impetus he required to move his feet. He replaced his hat and allowed her to drag him through the door until they were once again on the street together.

He stared down at her. "I make it a practice never to ask about a lady's private affairs, but—"

"Half a moment, I pray you, sir!" she interrupted. She sped hurriedly down the street, tugging him by the arm as if he were willingly escorting her. He was *heavy*, dragging his feet the way he did at first, but within a dozen strides, he was managing his long legs tolerably well. Once they had gained the corner, Elizabeth slipped around it with her escort in tow and then quickly glanced back to be sure that none had noted or followed them.

He was still staring incredulously at her hand on his sleeve—eyes wide and horror-stricken at her unexplained assault on his person. Elizabeth cleared her throat and dropped her hand. "Forgive me, sir," she excused herself.

"Madam, are you in some danger? Though we have hardly been introduced, far be it from me to permit a lady to suffer at the hands of another."

"The only danger I am in is that which is common to every lady whose feelings outweigh her resources."

"I do not understand. Has someone threatened to harm you?"

She chuckled wryly. "I would deem it harm, though most would not agree with me. I am fortunate to have secured the support of my father, for as far as it will go. Please ask me no more about it. Think only that I decided to escort you to my uncle's office myself."

"If you intend to do that," he gestured before him and took up a position half a step behind her. "Perhaps we would draw less attention if I am seen as your manservant. I do not wish to be remarkable any more than do you."

She lifted her shoulders. "Very well. Come along, my good fellow."

~

She had a rather light and pleasing way of moving.

Darcy had never in his life walked—simply *walked*—behind a lady, save his own mother, but he decided at once to make an effort to do so more often. There was something quite enjoyable about watching the way her skirts played about her ankles, the delicate arch to her shoulders, and even, Heaven help him, the tantalising sway of her hips.

For the first time in years, Darcy permitted himself to admire a woman for her native feminine charms, rather than fearing her manipulative arts. This particular woman still did not know the measure of his wealth and had nothing to gain by attempting to seduce him. Nor did she seem inclined to try. She was simply a… a puzzle. An unpredictable, unaffected… distractingly appealing woman, despite her glaring faults, whose easy manner utterly unravelled all his previous perceptions of feminine confidence.

Darcy suddenly found it necessary to swallow, for there was a sensation in his mouth very much like that feeling when he anticipated savouring a fine roast duck. She turned her head slightly as she examined the row numbers they passed, and to his continuing mortification, he thought her profile rather more striking upon further examination. He forced himself to look away as Richard's laughter echoed in his ears. Well, hang the man. There was no crime in looking at a woman, particularly not one who expected him to follow her. Where else could he look?

Once, when her head turned a little farther than on previous occasions, she seemed to self-consciously catch herself and turned slightly more to look him in the eye. "My uncle has taken a new building recently, and I have only been here once," she apologised. "I remember the number, but I wish to be careful not to pass it."

"Naturally. I presume your uncle is some manner of textile merchant? We are presently among the cloth distribution warehouses."

"That, and a number of other things."

He caught the faintest blush as her head turned again and waited for her to continue. "Will you think the less of me if I demonstrate some basic knowledge of his business? Shall you think me unladylike and then feel yourself free to despise me?"

The gentlemanly answer would have been to deny her suspicions outright, but there was that knowing twinkle in her eye, and then a whisper of conviction in his own heart. Yes, he would have thought the less of her—an hour ago he would have. Her erratic behaviour and unsettling disregard for gentle manners had done little to enhance her appearance of dignity, and he would have had to confess that to her, the distinction of a fine lady was dubiously applied at best.

However, she had helped him. And she continued to help him, though she still knew almost nothing of him. His mouth firmed in resolve.

"I will not think less of you," he declared. "Rather… I might say that a lady's knowledge of her uncle's affairs shows an affection for her family and an interest in practical matters which is very pleasing."

She paused, glancing over her shoulder once more with an expression which was somewhere between amusement and disbelief. "Very well," she stepped on again. "My uncle also trades extensively with America. At present, he has found success with tobacco and beaver pelts."

"And you have lived with him for a long while?" he asked politely.

"Oh! No, I am only visiting. I live in Hertfordshire, near Meryton, and I am to return home on Friday."

"Hertfordshire? Are you familiar with estate known as Netherfield? I understand it is rather large and situated not far from the town called Meryton."

The lady laughed, then turned to look him full in the face. "I have heard we are to have a new tenant in that house at last. You may well imagine the high hopes of all in Meryton that he will prove a charming neighbour. Oh! Here we are." She gestured to a door. "My uncle's office, sir."

"I hope you do not feel it a very great imposition that I ask of you—a lady entering a warehouse, that is."

"I do not think it an imposition to speak with my uncle, and his office is *in* the warehouse, so I make no objection. However, would it not be more proper if you preceded me up the stairs?" She tipped her head toward the steps.

As it happened, Darcy would much rather have followed her—all the better to admire the smooth play of muslin over long legs, the slim turn of ankles peeking beneath her garments… *What am I thinking!* "Indeed, madam," he almost coughed, "I thank you."

Darcy had never before entered a warehouse office, and it was with some mild degree of surprise that he reached the threshold and found no footman waiting to open the door for him. The lady arrived presently beside him, and she lifted her brows in silent inquiry. Not wishing to appear the most hopeless mollycoddle in all of London, he was forced to do the unthinkable.

He knocked on the door himself.

It was opened by a portly older man, with wireframe glasses and spidery wisps of grey hair poking out at odd angles from his skull.

Darcy hesitated. "Mr Gardiner, I presume?"

"Oh!" The man adjusted his glasses. "Dear me, no. Mr Haskins, at your service, sir." He stared hard at Darcy, then his eyes lit with some recognition on the young lady. "Miss Bennet! I am afraid your uncle has gone out."

"Gone out? That is unfortunate. I had counted on finding him here."

"He was, until only a few moments ago. It was a matter with his solicitor which required his immediate attention—something to do with import documents for one of the ships in port. I believe he expected to be several hours."

"Hours!" the lady lamented. She looked up to him apologetically, pearly white teeth nipping her lip. "I am afraid I am no longer of any help to you, sir."

"That is not strictly true."

"Did you not require a statement to clear your character? Will not matters become rather inconvenient for you if you do not have it soon?"

Darcy was chewing thoughtfully on his own inner lip. "Perhaps. But I do not wish to importune you any further, madam. It is not your problem."

"I feel badly on your behalf, sir, for I know something, or at least I think I know something, of the circumstances you face. I am not without genuine sympathy in the matter."

"I thank you for that. Unfortunately, sympathy will do very little toward solving my predicament. I may apply to your uncle again, but I am afraid for today, I must seek another alternative."

"Perhaps if you have nothing better in mind, we could go together to seek out my uncle in town?" she suggested.

He looked down suspiciously. "Why would you trouble yourself so? You owe me nothing. Ought you not to return to your home?"

"As it happens," she permitted a guilty smile, "there is another guest at my uncle's residence I wish to avoid. I find it preferable to enjoy the sights of London since I am not often afforded the opportunity. And who could object, as my safety has been secured by a proper footman?"

"I see. Well then, madam," he bowed gallantly and gestured for her to precede him back down the stairs. "Allow me to escort you."

Twelve

"Why, Aunt Catherine, such a pleasure to see you again." Richard gave a short, very proper bow before his aunt. "I came to call on Darcy, as I had intended. Is he at home?"

Lady Catherine looked him up and down suspiciously. "You still do not know his whereabouts? I have not seen him."

"The blighter! Oh, do forgive me, Aunt. I did not intend to speak so callously. I am merely affronted on my cousin Anne's behalf, and I fear my feelings overcame me."

"Richard Fitzwilliam, I believe you have been corrupted by your years in service," she accused.

"Alas, I fear that even General Wellington himself, the most gallant gentleman alive, is not quite so mannerly when he has just returned from a campaign. Pray, forgive my faux pas."

"I shall forgive a great deal if you can discover Darcy's whereabouts, so that I might have a word with him. Have you seen him at all?"

"Darcy? Why, the last time I saw him was... yes, I believe we had taken a carriage ride... to a part of Town I did not know well. But that was some time ago, of course. I have not seen him since."

"It matters little," sniffed the lady, "unless he has become indisposed or injured somewhere. Naturally, we are *most* concerned for his safety, but I think such a calamity unlikely. I am terribly distressed that he has not returned, for he must do his duty by Anne! Much must be planned, and he ought to consider his bride's sentiments before slighting her publicly as he has done."

"Of course! That was another reason for my call. I had hoped, dear Aunt, to express my very fondest congratulations to my cousin. Is she receiving callers?"

"She is in the blue drawing room, for it is warmer. She must be very careful of her health, after all. I shall attend you."

She led the way, commending her daughter's fine qualities and expressing her satisfaction that at last the dearest wishes of her departed sister were to be answered. He nodded politely as the door was opened to them.

"Anne, my dear, your cousin has called to offer his congratulations." Lady Catherine gestured what he was to do, and Richard did not dare disappoint. Anne rose, wrapping herself in a thick woollen shawl as she did so.

Richard squared his shoulders and pasted a courtly smile on his face. "Greetings, fair Cousin. How do you do?"

"As well as might be expected, with circumstances as trying as they have been," she sighed, casting baleful eyes to the gilded ceiling.

Richard appraised her person carefully as he approached to kiss her hand. She had still that sickly pallor about her that she had always possessed, but there was a certain flush to her countenance, a particular gleam in her eye which seemed altogether new. He took her hand to kiss it and found it ice cold. "I am certain you shall prevail, fair Cousin. I have always felt that your strength was generally underestimated. Might I add that you are looking remarkably well today? Darcy is indeed a fortunate man."

Even as he spoke the lie, he was shaking his head inwardly. Poor Anne! Saddled already with dismal health and an overbearing mother, fate had decreed that she also should be granted a figure which resembled a ship timber and a voice which grated on even the most weathered of ears.

These handicaps might have been sufficient, but alas, the woman had the feet of a horse and the teeth of a donkey, and owing to her persistently bad health, breath which could knock down either. Such deficiencies, coupled with the haughty bitterness of spirit which had always been her heritage, rendered her the poorest choice imaginable for the future Mrs Darcy. Richard began to hope fervently that Darcy might find himself far too entangled with his tradesman's daughter to escape an obligation from that quarter and thus be spared a hideous fate.

"Richard," she whined with dramatic flair, "have you seen Darcy at all? We must speak of wedding dates, particularly after everything…" Here, she batted her short little lashes and blushed suggestively. "After all that has happened."

"Darcy? Why, I do not know precisely where he is. I came here to call on him, as you see, but I fear I shall have to return another day. I wonder, might I instead have a word with his valet?"

Anne blinked to her mother. "His valet? Whatever for?"

"Ah, you see, there was this particular style of breeches he had which have become all the rage in the better circles. I am invited to a party next week, and

I had hoped dearly to cut a fine figure. I must speak with a tailor at once if I am to be ready, but I have no notion where to begin."

"Is it now the task of gentlemen to ask other gentlemen's servants how their clothing is to be made?"

"I should have sent my batman, of course, but I had assumed I would be able to speak with Darcy in person, you understand. My appearance shall be of the utmost importance that night, for there is a particular young lady with eight thousand pounds whose notice I have been wishing to attract."

Lady Catherine dismissed his excuses with a wave of her hand. "I have no interest in your intrigues, Fitzwilliam."

"I beg you would excuse me, then, Aunt. I shall enquire of the butler rather than troubling you. Now let me think, what was the valet's name? Williams? Willard?"

"Mr Wilson, I believe. I shall have him sent to you at once."

Richard bowed. "Thank you, Aunt. My mother and I are most grateful."

"Your mother! What can she possibly have to do with Darcy's valet?"

"Ah, well, she is most particularly interested in seeing me married off. I am duty-bound to oblige her, if I can persuade the lady."

Lady Catherine thinned her lips at his bit of frippery but clapped her hands lightly, and a servant came forward to do her bidding. "I have correspondence to attend, but Anne will be glad of your company while you wait. At least *some* in this family know how to pay their respects to a bride!"

"Then I am gratified to be of service," Richard bowed again as she left the room.

Anne offered him a simpering smile. "Will you be seated, Cousin?"

Richard accepted with good grace and was at once situated with a glass and something much stronger than tea to drink. He nodded his gratitude and saluted the lady. "My felicitations to you, Cousin. I say, I must confess to being a little surprised at you."

"Me? Whatever for?" Anne shrugged her heavily cloaked shoulders.

"Why, at settling for Darcy, of course. I had thought you could do much better."

"Better than a man with a large estate and ten thousand a year?" she scoffed.

"But no title," Richard pointed out. "Certainly, with a fortune such as yours, and being the granddaughter of an earl, you might have caught someone's eye."

She flicked her fingers. "Darcy is as fine as any other man."

"Ah, that he is, but I never thought you wished to settle in Derbyshire. Is not Lord Wharton from Hampshire? And Viscount Hallstead, now he is from Kent like yourself. Is not the weather much more agreeable to your health?"

"What matters the location of the estate? I have no intention of living there, save for a visit in the summer when it is at its finest. I shall remain in Kent, of course, or London during the season."

"Naturally," Richard agreed, "it is far better for your constitution, I am sure. Although, I am rather surprised that Darcy agreed. He is rather unreasonably attached to that miserable county in the north. I congratulate you on prevailing, Cousin, for I know few who can against him."

"Darcy is hardly an ogre, Richard."

"Perhaps you have little seen this side of the man as yet, but I assure you, he gives small credit to comforts. Why, poor Georgiana once rode astride for two days together because Darcy would not slow their journey north by taking the carriage."

"Richard, do not be ridiculous. He would never set Georgiana on a horse to travel and certainly not astride for such a trip."

"I assure you, he did, and when we arrived at Pemberley, no rest was awaiting us but several days of work, for the fields were flooding that spring. Why, even Georgiana had a list of tasks. Darcy did permit her a pair of Wellingtons for her work in the field…."

"Richard, I do believe you are teasing me. Georgiana wearing boots and working in the fields! Preposterous."

"Nothing of the kind, dear Cousin! I would never speak an untruth about Darcy, for I love him like a brother, for all his peculiarities. I must, or I certainly would never have arranged quite so many affairs for him."

"Affairs?" Anne laughed. "Forgive my rudeness, Cousin, but what could *you* have possibly arranged for Darcy? I always thought it was the reverse, for I am certain you have had access to his purse."

"On occasion, indeed, both assertions have been true, but… well, it is hardly fitting knowledge for a lady. I suppose as you are to be his wife, you will discover soon enough what his ways are. There are certain matters for which a less refined sort of expertise is necessary."

"Richard Fitzwilliam! If you intend to imply that Darcy has had his indiscretions—"

"Indiscretions! That is a mild description. I have certain knowledge that he spent the night, just recently, mind you, hiding in the servant's quarters with one lady—or perhaps 'lady' is too strong a descriptive."

"It matters not, for I am to be his wife, so all that must be in the past."

"Oh, to be sure, Darcy is a fine man and will certainly never disgrace his wife… at least, not intentionally. There may yet be some bother with that one from…." Richard stopped, affected a frown, and then shrugged. "Certainly, it must not matter to you, so I should not repeat it."

"Which one?" Anne insisted.

"Well, it is only hearsay, after all. There may be little truth in it."

"And do I not have the right to know what is being said about the man I am to marry?"

"You do have an excellent point, fair Cousin. It is only that some say Darcy visited the home of a certain paramour just after his interlude with you last evening. I understand he—"

"Richard Fitzwilliam!" Anne stood, shaking and white, as she pointed one of her talon-like fingers toward his chest. "These are the basest, vilest of accusations!"

"It is nothing but the truth. You desired to know of his habits, and rightly so, for you are to be stuck with the man."

"I did not wish to hear jealous slander," she sniffed.

"Slander! All the men at the club have nothing but the highest regard for Darcy and his exploits."

"I care nothing what the gentlemen at the club think! My interest in him is that of a respectable lady toward her future husband."

"Do you think you can live with a man and remain ignorant of his secrets? If you do, I pity you, Cousin, for your disappointment will come as a rather wretched surprise."

"Nonsense! I insist you leave this house at once, Richard, and do not return until you have recanted these odious defamations."

"I beg your pardon, Cousin. I fear I have overstayed my welcome." He bowed a proper farewell, rolling his eyes as his face was hidden from her. "May I only beseech you, dear Cousin, consider carefully and enter this marriage with all due contemplation. I am naturally concerned for your happiness and would wish you to know something of the man before you take his name."

As he turned to go, leaving her scowling and turning pointedly away from him, a footman opened the door. Just in the corridor stood Wilson, looking expectantly to him with a hopeful eagerness in his face.

"Ah! Excellent timing, Mr Wilson. I was hoping you might have the name of Mr Darcy's tailor for me."

Wilson bowed and extended paper, catching Richard's eye with a significant expression. "I understand, sir. I have written down the direction. Please inform me if I may be of further assistance."

"Very good, thank you, my good man. I think this is sufficient to the moment, but I shall not hesitate to enquire if I have forgotten something."

Turning back to his cousin, he inclined his head. She ignored him, but he bade his farewell all the same. "I wish you a very good day, Cousin. Please do give my regards to my aunt."

She never answered.

~

Darcy shifted the parasol in his hand, trying to discover how to carry such a device and not feel himself the fool. "How, precisely, do you propose we find your uncle? I appreciate your willingness to be of assistance, madam, but there are any number of attorneys on a single street in this part of Town, and we were given very little direction. I think perhaps we would do better to return to Gracechurch Street to await your uncle."

"That will not be until this evening, and he is likely to be occupied when he does come home. You know, you ought really to put your hand out if we wish to summon a hack chaise, for it looks rather badly if I should do so when I am accompanied by a perfectly good footman."

Darcy groused and gave a half-hearted toss of his hand at a passing hackney, but it was already occupied. He turned back to her in near defiance, relieved that he had not truly gone so far as to summon a carriage like a common domestic.

"If your uncle is late returning," he protested his earlier point, "then will it not be because he has been honestly detained? That is yet another reason I am reluctant to disturb him. If he is about other business and I insist upon his notice, he may not be well disposed toward me. It is a ridiculous predicament, but I am forced to depend upon his goodwill. I would rather not approach him at all than to offend him and further complicate my circumstances."

She smiled back at him. "You are accustomed to high-mettled gentlemen of the *ton*, I think—easily offended and quick to set themselves against one who might impose upon them. My uncle is not of that disposition, and you have no need to fear his censure. In fact, it may profit you greatly to make your request in the presence of his legal witness, for he will certainly see that it is drawn up properly. As to discovering his whereabouts, that is simple enough. He always uses the same attorney for business matters. My other uncle, do you see, is an attorney in Meryton and he has a partner here in London."

Darcy felt his face twitching. "Your uncle is an attorney? And the other is…"

"A merchant, yes, we have already canvassed this. I am afraid I cannot produce any lords or even knights from my pedigree to make your acquaintance." She glanced back with a look which was hardly apologetic for her poor connections. "My uncles both labour for their livings, but that fact renders them no less agreeable in my eyes." There was an iron in her gaze and heat to her tone which Darcy did not dare contradict, however much he might cringe at her situation.

"I am certain they are perfectly respectable," he agreed unevenly. "But… what of your father?"

"I could tell you much of his situation which might sound flattering, but I have no interest in leading you on to some pretty images of great houses and lands. My father is a good man, but I can boast of little in the way of connections by him. I am certain that so discerning a fellow as yourself would find our house, as well as its master, beneath your notice."

"A gentleman does not judge another man by the size of his house, but his management thereof, and his attendance to his duties," he clipped out, with a tightness to his voice which, if she cared to notice, could not help but betray his own uncertainty on the matter. "Pray do not suspect me of thinking meanly of a man I have never met. You have already informed me that he is a fair and reasonable father. Surely you and your sister have no cause to repine."

"Which sister? For I have four of them."

Darcy stumbled to a halt. "*Four?* There are five of you, altogether?"

"Of which I am the second, and I shall spare you the indelicacy of enquiring after my brother, for I have none. Do keep walking, sir, for it looks odd that a lady's footman should fail to keep pace on the street."

Darcy forced his feet into motion again. "But your father must have a brother, of course. Someone to care for his family, should the unforeseen strike?"

"Not one, and I would hardly call a man's eventual demise 'unforeseen,' for as you know, sir, none of us escape this world alive. My mother has a holy terror of the hedgerows, but perhaps that is unwarranted, for my father does have a relation. He is a man of the cloth and has vigorously sought to amend that breach… it is only a pity one cannot tighten that cloth a *bit* more snugly about his parsimonious neck!"

Darcy made a strangled noise in his own throat, perhaps in sympathy for the unknown gentleman who had also fallen victim to this lady's barbed tongue… or perhaps in unwonted laughter. She, however, seemed to understand him to be commiserating with her, for she offered a mischievous little smirk over her shoulder.

"Ah! I am irreverent, and I know it very well. You see, however, something of the predicament in which a lady may find herself, quite apart from any fault of her own. Agreeable gentlemen can be in rather short supply when ladies are so bountiful."

Good heavens, Darcy's chest froze. *Bingley!* To such a family, in such a neighbourhood, his friend would be as a prize bull…. No, not a bull. Not Bingley. The fool would be little better than a bleating lamb with wide, innocent eyes, happily trotting toward the slaughter.

"Madam," he enquired hesitantly, "what of your neighbours? Have you," he coughed, "any acquaintance among the local gentlemen?"

She looked back to him again. "You must cease calling me 'madam,' for it really does sound ridiculous. Miss Bennet will do nicely, as my older sister Jane is not present. It is a pity, for I think you would have liked her—everyone does—but Mama desired her to remain at home when word was had that Netherfield's new tenant might be a person of interest."

Darcy's stomach knotted. *Damnation*... one lady already being groomed to be thrown into his friend's path, and he had yet to even take up residence in the county! Yet even if this elder Miss Bennet had warts and a witch's cackle, Hertfordshire was apparently overrun by ladies. There would be entire legions of simpering misses, no doubt led by a battalion of strategising matrons such as would do His Majesty's army proud! Bingley would not have a prayer. He would declare the first lady he danced with an angel and would host the very enemy upon his own doorstep if it meant some fair creature would spare him but a smile.

"My eldest sister," continued the dark-haired vixen, just as if she could have read his thoughts, "is the sweetest, most generous person alive, not to mention the most beautiful lady in the county. I have the greatest affection for her. I am not of the persuasion of some, who might be led to act out of desperation to preserve her family, but I do earnestly hope matters resolve to everyone's satisfaction. If anyone deserves her happiness, it is Jane."

"Not yourself?" he could not help but ask, then bit his tongue. If he were not careful, he would end up no better off than Bingley!

"I have not half of Jane's goodness," she answered plainly. "I do have such a habit of letting my tongue run on, and occasionally it is rather sharp. My sister possesses every virtue I lack. She is as genuine and true-hearted as she is beautiful."

"Warm praise for a sister, Miss Bennet. I wonder if anyone can truly be deserving of such high esteem, for such has not been my experience."

"Such a cynic, sir! Surely there must be someone you admire without reserve. Perhaps a near relation?"

He found, much to his chagrin, that he was beginning to smile. Unlike most ladies, she was not *easy* to talk to, in that she eschewed the banal, safe topics and forced him to defend his position, but he was growing to be at ease in her presence. She was interesting, at least, a thing which could be said for few among his acquaintance, almost none of whom were female. "I must confess to the very sincerest affection for my own sister."

"You have a sister? Will you tell me something of her? Has she your grave turn of countenance, or is she agreeable?"

"You think me disagreeable?"

"I think you are inclined to a more generous opinion of yourself than others might accord you," she returned tartly, but not without a teasing lilt to her voice.

"I think I am justified in punishing you for that remark. Therefore I will refuse to answer your question regarding my sister."

"Ah, but you have no choice, for you see now I am free to think the worst of her. Shall I assume that she is sour, ill-favoured, and lacking in all talent?"

"You may not, for she is none of those things."

"Then is she perhaps of an unpredictable temperament? Given to fits of melancholy, or rage, or scandalous behaviour?"

Darcy dropped his gaze and stubbornly followed in silence, refusing to allow her the victory.

"Oh, dear, I have touched a little near the mark," she apologised, all the animation and playfulness gone from her voice. "Forgive me, sir, if I have spoken when I should not have."

"You mistake my silence for a confession," he replied quickly. "I assure you, my sister has a very generous and mild disposition. I would not have you think otherwise. She has, however, fallen victim to the pretty words of one who is insincere, as young ladies occasionally do. Her spirits have been slow to recover from such an injury."

The lady walked on with a lowered head. "My apologies, sir," she murmured after a moment. "I can see that you are very fond of her, and she is not the first to make the acquaintance of a false friend, lady or gentleman. I ought not to have teased you."

"You did not know," he answered matter-of-factly. "None do, save my cousin, whom you met before."

"And I know nothing either, as I do not know the lady's name and I will nobly forget your cousin's. There, she is quite safe from me. I am certain she is a lovely girl and will recover well in time."

Darcy smiled in earnest. "I hope so. I have endeavoured to guide her as best I may, but there is much an elder brother cannot understand."

"Yet your concern for her does you credit," she replied warmly. "It almost makes me envious that I have no brother. Oh! I should not confess the turn of my thoughts, but you are harmless, are you not?"

"Far from it."

"Only one who intends to *do* no harm would speak so. I was only thinking that if I had a brother, I would not be walking over London to avoid my aunt's guest. I would have remained, and he and I would be agreeably engaged in concocting all manner of mischief to torment a respectable man."

He stifled a chuckle. "It seems, madam, that in half a morning's time, we have come to know both everything and yet nothing about each other. You have only insinuated, not fully confessed, the reason you wish to remain at large rather than returning to your relations."

"My good fellow, I must protest. In the time we have been walking as lady and servant, all while secretively chatting about sisters, you have let at least three vacant hackneys pass. As we must go some distance yet and you are in haste, I insist you catch that next one, or I shall be forced to reconsider your employment."

The corner of his mouth twitched helplessly. "As you wish, madam."

Thirteen

"No. I will not do it."

Elizabeth rolled her eyes. Again. "The footman rides on the back of the coach! It is always so!"

"I am perfectly aware of this, but I will not do it."

"Well, you certainly cannot ride inside the coach. What will passers-by think?"

"If I am inside, they cannot see me."

"They can see me, mounting and dismounting the box with you. I will tell you what they will think! We will be presumed to be entering an assignation—a lady and a lover dressed as a servant to evade prying eyes at home! You wish to avoid drawing attention? That would certainly do the opposite."

"We must simply wait for a coach that is better suited."

"You have dismissed two already. We will never make half a mile at these odds." Elizabeth blew a huff of frustration. "How can you have lived so long in the world and yet remained so innocent to its realities?"

"I am not a simpleton. I know very well the realities of the world, I thank you, but bouncing on the rumble seat of a hired coach through the busy streets of London, knowing that at any moment the horseflesh I stare backwards at could very well seat itself in my lap, is not an appealing way to travel. Even worse to cling by the straps, standing on a step no larger than a stirrup iron. Have you ever examined the hand grips on the rear of coaches? I have no wish to meet my death today."

"I suppose you must own some manner of carriage? After all, you have confessed to fewer details of yourself than have I, but if you are not some manner of a gentleman, you would be the most worthless manservant in the house. I pray you truly are a man of means, for your own sake."

His eyes darkened, and even his nostrils flickered in annoyance. Elizabeth tried not to smile. He was so *easy* to goad.

"I do have a carriage, madam, if I must confess so much. More than one. What has that to do with the issue at hand?"

"If you object so strongly to the usual accommodations for a footman on the back, I presume you have suited your own carriages with better provisions?"

She watched his jaw tighten. His lips were twitching into a frown, and he glared at the pavement for half an instant. Elizabeth tilted her head and waited.

He turned then, without a word to the contrary, and lifted his hand to the next hackney as it approached. It drew to the curb, and her dark stranger shot her a look that demanded she appreciate his efforts. He opened the door, appeared to sniff the upholstery, then nodded curtly to her. As she approached, he put down the foot block and held the door for her to mount the box. Elizabeth dipped her head in a scant approximation of a full curtsy and raised her foot, then found that he had caught her hand to help her in.

She met his eye in surprise, but his expression was grave, yielding nothing. She drew a sharp little breath and stepped up, feeling his strong arm assisting her more than she was accustomed to. Even through the gloves they both wore, there was something reassuring about the firmness of his grip as he steadied her. She seated herself and looked back as he put up the step and closed the door. She heard his voice outside, giving the driver the direction, and then there was a creaking just behind her as his weight settled into the rumble seat on the back.

There was a small, darkly soiled window between them; evidence that this particular coach had been rather fine in its youth. Elizabeth turned to peer through it, finding it completely obscured by his broad shoulders as they rocked through the busy streets. He was forced to press his back directly against the thin panel which separated them, and she could hear through the glass the soft scraping of his clothing against the wood.

It was slow going, traversing the busy streets at any time of day. Elizabeth began to wonder if they would not have done better to walk, but the few places where the horse jerked into a faster gait more than made up for any stoppage. She had ridden in her uncle's carriage often enough, which could boast a clever driver, but this master of the ribbons did not seem to hold with finesse over practicality. Quite often she was forced to grip the seat for balance as the frantic driver dashed his jaded vehicle through holes in the way which were far too small. She gritted her teeth, resettling her bonnet after one particularly rough lurch. The chaise had skidded to a sudden halt, forced to wait on traffic. There was a grunt from behind her, but the shoulders still darkened the window, so he had not fallen off.

Unable to resist, she knocked on the glass. "Is there a horse in your lap?"

"Two," was the dry retort.

"Perhaps you should step onto one of their backs."

There was a pause, and Elizabeth tried to imagine what expression would be crossing his face. Alas, she did not know him well enough to predict his response. More was the pity, for the facial reaction was always the most entertaining part of any exchange.

"I doubt the two together could hold me," came his muffled reply. "The pair of nags can barely pull their own cab."

Their vehicle jerked again, and the rattling of the wheels made further attempts at conversation impossible. Elizabeth turned to face forward, giggling as she did so. Oh, he was the most haughty, insufferable man, and she would be well rid of him soon, but he was not without his abilities. Few apart from her father could truly banter with her, giving rise to this bounding sense of playfulness she felt when speaking to him. Uncomfortable he clearly was, for a variety of reasons, she could imagine, but he was intelligent. Such a shame that more gentlemen were not so well read and spared so little time for serious thought. And such a shame that this particular man's good looks and fine figure belonged to a personality so brooding and prideful!

In due time, they had reached their destination. Elizabeth settled her bonnet once more, just as the door was opening. He was frowning down at some bit of mud sprayed upon his shoes but straightened as she bent toward the door. Once again, that strong hand took hers. She stared at him curiously as she lowered herself to the pavement, and he gazed back, dark brown eyes unflinching. He remained so, ensuring that she was safely upon her own two feet, for an uncomfortable second longer until the driver coughed.

Elizabeth shook herself. She drew out her reticule to pay the man, but as she extended the coin for her "footman" to pass to the driver, his hand touched hers again, staying it. He turned to pay the driver himself, then came back to her with a slight bow. "At your service, madam."

She arched a brow. "Miss Bennet, please, or Miss Elizabeth suits me, as well."

There was a faint softening about his mouth. "Very well, Miss Bennet. I hope you know where to go from here."

Elizabeth looked up at the buildings. "I have never been here, but I believe it is nearby."

"Nearby?" his tones rose. "How did you give the direction if you do not know the exact location?"

"I overheard my uncle Philips three years ago when he first formed the association. He told my father and my uncle Gardiner the cross streets, which were Charlotte and Castle Street near Long Acre, so…." She arched on her toes and scanned up and down the street.

"Three years ago!"

"Yes, but I have an excellent memory, sir, for you see my dearest friend from Hertfordshire is named Charlotte, and Long Acre is quite similar in sound to—Oh! I think that is it. Yes, Harrogate and Smith, in the fifth building down on our right. That sounds familiar."

"You are not certain?"

"Reasonably so."

She could see his jaw clenching and his fingers working into a tight knot. "Let us proceed, then."

Elizabeth found she could scarcely keep ahead of him when he lengthened his strides toward an objective. She glanced over her shoulder once, and he drew back, but his impatience could hardly be denied.

They were still two streets away when three men, deep in conversation and appearing in much haste, came out of the building they approached. "Ah!" Elizabeth exclaimed. "You see, there he is, my uncle! You need not have feared, for I was correct after all, and this is the right place. That man in the green is my uncle."

"Your uncle is leaving!" His strides lengthened again.

"Oh. Indeed, he is. Uncle Gardiner!" she cried, but her companion put out his hand and called in his own deep voice.

"Mr Gardiner, sir! I would speak with you—Mr Gardiner!"

But neither Mr Gardiner nor his companions heard. They mounted a waiting carriage, apparently all in some great hurry, and the horse was moving away.

Elizabeth's escort was nearly running now, his walk looking more like a sprint as he left her far behind in his pursuit of the departing carriage, but the street here was clear, and the carriage was gone. Still, it took him at least thirty paces to admit defeat. By the time Elizabeth caught him up again, he had slowed to a dejected gait before the very building her uncle had left.

"Bad luck," she bit her lip, and hesitantly peeked at his face.

His cheeks were flushed to a deep crimson, and she doubted that it was from the exertion for so fit a man. "Luck!" he spat. "I have been cursed from the moment I drank that brandy!"

"I beg your pardon?"

"It is none of your concern," he snapped, all the while glaring down the street. "This has been an absurd waste of my time. I must have been daft to agree to this scheme!"

"See here, sir, there is no cause to become irritable with me! I have done what I could, and I daresay more than any other would have—certainly more than any rational person would have bothered with, for you are a testy, disdainful man. I do not expect you to kiss my feet in gratitude, but a man who claims to be a gentleman would not behave with such incivility!"

He whirled, his gaze heated and intense. "You think me uncivil! Have I not some provocation? I could have been about something useful these two hours, something which might have done me some good!"

"Spare your energies for the party who has wronged you, for it was not myself. How was I to know we would scarcely miss him? Now, if you will excuse me, sir, I believe our business is finished, unless you are fast enough to catch that carriage."

She turned on her heel to march toward the corner, thinking of hailing another coach, but he was at her elbow in two strides. "Where are you going, Miss Bennet?"

"Back to Gracechurch Street. I have just had an epiphany."

"And what is that?"

"That if I seek to avoid the demands and company of irksome gentlemen, I would do better to tolerate my aunt's guest. At least he is witless enough to be laughed at."

"I am glad you do not think me witless, but I apologise if you found me irksome just now. I have seldom been so frustrated by circumstances."

"I suggest you accustom yourself to frustration, for it is the way of the world. The rest of us cannot afford to orchestrate our lives without some level of inconvenience. Consider it an exercise in character development."

"I have character enough, I thank you. Come, Miss Bennet, I have apologised once, and I never do so twice, but I do so now. It was not my intention to insult you after you attempted to help me."

She stopped, glanced at the hand he had touched to her elbow to catch her attention and looked back to his face. He dropped his hand as though she had scalded him, seemingly as surprised as she was to find that he was touching her again.

"A gallant apology does not compensate for the arrogance of the trespass. You are too quick to assume an inconvenience as a personal affront."

"And you are too quick to wilfully misunderstand. My frustration was of a more general nature. Toward you, I have expressed my indebtedness."

"A strange way you have of doing so!"

"Must I apologise a third time? I believe I have given you to understand the gravity of my situation. Is not my annoyance at least somewhat justifiable? Would you not—or, rather, *have* you not—suffered a like circumstance?"

Elizabeth sighed loudly. "Very well, I can find it in my heart to forgive you, but I am afraid that nothing more can be done here. I shall return to Gracechurch Street, for my family will eventually begin to wonder where I am."

"I do not doubt it. Surely, however, before we go, there must be someone in that office there who can tell us if your uncle is expected back soon or, perhaps, where they have gone."

"Did you not see that third man? The one with the brown coat turned and locked the door. There will be no one there. I am afraid we must concede.

Perhaps if you leave with me your direction, I may speak with my uncle this evening when he returns home. Surely you can find some other way to avoid your... entanglement... for just one more day? The parson will certainly not be waiting on your doorstep!"

His eyes rolled upward in thought. "I doubt that I can, for the moment I do return to my house, I shall be set upon by a score of angry relatives demanding my capitulation. I shall not trouble you with the particulars, but even my staff are not to be relied upon. If I have not some evidence for my own protection in my hand upon my arrival, it will become all but impossible to deny their claims."

"Would that a lady's testimony would do as well as my uncle's!"

He gazed down at her for a long moment, appearing to contemplate something very deeply. When he spoke again, it was in a soft voice. "I believe we both know what other complications would arise in that case. I would not wish it upon you, Miss Bennet."

She coloured, looking away. "My aunt is a respectably married woman. Surely, her testimony—"

"Would be considered that of an interested party with two unmarried nieces under her roof. No, Miss Bennet, it is impossible. It was enough risk to consider your uncle's word, but a lady's... it is out of the question." He sighed, his gaze wandering toward Saint Paul's Cathedral in the distance. "Perhaps Wilson or Fitzwilliam has discovered something I might find useful, for that is my best chance."

Elizabeth smiled regretfully and dipped him a curtsy. "May I wish you the very best in your search, sir. If you still have need of my uncle by the morrow, we would be happy to receive you."

"You speak as if you are abandoning me, Miss Bennet."

"I think it for the best, sir. You do not need the additional scandal of being recognised with yet another lady, and I have my own reputation to consider."

"I am ordinarily inclined to agree with you, Miss Bennet, but under the circumstances..." he looked over his shoulder, across the street from where they stood, to a hotel. "I have hardly eaten today, and I believe some fortification is required before I mount the back of another carriage."

Fourteen

"My Lady," Mr Collins scraped humbly before his patroness. "I am most honoured to be of service in whatever way your ladyship should desire. How deeply moved I was to receive your note yesterday while I was visiting in Hertfordshire! My gladdest wish is answered, for the very joy of my heart is to carry out your every request. How may I be of service, my most esteemed and revered Lady?"

Lady Catherine glanced to the door, which was guarded by none other than the butler himself. "I will speak to the parson in privacy," she informed the man. He looked about, bowed his respects, and closed the door between them.

Collins was still standing and bowing every few seconds as if he had forgotten that he had already done so, with his dumpy hat still in his hands from his travels and that wheedling smile overtaking his pasty features. Lady Catherine could barely restrain a sniff. He was useful, if a cloying, laughable excuse for a parson, and he did not trouble her with spiritual trifles or expensive ethics.

"I want you here," she glided about the room, her hand lifted expressively, "because I have glad tidings. As you know, my nephew, and consequently Anne's cousin, is Mr Fitzwilliam Darcy, a gentleman of remarkable fortune and good repute. It is his house in which you are presently a guest. My daughter has been betrothed to him since her infancy, and I am pleased to report that the marriage will be solemnised imminently."

A look of childish pleasure beamed upon the parson's sweating face. "Oh, My Lady, that is the very gladdest of news! Only to think that I had expected to delight your ladyship with news of my own engagement, but the fair Miss de

Bourgh's happiness is more dear even to my heart than my own. This is indeed a blessed day! Does your ladyship request that I humbly offer my services to the betrothed couple, to lend spiritual counsel in preparation for marriage? Shall I guide their steps as they ready themselves for this all-important station?"

Lady Catherine flicked her hand, demanding that he cease speaking long enough for her to make her desires known. "I intend for you to perform the service. A special license has been obtained and has been delivered into our hands only an hour ago."

Collins' eyes grew wider, his ungroomed brows forming one bushy line in the midst of his pale forehead. "Such eminent foresight! Your ladyship has taken every precaution to see that Miss de Bourgh is not troubled by a long ceremony in a draughty church! One can never know if another church has been properly aired or thoroughly warmed. I bow to your wisdom, My Lady."

"Is anything less due to the daughter and heiress of the de Bourgh family heritage? This marriage shall see the uniting of two of the finest families in the kingdom, unifying the two great estates and securing what has long been promised as her birthright. I would not risk her health in any public setting, no matter how fine the architecture or prestigious the bishop. The ceremony will be performed in this very room."

"Your ladyship is a fount of wisdom! If only my parishioners could witness your sterling example of humility. What are a gilded ceiling and stained glass when the sacrament of a bride's duty might be imperilled?"

"Indeed. You shall appreciate that proper forms have already been procured, thanks in great part to Mr Darcy's thoughtful provisions for his future bride. I had them set out for your examination."

"Indeed, My Lady, I am certain that everything has been done properly. There shall be no need for my humble eyes to examine them if your ladyship has already deemed them satisfactory. When is the ceremony to take place? I have not my proper clerical robes…."

"This evening, as soon as my nephew has returned from his business."

"This… this evening? Why, of course! It is outside the canonical hours, but a special license has been procured, and perhaps your ladyship is wise to impress that distinction. The heiress of the de Bourgh legacy need not submit to form!"

"And the Earl of Matlock shall witness. The marriage will be solemnised and consummated at once, so that no objection may be made by jealous Society."

"But My Lady, would not Miss de Bourgh prefer a proper courtship period? Perhaps a ball hosted in her honour, to announce her impending happiness?"

"No such trivialities shall be necessary. Anne, of course, would be the most celebrated dancer in Town, had she learned, but she has not the appetite for revelry. Neither does she have need for a larger trousseau, and Darcy shall see that she is properly honoured wherever she goes."

"A thousand apologies, for I have again underestimated your beneficence, My Lady! Miss de Bourgh is the most fortunate young lady, and we who wish her well shall be the most blessed of all witnesses."

"Naturally. Now, Collins, I presume you have found some lodgings in Town?"

"Indeed, I have, My Lady! You see before you the happiest of all men, for I have been most graciously received into the home of my future relations, and Miss Elizabeth Bennet, who shall be my bride, is also a guest in the same house. I am most eager during my stay to bestow upon her those little attentions which ladies find so agreeable, that our own humble felicity may be assured when the happy day comes."

"You may return to your future relations until you are sent for. I have no present need for you, and it would be hardly suitable for you to linger about this house before the bride and groom are prepared to meet. However, when you return to conduct the ceremony, I insist that you bring your betrothed to pay her respects to the bride."

"Your ladyship is as gracious as you are wise," he bowed.

~

"I confess, it did not occur to me that I would not be welcomed in my present attire." Darcy stood uncomfortably on the pavement, glancing up the street.

"I had wondered at your intentions when you walked into the hotel and ordered a table but thought it better not to ask," Miss Bennet replied with a poorly disguised grin.

"Nothing is stopping you from taking some refreshment. I will wait here for you, for I would rather not loiter in the back with the... ah... with men I do not know."

"It was you who first mentioned your hunger, not I. I can well imagine why, if you have not eaten since that bit of biscuit and coffee this morning. I can manage until I return to my aunt's home. However, we must think of something for you, for it will be almost an hour before we will have returned to Gracechurch in the mid-day traffic. I would not like for you to faint off the back of the coach. Heaven knows the trouble I should have in dragging you off the streets a second time!"

Darcy felt his stomach tighten. Blast the woman, but she simply *would* tease him, and he could no longer pretend that it annoyed him. Far from it, in fact. He looked down into her composed expression and detected that spark of mirth in her eyes, the laughter threatening to bubble from her lips. It was quite simply too tempting to banter with her, and he had had enough of fighting for the day.

"I doubt a public coachman will be so obliging as your uncle's must have been. You would be forced to leave me to be trampled underfoot."

"And heaven knows, we cannot have that! Only think how disappointed your family would be."

The inflexion she placed on the word *family* was hardly to be missed. "Upon consideration," he mused with affected gravity, "perhaps your suggestion has some merit. I might even consider it a lucky escape."

"Yes, but if you fell, the traffic on the street would necessarily draw to a stop, blocking the carriages for hours, perhaps. I am certain that such a fastidious fellow as yourself would take issue with creating such a fuss."

"You have judged me rightly, Miss Bennet. It seems that fainting off the back of the coach is not an option worth considering. I shall simply have to walk, and pray that starvation does not overtake me before I can re-join my cousin."

"Where does he live, if I may be so bold?"

"Mayfair, but I dare not show myself again at his residence. He was to meet me at the park on Elm by two o'clock. That is just over an hour, which leaves not enough time to return to Gracechurch before meeting him. I hope he has been able to learn something from Wilson."

"He is certainly an obliging fellow if he exerts himself so on your behalf."

"He is, but I do not persuade myself that it is for my sake alone that he does so much."

She pursed her lips, obviously curious, but unwilling to ask what he meant. "And if he has nothing to report?"

"Then I must find some means of biding my time until your uncle returns home and I am able to produce something to my own defence. Unfortunately," he glanced around, "I cannot think of any home in which I could seek quiet refuge without being found out and harangued by someone connected to… well, it is nothing I ought to trouble you with." He finished speaking and looked over her head, toward the street, scarcely suppressing a hiss of frustration. Of all the misbegotten, cursed woes, to be so helpless when the stakes were his very future!

She tilted her head. "Has it occurred to you sir, that not all prospects are so dismal?"

He arched an eyebrow in interest. "How so?"

"Sir, you give the impression of one who has always borne the weight of serious matters. Have you ever been forced to spend your time at idle pursuits?"

"I positively loathe such an imposition."

"Oh, that will not do! Do you not know how to relax?"

"No."

Her eyes widened at his blunt response, and she began to chuckle. "Well then, you must learn. No, do not scoff, I tell you this in all seriousness. My uncle Gardiner, industrious man that he is, suffered a health crisis two years ago. He works too much, you see, and I fear he is beginning to do so again. My aunt wisely insisted that he take a holiday to the Lake District, and he returned a different man. They now try to go somewhere every summer. I believe it did wonders for his health, for the simple fact that he was not able to set himself about his appointed tasks as he had been used to and was forced to look about for other amusements. He is now a proficient angler and finds it such an enjoyable means of passing the day that he has even shared his passion with me."

"With you? You enjoy fishing?"

She flinched. "Oh, dear, I was not to speak that aloud. I hope you do not think me any more a hoyden than you did a moment ago."

"A good deal less, in fact."

She lifted a brow. "You intrigue me, sir, but let us not lose the point. Perhaps this crisis which you can do nothing about at present is Providence's way of setting you down for a moment of perspective."

"You have the most curious notions, Miss Bennet. You think that I ought to take leave of my troubles for the day? That is the surest way to see them multiply! I tell you, nothing would set my mind at ease so well as seeing this matter resolved."

"But as you have already told me, there is little you can do, for you must wait on others. Why should you fret yourself into illness? Can you, by one moment's worry, change what is beyond your control?"

"I can do all that can be done and rest in the knowledge that if I failed, it was not for want of effort," he insisted.

"That you have already done. We have tried and failed to secure the witness from my uncle. There is nothing to do now but to wait patiently. Unless you are comfortable trusting to your luck without my uncle's word, my advice to you, sir, is to take the opportunity to enjoy the day, perhaps in some activity you might not have otherwise done."

"Such as what? You puzzle me exceedingly, Miss Bennet."

"When was the last time you simply sat under a tree to read a good book? Or admired the rose hedges in the public gardens?"

His brow furrowed. "I was probably twelve."

"There, do you see? You, sir, are too responsible."

"This is a bad quality?"

She laughed, a joyful, artless sound he could have listened to for hours without tiring of it. "I am giving you sound advice if you will heed it."

"You call it sound advice, to tell me that I must neglect my responsibilities?"

"Precisely. For one hour, do something you have never done before. Stop and talk to a hackney driver, sit on a park bench with no object but to watch the birds, buy a flower on the street corner for your sister. And when you have finished torturing yourself in that way, you may resume your search. By then, I might even be able to introduce you to my uncle."

"I have had enough of hackneys for the day, thank you. I would go mad sitting on a park bench watching birds, and my sister is safely out of Town just now. What, then, do you recommend, if you are so insistent on me taking my leisure?"

"Well, sir, you did mention your hunger. What if you were to walk into a bakery for a bit of bread, just as any manservant on an errand for his mistress? You could then take a pleasant stroll to that park to await your cousin and find some little spot where you could eat in privacy. After that, I give you leave to act responsibly again."

"That would satisfy your notion of doing something I have never done before? Taking a loaf of bread to the park? I am no stranger to a picnic, madam. I have taken my sister often enough."

"But I warrant you have never done so without extensive planning, never dressed as a footman, and I doubt you have ever had to purchase the bread yourself. You shall have to speak to the baker, you know, and imagine the horror if, while seated at a public park, some passer-by happens to glance at you while you have breadcrumbs upon your fingers? Perhaps it is not the most shocking activity you could engage in, but yes, sir, I do believe it would do wonders for you."

"You have a most peculiar way of considering what is good and helpful for a man."

"Indeed, I have. Come, there is a bakery just there. I challenge you to put the scheme into action before I leave you to your own devices and return to my aunt's house."

"Oh, no, Miss Bennet, you cannot leave me with such an assignment and then merrily go about your way! You must see that I do not expire from the strain of doing nothing."

"Sir, I have already spent far too long alone with you."

"So, you would travel unescorted the two miles through the busy hours of London traffic?" He shook his head gravely. "You would do far better to wait for your faithful footman to attend you, which he is most willing to do as soon as he completes the task you have set before him."

"Sir," she hesitated, looking down for an instant, "surely you can see that I cannot simply sit with you in a park. You have given me no cause to be ill at ease, but in the partial seclusion of the trees... perhaps it is as well that I tell you frankly that I am not a lady of easy virtue."

"I am relieved to hear it. Be easy, Miss Bennet, for you are as safe with me as with your uncle. Indeed, I have as much reason as you have to be cautious of my associations; therefore, we will take care that appearances are as they should be, and you will be well protected."

"Ah, the wolf declares he has no fangs. I am comforted now."

He smiled. How many ladies would have gone nearly rabid in the attempt to lure him into the secret parts of a park? "Miss Bennet," he placed his hand over his heart, "on my honour as a footman, I vow to return you safely to your relations, as virtuous and impertinent as you are now. I will even hold your parasol over you as we wait. How could you refuse such an offer?"

She glanced uncomfortably over her shoulder, her lips pressed in thought. "Very well, sir."

Fifteen

Elizabeth had watched in patient amusement as her "footman" entered the bakery, looking as lost and helpless as a puppy. She had remained just outside the door, so she could not hear the exchange that took place, but it seemed to take an inordinately long while to make a simple purchase. Fully ten minutes later he emerged again, his cheeks dark with mortification, but he smiled in triumph when he saw her. He hoisted a long brown parcel, bestowed a crooked grin on her, and announced, "To the park with us, Miss Bennet."

It was fortunate that the destination was only a short distance away, because the constant rustling of the parcel wrapper as he tried to find a natural way of carrying it, and the intoxicating aroma of the hot bread itself, threatened to drive her mad. "Where do you think we should sit?" she asked over her shoulder.

"There," he gestured decisively.

Elizabeth looked and found a stone bench in clear view of the rest of the park. It was cleverly situated, for it faced in the opposite direction and the foliage near it discouraged others from taking seats nearby. It also boasted just enough coverage from a neighbouring tree that it felt more like an outdoor pavilion than an exposed corner, which seemed far more comfortable for a picnic. It was both public and private, and suited their wants perfectly.

He helped her to her seat, then took up a post behind her bench to unwrap the parcel. "I hope you like manchettes," he extended a palm-sized round to her. "These are a favourite of my sister's."

She thanked him and accepted his offering. "You seem to think quite often of your sister."

He looked down. "She is my primary concern at present."

"You must be wonderfully attentive. I am certain she can have no cause for complaint."

He still did not look up, but she could see a wry smile tightening his mouth. "I doubt she would agree with that assessment, Miss Bennet."

Elizabeth tore off a bite of her bread and chewed it contemplatively, still watching him. "Ah, I can see how it is," she declared after a moment. "Mr Responsibility has thrown a pail of water over something she wished to do, something which seemed eminently more exciting than the path you proposed. Am I correct?"

He was gazing at her now, a peculiar expression on his face. "More so than you can know, Miss Bennet."

"Was her desire really so reckless? I believe we have established that you must learn to accept that not all things are under your control."

"It would have been disastrous, leading to a life of misery and disgrace."

Elizabeth frowned. "Then I suppose it is as well that you do enjoy settling matters to your liking."

"Why do you assume I take pleasure in giving my sister pain?"

"That is not quite what I meant. Other guardians would be less diligent about those in their charge, for the inconvenience to themselves is too great to stir them from their complacency."

"I would consider that the most reprehensible abuse of the position, and the young lady would be the one to suffer for it. If the proper guardian will not take an interest, who is to do it?"

"Who, indeed?" Elizabeth sighed. "But happily, your sister shall not be such a one. She may still be grieved with you, but as you have noted that she has a generous nature, she will forgive you in time. This must have been a very recent disagreement between you."

He pressed his lips together and made a low humming noise between his teeth. "Very recent," he confessed reluctantly. "Yes, I am confident that she will see the wisdom of my advice, in time, but she has not fully done so yet. Her fragile state only heightens the stakes of the present crisis and makes my own position the more precarious. I cannot…" here he shook his head and looked away. "Forgive me, it is not your concern."

"I should think that the troubles of those in my employ are indeed my concern," she informed him archly. "It would be dreadful to think I would lose the services of a perfectly good footman due to some personal difficulties."

A slow, cautious smile appeared… oh, why must the man have dimples? Elizabeth flushed slightly and found it difficult to hold his eyes for more than a second or two with such an expression on his face.

"You are rather enjoying this charade, are you not, Miss Bennet?"

She lifted her shoulders nonchalantly. "It is the first time I have ever had a manservant dedicated exclusively to my own delights. I believe I could become used to it."

"It will cost you dearly. My services do not come cheaply."

"In that case, perhaps you should look for a better position!" she laughed. "I have just enough pin money for a few new bonnets from town before I return home."

"But as you have already informed me, my skills are somewhat lacking. How shall I find suitable employment without further practice and a solid reference?"

"In that case," she leaned back and lifted her hand with a flourish, speaking with an exotic trill to her voice. "I fancy another manchette. Would you be so good as to pass me a bit more of the fine luncheon that Cook has so courteously sent up from the kitchens?"

He was smiling again, and Elizabeth felt her cheeks warming just a little more when his dark eyes sparkled in her direction. He bent over his bread parcel and carefully withdrew another generous portion. "I ought to have procured some butter and preserves for milady."

"One must learn to endure some inconveniences on a proper picnic. Do you really intend to stand behind me the entire time holding my parasol?"

He looked over his shoulder. "Indeed. I know our faces are not obvious from here, but it is remarkable enough for a lady to be reclining in the park with only her servant. I do not think most would consider our position *too* scandalous, but I do not desire that anyone should perceive anything out of place. Have you any anxiety about what your relations might be thinking of your whereabouts?"

"I had left a message that I would be at my uncle's warehouse. It would not be so unusual for me to visit his offices at least once during my stay, and I think under the circumstances, my aunt will know why I wished to be away from the house. She will not suffer any anxiety…" she frowned again, "…unless he returns before I do. But surely he will not."

"I apologise, Miss Bennet. I have caused you a very great inconvenience."

"Indeed, you have, but it does not necessarily follow that the inconvenience is an unhappy one. You have provided me with an excellent diversion, and for that I thank you. I have all London's delights at my fingertips and a handsome footman to attend every one of my whims."

One side of his mouth curled, revealing a flash of white teeth. "You think me handsome?"

"Surely it is only an effect of the dashing livery," she took a slow, deliberate bite of her manchette and chewed it thoroughly before continuing. "Perhaps that is why my sisters admire a red coat. That gold braid and fine cut lend *any* man an air of distinction."

"I am glad I am capable of impressing you in some measure," he answered dryly.

"You would be a poor candidate for a footman if you could not," she informed him, "but here, we are talking of silly matters when you had an assignment to complete. So far you have not observed so much as a leaf or a blade of grass. If you do not like watching birds, perhaps there are some squirrels in this park for you to admire."

"I think the wildlife here is rather limited," he paused and levelled a pronounced smirk in her direction. "Save for one decidedly curious creature with an affinity for saucy remarks and a penchant for changing the subject whenever it suits her. Would you like another manchette?"

Elizabeth laughed. "Thank you, sir, but no."

"Then you are ready for dessert." He unwrapped his parcel completely, his countenance darkening with frustration when bits of the brown paper stuck to his fingers. He picked out what he desired, all while holding each finger daintily apart from its fellows, lest they stick to one another.

Elizabeth bit back a snicker. He really was the drollest man; so staid and eminently masculine, yet so fastidious. He would have been an entertaining puzzle to study, had she a better opportunity.

"Do you like sweet rolls?" he asked, after freeing one of the said treats from its wrapping. "They are another favourite of my sister's, and I thought you might enjoy them as well."

"How very kind of you, sir!" She took it gingerly, smiling in gratitude for his thoughtfulness.

He turned his attention to extracting another sweet roll from the paper for himself. "I apologise that I have no tea for milady, nor even a proper napkin for you to clean your fingers."

"It is no matter," she finished the small treat, then delicately nibbled the sweet residue from her fingers as she blinked playfully back to him. His eyes rounded as he watched her, apparently transfixed by her dreadful manners. He turned jerkily away, clearing his throat at least twice.

Elizabeth ought to have been ashamed of herself, but really, what else was a lady to do? She could not have refused the sweet roll in good conscience, nor could she have gone about her day with sticky fingers! Perhaps she might have done it more discreetly, but rarely had she found anyone who was so much fun to tease. Besides, it was not as if she had any intention of impressing him, nor even any expectation that she would ever see him again.

He put away the wrapping papers with fingers of his own which were now mysteriously clean, coughed one last time, and addressed her in a perfectly civilised tone. "It seems we have little more to do but converse, so may I be so bold as to ask what is the nature of your visit to Town? You have spoken more than once of wishing to enjoy the city as if you have never before had the opportunity. Yet, you seem familiar enough with our surroundings."

"I may have–" she sighed, the last traces of sweetness fleeing from her tongue as pleasant thoughts evaporated. "Let me simply say that the future is uncertain, and I wish to enjoy my life as much as I can before I shall find it necessary to make some difficult decisions."

He fell silent for a few moments, and occasionally she felt those dark, thoughtful eyes turning her way, but he held his peace. After a bit of quiet reflection, he suggested in a lighter tone, "Perhaps milady wished to see something beyond this inauspicious little park. I hope I have not dashed your entire day."

"I have no great designs. We saw a performance at the theatre last night, and I had hoped today that we might explore Vauxhall Gardens, but as the day has seemingly gone so poorly for my uncle, I think it impossible. It is a pity, for I doubt we shall have another opportunity during my stay."

"Vauxhall? You do know that the Gardens are in a state of decline, do you not? I do not wish to be the bearer of bad tidings for one who has heard but never seen, yet they are nothing to their heyday of my father's generation."

"Nevertheless, they still boast sights I could not see in Meryton. My aunt and uncle have very kindly engaged themselves to fulfil my silly wishes as best they can. Though it may be impossible, and even a disappointment if I should go, I am grateful that they have tried. Perhaps you can tell me something of the Gardens, so that I may enjoy the scene vicariously. You have been, have you not?"

He turned to extract the coin purse from his pocket and then drew out a small medallion. "I hold a season admission, but I have not been there in five years."

"But you carry the token in your pocket at all times?"

"It is a memento of sorts. Perhaps it is odd, I confess. I purchase one every year, but I have no desire to go."

"That is a pity! Would not your sister relish the chance to spend the day with you in such an environ? It seems to me that giving her a day of pleasure in your company might do much for relations between the two of you."

"Perhaps it would," he admitted as he replaced his coin purse. "I confess, I had never thought of it."

"Do you think she would like it? What would be her favourite part?"

"The Garden walk, most certainly, and the Cascade, I suspect. But she would take the most pleasure from the bucolic setting. She enjoys flowers, a trait she inherited from our mother. She has a quiet, contemplative nature, and I believe she finds them peaceful."

"I had expected you to say she would enjoy the musical entertainment and the acrobatics. There are still performers, are there not? Are they really so marvellous as I have heard?"

"Yes, and she would certainly take her delight in them, but she would tire of the noise quickly. I do not mean to imply that she is a recluse, but she does not enjoy crowds of people."

"I wonder if that is also the reason you no longer attend, sir."

He peered cautiously down at her. "Miss Bennet, you have a disturbing capacity to sketch my character. Are you always so perspicacious?"

She laughed. "I believe, sir, that your words are really less a confession than an attempt to distract me from asking more personal questions. You cannot pretend that you never enjoyed the Gardens yourself, not with that token in your pocket, so what was your favourite part? Remember, you must describe it very clearly, for I may never see it with my own eyes."

A wistful smile warmed his face, and he gazed into the trees. "I expect you will think me a sentimental bore."

She gestured expansively about their little nook in the foliage. "We have nothing to do but wait, and I would very much enjoy hearing your tale."

"There is not much to tell. When last I visited, I was in the company of my father. He died less than a month later. It had been his wish to visit one last time because he had such fond memories of my mother there from the early days of their marriage. I am afraid I have not been back since."

Elizabeth fell into silence. His expression had turned sombre, and he still gazed into the treetops. "I think—" she ventured. He looked back to her, one brow raised as he waited for her. "I think your parents were fortunate indeed. It is a fine thing to treasure one's life partner."

The lines around his mouth softened in pleased surprise at her observations. "Fortunate they were, Miss Bennet. Would that all others could be so blessed."

"Ho! There you are!" called a voice behind them.

Elizabeth and her footman both turned. The man she had seen earlier in the morning, Fitzwilliam if she remembered properly, approached with long, jaunty strides and a cheerful smile. He removed his hat with a flourish as he entered their little alcove under the tree. "Miss Bennet, it is a pleasure to see you again. I wonder, might I share a word with your manservant?"

Elizabeth glanced at the taller of the two and could not help but chuckle slightly at the dark look of annoyance which had passed over his features. "Indeed, sir."

Sixteen

"**I** see you have won the favour of your fair lady," Richard jerked his head back toward the bench where Miss Bennet sat. "At least she was smiling this time, rather than threatening to slap you."

"She is not 'my' lady, and she would hardly be so vulgar as to assault a man."

"Ah, you are defending her already. This is promising, Darcy! Tell me, did her uncle defer to her father, or are you already secure of his blessing? I can see it, your imagination has already leapt from admiration to love, and from love to—"

"Richard, desist!" Darcy snapped, glancing over his shoulder at the lady. "You know what you suggest is impossible, but Miss Bennet is a respectable woman, and I will not hear you jesting about her."

"Fair enough, Darcy," Richard held up a hand. "But it will be your loss. So, was this Mr Gardiner able to provide you with what you needed?"

"I have not yet been able to speak with him. Apparently, his business has demanded his attention in various parts of town today."

"Oh." Richard frowned. "That is… unfortunate."

"A temporary setback," Darcy agreed. "But not an insurmountable difficulty. Miss Bennet assures me that he is an amiable fellow and will not object to speaking on my behalf once we do find him."

"I hope you are correct, Darcy. Your valet had some rather choice words regarding our aunt's actions today."

"Such as?"

"Apparently she has been receiving numerous callers and has sent a flurry of notes among her acquaintances."

"I would have expected no less. Does he know any names?"

"No, but a dressmaker has been sent for, a solicitor has called twice, and Aunt is making inquiries about a lady's companion—for Georgiana, I presume. That was all before mid-morning tea. Another caller had just arrived when I was being shown to the door, but I could not learn who it was."

"And what of the other servants of the house? What has he learned?"

"You will not find anyone to vouch for you. Aside from your head groom, who was apparently not worth the trouble, our aunt has purchased the loyalties of everyone else. Even should you call them to task and threaten their employment right now, I would not trust any."

"Nor would I," Darcy scowled at the ground. "Not after one betrayal. I will have to dismiss everyone, it seems. I still intend to make my position clear and to demand a truthful witness, but since I will not offer a second chance at employment, I cannot depend upon anything that anyone will say. Some might even concoct a worse tale out of revenge for the loss of their position! How could Lady Catherine have so thoroughly swept the house's sentiments?"

"There are probably a few kitchen maids and dust boys who are innocent, but they could not be expected to know anything. They will be of no help to you."

"Indeed. Richard, this is preposterous. I intend to go to the house at once to confront her. She cannot bring her will to bear by means of deceit, and I will not stand for it. It is my house, my staff, and my future she has taken into her hands!"

"Very well, then Darcy, what do you intend to say to her? Remember my father's order, no public fracas will be tolerated. You must find a way to do this and still keep the peace, or the entire family becomes the talk of the *ton*. For myself, I would not care, but I would think you—"

"Yes, yes," sighed Darcy. "Perhaps I will speak with Anne and discover what may be done. Perhaps *she* might be worked upon."

"It would be so much simpler to shun a presumptuous young lady if she were not a relation," Richard mused. "You have certainly proved that often enough with Miss Bingley, among others. But as to Anne, I have anticipated you somewhat."

"How do you mean?"

"Oh! Just a bit of judicious slander, a few well-placed insults to your character—you know, the sorts of things that a lady would not wish to hear about her future husband. You can thank me later."

Darcy groaned. "Surely there was a better way...."

"Do not doubt my strategic genius, Darcy. What could be better than to cause the lady to rethink her own wishes? Perhaps she will refuse to marry you!"

"Or perhaps she will be led to search more deeply into my personal affairs and discover a way to compromise me further!"

Richard's face crumpled in thought. "You do not think—"

"It is not impossible, but I think unlikely. I have been very circumspect as you can imagine, and the solicitor I employed for that affair was one our aunt does not know of. I made certain that none connected with us have done business with him."

Richard sighed in relief, then his brow wrinkled again. "Wise precautions, but you did not see the corruption in your own household until it was too late. Could you not be mistaken there, too?"

"They are vastly different things, but I do not intend to be blinded by the assumption of invulnerability a second time. I must bring this matter to a conclusion before any further damage can be done, and I remain convinced that a confrontation with Lady Catherine is inevitable. Since I must wait a little longer before obtaining the word of Mr Gardiner, I think the wisest course at present would be to escort Miss Bennet home, and then return to my own house to do what must be done."

"I think perhaps you are a little premature. You are correct that matters will only become worse without intercession, but wait and see what more your valet learns. The man is a crafty one, and he has Aunt Catherine's ear. She believes she can succeed, and I have yet to discover why. It is not as if you are a man easily swayed by belligerence, but she has some reason to think you will eventually capitulate. Additionally, I have never seen her so incensed as she is now that you have not returned. If you want my opinion on the matter, I recommend that you do not give her what she wants just now, which is you."

"And what am I to do? Sit here in this park until such a time as I may reasonably expect to meet with Mr Gardiner?"

"Perhaps you do not have to stay in this same park, per se."

"You are serious!"

"Perfectly. Darcy, she is searching for you. That was the last thing your valet told me. She has sent men round to all the clubs, fencing parlours, and every fashionable place she could think of. Now, would she do that if she thought she needed to beg and plead? No, Darcy, I tell you, she has some notion of how to force you, even beyond the supposed compromise. You may need far more than an alibi by the time you return to the house."

"And how am I to know what that is?"

"As I said," Richard grinned and clapped him on the shoulder, "let your valet sort that. When this is all over, you should buy that fellow a country house of his own. Meanwhile, Darcy, I suggest that you continue to make yourself invisible. By the by, you look as if you have a capital little situation here, not to mention agreeable company. Is that a bakery parcel I see over there? How very thoughtful of you, Darcy!"

"Hold here, you cannot truly be advising me to remain away, doing nothing at all."

"Why not? There is nothing else you can do at present. When was the last time you took a holiday?"

Darcy narrowed his eyes. "That is precisely what Miss Bennet asked me."

"Hah! I am liking that young lady better and better. Now, shall we escort the lady to her home?"

"*We?*"

"Indeed. I should like the chance to know her, and you need a chaperon. What is she calling you—have you at last given up your name, or were you afraid she would attempt matrimony upon you as well?"

Darcy raised his brows in a short laugh. "She did not even wish to know it, claiming that matters were simpler for us both if she only knew of me as a footman. An enigma, she is. I have never known her like."

"Truly! Well, then if I must address you directly, I shall call you 'William,' as Georgie does—no, do not look at me like that. I intend to enjoy this."

"Richard, wait!" Darcy hissed, snatching once more at his cousin's arm as the other made to move away. "I will not have you teasing the lady and leading her on to false presumptions!"

"No one is doing any leading but yourself."

"I have not lied to her," he growled reproachfully. "She knows something of my situation, or as much as either of us felt comfortable with disclosing."

"Then I suppose that is enough for now. Let us enjoy a pleasant afternoon with an exceedingly charming companion. After that, you can obtain from her family what you need, then part from her acquaintance with no regrets and no cause for censure by anyone." Richard turned and walked decisively toward the bench.

Darcy raised a futile hand again, watching his cousin approaching Miss Bennet. No regrets….

~

"Mama, where can he be?" Anne pouted. "It is not like Fitzwilliam to ignore his duties."

Lady Catherine snorted aloud—although she herself would have described the sound as something far more refined. "And what has he done for the past eight years, but ignore his duties? I shall see an end to this, for my own dear sister's son must learn his place."

"You do not think he has left Town, do you? Perhaps some elaborate scheme to claim he was never here, or even…" Anne's eyes widened, and her mouth rounded in a horrified gasp. "He could not have eloped with some other woman to Scotland, simply to avoid our marriage!"

Another indelicate sound escaped her lady mother. "Darcy is a selfish boy, but he is not a fool. He would never court such disgrace."

"But he is wilful, Mama. How shall I ever manage him? He will be sure to make my life a misery if he does not get his way."

"Never mind that. Even Darcy can be made to know what is best; you shall see. I depend on you to do your duty, and I shall see to it that he does his."

Anne shuddered in distaste but said nothing.

"What is this?" her sharp-eyed mother remonstrated. "A man knows when a woman does not welcome him, Anne. You would do well to remember my directions. It is not as if Darcy's person is objectionable! Many men have less than half his attributes."

"That is just it, Mama. He is… rather large and strong. I should have preferred a more gentle-looking sort."

"Let me hear no more of this! I know your preferences, but it will not do! Think you *that* sort could make a proper husband?" The lady sneered in disgust. "Darcy will correct the errors in your proclivities."

"But he is hardly courteous! He has never once paid me a real compliment, other than what was expected of a cousin, and from what our cousin Richard has said—"

"Rubbish! You should not listen to a soldier's account of a gentleman, Anne. Men have their sport, of course, but Darcy has been trained from his infancy to conduct himself properly in decent society. He will treat you as the daughter of a knight and a peeress deserves."

"Even when he learns… you know?" Anne whispered.

Lady Catherine's eyes flickered in rage, and her lip curled over clenched teeth. "He will have no choice," she hissed, "and we will not speak of this again!"

Anne subsided, toying with the lace of her shawl. "I only hope he does not make too much of a scene when he returns." Then she shivered and drew the shawl more tightly around her shoulders.

"My dear, have you taken a chill?" Lady Catherine demanded in alarm. She cast about, and spying the shoulder of the footman standing at the door, summoned, "Here, you! Send for more wood for the fire, and have another blanket brought!"

"Mother," Anne protested, "It is August!"

"It is the *end* of August, and there is a pronounced nip in the air in the mornings. Would you risk your health on the very day of your wedding?"

"*Today?*"

"Of course, today! Why do you think I sent for Collins? The license is prepared, the parson awaits my call, and I would see the matter settled at once. We cannot afford delay, and I would have Darcy's word sworn the moment he returns to the house."

Anne sighed and surrendered to the arrival of a maid with a new blanket for her. A footman stoked the coals back into a roaring blaze, and her mother appeared satisfied. A moment later, another servant appeared and bowed his obeisance, waiting for permission to speak.

Lady Catherine appraised him with interest. "Wilson, have you something to report?"

Darcy's valet placed his hands behind his back and straightened his shoulders. "Yes, My Lady. The washerwoman who tends to some of Mr Darcy's linens received word from a kitchen boy, who was told by—"

"Never mind the chain of hands the message has passed through. What word do you bring of Darcy?"

"Mr Darcy was seen calling on the Earl of Matlock, My Lady."

The lady scoffed. "I had word of the same two hours ago! My brother, the earl would not have neglected to tell me so much. What I wish to know is where he has gone after that. I thought perhaps he was in the company of Fitzwilliam, but we have seen the colonel since then."

"Yes, My Lady, I spoke with him myself. I am quite certain that the colonel is doing all he can to assist your ladyship, but after hearing that Mr Darcy had been calling upon the earl, I believe I may have discerned what he might be about next if your ladyship wishes—"

"If I wish! Out with it, man. Where would my nephew have gone?"

"I believe he has gone to purchase a horse."

Lady Catherine's eyes bulged. "A *horse?*"

"Or rather a matched pair. I have heard him recently to lament that his bays were looking rather aged this year, and the earl himself even recommended a more fashionable turnout, with the higher heads and steps which are so much in favour now."

The lady was still glaring in astonishment. "A pair of carriage horses? When he has abandoned Anne... Mr Wilson, I believe you have taken leave of your senses!"

"Not so, Mama," Anne interjected. "Fitzwilliam remembers how well I like a drive behind fine horses. You know I do not care for walking out. What a capital notion!"

"Indeed!" Wilson nodded vigorously. "Miss de Bourgh speaks well, for I have good reason to believe the master has gone to procure a gift for his bride. No doubt the earl recommended it, and Mr Darcy set about it without delay."

"Preposterous! Mr Wilson, I am of a mind to dismiss you at once. It is clear to me that you possess no true information and are grasping at whatever notion strikes your fancy."

"I most humbly beg your ladyship's pardon," Wilson bowed from the waist. "However, it would not be out of character for Mr Darcy. Only a month ago, when he wished to deeply apologise to Miss Darcy for some transgression—it was not my business to know the nature of the affair—he set out without a word and was away the whole of the day. When he returned, he presented Miss Darcy with a new pianoforte, as well as a new phaeton which was to be taken directly to Pemberley for her exclusive use. She forgave him most graciously for whatever his infraction against her goodness might have been."

"I am sure you are right, Mr Wilson!" Anne seconded with feeling. "Why, now that I remember properly, he did ask me last evening just before dinner if I did not wish to go driving in Hyde Park while the weather was still fine. It would be just his way to do his penance by the purchase of some elaborate gift. Mama, you do remember how he had that beautiful new rug sent from India after that summer when he and Richard bled all over your old one? I think they had been shooting and one of them fell down an embankment and nearly killed himself on a stick… I forget now which, but I do remember how put out you were with them for the blood."

"It was Fitzwilliam," the lady pronounced crisply. "Although Darcy was covered with nearly as much blood from carrying him. Mr Wilson, I can hardly credit this notion that he has gone now to purchase horses for Anne. After he has been away half the night and the whole of the morning, to excuse him now by the assumption of generous motives is sheer lunacy! If he wishes to honour his bride, he ought to be here in person to do so."

"I am quite certain he will be soon," Wilson bowed again. "Mr Darcy is a judicious sort, and no doubt since he was in the company of some friend since last evening, they have been detained for various reasons. I am sure they are making a properly thorough search for just the right pair to suit Miss de Bourgh. Your ladyship might consider sending word round to the stables to make ready for the new horses, if Mr Darcy has not already done so. I would be happy to carry word to the head groom myself."

Lady Catherine made another guttural noise, eloquently expressing her scepticism. "Go then, if it suits you, but I grow impatient. If this 'friend' knows what is good for Darcy, he will cease to importune my nephew and either send word or return him here forthwith!"

Seventeen

"I s there no one at your house to whom you must send word of your whereabouts, sir?"

Elizabeth formed the apex of some odd social triangle—walking after a fashion beside the colonel and before the "footman." It made conversation stilted and awkward, for the colonel persisted in light-hearted small talk, but the other's eyes seemed to burn into her shoulders with the weight of all that he was leaving unspoken. In an effort to bring some genuine levity to all members of their party, she frequently turned to engage him in pointless questions.

He had been staring fixedly at her back, his eyes blank and his steps mechanical as he followed with her parasol. He blinked, as if only then understanding that she addressed him again. "What? My house?" He then glanced at the colonel, who was looking over his shoulder just then to catch the reply.

"Wilson, perhaps, but I know not how to send word again to him or to receive a message in return without exposing his position."

Elizabeth felt her brow creasing. This all sounded a good deal like espionage! All to avoid an undesirable marriage? She shook her head. Well, if she had not an ally in her aunt and sister, she would scarcely have been less circumspect about returning to the house graced by her would-be suitor.

"Sir, perhaps this Mr Wilson has some connections of his own. A shopkeeper with whom he does business, or perhaps an old friend who is trustworthy?"

The dark eyes brightened when she glanced back a second time. "Miss Bennet, that might be the very thing. There is a cobbler who was to send a pair of new boots this week, and naturally, Wilson would receive them."

Elizabeth's eyes widened again, this time in play. "This Mr Wilson is not so uncharitable a fellow as I had once made him out to be, for when I first met you, sir, you were suffering from inadequate footwear. I am glad to hear your employer has already seen to a remedy."

The colonel to her left broke into a scarcely controlled bellow of laughter. She did not look back over her shoulder to see the expression on the taller gentleman's face, but she thought she heard some manner of grunt. Well and good, let him learn some humour in his circumstances!

"Miss Bennet," chortled the colonel, "I do believe you have once more set my cousin at a loss for words. I assure you, I am taking notes, madam, for I intend to learn how it is done."

"It is not my intention to bewilder. I have begun an experiment, you see. My good manservant here has a rather charming smile when he employs it; one which cannot help but give him some advantage in whatever he endeavours. However, Colonel, I find that he so rarely makes use of the expression that I have taken it upon myself to aid him in practising." She glanced over her shoulder. "I should say that so far, my experiment has met with the very greatest success."

"No true proficiency can be gained without practice, as my aunt would say," agreed the colonel, in a perfectly sombre tone. "I wonder, do you think he has caught on to your little game yet?"

"He has," came the deep voice just behind her.

Elizabeth's neck prickled at the grudging amusement in those rich tones. It was as if he were walking close enough that his breath might have caused the small hairs above her collar to shiver, but when she turned round again, he still walked at his respectful distance, her parasol tipped lightly in his hand. She drew breath to gather herself, then pursed her lips and raised her brows in an unspoken question.

"And he makes no objections at present," he finished, shooting a slightly defiant look toward the colonel. "Far be it from me to suspend any pleasure of my lady's."

"Well spoken, sir!" affirmed the colonel. "Miss Bennet, if you do have no intention of keeping your manservant on, perhaps I might consider offering him a position myself. Such a clever fellow might prove himself useful."

"Ah, but Colonel, he insists that his wages are rather costly. I might advise you against taking him on, for though he does suit the livery quite nicely, he is far from the most proficient manservant of my acquaintance."

"I yield to the lady's advice," the colonel bowed his head, his lips still quivering in silent peals of laughter. "But do forgive me, Miss Bennet, I believe I have already forgotten the name of your street. Was it Lombard?"

"Gracechurch, sir. On the next street."

"Ah! Indeed, we've nearly another quarter of an hour. Are you not fatigued, Miss Bennet? I will quite happily hail a chair for you."

"I am accustomed to much walking, sir, but I thank you. I believe we might find a carriage uncomfortable."

"I believe your footman would find it uncomfortable, at the least," the colonel glanced over his shoulder again with that wicked grin on his face. He was enjoying his cousin's discomfiture far too much and seemed in no way repentant for it. "Very well then, Miss Bennet, we shall continue on foot. Oh!"

Elizabeth glanced to him in surprise and saw the gentleman flushing very slightly. "Is something amiss, sir?"

He blinked, seemed to gulp, and then turned his head very slightly over his shoulder. "It is Miss Wakeford."

Elizabeth looked where his attention seemed to be diverted. Miss Wakeford, whoever she was, appeared to be just stepping down from a carriage with a female companion. The colonel was clearing his throat and surreptitiously tugging at the front of his jacket, but his lady of interest had not yet noticed him.

"Miss Bennet," the voice in her ears caught her attention, "would you not prefer to cross? We shall have to do so soon, and the other side of the street offers some very charming shop windows."

"Yes, excellent advice," the colonel stammered, still looking straight ahead.

"Will you not be attending us farther, sir?"

The colonel darted a guilty look at each of them. "I think it for the best that I… will you be well enough, Miss Bennet?"

Elizabeth declared she would and heard the steady, reassuring footsteps behind her begin to turn. It seemed she had little enough choice, for both gentlemen seemed to have their disparate reasons for parting company—one so that he could speak to the lady of his preference, and the other so he would *not* have to speak to her.

Once safely across the street, she caught a glimpse of the colonel between passing carriages. It seemed that he was well received by the lady, but if she wished to know more, her curiosity was to remain unsatisfied, for her escort seemed relieved to have avoided the meeting. "Do you know, sir," she spoke without turning her head, "did I not know better, I should suspect you to be a haughty, unsociable fellow."

"What makes you believe that I am not?"

"Your sense of humour is far too incisive. Clever fellow, you must have fooled a number of people with that brooding scowl of yours, but there is much lurking beneath the surface."

"You are quite determined to create intrigue out of my character, but I assure you, there is none."

"Indeed? I am not convinced, but then, I am certain it is no concern of mine."

"You would proclaim my own character a puzzle, when you, madam, have proved the greater mystery."

"I? How so?"

"I do not believe I shall grant you the satisfaction of a reply at this moment. Perhaps if we meet again in a setting more agreeable to conversation, I might elaborate for you all the points at which your nature eludes me."

Elizabeth laughed, glancing back and just catching the gleam of humour in his eye. They were approaching an intersection, and the walkways were somewhat fuller now, so they fell into an easy silence for the remaining distance to Gracechurch street.

As they came upon the house, Elizabeth's steps began to slow. She bit her lip and drew a long sigh as her eyes scanned up the windows facing the street. She could see her own, and that one just down the way from it must be where her cousin awaited her return like a vulture. He would be upon her the moment she had set foot inside the door, and no quantity of veiled hints or even stark objections would be sufficient to discourage him.

"Miss Bennet, are you unwell?"

She shook herself. "No, merely... reluctant. Pay me no mind."

His lips thinned unhappily, and he paused, indicating with a dip of his head that he waited upon her pleasure. Elizabeth could not help a slight smile. The gentleman was learning his trade, after all.

Her brief, pleasant thought shattered an instant later, for there, standing on the pavement, was a boxy frame in black, slightly stooped and crowned with a floppy parson's hat. The figure was speaking, stopping everyone who passed by with a raised hand and a wheedling voice. And it was her name he was plying.

Elizabeth gritted her teeth, and a low, whispered word escaped her which, fortunately, not even her companion could have made out. For his part, he had jerked to a halt in dismay, aghast at the scene created on the street and the repeated references to her name in such a public venue.

Elizabeth spun away, her face growing hot with shame and anger, and found herself almost colliding with the strong arm which held her parasol. His voice was low in her ear as he asked after her well-being once more. She groaned, unable to claim that she was not humiliated, yet likewise too ashamed to allow him to see her so deeply affected by the actions of a fool. How she longed to set Collins down with a proper tongue lashing, but not on the street, not with nowhere to escape to afterwards but the same house, and not before *him*, so that she might feel ever more keenly the shame.

She felt his hand gently close around her elbow, and he guided her to stand near the steps of another house while she composed herself. A handkerchief found its way into her hand, and though she was far from tears or fainting, she was not beyond shielding her face with the article to stop a torrent of furious words which would not have improved the situation.

"You there! Ah, yes, perhaps your mistress can help me."

Elizabeth cringed at that oily voice, and she felt the sun strike her more fully as her parasol turned slightly.

"I beg your pardon?" Elizabeth's companion sputtered.

"Yes, I was speaking to you, man! You are with your mistress, are you not? I must ask her if she has seen a young lady, for I fear she may have met with some accident. Do you know Miss *Eliz-a-beth Ben-net*?" At that last question, Mr Collins' voice raised, and his words slowed, as though he were speaking to a child or trying to make himself understood to a foreigner. "It is most urgent that I find her. Miss… ELIZABETH… BENNET."

Elizabeth could not bring herself to turn round and look at the fool. He did not deserve to find her! Gratefully, she sensed the tall presence step nearer and gloried in his clipped tones when he replied.

"And who are you, sir, to be making inquiries after a lady of strangers upon the street? How have you the right to presume information of… this lady? Do you believe your actions in any way favourable to the lady you seek?"

"I am the betrothed of the lady in question!" Collins blustered. "I am perfectly within my rights to seek after my future wife, for it is most distressing that a young lady should be so long away without her escort. I came to London specifically to see her and make her known to my patroness, and she must be in the neighbourhood somewhere. Ask of your mistress if she knows Miss Bennet."

"I shall not permit this lady to be imposed upon in such an indecent manner," Elizabeth's companion retorted. "Good day, sir."

Elizabeth felt the shade of the parasol fall, then a hand guiding her elbow once more. Without thought, she suffered herself to be led away, still too mortified and incensed to allow her face to be seen by that bombastic oaf. Behind her, she heard Collins importuning yet another passer-by with a demand for anyone who knew Miss Elizabeth Bennet.

"You may lower the handkerchief, madam," was the murmured assurance at her side. "He is safely behind us."

Elizabeth swallowed and slowly complied.

"*That* was the reason you did not wish to remain at home this morning?"

She released an unsteady breath, tasting the copper tang in her mouth from so long biting her tongue. "Indeed."

"I believe, madam, that your character is less a mystery to me than it was a few moments ago. I perfectly understand now why you would not wish to expose yourself to… that."

She could not help a bitter laugh. "*That*, sir, was my father's cousin, and his character does not improve upon closer acquaintance."

Her companion fell silent for a moment. "I regret the mortification such an incident may have caused you."

"He has no right to abuse my name on the street like that! Yet, if I am provoked and speak against him, it should be myself upon whom the censure would fall."

"I presume that when your uncle learns of the man's conduct, he will be severely reprimanded?"

"Naturally... when he *does* learn of it. But that will be perhaps hours. How am I to tolerate such a buffoon until then?"

"Perhaps there is no need," he suggested.

"I cannot avoid it!"

"Why can you not? You have advised me, now I shall do the same for you. Wait for your uncle, and do not put yourself within reach of a fool without some protection in place."

"That may do very well for a..." she looked him up and down... "gentleman...."

He smiled, and Elizabeth nearly forgot what she had been about to say. Those dimples again! She cleared her throat. "...But I have already behaved scandalously enough for one day. You cannot truly be suggesting that I continue walking the streets of London until this evening!"

"Would it make matters worse if you did?"

"How could it not?"

"Your aunt and sister do not presently fear for you—as you have said, they expect you to be in the company of one who would look to your safety, as you are at this very moment. Is it not true that the only person fretting about your whereabouts is... that man?"

"Mr Collins. Yes, I suppose that is true."

"And would it distress you to be at odds with him until your uncle may intervene?"

Elizabeth stifled a grunt of wry laughter. "Not in the least! Think me a wretch if you will, but I would rather enjoy frustrating him."

He smiled again. "I cannot think so ill of you, Miss Bennet. Come, I believe I will make use of your notion regarding my bootmaker, and then, may I have the pleasure of introducing you to some of the more memorable sights in London?"

She stopped and stared at him. "You are serious?"

"Quite so. As you have noted, we are both of us in need of a holiday. As we presently find ourselves with little opportunity to improve our situations, let us spend the afternoon reviving our spirits. I will look to your safety as if you were my own sister, and I shall depend on you and your parasol to keep me from being recognised."

"Sir, I cannot claim to know you at all, but I have the sense that such a proposition would normally have caused you no small degree of horror."

"You are correct that it is… out of character for me. But that only makes the suggestion all the more intriguing—not to mention that none would ever suspect how we passed our afternoon. I find it almost irresistible, do not you?"

Elizabeth arched a brow, a hint of mischief bubbling in her breast. "Irresistible, indeed."

Eighteen

M iss Bennet baulked at the door. "Are you certain this is a good plan? I
have never even heard of such a scheme!"

"I assure you, it would not be the first time I have seen such arts
employed. You might well be astonished and scandalised by some of the means
essayed by the more creative among your sex. At least this time, it is done with
the best intentions."

"But I am not certain I have it in me!"

"That is why I know you will succeed," he informed her warmly. "You have
an honest face; therefore, none could suspect you of malice. The additional
incentive of which we spoke will no doubt be of assistance as well."

"It is not that, nor my appearance of honesty that I doubt, but my ability to
behave the convincing flirt. My sister is the expert in that art."

Darcy narrowed his eyes, once more thinking of poor, simple Bingley. "The
elder sister you praised so highly?"

"Heavens, no! Jane is far too modest. Why, if she liked a man, he would be
the last to know of it, for she is so reserved. Sadly, it is my youngest sister who
leads in this way." She sighed, shaking her head in seeming regret. "I suppose
if I recall her example and try to behave as she, perhaps I could be persuasive
enough."

"It would be better if you do not act the coquettish naif. You have a
sophisticated manner, and I would invite you to employ it. Most who would
consider this sort of scheme do not think of themselves as girls just out of the
schoolroom."

"Are you truly in earnest? You have seen such a trick?"

"More than once, and sometimes far more desperate measures than what I
propose. If you wish to know whether it has ever produced the desired result,

you would have to apply to another, but it has not stopped many from making an attempt. If you truly dislike the notion so much, let us think of another way, but I doubt that I, dressed as I am….”

She nodded slowly. “I understand.”

Darcy held the door for her and stood aside, just as he had seen his own male servants do on so many occasions. How natural it seemed already, to attend this woman who met every gesture of service with a graciousness that displayed appreciation, rather than expectation. And how easy he felt when the eyes of the room were not upon him, but on her! He could breathe in her company, and even enjoy all he saw as if through eyes not jaded by years of careful observance of all Society’s pointless mores. How she had, in the course of one frenetic, turbid morning, somehow taught him the simple pleasure of *being*, was a mystery certain to baffle him for a long while.

She cast him one last nervous glance, fumbled slightly with the tips of her gloves, then arched her shoulders and stepped forward into the shop. The proprietor of the boot shop met her with a discreet bow of humility. “How might I be of service, madam?”

Darcy stood stock still behind her, his profile turned so that he appeared ready to reach for the door, but his eyes were following her every movement… a little sliver of tongue which nervously touched her lips, the maidenly flutter of lashes as she withdrew the slip of paper he had given her from her reticule. She seemed to draw herself up then, and with cheerful, serene confidence, made her request.

“I beg your pardon, sir, but I understand you have a parcel to be delivered to this address.” She gently touched the paper to the counter and slid it to the cobbler.

He accepted it, and his forehead wrinkled when he read the street number. “To this address? Madam, I often deliver to this address, for the gentleman is one of my finer customers.” He dropped his voice significantly, then handed the paper back to her. “I would not like to displease the man in any way,”

“Nothing of the kind, I assure you. I simply desire to send a message to the servant who will receive the parcel.”

The proprietor began to shake his head in denial, lifting his hands, but when Miss Bennet drew out the second paper and laid it down with two silver coins, he began to show more interest. “I understand the parcel is to be delivered today?”

“The boots are ready, madam, and the delivery only wants my boy’s return from his last errand so that he can carry it.”

“I thank you most kindly for the information,” she tipped her head grandly, as if she were any fine lady in a ballroom accepting champagne from her partner.

The bootmaker cleared his throat, and the silver coins disappeared. “Anything to please a lady,” he returned gruffly.

She turned with casual elegance and strode to the door without so much as a glance at his face, just as any lady out with her servant would have done. Darcy almost chuckled at the sight of her, so assured and composed, but the moment her feet touched the pavement and the door jingled closed behind them, she released a great sigh and then an astonished little laugh.

"I cannot believe I just did that! Do you not think it was wrong, to do something in deceit?"

"Whom have you deceived? You told the man nothing about yourself, real or imagined, nor anything of the message you conveyed. The person receiving the message, which was written in *my* hand, not yours, will benefit from the intelligence gained. You were not attempting to form an assignation or to injure anyone, and I myself hope to be the beneficiary of the communication once it is received properly."

"What precisely did you tell this Wilson person?"

"Where I expect to be found throughout the remainder of the day. If he does have anything of interest to report, he will need to know how to send word to me."

She paused, tilting up her head and narrowing a single brilliant eye. "You are a mystery to me, sir."

"I imagine I must be. Shall we have a formal introduction, Miss Bennet?"

She cocked her head the other way, white teeth just catching her bottom lip in thought. "I am of a curious nature, sir, which you have no doubt discerned. Moreover, I enjoy watching people and discovering their foibles and peculiarities. You are among the more unique individuals I have encountered. You walk about town dressed in clothes that I know very well are not your own, you seem to wish to avoid anyone of your own circle, yet in all other respects, you behave as someone with… abundant resources at his disposal."

"It is true, Miss Bennet," he answered slowly. "I will tell you anything about myself you wish to know, for I believe you deserve honesty."

"And what of you? Do you not risk exposure, if I were to learn of your name and consequence? Do you not fear that I might bring harm to your sister or attempt to compromise you as someone else has done?"

He smiled, enjoying the answering twinkle in her eyes. "I am not afraid of you."

"Are you not? For though I may not be of noble blood, I do have a reputation to lose, after all. Have you no fear of reprisal for spending the day with me?"

"Have you?"

She seemed to pause. "I fear having no choice in my fate."

"In that," he answered gently, "you are not alone. Since we have both agreed that at present, we do have some choice in remaining away from our residences, where certain unpleasantness awaits us both, let us content ourselves. We shall be discrete and protect each other from those who would speak slanderously of either of us. Do you wish to know my name, Miss Bennet?"

She looked down to the pavement, toying slightly with her reticule. "I expect," she answered in a low voice, "that you do not mingle with many tradesmen's families."

He shifted on his feet, aware once again of the poorly fitting shoes. "No."

"And you do know this about me for a certainty. Whatever else I might claim for a pedigree, my people are not of your circle, whatever that is. Can any good come from knowing you as other than a footman?"

He felt his chest tightening strangely. "It is not likely," he confessed, but even as he agreed with her, he felt a ripping through his core. She was right, and he knew it… but what he would have given at that moment to hear her reveal that she was, indeed, the daughter of one of his equals! Were her last name Cavendish or Fitzherbert or Ashby, he would at least be able to speak with her again after this dreadful day had ended.

She gave a short nod, blinking for just a moment. "Then do not tell me more. I would only ask your Christian name, for I cannot continue calling you 'sir.' Any lady would know her footman's first name."

He smiled again… could not help it. In fact, he could hardly look at her without smiling, but he did not like to think on that, considering their agreement. "My sister calls me William. Will that suit, Miss Bennet?"

"If you will call me 'Miss Elizabeth,' for I keep looking about to see where my sister is when you call me 'Miss Bennet,'" she laughed.

He bowed from the waist, right there on the pavement outside a boot shop. "I am pleased to make your acquaintance, Miss Elizabeth."

"I as well, William." She dipped a modest curtsy. "Well, now, that is settled," she brightened at once, "where are we expected to spend the afternoon?"

"I thought you would never ask," he grinned and put his hand out to summon a hack coach.

~

Elizabeth could not remain sedately in her seat. She leaned forward, touching eager fingers to the window as each famous sight rolled by; The Strand once again, with that hotel which had refused them service; Charing Cross with its awe-inspiring statue of the troubled King Charles I; the humble Scotland Yard, followed by the pristine buildings of White Hall. This was a part of Town she rarely saw… and might seldom, if ever, see again. She blinked away an unwelcome bit of emotion from her eyes, determined to wring every bit of enjoyment from this day that it had to offer.

There was a thumping from the back wall of her coach, and she leaned back to press her ear to the panel. "Look to your right," came a muffled voice.

Chuckling, Elizabeth did.

"Behind the Horse Guards buildings," he urged when she did not respond at once. "Do you see it?"

Elizabeth craned her neck, trying to see better from the moving carriage. She knew well that St James' Park, in all its dashing splendour, lay just there to delight the eyes and stir her deepest yearnings. There, beautifully dressed ladies walked on the arms of their sensible-looking husbands, military fanfare dazzled the young and swelled the hearts of the aged, and classical architecture and verdant bowers melded into one gracious Walk. She sighed, her chest squeezing just a little. What she would give to admire it at leisure, knowing that at any time she could return to indulge her senses just a little more. But it was no good to long for that which could only make the choices before her seem more miserable than they already were.

"Would you like to stop?" she heard through the carriage wall.

The smile returned to Elizabeth's face. Her escort was attentive, whatever else might be said of him. And this time, he had not permitted so much as a facial twitch or a cough of ill humour when one of the oldest carriages in all London had answered his hail. It was clean and safe, that much he had assured them both, but his voice from without could hardly be heard over the squeaking of worn leather and wood.

"No, thank you," she called back to him, pressing her cheek to the panel so that he would be certain to hear her. "I would prefer to go on."

He did not answer directly, so she rapped her knuckles against the wall, just as he had done to attract her attention. He replied in a quick, staccato beat just behind her ear.

The carriage slowed briefly, and Elizabeth tried speech once again. "Are you quite safe back there?"

"I have made a bargain with Fate," his muted words filtered through the panel.

"And that is?"

"If this foot peg breaks under my weight and I am trampled by that fine pair of chestnuts behind us, I shall never again have to wear such uncomfortable shoes."

Elizabeth giggled, and could nearly see that faint twitching round his mouth, the mock gravity crinkling his eyes as he spoke. "Let us only hope the carriage behind us belongs to no one you know."

"It does. I do not think they would drive to the curb simply to avoid my body."

"Then I dearly hope your hands are strong!" she laughed, then playfully knocked again near the place she had heard his last thumps. To her childish delight, he replied in kind.

The carriage rocked forward again, and for several minutes the traffic moved ahead at a moderate pace. She could not have heard him then if he had tried to speak, but there sounded another knock on the left side of her head as they approached Westminster Abbey. Elizabeth looked on, breathless in admiration for yet another building she would dearly love to explore.

Their driver chose a meandering route through the back streets—or perhaps he had received the direction from her escort—and Elizabeth was treated to several more quaint views. Then, as if by magic, London fell away, and they began to pass fields of wheat and fruit orchards. The cobblestones still rang loudly beneath the horse's feet, but there were fewer of them, and the carriage seemed to roll more freely. A lad of perhaps eight or nine, standing amid a golden wheat field with a sickle in his hand, waved energetically as they passed. Elizabeth waved back but realised belatedly that the boy had not been offering his civility to *her*, but to the tall man clinging to the back of the carriage. Elizabeth leaned a little farther to the right, searching the ground, and could see the shadow of his hand lifted in greeting to the young farmer.

She drew back again to the seat, her cheeks almost weary from the constant smile they bore. Such a peculiar man, this William! When he had uttered those first, disdainful slurs in her presence that very morning, she would have sworn that he was conceited, arrogant, and cared nothing for the feelings of others. How wrong had been that first impression! She could not help but wonder what his usual manner was when among his equals in society. She would have wagered the last of her pin money that he did not mingle and cavort freely, as did those gentlemen who were usually deemed "amiable." Yet, there was a gentleness in him, and a deep feeling akin to sincerity and kindness, if one took the time for a second look. Was that not, to her tastes, more amiable than the sort of man her mother had taught her to admire?

She felt herself sighing again and shook her head. "You must stop," she muttered aloud. There, she had spoken it, and must now heed. She could not afford to think of him, even if he would ever look at her. She had been given one day to peer beyond the veil of her own destiny, one day in the presence of the very sort of man who could teach her that they were not all fools. She must content herself with that. She must continue to treat him as a kind stranger, one whom she would never see again after this day had ended.

Within minutes of this resolution forming, it was tried. The carriage drew up to a queue, and she felt the ageing springs give way as William bounced down from the back. His steps crunched on the gravelled earth, and she heard him paying the driver. He opened her door and greeted her with an expression that threatened to rob her of breath. There was a boyish delight there, a flickering of the youth he must have suppressed long ago, but kindling beneath it was something fuller, richer, and simmering with flavours of the forbidden.

Elizabeth paused, her lips parted as she surveyed him with eyes opened to a new depth of awareness, and the back of her neck prickled. His chest swelled proudly, and with one hand he gestured toward the Thames River, while the other crossed over his abdomen in a stately bow.

"Miss Elizabeth, Vauxhall Gardens await."

Nineteen

It was well into the middle of the afternoon when Edward Gardiner returned to his warehouse desk. This day had decidedly not gone as intended! He felt like a winded racehorse who had a heat yet to run. Wearily, he tugged his pocket watch forth to stare at its face and shook his head.

"Haskins," he signalled to his clerk as the man walked by, "will you have a note sent to my house, please? I am afraid I must disappoint Mrs Gardiner and my nieces this evening. I ought to send word, although they likely already expect it by now."

"Sir, Mrs Gardiner has already sent word here for you. There is a note on your desk from her. Oh! And Miss Elizabeth called while you were out."

"Lizzy? Why would she have come here?" he wondered, turning to find his wife's note.

"She did not say, sir, but it seemed to be some business connected with one of your household servants."

"How strange!" he murmured, then his fingers tore into the sealed paper. He had not read more than two lines before he groaned audibly, and in the tones of a man in genuine pain.

"Sir?" Haskins stepped back into the room in concern. "Are you unwell?"

He glanced up, barely suppressing a grimace. "As well as a man with an infested household can be."

"Infested! Sir, I know of an excellent rat catcher. He set my mother's house right last winter. Would you like me to send for him?"

"Unfortunately, it is quite a different sort of rodent which has installed itself at my residence. I think I no longer regret the additional hours this shipment crisis has required of me. But my poor wife and nieces!"

Haskins looked politely unconscious of his employer's musings. He knew nothing of what Mr Gardiner might have meant, and so he went on about his tasks as if nothing were amiss until his attention was called back again.

"What is this?" Gardiner had reached the bottom of his note and looked up to Haskins in confusion. "What time did Miss Elizabeth call?"

"I am not certain, sir... I believe it was just before eleven. Half ten, perhaps?"

Gardiner stared at his note, his features pinched. "And she had one of my servants with her?"

"Yes, sir, a strong-looking footman. I am sure she was quite safe, sir."

"Oh, it is not that. Mrs Gardiner said Lizzy had left the house, and that I should try to keep her busy here for the remainder of the day, for she would spare her some of the company at home. But you say she left directly when she learned I was out?"

Haskins frowned in thought. "I believe so, sir. She may perhaps have sought the newest book shipment in the warehouse before she left. You know how she indulges that enjoyment upon each visit. Perhaps one of the stock boys might have seen her."

Gardiner turned the note over, scratching his head. "No, more than likely she returned to the house directly. When did this note arrive?"

"Not ten minutes after she, sir, I am quite certain of it. Perhaps she passed the messenger on her way."

Gardiner grunted and tossed the note to the side, then drew a stack of invoices into its place. "Yes, I am sure that is it. Poor Lizzy! Stuck all day with such a disagreeable fellow. It is a pity I could do nothing to get her out of the house this evening."

~

"Have you never been on the water before?" Darcy was watching his feminine companion in some amusement. The barge which was to carry them across the Thames was met with equal parts delight and trepidation, and once aboard, she had secured the hand railing as if her very life depended upon its stability.

She offered him a guilty smile. "Only small fishing boats, in shallow streams. I have always found them somewhat unreliable, even when piloted by skilled hands."

"And you find this craft to be less seaworthy than they?"

"Oh, I should think not, but the water here is deep and unfamiliar. Let me accustom myself to the rocking below my feet before I let go this railing, then, I promise, I shall enjoy the crossing." She closed her eyes then, as if she were insisting upon absolute silence during this moment of reflection and composition. Her fingers gripped and readjusted themselves on the rail, and her shoulders rose and fell in deep, rhythmic breaths. After a moment, her eyes cautiously blinked open.

"Better?" he asked, helpless to keep the laughing smile from his face. She possessed all the seriousness of a sage when she chose, and then the mercurial capacity to will it away at an instant's notice. He had never known anyone more intriguing, and it was all artless sincerity on her part. It would be a long while before he tired of her company.

She ignored his question, perhaps because of the playful note in his voice when he had asked it. Instead, she was slowly stretching her frame, standing taller and daring to throw back her head slightly to admire the sky and trees lining the river. There was a lithe, graceful quality to her bearing—almost as a dancer in repose, or a yearling stallion just discovering his own charisma. Darcy sensed that strange magnetism again, the longing to savour and indulge, to discover and claim….

He shook his head, feeling as if some physical force had commandeered his senses. His vision was even dazed for an instant, so harshly was he bound to reprimand himself. The sudden thickness of his tongue gradually subsided, but the stirring from other regions of his being was more difficult to ignore… and none more so than the pang in his chest. What could he possibly be thinking, even to look at her? He had settled with himself at first glance that she would be unsuitable as a wife, and he certainly would never ask anything less honourable of her. Why, then, could he not look away?

He clenched his fists, biting his lip and trying to turn his head even as his eyes stubbornly locked on her, admiring the energy and life sparkling in each look and gesture, and seeming to snap even in the air all about her. Perhaps if he punished himself severely enough when standing beside her, the arrangement would become less appealing. His nails dug deliberately into his palms, and his tongue began to bleed.

"William, are you also distressed at being on the boat? See, we are well over halfway across. It can be only a moment more, and we will be safely on dry land again."

Despite himself, the corner of his lip curled upward even as he tried to straighten it out from within by clamping it with his teeth. The wicked enchantress, did she not know that it was not the boat ride which caused him to quail in his dreadful shoes, but she herself? And she had the temerity to speak gently to him! Would that she would behave, even for one moment, as the debutantes and heiresses he had met. A glimmer of some dross tainting the sterling, something less than her quaintly charming virtues, so that he could recover his equilibrium and treat her with the proper disdain.

"William?" She touched his arm, true concern in her voice.

Damn.

He drew a slow breath, gave up fighting the impudent smile which had mutinied against his directives, and opened his eyes. She returned the warmth he felt from his own traitorous face like a ray of sunshine dancing on the waters behind her.

He was in grave danger. *This* was why his father had cautioned him so sternly against permitting even the breath of suspicion in his associations! All his life, he had assumed those words as a warning against those who would take advantage of him, but now he was in as much danger from his own sentiments as from anything his aunt could devise. And he was enjoying it.

"William, look!" Innocent to the turmoil within his own mind, she pointed across the water to the white steps which led up the river bank to this fantasy land she had so longed to explore. "What shall we see this early in the day, do you think?"

Darcy adopted an air of conscious nonchalance, not a little unsettled by how well he liked hearing her using such an intimate name. It was safer, he decided, to play the all-knowing guide rather than the comrade in adventure, so he tipped his brow upward and frowned thoughtfully. "Oh, many of the performers will already be about. Have you ever witnessed magic tricks or a man who can turn flips?"

Her eyes widened. "Do you mean he…." She turned her index fingers over one another in a circular motion. "There really are men who can do that?"

"And women too, but I doubt we shall see them today. Of course, they sell their famous punch and 'invisible' ham at almost all hours, so we may find our purses lightened, but we shall not be hungry. Oh, and like enough we will see a few painters out during the daylight hours, trying to pretend they are communing with nature here in the city, and selling their work for far more than it is worth."

"And musicians?"

"Perhaps, but I would expect little in that way until later. The real evening entertainment usually begins about an hour before sundown."

Her face fell slightly, but only for an instant. "And we shall have to depart well before that. We ought not to stay long, of course, but a small sampling of the sights will be a great treat."

"On the contrary, I told Wilson that this is where we would be found. Perhaps we would be foolish to leave it too soon."

"*We?*"

Darcy looked uncomfortably down into her face. "I did not mention that, I suppose. Yes, I told him of your name and your uncle's address, so that if the need arose, your family might be contacted. I do not expect that to happen, for

I should not like to give undue alarm, but I did not like leaving it to chance. I hope you have no objections, Miss Elizabeth. Wilson is trustworthy and discreet."

She turned from him and gazed over the remaining few feet of water, watching the boat hands as they began the task of drawing up to the bank. "I wish you had said something before potentially exposing me. You had no right."

He winced. "No right?" he asked with slight annoyance, but her tone had been gentle, so he took care that his was as well. "I view it as a responsibility, Miss Elizabeth. I promised you that you would be safe in my company. Should circumstances demand my immediate presence elsewhere, I would insist that you be given proper escort and security against malicious talk or bodily harm. Wilson has not the authority to act on his information, save at the point of greatest need."

She drew a long breath, her fingers flexing on the rail, and he could see that she was clamping down on her own lip to prevent any unseemly outburst. After a moment, she was steady enough to answer. "I believe I can understand your reasons, but that does not change the fact that you did not consult me on something so materially important to my own interests. Were I any less convinced of your good intentions, I believe you would have seen a bit of my unfortunate temper."

"I am sorry that my actions gave offence. It was not my wish, Miss Elizabeth."

She turned back to gaze up at him, a light of cheerful absolution in her eyes. "It was apparent to me from the first this morning that you were accustomed to your own way. At the time, I supposed it pure arrogance, but I could be persuaded to understand that you are not in the habit of sharing responsibility or losing control."

"Losing control can prove disastrous, and as for sharing responsibility, I have never been able to cast all my cares on another. Their weight is too great, and the consequences too severe."

"And we established this as the reason that you are in great need of a day of amusement. Come, let us speak no more of unpleasant things now, for the boat has docked and the other passengers are stepping off." And just that swiftly, their little argument ended.

Darcy marvelled, shaking his head and laughing silently to himself. He fell easily into the queue behind her as the handful of others made their way off the barge. They followed up the steps to the main Vauxhall Walk, and he tipped her parasol back so that she could look all above and beyond the heads of those in front of them. They approached the imposing brick edifice which stood as the last barrier before them of the sombre, everyday world, and Darcy drew out his coin purse. A silver tag embossed with the mythical Atlas on the front and his name on the back for himself, and a polished shilling for her. Before she could trouble herself to search within her own purse, he had paid their admission, and in such a casual manner that the bored attendant never bothered to check the name on the back of his tag.

She caught his eye in sweet gratitude, but he directed her gaze forward again. Through that grey portal could be seen an expanse of glittering pavement, bordered by towering elms. "The Grand Walk," he murmured lowly to her. "And there on the left is the Rotunda, where my father and mother would take in the concerts on occasion."

She seemed to surge forward, as if she wished to admire everything at once, then, within a few steps, she slowed. They were well inside the gates now, and the passers-by circulated easily around them as her steps drifted to a halt. She turned, looking puzzled and not a little disappointed.

"Miss Elizabeth? Is something amiss?"

"I suppose I had built it up so in my imagination," she sighed. "It looks... rather tired, does it not? The grass is a little unkempt, that paint there is peeling...."

"I did relate that the Garden is not what it was in its glory days."

"I ought to have listened!"

"Only think, Miss Elizabeth, how it appears at night. That arch there," he pointed to the right, "will be adorned with blazing torches, as will the Pavilion there," he gestured to the distance on the left. "Everything will be cast with mystery and intrigue, and the music will be gay, the entertainment lively. What matter a bit of dead grass and peeling paint? Are they vital to your enjoyment?"

She chuckled. "You begin to sound like me."

"That is well, for you frightened me when your words sounded a little too much like my own."

"A travesty, indeed!" she laughed more heartily. "Very well, I shall look beyond superficial appearances and appreciate the venue for what it is; a chance to set my cares aside for a while and to mingle among those I might never meet otherwise. Shall we, William?"

Too late, he caught himself. He looked down into her face, felt the unbridled pleasure beaming from his own and the lump which seemed to swell in his throat. *Devil take it.* He had never wanted anything more in his life than to please her. An hour. Two, perhaps. Three, at the outside; he would be hers for a short while, and then he would be rational again.

He gestured before him, down the length of the Grand Walk, and adjusted the white parasol so that it offered her the appropriate shade in the afternoon sun. "I am at your service, Miss Elizabeth."

Twenty

Elizabeth had not long to suffer in dismay over the dandelions or the drooping elms, for within a very few steps, their promenade had carried them to the heart of the Gardens. To her right was a square, planted all round with towering giants and dominated in the centre by an orchestra stand, which was, at present, still vacant. She marvelled for a moment at the detail and splendour in the construction, even if the paint was somewhat faded. She could easily close her eyes and imagine the classical frontage ablaze with the glow of coloured glass lanterns and candles, and made ethereal by the music it hosted. If only they could stay long enough for her to hear just one melody!

As if he had read her mind, William spoke at her elbow, "The orchestra tends to start a little earlier than the supper. Within an hour or so, the musicians will arrive."

"Are you suggesting that we might stay so long?"

"At what time of the day does your uncle typically return from his warehouse?"

She frowned. "That is just the trouble. He is not usually there all day, nor even half of it. Today must have been a very bad one for him, so I cannot tell you what we ought to expect. I should not think him much later than six or seven in the evening, for he will wish to eat his supper with my aunt."

"Then if we have no word sooner, we should time our arrival to coincide with his. Any earlier would seem nonsensical, for you would be entering the house again without protection from your...." He cleared his throat and stopped.

"He is *not* my betrothed, nor, I hope, shall he ever be," she clarified firmly.

"I am relieved to hear it. He did seem an audacious sort of fellow to make such a proclamation when the lady's intentions are not similarly engaged."

Elizabeth dipped her face down and away from him, but some outspoken nerve tasked her not to keep silent as her good sense would have allowed. "He has reason to think that he has a chance of success." Then she stopped herself, turned and tilted her head, so that shade of the parasol fell over her eyes. "Let us talk no more of Mr Collins, please."

He inclined his head, and there was a stately serenity to his countenance when he suggested, "Perhaps you would like to view the supper boxes or the Temple of Comus?"

She looked in half-interest over his shoulder at the larger of the two dished colonnades, this one graced with a Rococo spired pavilion, then smilingly shook her head. "If our time is to be limited, I think I should like to see the arches I have heard of. Are they not there?"

"Indeed, the southerly walk parallels this one. Some parts of it are also called the Italian Walk, for the architecture. We may cross over here and walk the length of the Grove, then we should have an ideal prospect of the arches."

Elizabeth's eyes feasted on every facet as they slowly wandered the few steps in that direction. At the edge of the Grove, a few acrobats cavorted about, plying the late afternoon revellers for a few pence in appreciation for their efforts. She laughed outright as one flipped directly into her path and tumbled into what appeared to be a clumsy bow. He then snapped upright again, only to snatch the hat worn by her tall, sombre companion and cartwheel away with it in his teeth. William's exclamations of dismay in the face of such effrontery were lost in the general approval of the sparse audience. The tomfool landed several paces away, twirling the plain chapeau about his finger and grinning daringly at Elizabeth.

"Allow me to redeem your lost item, my good fellow," she chuckled, gesturing for her escort to remain at peace. She felt the rather fine lady, paying to recover the dignity of her "servant," and laughed merrily when the acrobat accepted her penny with a flourish and a gallant kiss to the tip of her glove. The hat was returned in much the same manner that it had been pilfered, and the colourfully dressed fellow whirled away in search of more good-humoured guests.

"Are you quite recovered?" she asked of him.

"It seems the heavens have today determined that I possessed a bit more pride than was good for me," he grumbled, but not without something of a twinkle in his eye as he took in her own amusement. "It is doubtful that I will ever be recovered, but I believe I shall survive the ordeal."

Elizabeth laughed and drew a little closer, the better to share in the benefit of her own parasol. "I expect that few take such liberties with your person under normal circumstances."

He was silent for a moment, and when she turned up to look at him, his face appeared deeply thoughtful. "That is true…" he hesitated. "At least somewhat. Those liberties which are presumed on occasion are never so innocent."

He said no more, and Elizabeth was left to ponder yet again what singular occurrence had sent such a man into hiding from his own household. In an apparent attempt to change the subject, he gestured to a particularly handsome rose hedge lining the rows of supper boxes. She gave it due appreciation as they passed, and out of respect for his privacy, she left the question alone.

Together they turned left and proceeded a little way up the gravel path. From this angle, they could look down the arrayed arches for what seemed a greater distance than the thousand feet she had been told it was. The illusion was so convincing, the placement and antiquated style so evocative, that even during the prosaic light of day she could fancy that she had been transported to an ancient world.

"The ruins at Palmyra," William indicated the far extremity of the Walk, and indeed a decidedly realistic painting formed the background of the final arch.

"It is astonishing!"

"Perhaps from this distance," she could hear the faint smile in his voice. "A nearer view might render it less remarkable."

"Ah! There you are, the pragmatic one again. It shall not work, for I am determined to be pleased and, therefore, most certain of being found so. However," she squinted and tilted her head, "it *would* look far more convincing at dusk."

There was the softest hint of laughter in her ear. "Come, Miss Elizabeth," he touched her arm with his free hand, "let us turn from the main path just before the last of the three archways. There is a smaller path there, and you will be spared the shattering of your pleasant illusion by too close an appraisal. Perhaps we could admire the golden statue of Aurora or simply take in the trees."

He was walking more beside her now, the better to point out all the items she might find of interest, and she almost felt it would have been more comfortable for her to take his arm as they walked. Her last vestiges of decorum checked her, but she did not object to the fact that she did not have to turn so far to ask her questions of him. It was amusing, too, to find from the corner of her eye that their gazes seemed to be united, seeking the same objects wherever they turned.

"Is that another walkway there, through the trees?" she wondered aloud. She did not need to point, for he had been looking that way with interest as well. The path was some distance through the thicket and far narrower than the one on which they walked. Any less daylight than they presently enjoyed would have rendered it almost invisible from their position.

A low noise sounded in his throat. "We will not be viewing that path. It is one of the Dark Walks that border the Gardens, venues where certain illicit doings are known to take place. It would be… inadvisable for us to venture there."

"Ah." She could not help a faint blush, for indeed, she had already seen two or three women of uncertain age who appeared to have been wearing a deal too much rouge. Their purpose painfully clear, she tried her best to put them from her mind. These last weeks, that subject had become a touch too real for her, and a woman's security, far more fragile than she had formerly wished to believe. Her own virtue, if her little pleasure tour were ever discovered, troubled her far less than it should have, had not other matters already sunken lower than she might have imagined they could ever do.

"There is the hermitage," her companion announced, distracting her from her guilty musings. "Would you like to have your fortune told?"

She looked back with a quizzical frown. "You do not believe in that superstition, do you?"

"You must not mock the hands of Fate," he informed her seriously. "But you can learn its will, for the modest sum of a sixpence."

"Then, by all means, let us learn what destiny lies ahead."

He guided her, most chivalrously, to a small, dank-looking hovel which had been arranged to look as if some forest-dwelling hermit had made it for his home. The humble door stood ajar, and within the false abode, a very convincingly costumed individual puttered about. Just outside the door were positioned some roughly carved seats, and into one of these, he helped her settle to wait.

The hermit took no notice of them for at least two minutes, keeping up the act of poring studiously over what appeared to be a crumbling old tome, and mumbling something unintelligible. She almost began to grow annoyed with his intentional delay, for it was clear he had seen them, but just before she would have spoken aloud, she saw William's hand moving at his knee in a calming gesture. "Patience," he whispered. "It is all a part of the amusement."

At last, the old man stretched, rose, shuffled out of his door, and took in their presence with a convincing degree of surprise. "Ahhh," he sighed, his eyes seeming to mist over when he looked at Elizabeth, "what elusive fortune has brought thee hither?"

Elizabeth drew out her coin and dropped it into the bowl he had so nonchalantly carried out of the house. He pretended not to notice, his eyes rolling back into his head as he stumbled to a ragged chair himself and deposited the bowl on the ground. He held out his hand, and when she hesitated, he became agitated and grunted his displeasure. She glanced at William, who nodded, and gave her gloved hand into the crusty fingers of the hermit.

"Mmm," he mumbled. "Ah. Ohhhh." He groaned as if he were in pain, and his brow furrowed. Then his eyes flew open, and he stared hard at her. "Thou art more than thou appearest!" he gasped. He closed his eyes and sought her other hand, and a grimace crossed his features.

Elizabeth rolled uncertain eyes toward William, but he was leaning intently forward, apparently enjoying the performance.

"Eeee," the old eccentric continued, "a treasure too well guarded is never found. That which thou seekest is before thee even now. Lift up thine head; never lookest thee down. Faint not, nor touch'd by shame art thou; thine dearest wish shall come round."

His hand dropped hers, and he drew back in a stretch as if waking from a long nap. Elizabeth turned a bewildered expression upon her companion, feeling as if she had just paid good coin to hear the made-up ramblings of a crazy old man. William's own brows were quirking in similar confusion, and he lifted one shoulder as if to say that he, too, was baffled. He began to rise to assist her to her feet when a withered finger shot straight into his face.

Elizabeth jerked back in amazement, wondering precisely how her stately companion would perceive this bit of theatrics. It seemed that he was as astonished as she, for he tumbled back into his seat, his dark eyes wide.

"The fall!" the hermit almost shrieked. "Hard it is when cast down thou art from artifice and pride! Seekest thou not pleasing lips and hands that lie. Woe upon thee, if thou learnest not, for verily the price is thine love and life!"

Elizabeth felt her hand snatched in unequivocal demand for removal, and the next second, he was pulling her to her feet and down the path, away from the wheedling howls of the backwoods prophet.

~

Wilson stared once more at the note his master had hastily scrawled on a bit of... bakery parchment? Wherever had Mr Darcy found that? Matters must have turned badly for him indeed if he was draughting such disgracefully penned missives and secreting them into boot boxes. And Vauxhall? The man must have lost his senses!

Then again, perhaps not, for if Wilson were astonished at Mr Darcy's present whereabouts, all others would think it an outright falsehood. And who was this in his company... *Miss... Eliza?* No. He squinted, trying to smooth the paper, but some grease still clinging to the sweet-smelling parchment had smudged the writing as it was folded. He tilted his head and made out the rest of the name. *Eliza Benwick.* There were some more words blurred, but he could make out a few here and there. *Cannot... home... Uncle... witness... 23 Gracechurch... inform... whereabouts... Edward Gardiner... send word... escort home... do not... until I send... Please advise... Lady Catherine.*

Wilson blinked and scratched his head. He read the note at least twice more, only making out about two more words. *Evening… compromise.*

Whatever that meant. He sighed, turning the note sideways as if he hoped it would make it easier to read. Clearly, Mr Darcy was requesting him to contact this Edward Gardiner person on Gracechurch Street, and for a mercy, the address was intact. He also seemed to desire that a messenger be sent to him directly at the Gardens, but if he had listed a place where he might be found, Wilson could not read it. Surely, however, Mr Darcy would be watching out for such a man and would make himself easy to locate. Wilson secreted himself in the semi-seclusion of Mr Darcy's dressing chambers, on a small little desk kept for his own purposes, and checked his pen.

Dear Mr Gardiner,

My master, Mr Fitzwilliam Darcy of 16 Grosvenor Square, desires me to send word on his behalf that he is presently in company with Miss Eliza Benwick at Vauxhall Gardens. I believe she is known to you and may perhaps be awaiting your arrival, or simply wishing to assure you of her safety while in the presence of other companions.

I do apologise for the shock such a note must give you, sir, and I wish I could be more concise as to the details of why the lady wishes for you to be informed. My master's note to me was damaged and only partly legible, but he would not have made such a strange request were it not of some import. I obey to the best of my ability. If you are the guardian of such a young lady, as I believe his note must have implied, I can only assure you that my master is a man of honour and seeks to inform you out of goodwill and sound intentions.

Humbly,
Mr Henry Wilson,
Gentleman's Valet

He cringed when reading his own note, but it could not be helped. It was a mercy that he would likely never have cause to see this Edward Gardiner face to face if the man lived in Cheapside. He dipped his pen again and started the second note.

Mr Darcy,

I shall keep this note brief so that it might be sent the sooner. I have indeed sent word to Miss Benwick's family, as you requested. I hope I have been able to read the direction properly, as your note was only partially legible due to the sort of paper on which it had been sent.

Lady Catherine has sent at least half a dozen footmen out on various errands, but I do not know for what purpose. A solicitor has called again, and I heard some inquiry being made about Miss Darcy's settlement. Additionally, there is a parson who called earlier in the day and held a private conference with Lady Catherine. I believe he is her own rector from Kent, for he paid her the most gracious homage.

I have learned that Miss de Bourgh is indisposed. This condition came upon her rapidly, following an unannounced caller. He had the appearance of a gentleman but was not well received by Lady Catherine or Miss de Bourgh. I was near the room where the short conference was held, and though the words seemed carefully chosen for the purposes of obscurity, I was able to discern that this man holds some knowledge of a private affair directly involving Miss de Bourgh. He was dismissed and, dare I say, roundly abused by his hostess. I know not what such a visit might portend, but I presume it was not insignificant.

Please advise, sir. I do hope you have been able to recover the information you required.

With respects,
Wilson

Wilson tucked the notes he had written, as well as the one from Mr Darcy, into his breast pocket and stole out of the house, toward the mews. It was short work to persuade the head groom to send two of his sharpest errand boys in opposite directions with the notes, although Wilson now had one less flask of his stash of spirits to look forward to as a consequence. No matter, for if he were successful, he was certain that Mr Darcy would amply make up for the deficiency.

He returned to the house, feeling rather accomplished, but three steps after he had left the servant's entrance, he was arrested by the glowering face of the head butler. "Well, now," he frowned down his long nose, "taking the air, Mr Wilson?"

He straightened and dipped a short bow. "Only attending to my duties, sir."

"When did a valet's duties include a secret trip to the stables?"

"Lady Catherine had requested that I speak personally with the head groom about some new horses—"

But the butler was not listening. He extended two long fingers and withdrew the barely visible tip of paper from Wilson's breast pocket. "Here, what is this?" He held it out in some distaste, rubbing his fingers against one another and finally withdrawing his handkerchief so that he might not be sullied in touching it.

"It is nothing, sir!" Wilson lied quickly. "Only a baker's order; one of the kitchen maids had asked it to be carried."

The butler unfolded the note, and his bushy eyebrows lowered. He looked over the edge of the paper at the cowering Wilson and shook his head. "I imagine Lady Catherine will find this most interesting. You, sir, shall confine yourself to your chambers."

As if this disgrace were insufficient, the butler nodded to one of the footmen standing at the end of the hall. "See that Mr Wilson is kept in comforts in his room until he is called for."

Twenty-one

He could not explain himself. The words of the old madman in the Hermitage had shaken him more than he would confess, and for no reason he could comprehend. Miss Elizabeth did him more justice than he deserved, for she declined to question him very seriously about it. She, too, appeared mystified by the riddles spoken by the odd little man, but she seemed to brush it off the more easily.

It was several minutes before he felt secure of his powers of speech once again, though when he ventured so much, he only managed an inarticulate, "There," when they passed the spectacle of the golden statue of Aurora. She paid it little more notice than the rose hedges among which it was situated, for her eyes frequently turned up to his face to see that he was, indeed, well. Again, he felt a warmth spreading through his chest. No woman of his acquaintance had ever been quite so sensitive to his moods, save perhaps his mother.

There was no time to reassure her that he was not displeased or offended by something, for in their path stood a curious personage. He was dressed in an affected manner quite similar to a penguin, complete with his long tails and frilly white cravat. CH Simpson himself, the self-proclaimed master of ceremonies at the Gardens. Darcy suppressed a groan, and would have tugged Miss Elizabeth off the path and in another direction, had he been escorting her as a proper gentleman. However, as he held only her parasol and not her hand, the odd fellow was upon them before he could protest.

Arching his back and placing one foot forward with dramatic flair, Simpson tipped his hat and bowed gallantly before Miss Elizabeth. "Greetings, gentlefolk! Welcome most humbly to our fair Gardens, where you may seek any pleasure, revel in any delight which might suit your most excellent fancy."

Darcy bit back a sigh and could not help a roll of his eyes. Simpson was a useful sort of buffoon, no doubt, as some parties simply adored being fawned over, and others had their grievances diffused by such obsequious absurdity, but Darcy could not tolerate this brand of nonsense. Perhaps it was all an act, but when a man spent every day for the whole of his life affecting the manner of a toady, he could not help but become one.

Simpson was addressing only Miss Elizabeth now, bowing and scraping once more with that flamboyant touch which was his own trademark. "My dear lady, what a fair afternoon to grace us, so condescendingly, with your magnanimous presence! How wise you are to partake of the delights of the floral gardens before the evening entertainment renders them less beautiful by comparison. Pray," he bowed again, "if there is anything that can be done to enhance your enjoyment of our fair Gardens, you have but to call for Mr Simpson! And so that I might know to respond with all due alacrity, might I have the pleasure of learning who might summon?"

Miss Elizabeth smiled; the patient, bemused smile of one who had decided upon humour rather than annoyance, and that soft little chuckle of hers bubbled fourth again. Darcy hated to confess it, but he had become rather fond of that sound this day. It was no mindless giggle like so many young ladies, nor rather was it the braying laugh of the courser sort. It was simply an effusion of delight, simmering up from a heart of which he had come to think the impossible: genuine, unaffected kindness, bound up in a soul of wit and fire, to forge the sort of woman who might have stepped from mythical pages.

She curtsied in reply to the officious greeting, then with a playful glance his way, she introduced herself. "I am Miss Bennet, and my attendant here is named William. We are most pleased to be received so graciously. I thank you for your kind attention, but we are not in need of anything."

"Oh!" he protested, "but you have no refreshments! My dear Miss Bennet, this simply will not do. We have so much to see here and so many wondrous events this evening to delight the eye and uplift the spirit. You simply must be properly restored so that you may not weary before you have experienced all!"

"I thank you," she was smiling in that cheerful, yet dismissive way which seemed to beg off, "but that will not be necessary. We cannot stay long, and indeed, must depart before the greater share of the evening's events."

"Indeed, this is a travesty!" he declared. "For you simply cannot properly appreciate all without at least witnessing the Cascade, or the Ascents, or even sampling our delicious fare. And the fireworks! You must not go before the display. Pray, Miss Bennet, will you not alter your intent?"

She began to deny his wishes, but even as she opened her mouth, another voice interrupted.

"Miss Bennet? Did I hear Miss Bennet?" The voice came from somewhere behind Darcy, but it rapidly neared as a generously proportioned figure of a woman happened upon them. When her eyes found his Miss Bennet, she lifted her hands in the greatest joy, as if she had recovered a long-lost relation. "It *is* you, Miss Bennet! I thought I heard your voice, and I was certain of it when I overheard your name!"

Elizabeth seemed to start, and a curious expression crossed her face as if she did not at first recognise the voice or its bearer. Then her eyes cleared, and she smiled warmly. "Mrs Jennings, what a pleasure to meet you again!"

Then—God bless the woman!—she glanced quickly to him and raised an eyebrow in question. With the greatest relief, he was able to shake his head very subtly. No, he did not know this woman; it was, therefore, safe for her to carry on a few moments' conversation with her acquaintance in his presence.

"Miss Elizabeth, I cannot tell you what delight this happy circumstance gives me! Why, I was only telling my daughter Charlotte—that is, Mrs Palmer, the one I told you of last night—not half an hour ago of the delightful time we all had at the symphony. Did you not love it, my dear?"

"Indeed, I did," Miss Elizabeth averred, "I always do enjoy music."

"Oh, one does not go to the symphony for the music but the company! And how happily seated we were—why I never go but that I find myself beside the most agreeable new faces. I simply adored your Mrs Gardiner, and Miss Kitty was perfectly enchanting. As for yourself, I have never been so delighted to meet any young lady. I was just praising you to my dear Charlotte, was I not, my love?" She gestured to a plump younger lady walking beside her, who had not spoken but had announced her arrival with numerous quiet giggles.

"Indeed, Mama, you were saying that very thing. Miss Bennet, I am so pleased to meet you!"

Miss Elizabeth curtsied to the young wife, but whatever duty or pleasure she might have expressed was lost in the next moment, for Mrs Jennings was speaking again.

"Now, my dear, do you not agree with me when I said how handsome she was? And clever, too—why I cannot recall the last time I laughed so! We simply must exert ourselves on her behalf, for I shall not see such a young lady passed over."

Miss Elizabeth looked confused and turned toward the daughter to make sense of the mother's words. Her dismay was evident when all was explained.

"Oh, Mama is so droll, is she not?" Mrs Palmer enthused. "She always fancies herself the matchmaker, and she's a ready eye for any young lady in need of a husband. A handsome girl and a wealthy man, that is her prescription for bliss, and I daresay she is never wrong!"

"I—" Miss Elizabeth protested weakly, "I am sure I am grateful for your consideration, madam, but I have no need—"

"Nonsense!" Mrs Jennings laughed. "Oh, come now Miss Bennet, no need to be so missish. Have not all young ladies the same requirements? But never fear, for I have no intentions of setting you up with any man just yet. Why, I have only just met you! I've no idea the sort of man you would like, nor even if there are any you have set your hopes upon, but a half an hour's chat shall suffice to know all. Let me see, is there such a young man who might have already captured your fancy?" She touched a finger to her lips and stared pensively, the better to divine what no properly brought up young lady would dare confess.

"No, indeed!" Miss Elizabeth shook her head, her cheeks flushing rather becomingly. "But I thank you for your kind interest, madam. As it is, I am afraid I cannot tarry half an hour."

"Oh, now you may not brush me off so quickly. The evening has not yet begun, and we have all night to sit together and talk this over. Now I suppose your aunt and sister are here somewhere? Sure, taking another of the walks, no doubt. Well, no matter, they can find us when they come to the supper boxes. Come, you simply must join us, I will not hear any objections! Am I not right, Charlotte?"

"Oh, yes," Mrs Palmer agreed. "It is a such a large box, and our company is so small this evening. I can scarcely abide not having a great variety of company, but we heard on the way here that Sir John—that is my sister's husband—was taken ill and could not come. We've other friends we tried to persuade, but alas, they have only just married, and they are of no use whatsoever as companions just now. Pray, do join us, Miss Elizabeth, and Mama will be vastly pleased. Oh, and I simply must have you meet Mr Palmer, he is so very droll!"

"I am very sorry," Miss Elizabeth shook her head, "I am afraid I cannot stay. My visit today was to be of very short duration, and I am expected home soon. As soon as we have completed our circuit of the walking paths—"

"Oh, no! I simply must protest, for you cannot go so quickly! Why, it is not even half dusk, and you know there is nothing to the Gardens when they are all lit up at night. Is that not true, Charlotte?"

Mrs Palmer shook her head vehemently.

"Now, I see you have a manservant to escort you, that is very good. He can certainly see to your safe return to your party if they do not arrive shortly, but you simply must dine with us for a little while, at the least. We are going to take some early refreshments, for my daughter's condition demands such, and Mr Palmer's humour is much improved by food and drink. No, no! Your modesty does you credit, Miss Elizabeth, but I will not hear another objection! Upon my word, if you are not so very much like a young lady of my acquaintance! Always trying to be so sensible, but even the sensible are often possessed of some deep feeling they will not confess. Therefore, I shall spare you the trouble of keeping up the pretence and insist that you join us until your party returns to the main square."

Mrs Palmer giggled again, and Miss Elizabeth was left with no means of objection. Darcy watched her nibble her lips nervously, then glance at him to silently ask his approbation of the scheme. Darcy lifted just one brow as if to say that a small delay would be of no great consequence. It was not as if Mr Gardner would be ready to receive them quite so soon, and a little refreshment seemed harmless enough. Additionally, he could not help but believe their own presence, as a single lady and footman, would seem the less remarkable if they appeared to be a part of a larger group. And so, to take refreshments, they adjourned.

~

Richard Fitzwilliam had returned to the earl's townhouse to resume the aborted call he had tried to pay on his mother. She would have considered it ill-bred indeed should he cry off entirely, and he had now some motive in asking for an audience with her. Miss Wakeford's words alluding to her father had inspired in him the resolve to speak more seriously to his own family about certain matters.

Unfortunately, once again he was not the only caller to the drawing room. Only moments after he had settled by the hearth to await his mother, Lady Catherine was shown in. Her arrival had come as little surprise by the time he saw her, for her strident protests had echoed soundly in the hall for some minutes already. Accompanied by avowals of, "He shall hear my thoughts on the matter!" and "I intend to carry my way!" the lady herself blustered into the room.

Richard stood and bowed. "Good day again, Aunt Catherine."

She turned accusing eyes toward him and pointed a recriminating talon directly at his heart. "And I shall have my satisfaction of you as well, Richard Fitzwilliam! I know very well what you have done."

"I? Forgive me, Aunt, I was not aware that I had given any offence."

At this moment, both the earl and countess arrived, and Richard felt himself the nexus of three very heated glares. "What have you done, Richard?" his father demanded.

"I cannot know, sir. I merely called to speak to Mother about visiting Mrs Wakeford and her daughter—"

"Darcy's valet," interrupted his aunt, her voice and manner a conflagration which might have smelted iron, "confessed all! He has been sending word to Darcy in secret all day. In short, he has been spying on my actions, and your son, Brother, has been one of the messengers!"

Richard's mother sent him a scathing glance, then looked away, and he felt his prospects toward Miss Wakeford beginning to dim. His father, however, was now staring at Lady Catherine in confusion. "Darcy's valet knows where he is?"

"As do I, by now. He has gone to Vauxhall Gardens, that disgraceful haven for miscreants and derelicts. No doubt he has sought his amusement in the darker reaches of the park, and cares nothing at all for his duty toward Anne! I will have him brought back at once!"

It was Richard's turn to appear flustered. "Darcy at Vauxhall? Aunt, I think there must be some mistake. He despises the place, I have known him to denounce it in my own hearing."

"I have it in his own hand." Lady Catherine produced a greasy bit of parchment and thrust it before the earl's nose. "There! Can you deny it? He has played me for a fool, traipsing off to some sort of holiday while the most pressing obligation of his life awaits at his house! And not only has he behaved utterly out of character, but he has taken some tart from Cheapside as his companion, as well as named her guardian so that all should know of her ruin! There shall be no end to the rumours when he has had his day with her! He has done this on purpose, with the intent of disgracing Anne and shirking his engagement. The shameful knave! He has left me with no other alternative."

The earl was rubbing his fingers together in distaste, but his expression was grave. "This *is* Darcy's hand, what there is of it that is legible," he confirmed. "What do you propose, Catherine? For clearly, something must be done. This is a deliberate insult to the family, and I will not stand for Darcy to create some scandal merely because he was displeased with his choice of bride."

Richard was glancing between them in growing alarm and sent his mother a beseeching look in hopes that she could stem the tide of the Fitzwilliam clan's outrage. He was horrified when she looked coolly away from him and allowed her eyes to rest upon her husband to await his decree.

"He must be found, of course! I have sent some of Darcy's male servants there in search of him already, but I would ask your support as well. The Gardens are large, and he could easily escape detection if night falls before he is discovered. I would have ten of your sharpest men at once."

"You may have them," the earl scowled, frowning first at the note, then at his son. "And I shall accompany them."

Twenty-two

Mrs Jennings' party had secured the use of a supper box near the statue of Handel. There was a gentleman seated there already, and he looked as little amused as Darcy might have done himself, if dragged unwillingly to a frivolous venue and saddled with such a silly wife and over-bearing mother-in-law. He had brought his own paper to the Gardens and apparently found it far more interesting than the sights or the people.

"Mr Palmer!" his wife exulted, lending every energy to her manner which his lacked, "Come, I simply must have you meet Miss Bennet!" She turned back to Elizabeth with a proud smile and even bobbed a little in excitement when her husband obliged.

Mr Palmer glanced over the edge of his paper with eyes that showed no flicker of interest. "Hmm. A pleasure." He glanced back down and continued his reading.

"There, Miss Bennet, did I not tell you? He is absolutely the drollest fellow! I simply never know quite how to take him. I think he likes you very much, for he smiled, did you see? Here, you must sit beside me."

The supper boxes were arranged in something of an inverted "U" shape, with a long table amidst the benches and three walls about to create a sort of half-room. There was comfortable seating for perhaps ten persons at the table, and a waiter promptly brought himself to attend them.

"You have never been here, have you? Oh, you simply must try the rack punch. Legendary it is! No one may visit without taking some. And, of course, the ham, for you have never seen the like. You will not believe how thin it is! Why, I think a half pound could paper my entire house."

Mrs Jennings was somewhat behind her daughter in settling at the table. She was so much red in the face from the exertion of walking that when she at last poured herself into the bench beside them, she readily seconded her daughter's request for the beverage. The waiter bowed smartly and returned a short while later with the repast.

"Now, Miss Elizabeth, let me know more of you." Mrs Jennings' curiosity had lent her the strength to recover her breath miraculously well. "I was not able to learn many of your particulars last night. You said that you have family in Hertfordshire?"

"Yes, ma'am, my parents and four sisters, one of whom you met last night."

"Four sisters? And no brother? Such a pity! But it is not a hopeless case. Why, I have just seen the happy conclusion of some courtships which none could ever have thought possible. Two young ladies, poor as church mice, but both very good sorts of girls. One of them was quite taken with a blackguard, the other with a sweet fellow who was nearly trapped by a youthful vow. What do you think? It all came right, and so it shall for you.

"I daresay you are not quite so handsome as Miss Marianne, nor so easy tempered as Miss Elinor, but a young lady in possession of such a pretty face and such an engaging wit as yours should encounter no more difficulty than they. Let me think…." She tapped her fingertips on the table and her eyes rolled up in serious deliberation.

Darcy was standing at the end of the table all this while, positioned opposite the other family's footman, and trying to keep his countenance. Surreptitious glances informed him of Miss Elizabeth's discomfort with this blunt line of questioning, but her patience was not entirely spent. She was blushing most prettily, but in evidence also was a small quirk to her lips which indicated an equal measure of amusement at the well-meaning busy-body. How such a woman as his Miss Elizabeth might fare at the hands of Lady Catherine, he could not help but wonder! Could she be so gracious as she was now? Perhaps even diverted enough that the price of enduring his aunt's company would be well compensated?

His musings took quite a different turn at once, for the question of seeking a mate for Miss Elizabeth was not one that their hostesses were inclined to neglect.

"What of Mr Spencer, Mama?" Mrs Palmer smiled, looking vastly pleased with herself. "He fancies ladies with darker hair, I believe."

Mrs Jennings tilted her head, studied Miss Elizabeth for about three seconds, and then shook it firmly. "No, not half good enough! He is a simpleton, and she would soon tire of him."

"Mr Irving? Oh, now there is an intelligent man!"

Mrs Jennings made a face. "A homely sort, although a good enough fellow. But no—you would not pass for a parson's wife, Miss Elizabeth. I am sorry to say it, but it is true. You would upset half the ladies in the parish and be called irreverent, though you and I both know you mean no harm by it."

Miss Elizabeth's brows arched and she almost smiled. "Thank you," she commented mildly.

"Oh! Mama, I have just the perfect notion. Do you remember Mr Bradley? He has just inherited, you know, and he will be seeking a wife this season."

Mrs Jennings pursed her lips and appraised the hapless young lady with new interest. "Indeed, a capital notion, my dear! He will have an estate to manage, though it is a small one. In Devonshire, my dear, so you would be my neighbour! He is not often among society, and I think he would not object to a lady of lesser family, but he would be quite taken with one of Miss Elizabeth's cleverness. Yes, it might be just the thing! Perhaps I ought to host a house party this fall, and you must come, Miss Elizabeth."

Darcy coughed, two or three times. It was preferable to the bark of objection that he repressed, but it drew notice, nonetheless. But, hang it all, Miss Elizabeth and Joseph Bradley? If it were the same man he remembered from Cambridge, he would not wish the fool's boorish company on any woman, let alone one of Miss Elizabeth's calibre.

She was looking at him now, a slight concern written upon her features. "Mrs Jennings, may I order some rack punch for my footman? I believe his throat is dry from our wanderings in the Gardens."

"By all means, my dear! He must have some of the ham as well, for it shall be a long evening." At a wave from the good lady's hand, Darcy found himself almost instantly suited with a glass and a plate. He bowed his gratitude and proceeded to drink of it slowly—more to conceal his chagrin at the thought of Bradley and Miss Elizabeth than to soothe his throat.

"Upon my word, Miss Elizabeth…" Mrs Jennings was regarding him narrowly now, and he shifted his gaze slightly away from the tables. Still, he felt his face burning under the warmth of her scrutiny. What could the woman have noted? He searched rapidly through his memory, but he was certain he had never seen her before.

"Ah! There it is. My apologies, Miss Elizabeth, but your footman is terribly familiar to me. I had thought perhaps I had seen him before in the house of another. Is he new to Mr Gardiner's employ?"

She cast him a conscious look, but quickly returned her attention back to Mrs Jennings. "Rather, you might say."

"Sure, that is it. I am certain I have seen him in Marylebone somewhere, perhaps at a house party. One does not quickly forget such a handsome face, be it footman or gentleman, am I right, Charlotte? Now, as I was saying, Miss Elizabeth, you simply must come when I give a party of my own, for I shall invite all manner of eligible gentlemen. Fear not, for I shall not make a spectacle of you. I know many other girls who would be pleased to come, for my door is always open to young ladies. I do enjoy the company of the young so! I will be certain to invite Mr Bradley, as well as Mr Smith, Mr Irving, Mr Bingley, Mr Grant… let me think, what other eligible young men are to be in town after the fall shooting?"

He started at Bingley's name, unfortunately drawing at least one pair of eyes back to himself. Perhaps this loitering in Mrs Jennings' box was ill-advised, after all, for if she had great enough familiarity with a man such as Bingley as to consider inviting him to a house party….

"I have it!" Mrs Jennings was shaking her finger with a knowing smile and staring directly at him. "Miss Elizabeth, your footman bears a striking resemblance to a gentleman I know of. I have never spoken to him. I would be beneath his notice, do you see, but indeed, he has the very look of him. Why, the pair could be twins!"

Miss Elizabeth held herself admirably well—far better than he was faring himself. While he might have dashed away in that instant, hiding his face from all with his hat, she had the temerity to laugh.

"How very amusing, Mrs Jennings! I shall be certain to tell my aunt that her new footman is, in fact, a high-ranking gentleman in disguise. Is he an earl's son? A duke's?"

"No, my dear! Only the nephew of an earl, but in his way, he is a finer catch than either of your suggestions. A young man, not yet thirty, in full possession of his inheritance. And such an inheritance it is! But I should not torment you with the details, for he is beyond my humble society and known to be rather taciturn. Therefore it is not in my power to introduce you. What is more, I read only this morning that he is betrothed elsewhere, so it will not do to think of him. But what do you say, my dear Charlotte, is he not the very image of—" Here, she leaned close to her daughter and whispered a name.

Miss Elizabeth was biting her lips and blinking in his direction as the two ladies conferred. He jerked his head to the side, an ardent plea for removal from the box, and she gave a short little nod of agreement. Their resolve, however, came too late to spare him the additional mortification of Mrs Palmer's appraisal.

"Indeed, he does, Mama! Why, I should never have noticed had you not said, for I have never been in the same room with the man, but I have seen his portrait. We toured that estate, you remember, on our return from Scotland. Mr Palmer! Do you not agree?"

Mr Palmer lowered his paper long enough to grant his wife a look of patent boredom. She cupped her hand round her cheek and mouthed something to him. He narrowed his eyes, glanced at Darcy with marked ennui, then replied, "I see no resemblance." The paper raised again, and nothing more could he be induced to say on the matter.

"Oh, is that not exactly like him!" Mrs Palmer laughed. "Indeed, I never know quite what to think."

"Well," Mrs Jennings lifted her punch dismissively, "I hope you will forgive us for sporting with your footman, Miss Elizabeth, but my son-in-law is quite wrong. But no matter, for my object is fixed, and I must not be diverted from it. You shall attend my party if your mother can spare you again from home, and we shall have a merry time of it. Bring at least one of your sisters; I absolutely insist upon it. Ah! I see the orchestra is arrived! Miss Elizabeth, where can your party have got to? They shall miss the music!"

Darcy's eyes went to her face, and once more he blessed her for her easy social graces. "Indeed, ma'am, and I think perhaps I ought to go and look for them. Perhaps they are somewhere waiting for me."

"Oh, then indeed you must go, Miss Elizabeth. We shall stay here, but do bring them back to visit and hear the music if you can persuade them."

"I thank you, Mrs Jennings, Mrs Palmer." She turned to look at him fully, extending her hand so that he might help her to her feet. He could not miss the significant widening of her eyes, the endorsement of a quick departure, and he hurried to concur.

~

". . .And the glazing on the Eastern wing alone cost in excess of—"

"My dear Mr Collins," Mrs Gardiner interrupted, "will you not take some more tea? I fear you will damage your throat, for it is quite dry in here, and a parson must take care of his voice."

"Oh! Indeed, madam, you are quite right!" He beamed proudly at the lady's condescension, quite easily forgetting that he had been unable to finish the afternoon's fifth recounting of the majesties of Rosings Park. "You are indeed too good, Mrs Gardiner," he bowed upon accepting the cup. "As my patroness so frequently asserts, true gentility is found in the address and manners of even those of lower station."

"I am sure I thank you, sir." Mrs Gardiner forced a smile. "Kitty?"

Kitty Bennet rolled her eyes and held out her cup for the third refill in the last hour. "Thank you, Aunt," she mumbled, thinking that she must excuse herself soon. A fourth cup of tea would all but ensure that she could legitimately part from Mr Collins' company for at least a quarter of an hour, and so she readily addressed herself to it, whether she craved it or not. Hopefully, he would soon find himself in a similar predicament.

"Now, as I was saying, Mrs Gardiner," Mr Collins helped himself to another serving of finger sandwiches, "there is nothing like a comforting blaze. Why, even in the warmest months, Lady Catherine advises that the fire be kept bright, for not only does it cheer the aspect of any room, but it does not do to leave the chimney cold. I can think of no surer way to invite unwanted pests to make their nests in the brick."

Kitty glanced over at the empty hearth, saw her aunt doing the same, and snickered. Mrs Gardiner was spared the trouble of excusing her domestic arrangements when her manservant entered with two notes on a tray, and she was able to pardon herself to take them. One of these was addressed to Mr Collins, and it was promptly given to that gentleman, while the other was for Mr Gardiner. Mr Collins relieved them of his company at once, for upon beholding the style and hand of the address, he coloured, held his breath, and rushed from the room to read his auspicious missive with the proper reverence of absolute privacy.

Mrs Gardiner looked at the one addressed to her husband in some puzzlement, turning it over to observe the seal on the back. "Kitty, my dear, have you any acquaintance in Grosvenor Square?"

"None at all, Aunt."

"How very curious! It is a short note, for it is only one page thick and folded in half. It does not quite have the look of an invitation, nor yet a letter of business. An introduction would require two pages, at the least."

"Perhaps it is someone of Uncle's acquaintance. Has he not friends who would write a short note? Perhaps a gathering at one of the gentlemen's clubs?"

"Perhaps," Mrs Gardiner conceded. "Though he is not a member of any, it might be some business friend or other. I shall lay it aside for when he returns home, though I do not know when that shall be today."

"I do hope he hurries because I do not think I can bear another hour entertaining Mr Collins. At least Lizzy was able to stay away, for it would have been far worse for her here. Even if she is sorting books in the warehouse, I am quite jealous of her. How angry she will be when she learns about Mr Collins shouting her name upon the streets earlier!"

Mrs Gardiner opened her mouth to reply, but the door to their sitting room burst open, and Mr Collins himself was panting his excuses. "Forgive me, Mrs Gardiner, but I am afraid I must leave your most amiable company. My presence is required by my patroness, and I dare not displease her by careless delay!" He turned and lumbered away, calling for a footman to help him on with his coat and to summon a carriage.

Kitty sighed and fell back into her chair, all pretence at drinking tea and reading Fordyce happily forgotten. "Good riddance!"

Twenty-three

"That went rather badly," Elizabeth confessed as they hurried away from the supper boxes. She glanced back, only once, and saw to her relief that good Mrs Jennings had already turned her attention to a very small roast chicken which was closer in size to a pigeon.

"It could not be helped," he answered in a strained voice. "It appeared to be a perfectly agreeable situation. I had no notion that I might be recognised by one not already known to me."

Elizabeth kept silent as they walked a little farther. His admission was as good as a proclamation, that he was indeed fabulously wealthy and considered a fine catch by many. To speak now of what he had tacitly confessed seemed to her to drip of manipulative intent, a desire to work upon her strange intimacy with him and his delicate position to salvage her own situation. Her mother would have commended it, and even her father would have merely laughed at her good luck. She glanced up at his face, and her heart stirred with conviction. No, even should she wish it—and she could no longer say that she did not—she would not do unto him as others had done. He deserved better.

"Miss Elizabeth, you have grown strangely quiet. Are you distressed?"

"Not at all," she forced a bit of cheer. "I was only thinking what a useful woman Mrs Jennings is."

His cheek seemed to darken, and she heard him catch his breath. "Indeed?"

"Why, of course. She clearly enjoys making herself useful, and she has such a pleasant way of going about it that none could be offended by her ordering of their affairs. Do you not know of others who enjoy giving themselves some purpose, to the point of becoming more of a burden than a help to the beneficiaries of their goodwill?"

"My aunt," he retorted. "Although I believe Mrs Jennings might have sought the benefit of *your* interests as much as her own gratification. I cannot say that for my relation."

"I believe she did," Elizabeth lightly directed him back to the less serious matter of Mrs Jennings and her follies. "And perhaps I would be wise to accept her advice. You can see how well-matched the lady's daughter and her husband are, which cannot help but proclaim all the evidence that is necessary of Mrs Jennings' abilities."

He stopped walking and was staring at her in astonishment. "You cannot be serious. I never saw a more mismatched couple in all my acquaintance than Mr and Mrs Palmer."

"Why so, sir? One has all the gaiety, and the other has all the seriousness. Perhaps the scales are weighted evenly."

He narrowed his eyes, tipping his head slightly as he tried to determine if she were in earnest. "Mrs Palmer is, I grant you, a kindly and sincere enough woman, but you could not wish such a silly-natured wife on a man of intellect."

"What makes you believe he is such? Reading the paper and avoiding conversation does not indicate that the person is intelligent, nor even particularly dignified."

"He refused to engage in a conversation which could only be termed as degrading."

"Do you think that was out of an offended sense of decorum or, rather, a prideful inattentiveness? Do you not rather think he wished to impress us with his disdain?"

"I think perhaps he wished to impress his wife, but she is insensible to correction and wilfully ignorant of her husband's preferences."

"You claim that his pride is under good regulation?"

He glanced away, seemed to contemplate the trees rather seriously, and made a careful reply. "I think it possible in theory, but perhaps his has been carried to extremes. He is more likely to give offence and make himself look the pretentious buffoon than to improve the mind of his wife." He turned slowly back to her. "I do not condemn another man, Miss Elizabeth. Indeed, I speak without any malice whatsoever, for I can easily imagine the circumstances which could drive a man to behave so."

Elizabeth pursed her lips in thought and began to walk on. "You do not consider his character flawed?"

"We are each of us flawed, Miss Elizabeth. It is how we prune our flaws, as well as cultivate our strengths, which determines our character. I would imagine Mr Palmer was never truly amiable, but had he chosen his bride differently, he might have become a tolerably civil sort of man."

"Or," she mused, "perhaps he is already matched to just the right sort of woman, but he will not trouble himself to mend his approach to her. My parents are not dissimilar, though rather than rudely dismissing my mother, my father makes a jest of her in the presence of her daughters. He is a clever sort of man who wants gaiety and liveliness to make him a perfectly agreeable companion. My mother's mind might have been improved, and her energies given proper direction, had either of them in their youth attended to what was fitting between man and wife."

He was looking at her strangely as they walked, his brow knit, and his mouth open as if to speak, but he said nothing. The idea appeared so shockingly novel to him that he was at a loss.

"Forgive my ramblings," she apologised. "You can have no interest in my family's affairs."

"You mistake me, Miss Elizabeth. Your insights are most profound, and something I had never considered. I shall take them to heart, for one day, of course, I must bind myself to a wife, and I may or may not have the choosing of her."

"I hope that you will not find yourself in an impossible situation of that kind. My words were meant merely as an expression of my own thoughts, for I hope to learn from the example and to avoid such disharmony if I may."

They walked on without another word for a few moments, giving only half their attention to the opening strains of music floating from the orchestra. They could no longer speak of such things without impropriety, no matter the strength of their mutual curiosity regarding the other's opinions. Yet they could speak of nothing else either, for the issue seemed too pertinent to the fortunes of both, too intimate for casual discussion elsewhere, and too serious for immediate dismissal to easily shift to another subject without giving it due introspection. It was the sight of Mr Simpson once again, bowing and welcoming more guests to the Grove which at last inspired a smile from Elizabeth.

"He reminds me of a slightly less offensive version of Mr Collins," she realised with a laugh.

William looked in that direction as well. "My aunt would approve of him."

They continued their leisurely stroll in no direction at all, but any watching them might have paused curiously when noting a tall footman laughing gaily with his lady employer over some private joke, and how frequently she touched his arm as they walked.

~

He was in the midst of it before he knew he had begun.

Somehow, this tradesman's niece had burrowed into the very tissues of his heart and nestled herself there. The thing was done quite without intent, and certainly without the knowledge of the lady in question, for she continued as lightly and disinterestedly as before… except that she seemed to have become rather comfortable in his presence.

So much more comfortable was she, in fact, that as the light grew longer and the crowds thickened, she made no objection to walking in rather near proximity to him. Why, she could only have been closer had their arms been entwined, a prospect which had lost all its horror for him. And when she turned to smile at him, or—*heaven help him*—laugh obligingly at some wry comment made in a pitiful attempt at a jest, he felt a nearly irrepressible desire to provoke another such response. Thus, within a quarter hour he had begun to feel himself rather witty, and indeed most of his friends would never have thought him capable of such a barrage of clever remarks or amusing anecdotes. In all likelihood, they would have been correct—he was not capable, not on his own. *She* had inspired him, and he drank in that fortifying elixir with near-manic devotion.

He was addicted to a woman he had only just met.

It was a craving of which he must deprive himself in short order. This he knew, but he was no more inclined to pull back from her now than he was to return home and wed the socially acceptable bride who awaited him.

One day! Surely, Fate could grant him one day of pleasure in a woman's company. One day which might salve the whole remainder of his life, for even if Anne were not forced upon him, the remaining prospects were dull and tarnished by comparison. Could Elizabeth be correct in her supposition that he himself held the power to make his future companion more agreeable? And if it were possible, could he imbibe enough of *her* to infuse that sparkling life into another?

She accidentally brushed his arm again, all innocent laughter at one of his boyhood exploits with Richard, and a sort of fire jolted through him. Awareness burned with the same sharp pain as the snow on his bare twelve-year-old feet from his story—a tale he had never even told Georgiana because he had considered it too compromising to his dignity. In that instant, he knew.

She was wrong.

Nothing within his power could ever make any other woman a suitable partner for him, regardless of her pedigree. He could guide, he could coax, he could speak gently and exert himself to approximate some degree of interest in whatever peculiarities such a woman might possess… but he could not make her become Elizabeth Bennet.

"Your cousin is indeed an accommodating fellow!" she was declaring. "I am surprised he submitted to your dare and attempted the distance in nought but your nightwear. And in the snow! I can well imagine it was a memorable holiday from school that winter. Who won the race?"

"He won the footrace to the stables, for he was older, and his legs were longer. Once we had secured our mounts, I overtook him and was the first round the appointed tree and back to the house. Richard was certain we were both to die of pneumonia, so cold were we, but it was nothing an hour by the fire and a cup of chocolate could not mend. My father probably learned of the prank, but never did he speak a word of reprimand."

"A wise parent. And did you soon after put such antics behind you, forever to become the grave and steady young master?"

He felt his expression cool, the unaccustomed smile twisting to a lifeless grimace. "I am afraid so. Only a few months later, my mother died giving birth to my sister."

How long ago that had been! So many years of mastery and resolve—over half of his life had passed since that hideous day that had robbed him of feminine care and thrust him into manhood before his time. It was a matter of course, nothing to cause sorrow after over fifteen years, but this recounting was different, somehow. Without knowing quite why, he found his eyes fastened unseeingly on the festive lights dazzling the great fountain, for fear that if he moved them elsewhere, he would find them unaccountably moist.

"William?" She placed her hand full on his forearm, squeezing gently as only a friend might, and she turned him slightly to face her.

He blinked, and indeed his eyes had misted peculiarly. Why now? Why should one triggered memory of his mother's last day suddenly evoke such feeling? He struggled for a tight breath and smiled. "It is nothing, Miss Elizabeth," he reassured her huskily.

"There is no need to conceal your feelings. You are grieved, and rightly so. She must have been very dear to you."

He choked on a short laugh, then sniffed back the sentiment. "What mother of grace and beauty is not the object of her young son's worship?"

She did not answer in words, but there was a sympathy around her eyes, a sort of tightness working in her creamy throat, which spoke eloquently enough of how deeply she was affected. She held his gaze a moment longer, enough for the shared feeling to settle round both their hearts, then dropped her gaze respectfully to the gravel. "I suppose," she idly brushed at a rock with her slipper, "that we ought to begin considering our return to my uncle's house."

"Perhaps," he agreed reluctantly. He did not like to think of that… a return to Cheapside meant an acknowledgement of the gulf between her station and his, a reversion to the impossible troubles which plagued him, and a renewal of whatever difficulties she faced in her own life. "If we take the Grand Walk back, it is shorter," he offered, "but if you can tolerate a few more steps, we can walk back through the arches."

"Or we could look inside the pavilion. Perhaps the doors are opened by now?"

He submitted to this indulgence with no complaints of his own. A few minutes more could do no harm, surely. The parasol was no longer needed in this less brilliant light, so he slung its handle over his arm and gestured for her to "lead" the way, a mannerism which earned another of her bewitching smiles.

It was not so bad walking slightly behind her, and he happily satisfied himself with looking on her form as she walked. She was no conventional Grecian beauty, but those curves… no man would regret her figure once he knew more of it. There was none now to protest his admiration of her, so his pleasant inventory of her many assets continued undisturbed as they walked. So contented was he in this pursuit that he was quite startled when she halted without warning.

"Miss Elizabeth?"

She was looking straight ahead. "William… that man there is wearing the same livery as you. I do not normally care to notice such things, but yours is… rather distinctive."

"What?" His gaze followed in the direction she indicated, and his whole being recoiled in horror. His jaw clenched, he felt his nostrils distend, and his fists curled. "He is one of mine."

She looked to him swiftly. "The messenger sent by your Mr Wilson?"

"No. That particular footman is not among those I would trust. Wilson would have sent someone from the stables, or possibly the kitchens, if anyone."

She was beginning to shrink back, closer to his shoulder. "We should walk the other way."

He nodded vaguely. "Indeed, you are correct. Come quickly!" He captured her hand, heedless now of appearances, and spun her in the other direction before his own hired man could recognise him. "There is nothing distinctive about the back of my livery," he assured her. "So long as we see no others before us."

This proved a vain hope, for halfway up the centre walk loitered two others in the same attire. They were glancing casually about, but Darcy was sure that one of them, at least, had appraised Miss Elizabeth's person as they approached. "Left!" he hissed into her ear.

She turned, but not sharply, as he would have done. Rather, she feigned interest in some of the flowers and casually drifted in that direction, placing her body strategically before his own so that the pattern of gold braid so distinctive to the Darcy livery would be hidden from them. The footmen did not seem to think anything conspicuous in her manner, for their eyes did not follow. He could not help a surge of pride in her and congratulated himself on having secured a clever ally in his plight.

"Where shall we go?" she whispered under her breath. "We've no way of knowing if there are more, nor how to evade them. What do they want?"

"Likely my aunt has sent them to search me out, which is unfortunate, for it means that my correspondence with Wilson has been discovered."

Her look of alarm was not unfelt, and he flushed with guilt. "I am sorry, Miss Elizabeth."

She drew a fortifying breath and stopped, after a short glance around to be certain that they were safe from witnesses. "Am I compromised as well?"

He set his teeth. "Not if I can help it. But we must be cautious, for my aunt would not scruple to destroy your credibility if she thought it might achieve her ends."

"Then we must leave here at once!"

"It may not be so simple. I have… a number of footmen in my employ, and my uncle will have still more. I cannot think that his help has not been demanded as well. We are in the depths of the Gardens and must navigate a maze of watchful men to find our way out. I wish I had a way of knowing where they were all positioned."

"Men move. They will be walking, will they not?"

"I doubt it. I believe they will each seek a strategic vantage to watch so that all the known routes will be covered. What we need is some way of seeing them before they see us."

She frowned and looked about as he did the same. Short of climbing a tree—he started when she seized his forearm. "William!" She extended her arm, and his gaze followed where she pointed. "Have you ever been up in an air balloon?"

Twenty-four

They had some little difficulty in persuading the balloon master to an early departure. "First flight of the evening is at seven," he had stated unequivocally. Until, of course, William had brandished several shining coins. These disappeared rapidly, and the man opened the gate to the basket.

It took only a few moments for the coal fire to be stoked to its proper heat, for the warming had already commenced some while before their arrival so the balloon's impressive silk display could advertise the attraction all over the Gardens. When the man gave the signal for them to board, Elizabeth accepted William's hand into the basket, then clasped the wooden railing. The little gate closed, bags of sand were hefted over the side, and the floor beneath her feet moved.

They had already agreed that from above, two passengers in a balloon were not terribly conspicuous. Anyone noticing their ascent would only be able to see them for a few moments before the greater height obscured their faces and granted a view only of the bottom of the basket. Those below, however, would be far easier to see. As a precaution in the early moments of their flight, William had arranged to stand behind her at the railing to conceal himself, but soon enough he should have the liberty to move about.

Elizabeth's heart was thumping wildly. Two feet from the ground... three... six! She had not accounted for the rapidity of their ascent, nor had she considered how terribly unstable the floor would seem. Each shot of heat from the coal furnace, each jostle of passenger weight, served to rock the basket more than she had been prepared for. Her fingers tightened on the rail.

William was already craning his head about, searching at each change in elevation for whatever new angles of vantage the balloon could offer. "There, Burk and Johnson. And there is Turner. Two more there," she heard him counting. "Blast. Two by the Kennington Lane entrance. I suppose all the gates are being watched."

She closed her eyes and prayed for courage. She *would* look at the ground, she would! She swallowed, gulped a hasty breath of air, and tried to lean forward.

The figures below her swam into one dizzying blur. Her breath was coming in short, airless gasps now, and she felt herself growing faint. Oh, why had she thought she could manage this? She had enough trouble on fishing boats and horses! Wherever she could see the plane below her feet and feel movement that did not connect her to the ground, she had always felt ill. Carriages were little enough bother, for they were large, possessed a stable frame all around, and she could see only the horizon. That motion she had grown accustomed to, but this… this was beyond her!

"One by the orchestra," William continued. "And the South pavilion… Miss Elizabeth, are your eyes sharper than mine? Is the light playing tricks on me, or is that another just there, near the first arch?"

He stepped to her right, leaning far over the edge of the basket, and the floor swayed with a sickening dip. "Miss Elizabeth, can you… Miss Elizabeth?"

The genuine concern in his voice was lost to her, for she could already taste the bitter tang in her mouth. In another half moment she was likely to mortify herself beyond hope of recovery, and if she tried to respond to him, she had not a prayer that she might be able to check the rebellion in her head and stomach.

"Miss Elizabeth, you are ill! We must set down immediately," he called to the pilot.

She tried to shake her head, but she dared not. "No," she managed thickly. "Still the north side!"

"Miss Elizabeth, we will find another way. I will not have you so distressed. Here, now, can you take a deep breath without difficulty?"

She clenched her eyes tightly closed and tried, but a gentle gust of evening air unsettled the basket. The breath she had tried to draw slowly came as an inward shriek and then was expelled just as rapidly in a cry of helpless alarm.

"Set us down at once!" William demanded again of the balloon pilot. "Can you not see, man? The lady is unwell!"

"I'm trying to, sir, but there's a decent wind about just now. It will take some doing—ten minutes to the ground, at least. It will go faster if you help me to wind the rope."

"Then allow me," she heard him retort.

At once a stalwart strength left her, and she began to quake. She had not even realised that she had been leaning against his arm, and now bereft of that support, a new panic rose in her breast. No longer was she afraid of physical illness, but a mortal terror overtook her. She trembled from head to foot, and a series of frantic moans, wails, and sobs shook her.

"Miss Elizabeth!" William cried from half the world away, "You are only rocking the basket more. You make it far worse than it must be!"

She could not attend, however much she wished to. The music rising from the ground, so many fathoms below, told off the great measure of her fall, and nothing else could enter her mind. She knew she was shaking, desperately jerking herself about with her helpless spasms, but no force save the grounding security of firm earth could recall her.

"Miss Elizabeth!" William's voice was near now, just at her ear, and she felt him pulling her hands from the railing. "Please, you must hear me. Can you listen? Squeeze my hand if you can."

She could not. His presence was comforting—at least she would have someone else's hand to hold as she plummeted to her death over the side, if it came to that—but she was no more in command of herself than she had been a moment earlier. She clung more tightly to the rail.

"Elizabeth," his voice pleaded, low and earnest "release that. Hold my hands." He did not permit her to ignore his request this time. He was stronger than she, and with horror-stricken clarity, she felt him pry each of her fingers from the smooth wood, then substitute his own hands for the abuse of her digging fingernails. He tightened his arms, and she felt him pulling her back, her own arms crossing her chest, but still, she trembled.

Somehow, she would never know how, she felt him twisting her body, forcing her to turn to him rather than the deathly ground below. Her eyes were still sealed tightly, but she worked her hands free of his to knot them at his chest and buried her face between them. "William!" she gasped, "Oh, help me, please, take me down!"

"Be easy," he crooned, permitting only a faint hitch of concern to crack his voice. "We are going down. I will not let you go, you are safe."

But she was shaking her head, irrational fear still twisting her inner parts and clouding her mind. "We are going to die, I know it! The basket will fall. Oh, why does it rock so much? Please, I cannot breathe!"

He was trying to lift her head now, but she stubbornly held firm. "Elizabeth, will you trust me?"

A tremor passed through her. She shivered, then released a sobbing breath. She allowed him to lift her head, and very cautiously, squinted open each eye in its turn until she could make out his face.

"Lord help me, I am undone," he whispered.

He bent, and a searing peace claimed her mouth. She stilled. Dread was forgotten. Her panicked breaths were now an impossibility, for she found she must breathe in his rhythm, or not at all.

Over and again, his mouth soothed and caressed; urging gently, offering more than comfort, more than security—offering the forbidden, the one thing he could never give her, and she hungrily accepted. His arms were twined behind her back now, his hands fisted into pylons of succour against the terrors that lay behind her. Slowly, her trembles ceased, and her thoughts turned more sharply to the texture of his unshaven cheek, the tenderness of his lips upon hers, the delicious intimacy of being held by him than the certain death below her.

If Elizabeth was now calmed, it was because some of her agitation had passed to him. His chest had begun to heave deeply, a new disquiet shaking him. He drew back, his breath still warm upon her lips, and seemed unable to trust his voice. He simply stared down into her eyes, a tremulous quiver passing through him for a long moment.

Her body softened, and her vision filled with sheets of brilliant satin, sheer waves of heated air, and *him*. His expression, so gentle and broken, so full of the one feeling they could never share, shattered her heart. Never before had she desired anything so much, and only her lingering sense of unbalance kept her from standing on her toes to ask for just one more moment of heaven.

At last, he risked a hoarse, "Turn around, Elizabeth. Please."

She tried to comply, but his arms were still locked securely behind her back. She squared her shoulders against them and offered an apologetic smile. She would much prefer that he left his arms where they were, and he seemed equally unwilling to drop them, but slowly, he did so. She inched her feet about, and as she turned, she felt his hands capture hers from behind and clasp them at her sides.

"Hold on to me," he urged, his tones still rough. "Breathe, Miss Elizabeth."

Unsteady or not, his was the only voice in the world she could have trusted just then. She gripped his hands for her very life, and she forced herself to a long, shivering draught of fresh air.

The world exploded before her then, in violent and invigorating colours. The sky, she could now see, was beginning to streak with orange clouds to the west, and gradually darkening in each direction as she cast her gaze over the span of the horizon.

And she heard singing. Somewhere below, the Duke of York's band had struck up the Orchestra, and a thunderously approving audience had already gathered to hear. She stretched her body so she could look just over the edge of the basket, but her weight was firmly rooted, her balance anchored with William's. Safe, but daring.

It was glorious. She could see the tops of trees, spy little people walking about below her, and she felt sublimely aware and over all. The perspective of looking down upon the world, making all her reality smaller and seeing clearly that which she could usually only view through the thicket, caused her pulse to quicken.

"William, can we stay a moment longer?" she pleaded. Even now, the balloon master was still winding them down to the ground. Back down to reality, down to the dirty world with all its troubles and rules which dictated choices she never wished to make. No, she could not bear it! Not yet.

William spoke a word to the man, and for some while longer, the balloon held its stately position in the air. No longer was she clenching his hands for dear life—now her fingers had twined through his, sharing with him her newfound delight and sense of… liberty. Yes, that was it.

She lifted her hands with his, spreading them like the wings of a bird, and heard a low rumble of laughter behind her. Once, only once, she glanced over her shoulder to smile at him, and then he slowly began to turn them about the basket together, so she could see the whole world lying below.

She had never felt so free.

Twenty-five

"My Lady," Collins bowed, sweating and panting. "I am come as you directed, My Lady, and I pray most earnestly that I may be of service. I am not too late?"

Lady Catherine ceased her pacing, just long enough to curl her lip faintly. "You are two hours early. I did not summon you to arrive until later in the evening."

"Oh, My Lady, I must beseech you—"

She spun and marched to the window. "You may as well be of service while you are here. My daughter's spirits are distressed, and I will have you read to her. Smith!" she summoned.

A maid appeared shortly and bobbed her curtsy. "Yes, My Lady?"

"Is Miss de Bourgh well enough to receive a caller?"

The maid bowed her head. "Miss de Bourgh is asleep, My Lady. I may rouse her if your ladyship desires."

"No! Foolish girl, nothing but her wedding should rouse Miss de Bourgh. Never mind, Collins, I have no need of you at present." With a flick of her hand, she dismissed both servant and toady and resumed her pacing.

"My Lady," he protested, "may I not offer some comfort during this uncertain time?"

"Comfort! I want no comfort but my daughter's security."

"Indeed, My Lady, you are the most beneficent, wise, loving mother a young lady could desire. Would that all young ladies were so well guarded and provided for! Why, my own dear betrothed could not even claim the comfort of a proper governess, but her manifold charms and natural intellect will surely be found pleasing when tempered by your ladyship's kind condescension."

"No governess! Are there not five of them? A sordid lot they must be if all else you have told me of them is to be believed. Their father ought to be publicly disgraced, and their mother does not deserve any thought at all!"

He bowed. "Your ladyship honours me with her excellent memory! But I assure you, most wholeheartedly, that I have selected the noblest, the most intelligent among them, and her family's gratitude for my forbearance regarding other matters—"

He was never able to complete his speech, for the butler appeared behind him and nearly startled him out of his wits. He jumped, his hands patting his own chest in consolation for the fright incurred upon him.

"Forgive me, My Lady," the butler bowed, "but the gentleman has called again. He says his object is most urgent. Does your ladyship wish that he be sent away?"

"I have no cause to quail at his pleasure. Have him shown in, and my parson shall remain as a witness of his cruel intent."

A moment later a short, sharp-looking man entered. He was balding slightly, but his frame was lithe and graceful. He cast a disdainful eye in Collins' direction and addressed himself directly to the lady without preamble. "Have you considered my offer?"

"Consider! What is to consider? I am in no position to negotiate with a criminal."

"I am hardly a criminal! I offer you a perfectly respectable solution to your difficulties, My Lady."

"Respectable!" she snorted. "You ask for nothing less than nobility, and in exchange for what? A pretty song, a bit of tainted gold? You may as well ask for the crown jewels in exchange for a jig."

His face heated. "I offer you an alternative to abject penury, My Lady. You shall not prevail against the gentleman you have selected; his obstinacy is well known by all. Think you that idle threats and deception will work upon a man such as Mr Darcy? If that were possible, why has it not already produced the desired marriage? You have had all day, and still, he eludes you."

"Fitzwilliam Darcy will do his duty and redeem his cousin, have no doubts on that point," she snapped. "I know his precise whereabouts and have already dispatched a carriage to retrieve him. Moreover, I have all the inducement I require to see that he performs as expected."

The man shook his head. "Very well. You know where to reach me when your scheme fails, but I shall not wait upon you forever. My offer can only extend as far as your creditors will permit."

"Mr Barrett!" she whirled on him, her tone scathing, "our conversation is finished! Your name is abhorrent to me, and your family's connections so far beneath the de Bourgh heritage that your words are vile. Remove your disgraceful presence from this house at once!"

He frowned, cast one more look toward Collins, and departed without another word.

The lady was less easily silenced. "The lecherous slanderer! To think that I must give audience to one such as he, whose money has been made in such a manner! I shall have my satisfaction of Darcy. He has done this with intent to insult and wound! How could he have known to go there, of all places?"

"My Lady," Collins shook his head in that patient, long-suffering manner well-practised by all in his profession, "I am afraid I am most confused."

"Barrett is not worth a second thought," she assured him. "But Darcy! I will have words with him. How has he discovered it? Someone must have told him."

"I am certain it is all a mistake, My Lady, for how could any discern your ways? You are all that is wise and charitable, and your foresight is impenetrable!"

She snagged a greasy bit of paper from a nearby table and waved it in the air. "He has discerned it somehow and means to ruin me! And he has done it publicly, taking some girl to Vauxhall as his entertainment for the day. Why, he has even named her and had word sent to her guardians so that all may hear of it!" She sneered and read aloud from what appeared to be a stained, damaged note. "Eliza Benwick from Gracechurch street."

Collins' eyes widened. "I beg your pardon, My Lady?"

She continued as if she had not heard. "This Mr Gardiner shall receive not a word of notice from me. Serve him right if his ward is ruined. He ought to have guarded her better! His rights to satisfaction are nothing to mine."

Collins had grown pale, his limbs quaking. "My Lady... may I submit my humble services to help recover Mr Darcy for our dear Miss de Bourgh? Perhaps a man of the cloth might be able to persuade him where another cannot."

She turned and evaluated him with half a measure of approval. "A laudable notion, Mr Collins. Do go, and return this evening for my daughter's marriage ceremony. Be certain to bring your betrothed, for Anne shall require some manner of bridesmaid."

~

"Miss Elizabeth, a word, please."

She was already two paces ahead of him, almost fleeing from him as soon as the balloon had set them down. He could think of no reason for her sudden haste, for she had truly seemed to relish the latter half of their flight, and even graciously thanked the balloon master for his troubles on her behalf. There could be no cause now for her to put it behind her so quickly, other than himself.

"Miss Elizabeth," he pleaded again, "I beg you to hear me."

She slowed, and he could perceive a conscious reluctance in her profile as she looked down and to the side. "Oh, not now, please."

"I am afraid I must. I have behaved abominably, Miss Elizabeth, and I humbly beseech you to forgive me."

She turned, but only halfway. "Was it not I who was so little in command of myself that I nearly endangered us up there?"

"We were far from danger, at least of the mortal kind. It is another danger of which I speak."

"You must think me a fool!"

"Miss Elizabeth," he stepped around to her face, forcing her to stop. "I think nothing of the kind. You were frightened. Is there any disgrace in that?"

A fire had sparked in her eye, and she lifted her chin with a hint of defiance. "There *is* disgrace in tempting a respectable man to something abhorrent to him. I assure you, sir, it is not my custom to seduce men for my own purposes."

"Seduce? Abhorrent!" He almost laughed, but the matter was too serious for that. "You mistake me, Miss Elizabeth, for I find you quite the opposite."

"And what of my connections? Of my station in life? Can you deny that any such connection would be reprehensible to you, and to your family? Would any hold me blameless, when they knew of my circumstances, for grasping at a man so far removed from my own circles that it could only have been achieved by the vilest sort of compromise?"

"Miss Elizabeth, it was only a kiss," he reminded her. "And if I recall, it was I who initiated it, not yourself."

"Because my foolishness beguiled you into the act!"

He shook his head. "What is this, Miss Elizabeth? None forced me. It was my own inclinations, and I am sorry that I imposed upon you at a vulnerable moment. However, you were a willing enough participant and even seemed to enjoy the remainder of the flight holding my hands."

"Then you believe I make a practice of wanton behaviour?"

"I could never believe that of you."

His tones were so firm, so determined, that it seemed to jar her from her resolve to despise herself. She blinked, her lips parted, and her expression seemed to break. If he did not speak some other words of absolution, he feared that next, she would begin to cry, and that would prove his final undoing.

"Miss Elizabeth," he spoke more gently, "have you any notion of what other women might have done in your position? Were I dependent upon another's goodness—and I thank God that I am not!—would any other have befriended me, treated me with such unmerited regard, and bestowed on me such gentle reserve in all matters of import? No, indeed! I could never admonish a single act of yours. It is my own behaviour which troubles me."

Her eyes, bearing that peculiar sheen which caused his inner being to twist in torment, lifted to his own. "Fear not that I will make any demands of you, sir."

"William. I am your servant, remember?"

A hesitant smile blossomed, and she looked down to the ground. "Very well, then. William. You are quite safe from me."

Ah, if only she knew! He repressed a grimace of pain. "Am I forgiven, then?"

She sniffed faintly and smiled. "Quite. I believe I must thank you for finding a means to calm me when I had so far lost my faculties. I am utterly humbled!"

"I am afraid I hold the claim on that. My failing was not a mere moment of terror, but years of blindness and arrogance. Had I looked to my affairs better, we would not presently be seeking a way of eluding men who are in my own employ."

"I must confess to some curiosity on that point. I did not intend to ask about what is not my affair—"

"I believe it has become your affair. I have none but myself to blame, for had I not simply assumed my due, had I taken care to know the inner workings of my own house and not remained ignorant to any but my own personal cares, I might have apprehended the danger long ago. I imagine my aunt found the work easy because I made it so. Do you know, Miss Elizabeth, how mortifying such a discovery will be when word begins to circulate? I shall be the laughing stock of...."

"The *ton*?"

He clenched his teeth and held her gaze steadily. "Of everyone."

One side of her mouth curved. "It is not only you who have cause to regret poor relations in his own house. I have learned that bitter lesson only recently, and shall perhaps pay for the follies of another with my own future."

His brow pinched. "Miss Elizabeth, we have been rather close on the matter, but what is your trial? How can such a man as that Collins fellow have any thought of success with one such as yourself?"

She drew a slow sigh. "My mother's first object, when she found herself in possession of five daughters and no sons, was to marry them off respectably before my father could die or any of their daughters could disgrace the family. It seems that not all of us took to heart that caution about marrying 'respectably.' When one falls, four suffer, and when two are humiliated, three are shunned."

He closed his eyes. "I see."

She offered a tight little smile, forgiving and entirely false. "It is not your concern. Come, we must see our way out of this place."

He nodded, all business once more. "I believe I know the way, but you will have to trust me."

Twenty-six

"My dear!" Aunt Gardiner hurried from her sewing chair, "I had begun to wonder if we would see you at all tonight."

Kitty rose as well and watched as Mr Gardiner nearly staggered through the door of her aunt's sitting room, his shoulders rounded in exhaustion and his expression haggard.

"As did I. The import tariffs on my shipment from the East were raised and the whole lot impounded. I was required to haggle with the authorities half the morning over that, but the judgment stood. Now I have no idea how I shall make a profit on any of that silk. What is more, I learned that Bonapartists have captured half my stock of tobacco which was bound from America last week. Egad, but I wish for some tonic which might wash today away as if it had never happened!"

"Never mind that, my dear." Mrs Gardiner gently petted her husband's shoulder and led him to a chaise where he could receive a fortifying glass of brandy. "You have risen above worse before."

"Thank you, my love, although I expect your day was no less unpleasant. And now I suppose I've an evening of drudgery to anticipate! Where is our malapropos guest?"

"Oh! Mr Collins has gone off on some errand or other for his patroness. I do not know where. Has Lizzy gone above stairs to rest?"

He swallowed his brandy and looked at her with a polite sort of bafflement. "Lizzy? I expect she was doing her best to stay away from that Collins fellow, but if he departed earlier, why has she not come back down?"

Mrs Gardiner opened her mouth in confusion, but it was Kitty who answered. "Lizzy was not here all day, Uncle. Surely you saw her, for she was to spend the day with you at the warehouse."

Mr Gardner lifted his glass and stared at the purplish liquid as if it bore some kind of enchantment. "You must forgive me, my dear, but my head is rather fuzzy at present. I heard that Lizzy came to the warehouse and was even accompanied by a manservant, but she did not stay. I was out, of course, and I missed her, but I did receive your note. I had assumed that they crossed paths and thought no more of it. Are you saying that she is not here?"

Mrs Gardiner and Kitty exchanged sunken glances. "No," they answered in unison.

"Wait just one moment," Kitty's eyes widened. "Lizzy took no one with her. Did you say she came with a manservant? She could not have… oh!" Her lips rounded into a little heart shape, and she covered them with her fingertips. "It could not be!"

"Kitty, as you can see, I am in no mood for a mystery. Have you any notion of your sister's whereabouts? Is there cause for alarm? I cannot think Lizzy would do anything unfortunate or foolish, but could someone have harmed her? I must send for a constable!"

"Uncle, the only footman Lizzy saw today, I believe, was that fellow we dragged off the streets in Mayfair last night. I know she encountered him again while we were out walking. You do not suppose she has taken up with him?"

"So long as she is safe, I would be happy to believe almost anything!" he cried, jumping to his feet. "Mayfair, you say? I must call for the carriage. Which street? How shall I know where to begin?"

"Mayfair… my dear!" Mrs Gardiner caught his forearm. "There was a rather curious note which arrived for you earlier from Grosvenor Square. That is only one or two streets over, is it not? I thought little of it at the time, but perhaps it contains information tending to that very point. Oh! How foolish I was to leave it unread if it might pertain to Lizzy! I shall never forgive myself if something has happened."

She secured the note and presented it to her husband, who read it with all the panic which must attend the discovery of a young lady's disappearance. "I do not understand a word of this, and neither, I think, did its author. Lizzy gone to Vauxhall Gardens, alone but for the presence of some unknown gentleman? This must be some sort of a prank!"

"It lists the address of the gentleman," Mrs Gardiner noted, reading it over his shoulder. "Why, I know this name. The gentleman hails from Derbyshire and is well-regarded. You remember when we toured Pemberley a year ago, my dear? Certainly, if such a person is named, it must be true."

"But what would such a man want with our Lizzy? It must be some sort of a trick. Could it be a threat? This Wilson person claims his master is honourable, but he does not even know Lizzy's proper name!"

Mrs Gardiner was shaking her head in bewilderment. "What can have happened?"

"I do not know," Gardiner's voice had dropped gravely low. "But I shall be paying a call to the home of this Mr Darcy in Grosvenor Square, and I shall have a constable with me."

~

"There is a constable just ahead," Elizabeth whispered to her companion as they slipped from one corner to the next. "You do not suppose he might be of some assistance?"

"How so? Shall I tell him that I am fleeing the very men I employ to serve my person? And then shall I explain how I came to be dressed as one of them? I would spend the night in an asylum."

She scowled, only darkly enough to express her displeasure at his flippant dismissal. "I thought perhaps he or one of his fellows might prove useful to you once you have returned to your house."

He put his hand to a tree and leaned round it to look ahead. "As far as I know," he leaned the other way, "there is no law against winning the affections of another person's staff. There is certainly no law detailing in whose bed a single young lady must pass the night when visiting another's home."

"Good heavens!" Elizabeth ejaculated before she could recall herself.

He turned to study her in the light of a distant lantern, and an apologetic warmth lined his mouth. "I will be… most grateful to meet your uncle."

"Indeed!" she nodded jerkily, a little more of his predicament becoming clear to her.

"As for the constable… we ought to avoid him just now." He held up a hand as one of his men passed into view on the walk ahead of them. "Go," he whispered after a moment, waving to his right. "I am just behind you."

They fell into step quite casually, she carrying her own parasol low over her eyes even in the fading light. She walked easily, several strides ahead of him, as if she were unescorted and boldly untroubled by that circumstance. After a moment of practice, she even affected a slight sway to her hips with each stride and intentionally allowed her gaze to linger on any single gentleman she passed. One or two even lifted their hats in her direction, and another was so intrigued as to swivel his head about, gawping rather openly. It was likely that if she had not continued as if she had some other objective, he might have requested the pleasure of detaining her. Elizabeth shivered and suffered a hitch in her strides before she could continue on smoothly again.

After a moment she had caught up to the very footman whom William had followed. She would be quite safe, he had assured her—the man would know his business and would not trouble her while he was on his duty. She need only distract him for half a moment, keep his eyes on her rather than elsewhere, and she felt somewhat confident that she could manage. The footman had slowed as if he had a designated region where he should remain and had now come to the limits of that freedom. She passed him now, taking care not to do so quickly, and turned her head to feign a glance back.

He did not speak to her—would not dare, William had said—but she was certain of his attention. She walked very slowly, twirling her parasol, and she heard the unknown man clear his throat. Mere seconds later, just as her heart had begun to pound in uncertainty, she heard a strange voice from behind.

"Johnson! The master has been seen preparing to depart. He is bound for the river gate, and we are to follow and attend him."

Elizabeth faltered, but only for a moment. Her direction had been clear: she was to walk on at the same unhurried pace as if the matter did not concern her, but she could not help listening in fascination. How completely he had altered the tone of his voice, so that even his own man would not suspect him!

"What—er... Meriwether, is that you? Blasted trees, I can hardly see your face. The master has gone ahead you say? Why, what are we bothering about this wood for? Come on, then, no sense in waiting here."

"No, I was told to search out Wesley and Jones. You may as well go ahead of me, for the master will be wishing to take the first barge across. I am told that if he has gone ahead, we are to follow on the next available crossing. Will you alert Randall and Huxley as you pass through the Grove?"

"Well, then, if you have no need of me. Bloody glad I'll be to get out of this rat hole before I fall with some disease. Eh, Meriwether, do you see that fancy bit just there? I'd wager that one's a thoroughbred, eh, with a pretty neck like that? A pity we haven't time to dally!"

"Save it for the kitchen wenches. You could not afford her."

"And a crime it is!" The one called Johnson sighed loudly, and Elizabeth slipped into the shadows of some nearby trees to await his passing. She held her breath, afraid even to breathe and be detected. A moment later, there was a warm touch at her shoulder, and William was beckoning her without sound to follow in another direction.

"How did you do that?" she whispered. "I did not even recognise your voice!"

"I have not the least idea," he confessed. "I have never attempted any sort of disguise before, and am rather astonished at my own success. I hope the role I asked of you was not too distressing."

"I believe I can best summarise my feelings by respectfully requesting that this incident never be referred to by another living being."

"That," he turned to her in the semi-darkness, white teeth flashing, "is a sentiment we can both agree on."

"Which way do we go now?"

"Nowhere, for a few moments. I have sent Johnson to clear the way ahead of us, and if he is true to his orders, we ought to be able to promenade out with ease. We will allow them ample time to catch a barge, but not so much that their absence is noted."

"Twenty minutes?"

"Ten should suffice."

Twenty-seven

E ternity would not suffice.

It had been a hellish torment, standing beside her in the seclusion of a stand of trees in the growing dusk. Even after a long day of confusion, exertion, and such reversals of circumstance as would send any lady to her retiring room after ten minutes, she still smelled like a spray of lavender after a spring rain.

And that flirtatious manner she had adopted, so sensually enticing and yet so becomingly offensive to her maidenly sensibilities! A dignified Venus, a virtuous seductress…a man was more likely to find a unicorn. He would be a liar and a blackguard to persuade himself that his imagination had not instantly leapt to fancy how she might conduct herself in the privacy of her bedroom with a husband she desired.

It was devilishly unfair.

At last, he could bear the waiting no longer, and if he were honest, he was less impatient to be off than he was violently beset by improper urges. He *would* behave the gentleman! It could not be so very much longer now. A crossing on the barge, a bumpy ride to Cheapside where his head would be cleared as he clung to the back of the coach—he could not endure riding inside with her!—and then they would be in her family's home, and he would be safe.

With this laudable goal in mind, he gently took her elbow and guided her back to the main path. "We will skirt the edge of the Grove, walking just under the trees, but not near the supper boxes."

"Near the orchestra? Will there not be a great many people?"

"All the better for us to disappear among them. Half of them will already be intoxicated on the rack punch, and the other half well on their way to that same fate."

In a matter of moments, they had crossed the centre of the Gardens. Here, all faces were bathed in the brilliant glow of a thousand coloured lanterns, and lavishly dressed guests preened and displayed costumes which had been specifically chosen for such lighting. Elizabeth had seemed to tighten her shoulders together in a conscious gesture of inadequacy, for she wore only her morning walking dress. If only she could see that even in her simple muslin, she was a vast deal more handsome than those promenading peacocks!

Apparently, his gaze had once more been consumed by her form, for he was late in looking ahead of them. "William," she nudged him, "is that not one more?"

He looked where she had noted and groaned. Indeed, Paulson was standing stupidly there by the orchestra. Apparently, Johnson had overlooked him, and he was waiting on some order that was not likely to come. Darcy checked himself—Paulson was one of the grooms from the stables, but he had no way of knowing if he might have been trusted to carry a message from Wilson, or had been recruited to join the company sent by his aunt. He decided not to risk it. Were it only himself, he would flee from none of them, but for Miss Elizabeth's sake… no, her safety and reputation were paramount.

"Let us walk around the outer edges," he suggested. "Over there, behind the supper boxes and toward the Cascade. There is hardly anyone between those trees and almost no lanterns, either. We can cross behind the boxes."

It was some difficult work to make their way to the desired path, for everyone before them was caught in the throes of a lively dance. A raucous jig of some sort; perfectly distasteful in better circles, although the Vauxhall musicians were known to play almost any sort of music on any occasion, and never were they reprimanded for any of it.

To his immense relief, the music soon ended, and the crowd before them quieted just long enough for them to make their way through. Just as she had caught up with him and he had gestured for her to go on, another melody began to play, and the crowd was instantly swept up again.

Elizabeth stopped, then turned to gape at the crowd. "Is that a waltz they are playing? How perfectly scandalous! And how is it that so many know the steps?" She turned to him, her eyes wide and helpless with astonishment.

"Many young ladies of the *ton* learn it from their dance masters. As for the others, I can only conjecture that it is not a difficult dance to learn if one but watches it performed for a moment."

"Would you approve of your sister learning it?"

"She has already done so," he admitted.

"I am all astonishment!" she laughed. "You continue to surprise me, William. I would have thought you too fierce a guardian to permit something so shocking."

"She may tour the Continent one day, and I felt it a necessary part of her preparation—though only after she and her master agreed to my conditions."

"And those are? Pray, tell me what would set a guardian's mind at ease over such a scandalous dance?"

Darcy grinned. The little Pharisee, what he would give to be the man to introduce her to all the seductive delights she had been taught to view askance! "That she only practices the steps with one who is a trusted member of the family. Moreover, I insisted that she only dance with a male, not a female cousin or her companion."

"Not a female?" She shook her head. "Why ever not? I would have thought you would find that the safest alternative."

He smiled again, and caution gave way to longing. He leaned down to her ear and spoke softly, "That is because there is only one way to do it properly. May I show you? Only for a brief moment, here in the dark of the trees before we go?"

She looked carefully at his hand, then gave her own. "What is one more scandal to a day which has been rife with them?"

"What is it, indeed?"

He took her parasol from her hand and hooked it over a nearby tree limb. After he had shown her the most socially accepted posture, lightly holding one another's elbows, he stepped toward her. "Fall back, and allow me to guide you," he coached her. "Now, come to me... and back."

She proved a remarkable study. Whether it was her own natural talent or some kinship which allowed her to read his intentions, her body moved gracefully with his own, and they flowed easily about the edge of their private little ballroom. She was avoiding his eyes at first, looking down at their feet and nibbling her lip as if she feared the heavens would strike her down. But she was smiling.

This was the magic, and as her body began to meld to his, he sensed that she had discovered it as well. Man's strength and woman's grace, a perfect harmony of opposites, each complementing the other until together, they were more than the sum of two individuals. Into her embrace, he continued to step—turning her toward himself, feeling her answer by leading him on more deeply, enticing him... good heavens, she was looking up at him now, with such an innocent, playful light in her eye, that he began to feel slightly dizzy.

Somehow, she had lured him in close, and without quite knowing when he had done so, his hands had slid down her arms to lightly cradle her shoulders, and then her waist. She was blushing, but her own fingers grazed the collar of his livery as she swayed in his arms. Oh, where was firm ground? Only she was real: vexing, exhilarating, taunting, delicious Elizabeth Bennet and her lavender scent.

He had quite forgotten in which direction the gate lay. He had intended to ease her toward it, waltzing back through the crowd of revellers and then walking away, just as though he had not laid open his heart for her small feet to dance upon. The music was over now, but instead of facing the pavilion as he had intended, he broke from his reverie and saw only the fountain through the trees. He had taken her entirely the wrong way, somehow spinning her into the very darkest walk... and was unrepentant for his error.

She twirled to a stop, laughing with the sort of guileless freedom which had so intoxicated him from the first that morning. Her eyes, flashing in the early evening moonlight, were only for him; her hands, so intimately round his shoulders, her body, so invitingly close. He paused, staring and breathless, and something passed in their look which caught at his very soul. A moment later, he was utterly lost.

Her lips were so soft, so sweet, her smooth cheek so warm upon his own! How could any man release her now? Every request, she met. Each aching need, she answered in a tender exchange—her spirit for his gravity, her warm passion for his ardent sincerity—her heart for his.

He needed her. Oh, how to look on any other woman with equanimity, after this! His hands tightened round her waist, and she pulled his head yet lower until he could feel her pulse hammering against his own chest. Good Lord, was this what he had been created for?

He deepened his kisses, asking for more than he had any right to, begging what no maiden ought to surrender, and she answered with a sigh into his own mouth and a slip of her tongue over his lower lip. She must have at last frightened herself, for she broke away, and her cheek shook against his own with each panting breath.

"I should not have done that," she whispered between gasps.

"Probably not," he nearly growled into the hair just below her bonnet. "But pray, do not stop on my account."

One eyebrow arched, and those lips—*his*—curved softly again before meeting him once more.

Restraint was forgotten. Fear of discovery but a pittance. He pulled her up, supporting her delicious form against his body and allowing her to seek his hair, his neck, even his throat. Heaven have mercy, but he ached to devour her! And she seemed to hold no objections....

"Elizabeth," he rasped into her ear, "there must be..." *another kiss*... "is there some way...."

She drew to the side, nuzzling his jaw as she caught her breath. "What?"

Oh. Her fingers had entwined in the hair at the base of his neck, and his entire being shivered. There was no help for him now. "Some way," he repeated, his mind only half alert. "We could... I could protect you."

She dropped to flat feet, her hands still trailing down his chest. Her head tilted. "What can you mean?"

"I… I know that the relative position of our families would render it disgraceful, but there must be some manner in which we can… perhaps something can be arranged. You would not need to wed that fool."

Her hands fell away, and a suspicious note crept into her voice. "You are not suggesting what I think…."

He caught her hands, foolhardy bliss robbing him of rational thought. "Why should I not? We could prove the answer to one another's difficulties, and can you think on the prospect without hope for felicity? Would it not suit ideally?"

She tugged her hands from him again. "Not such a scheme as you propose. How could you even ask such a thing? Have I then disgraced myself so thoroughly?"

He shook his head. "I do not understand. I do not speak of compromise, where your choices are taken from you, but of an arrangement to your benefit, granting you the freedom to…. I do not know precisely how to say what I wish. You understand my meaning, do you not?"

"Perfectly." Her tones had hardened, her arms crossed over her chest, closing him off. She turned away from him, her shoulders rounded, and he distinctly heard a sob.

"Elizabeth? Tell me, to what can you possibly object? Is it myself?"

She spun back, hurt glittering in her eyes. "You have the audacity to ask me this? After such a day as we have spent, teaching me to trust you as a friend, you allow me to shame myself to such a degree that you believe such a proposal might be received with pleasure?"

"Why should it not be? And what is so shameful? Such connections are not uncommon, though there may be talk in some quarters. I care nothing for that, and it can be no worse than what you say you have already endured. I had thought we got on remarkably well, far better than any spouses of my acquaintance, and I am certainly in no hurry to make an alliance of *that* kind. Are we not well suited? Will you not consider it?"

"I cannot express the obligation which you might expect in this case." She covered her mouth—those lips which had so recently caressed his own—and her glorious eyes filled with tears.

"Elizabeth!" He drew near, searching for a handkerchief and dredging up every thought, every deed of the last minutes. How had he misrepresented himself, and how could she be made to see that they were formed for one another?

"Sir, I beg you to call me Miss Bennet. And as I saw a moment ago that my friend Mrs Jennings still occupies her supper box at the pavilions, I think it advisable that I request to join her party."

"If you wish," he lifted his hands in confusion, then turned to accompany her. What the devil had shifted? One moment she was kissing him as if her very life beat within his hands, and the next—

"Alone, sir."

"What?"

She tightened her arms about herself and shivered. "I think it best if you do not follow."

"El—Miss Bennet, I do not understand! Have I offended you with my proposal? What have I done?"

She startled and glared up at him as if he had overturned a priceless vase and then asked why his company had become suddenly odious. "If you do not know, then you are not the gentleman I had taken you for," she bit out. "I think we should not be seen together."

"You are leaving me now? But why? How will you travel back alone? It is too dangerous, surely!"

"I believe I can depend on the goodness of Mrs Jennings to see me safely home. I will have it no other way, sir. Do not follow me, for I shall not speak to you if you do."

"Is this all the answer I am to expect?"

He followed her out of the trees, back to the walk, and stood there; alone in a crowd, his arms held out in appeal, and waited for her to turn back. She did not. Nor did she walk slowly. His heart felt as if it had been ripped from his chest, and he was certain that all around bore witness to the haemorrhaging.

Fitzwilliam Darcy, the man who had never been denied anything, watched helplessly as the only woman he had ever admired walked away.

Twenty-eight

I *should have known!*

If there were people in her way, Elizabeth would never have seen them. She pushed through whatever lay before her, mindless in her determination to put *him* as far behind her as possible. How could she have been so bird witted? She, who prided herself on her perception and prudence, had fallen so abysmally into the stupidest sort of folly. How mortifying her descent!

She wanted to scream, to weep, and to run, all at the same time. She longed to hide in her bed for a month, and in the next thought, she could wish for nothing more than to strike something… no, not just *something*. She would strike *him*, right on that dimpled mouth, and wipe away that deceitful smile! How dare he masquerade as a gentleman? Hah! Likely enough, he really was nothing more than a drunken footman who happened to know a little Shakespeare, and the entire day had been no more than a ruse to take advantage of a naive country girl with no prospects of her own. What a fool she was!

He was not far behind, still calling her name and protesting his ignorance of her sudden fury. He had not ceased begging to know what he had done. Everything, that was all! Imposed on her, made her feel tenderly for him, and probably ruined her forever, if anyone ever heard a breath of the affair. And all so that he could make an indecent proposition!

She did not look back but pressed on faster. Gradually, his voice died away, but just before she reached the supper boxes once more, she paused and turned. It would not do for him to be trailing plaintively behind when she approached Mrs Jennings. What a tale to tell! She clenched her fists, her chin high, and looked defiantly round.

He was about thirty feet away, and she caught snatches of his forlorn figure as others passed between them. His arms hung slack at his sides, and a haunted look darkened his face. His mouth opened as if to speak once more, and he started to reach with an imploring hand, but she drew herself up, and he shrank. She held her challenging glare until he surrendered, blinking rapidly and still looking lost and pitiful. Had she still the veil of infatuation over her eyes, she would have yearned to soothe that broken expression, to reassure him that she, at least, was his friend… wretched soul was she!

He looked down, seemed to sigh, and then slowly turned another way. She waited until he had gone completely out of sight before she released the breath which had steeled her spine and hardened her face. Now, what remained but tears and humiliation? They stung already, but she could not dare to give way until solitude could afford her that luxury of berating herself for all her errors of judgment.

How ironic it was, then, that to gain solitude, she must first face one to whom that very notion would be abhorrent! Oh, how could she bear to speak now? And yet if she did not, Mrs Jennings' instincts would accuse her of despondency, and demand explanations she was unwilling to give.

She waited another moment, collecting herself as she gazed toward that kindly lady's box. One more moment. Two, perhaps. Three—just long enough for her pulse to steady and the tears to dry from her lashes. She drew a troubled breath, and took a step in that direction, only to be shaken anew.

"Miss Elizabeth! I had not thought it possible, but I find myself appalled!"

She flinched, her stomach twisting, and closed her eyes. Oh, how had *that* man found her, and here of all places? She groaned before turning to face him. Was she cursed this day?

"Mr Collins," she offered a demure curtsy. "This is indeed a pleasure, Cousin."

~

Welcome to Vauxhall Pleasure Gardens

Pleasure? Bah! Pleasure! The faded sign at the gates was a slap to a wounded face, for he could not recall when he had felt more miserable.

Perhaps he had not anticipated proposing marriage to a virtual stranger as he had done, but he certainly had never expected to be so harshly rebuked and soundly rejected! Did she not know enough of his character, enough of his circumstances to understand the honour he paid her?

She must, surely, for their few hours together had afforded them a familiarity almost unattainable between a man and a woman before marriage. It was inconceivable that she, intelligent as she was, would *not* have understood enough of what had remained cryptic between them to grasp the magnitude of what he offered, as well as the sacrifice he would gladly pay for her. And yet she was insulting!

What manner of woman would take righteous offence at a confession of love? Surely it was nothing he had done wrong…. He tried to recount each of his many sins this day, or at least those of which he was perfectly conscious, but none of those had earned her indignation upon their commission. No, quite the opposite! And when he finally did come to the honourable conclusion, that something must be done to satisfy their growing attachment to each other, she would hear nothing of it!

He shook his head as he stumbled forward. The finest woman, possessed of the least unstable mind he had ever yet encountered, yet even she defied all hope of understanding. A dashed monstrous thing was this, for if he could not comprehend even *her*, what chance had he of domestic harmony if forced to choose another?

He had wished very much to see her safely into the arms of Mrs Jennings, but she would not even permit him that much. That look, contempt bordering on open hostility, he would not soon erase from his memory. There was nothing else for it; she would have her way, and come ruin or harm, she would not accept another word from him. *Why?*

He trudged slowly, painfully to the water gate, caring not whether an army of his own footmen awaited there to escort him back to his own house. What could it matter? He might as well bow his head meekly to the noose, might as well have Anne de Bourgh, for there was no consolation prize, no second-place award when the only right woman would not have him. All the rest were on a level field, and all would be a bitter compromise to a man who had *almost* attained perfection.

His mood subsequently dark and cheerless, he was hardly surprised when he wandered back through the gate, empty and alone, and saw none other than his uncle, the Earl of Matlock, stepping off the barge. He sighed and could almost feel himself grow an inch shorter.

"Well, Darcy," his uncle growled, "I expect you have some sort of explanation for all this?"

Darcy pursed his lips, then dropped his eyes to the ground. "None whatsoever, Uncle. Let us go back."

~

"My dear cousin, I must protest. What inducement could have brought a respectable young lady to such a venue, and without a chaperon?"

They were safely aboard a barge now, and mercifully, William—if that was really his name—had been nowhere in sight on their path from the Gardens. She was free to hang her head all she liked. It was not as if Collins were perceptive enough to discover her melancholy! "Sir, I was not without such protection, as I have indicated. My friend Mrs Jennings was awaiting my return at her box when you happened upon me." That was half true, perhaps. She was invited but not necessarily expected. She doubted whether that semantic would trouble her thick-headed cousin.

"But who can such a woman be? I have not been introduced to her! Who is she, who could demand the attention of a lady of my family and detain her the whole of the day, keeping her away from her own family and her betrothed?"

"Sir," her teeth clenched, "our betrothal has not been made official. I will ask you to kindly not refer to it as such! I have still four weeks, as per the agreement with my father."

"My dear Miss Elizabeth," he adopted that grating air with which, no doubt, he issued his sermons, "you can have no possible objection to such an agreeable connection as I have proposed. Indeed, your circumstances are likely to decline still further in that time, and we both know the distress and worry you are certain to relieve in your most excellent mother by forming an honourable alliance. Your elder sister is certain to profit by our marriage, for the disgrace of your younger sisters might be overlooked the more easily."

"I am not yet twenty," she reminded him firmly. "My father has assured me that until such a date, he will afford me his protection."

"Protection! My dear cousin, pray do not speak as if I would take advantage of a young lady. My suit is honourable, as your good mother will attest. Moreover, it is only my very great forbearance and what I believed was your own excellent character which persuaded me to extend such an offer, for as my most esteemed Lady Catherine de Bourgh exhorts, we are to condole with those in trial and offer succour to those who suffer.

"I confess, an alliance in such a case is perhaps questionable to my own interests, but I feel it incumbent on my role as a clergyman to seek to aid the innocent while still pronouncing fit judgment upon the guilty. I am quite certain that your merits and My Lady's excellent advice will render you a perfectly respectable companion for a clergyman, and we have the advantage of distance from Hertfordshire in my quiet abode in Kent. Surely, all due circumspection and prudence dictate that our marriage should take place at once, the sooner your family's dignity may begin to make a recovery.

"It is, of course, my own generosity of spirit which leads me to offer to be the means of your family's salvation, and I flatter myself, no other would be so magnanimous in the circumstances. But," he comforted her, "where one ventures, perhaps another may follow, and perhaps by our excellent example of felicity, Miss Bennet and Miss Catherine may also one day be suited with respectable marriages. You must understand, Miss Mary and Miss Lydia," he spoke the names as an anathema, "must content themselves with their lot, but you need not suffer more than you have already done."

Elizabeth felt her cheeks burning. "Sir, as I have once informed you, you are the last man in the world who could make me happy, and I am convinced I am utterly incapable of making you so. I grant you my full blessing to withdraw your offer, with no recrimination on my part."

"I may be forced to do so, my dear cousin, much as it would pain me to be seen as the sort of man who would disappoint any lady! But I have heard the most distressing rumour, and it was that rumour which led me to find you in the very place I had feared. Are you here in the company of a gentleman? I beg of you not to dissemble," he held up a hand of generosity, his forgiving smile pasty in the darkness. "Pray, were you imposed upon or beguiled into a liaison? Fear not that I will publicise your disgrace, but of course, I must then break off our engagement and submit to your honourable father and most excellent uncle my reasons for withdrawing."

She sealed her lips and stared at the water.

"Dear cousin, I beseech you—"

"I was invited to be the guest of Mrs Jennings," she stubbornly retorted, unwilling to hear more of his self-aggrandisement. "I was not the only guest of her party, for there was indeed a gentleman I had never before met among her guests." Perhaps it was a slight stretching of the plain truth, but as Mrs Jennings herself would not have disputed that pronouncement, she felt quite safe. "Had you the decency to pay your respects to the lady, your anxiety would certainly have been relieved on that head."

"Impossible! For Lady Catherine has issued her decree, that we are to present ourselves at once, and no offence given to any person could be more of a transgression than disrespect to my great lady."

"I am not suitably dressed to meet such a grand personage," Elizabeth pardoned herself. "Another day must suffice, for I intend to return directly to my aunt and uncle. They must be concerned for me, even if you will not allow that my friend might be."

"What objection could any raise, if you are in the company of your betrothed? And pray, think nothing of your attire, for Lady Catherine is ever sensitive to the limitations of those of lesser station and is quite content to see the distinction of rank preserved by modest attire in other young ladies. As to going now, Mr and Mrs Gardiner, in their eminent wisdom, will think it nothing less than proper that you be presented at a time which My Lady decrees. Even your Mrs Jennings could not help but concur, naturally, if she knew all. I am quite certain on this point.

"You must know, my dear cousin, that another claimed your company this evening; a man whose notice of you could only be of a disreputable inclination, and this fact distresses me, my dear cousin, a great deal more than I am capable of expressing. My dear Elizabeth, pray assure me that you were not, in fact, in the company of a single gentleman for the whole of the day! For if true, this accusation betrays a temper disposed to manipulation and artifice of the most serious kind!"

"You may rest easy, for I was accompanied on my outing by a footman who came with me this morning from my uncle's house, sir." She crossed her arms and glared over the water. "Your information was inaccurate, for he was no gentleman."

"Your assurances give me the greatest comfort! Although it is very strange, rather shocking that any young lady should venture out all day in town, it was at least fitting that your safety should be secured by a proper attendant. But could Miss Catherine not have attended you as well? And where is this erstwhile manservant?"

"No doubt he has gone with his fellows," was her sour reply.

"But how is it then that my great lady's information named a young lady whose appellation bears a striking resemblance to your own and who was known to have issued from Mr Gardiner's house?"

"Where did your lady obtain her information? It sounds to me like hearsay. I did not conceal my face about town, and any number of persons might have seen me."

"Well," he nearly sputtered, "you may be assured that only the most reputable sources would have been consulted. But perhaps you are right, for, after all, I searched for you myself when I became concerned for your whereabouts, and perhaps not all witnesses are so exacting in the details as is proper. I am excessively attentive to matters such as these, for the safety of any young lady, be she relative or otherwise, must, of course, be the highest concern of any gentleman of her acquaintance.

"My dear cousin, pray, do not concern yourself that I shall condemn you harshly for a simple day of pleasure and enjoyment, for the amusement was innocent, and certainly the day fine enough to take the air. My good patroness, Lady Catherine De Bourgh, has more than once observed that young ladies who take pleasure in day outings are frequently possessed of the most flattering vitality and quite often are the soonest to bless their husbands with a little olive branch with which to bestow happiness on all her family. Rest assured—"

Elizabeth had ceased listening long ago. Strange, how easy it was to ignore Mr Collins when all her energies focused instead upon her humiliation at the hands of another. And what had she done to merit any better than a lumpy, sweating, ignorant beef-wit who liked nothing better than the sound of his own voice? She would receive precisely what she had earned, and she might as well become adept at neglecting one William Collins.

Twenty-nine

"**D**arcy, what in Heaven's name have you been doing? You came to me this morning proclaiming the vilest accusations against your aunt, and then you spent the day trading clandestine messages with one of your servants and traipsing about Creation? Have you gone mad? I am given to understand that you have been secretly gathering information against your very own relation! And what the devil have you been doing here without telling anyone of your whereabouts? Egad, Darcy, I never thought I should have to scold *you*. Stand up and face your duties like a man!"

Darcy clenched his fist and stared out the window of the carriage, refusing to look the Earl of Matlock in the eye. "I have no objections to asserting my manhood, but I do object rather violently to manipulation and deceit."

"Deceit? Deceit! Do I hear you properly? What are these clothes you are wearing, what foolishness have you been masquerading about all day? Preposterous! If your father could have seen you in this—this—"

"I must insist that you do not invoke my father's name! You are the head of the Fitzwilliam family, but for years you have done nothing to discourage Lady Catherine's abuse of her position."

The earl's eyes flickered in rage. "Have a care, my boy! Do you presume to dictate *my* duties to *me*?"

"I am not afraid to demonstrate to you your failings. I have deferred for years, out of regard for my mother's family, but Lady Catherine has trespassed against my goodwill in every conceivable way. Yet, when her actions are so blatant that none could consider her under the regulation of sense and decorum, you do not protest! You would hold me accountable for my aunt's desires despite their ruinous nature, see me perform her pleasure regardless of my own interests, and when I am delayed in seeking the proof of her falsehood that you demanded, I am accused of not performing my duty. Is it not you who ought to have borne the burden of checking her? Yet you claim the right to tell me that my father would be ashamed of my actions!"

"I have no need to tell you that, for your own conscience must inform you of it!" his lordship bellowed. "George Darcy would have done his duty, just as he did by my sister. By Jove! You did not see him disappear for a day like a spoilt child when he was given a bride."

"My mother did not force his hand with an intoxicated compromise."

"She did not have to. George knew what was expected of him and fell in love with my sister just as his father instructed. Anne did the same, and they were quite happy. There was not this weakling foolishness about the choosing of a marriage partner in our day! Why could you not do your duty? You are a selfish boy, Fitzwilliam Darcy, and I have nearly had enough of your objections."

Darcy scowled and turned back to the window. "That will suit me as well, for I too have grown weary of the conflict."

"And another thing… what the devil? You what?"

His stomach roiled in protest and his entire being recoiled, but he forced himself to spit out the words. "I will speak to my aunt about wedding my cousin." There was nothing worth fighting for anyway, since he had found the woman he sought, and she despised him.

"However," he interjected before his uncle could offer his congratulations that he had come to his senses, "I do believe I am owed some sort of explanation."

"Explanation? How so? I would counter that it is you who must explain yourself. What can you mean, going off without a word to anyone and in the company of some trollop all day, deliberately to humiliate your cousin?"

"I was with no trollop."

"Your aunt showed me the proof in your own hand! She even had a name… Benwick, something like that?"

Darcy shifted uneasily in the seat and, for a moment, longed for the safety of the foot pegs on the back of the carriage. "I know of none by the name Benwick. There must have been some misunderstanding."

"Well, I still say you have a bit of talking to do, for it is utter nonsense to me, that you should have gone off as you did like a petulant boy."

"What is nonsense is that my aunt was so insistent upon my immediate acceptance of my cousin that she would attempt to drug and then compromise me so that I might not escape with my honour intact. I would know the plain truth, for if I decide to bestow my hand on my cousin, whatever has been the cause of my aunt's desperation will shortly become my own concern."

"Her desperation, as you call it, is nothing more than frustration with your lack of commitment."

"And you do not think it strange that she attempted to impose upon me now? Would she not have had better opportunities on other occasions?"

The earl shook his head. "I have no interest in your intrigues, Darcy. When we walk in the door, I expect you to do your duty as a man of this family and act with honour. Do not forget, we still have Georgiana's future to think of as well, and I would see you situated first—for her good as well as your own."

Darcy ground his teeth. "I have not forgotten."

~

"Darcy! There you are, my dear boy. Come, let us greet one another as family and put this nonsense behind us. And my dear brother, of course, it is only fitting that you should have come as well, for I am excessively attentive to all manner of discord within a family, and we ought not to have any hint of that between us." Lady Catherine stood in the centre of his own drawing room, a caped dress spread opulently like a royal cloak and held court at his favourite wingback chair.

"Aunt Catherine," he acknowledged. "You will pardon me if I do not rush to kiss your cheek. I have a few plain questions to which I must hear an answer."

She looked hurt, her wrinkled brow falling and her lips trembling. "Darcy, you speak as if you have been the injured party. Would you accuse me, an old woman, of wronging you? I declare I cannot see how. What has anyone done that you ought not to have done yourself?"

He glared darkly, refusing to answer his aunt's plea. His gaze searched all round till it settled upon his butler, standing at a far door. The man's face reddened faintly when he felt his master's scrutiny, but he remained stock still, his hands locked behind his back, and his eyes straight ahead.

"Dawson! Have Mr Wilson brought, please."

Mr Dawson looked unhappy and glanced to Lady Catherine before he stammered, "Sir, Mr Wilson has been relieved of his duties and confined to his chamber for unseemly conduct. I should not like to expose any ladies or your distinguished guests—"

"Mr Dawson, who pays your salary? I know not what other compensation you have received, but your position in this house is retained at *my* pleasure."

"Darcy!" Lady Catherine objected. "What accusation is this? Do you suspect me of some treachery in your own household?"

He glanced levelly at the lady but did not give the satisfaction of a reply. "Dawson," he resumed, "I will also have Mrs White, and the cook brought."

"James!" the lady implored now, walking toward the earl, "hear you this? Does he intend to bring some sort of charges against me? I will not be thus spoken to! If he has some manner of protest to make, have I not greater? Has he not refused to perform his duty these six years since his majority? Nay, it has been eight since the subject was first canvassed openly, yet he refuses to oblige! That I should live to see the day my own sister's son should thus treat his family!"

"Darcy," the earl's deep voice cautioned, "we had settled that you intended to accept your duty. Do not delay or complicate matters by reluctance or pointless allegations now."

"I do not consider it pointless. The integrity of my household has been breached, my authority challenged, and my private affairs meddled with. If— and this point is absolutely conditional—I choose to offer my cousin my hand in marriage, I must have some assurances that such behaviour shall never be repeated."

"If!" Lady Catherine nearly erupted. "Have you no decency? Your cousin has been disgraced, and in your very own bed! How can you stand before me now and claim that you have some choice in the affair? The matter was settled last night!"

"That is the very point I would dispute, and to do so will require more honest witnesses than can be found in my own corrupted household."

"I will hear no more of this slander! Where is my daughter? Anne will be heard, for she is the wounded party here!"

A maid was thus dispatched, and the young lady brought from the very next room, but at the same moment she appeared, a footman bowed and announced a Mr Collins to see Lady Catherine.

Darcy, heated and offended as he was, could not help but be checked by such a name. "Collins?" he repeated.

"Indeed," his aunt smiled. "My parson from Hunsford. He is here to perform the ceremony at my request. I have already procured the license, and I will have satisfaction of you this very night before my daughter's ruin is made known."

Darcy knew not what to think. Outrage at his aunt's presumption and high-handed meddling was but one of the swirl of ill feelings plaguing him at that moment. Collins? Not... not *her* Collins, surely! He had not the opportunity to answer his aunt, for in the next moment, the very bumbling fool he had seen on the pavement in Cheapside that morning now bowed his way into the drawing room. And beside him, with her lovely eyes cast down over rosy cheeks and her hands folded demurely before her....

"My esteemed Lady Catherine," Mr Collins beamed, "it is with the deepest pleasure that I present, as requested, my betrothed, Miss Elizabeth Bennet of Hertfordshire, to help celebrate the nuptials of our dear Miss de Bourgh. May I again protest the very great honour bestowed upon your humble servants by giving notice of us at such a venerable occasion as the solemnisation of Miss de Bourgh's marriage to Mr Darcy? Your ladyship is too kind, to consider our satisfaction on sharing such a happy day."

He could not breathe. She had scarcely raised her eyes, but there could be no question that she had noted his presence. For no other reason would she stare so steadily at a bit of Indian carpet, but that she had been dragged here against her will by that idiot, presented as his unwilling affianced, and then confronted with none other but himself! He longed to go to her, to lift her chin and to bodily remove that simpering idiot's arm from hers, but all eyes were now on his Elizabeth.

"Your betrothed does not speak," observed Lady Catherine. "Is she so disrespectful that she cannot express proper courtesy at the introduction?"

"Oh, quite the contrary, My Lady! She is the most modest and exemplary woman, and I feel quite certain that she is merely overcome with gratitude for your ladyship's notice and condescension. Mr Darcy," he turned and bowed again, "pray, forgive my manners, for we have not been introduced. May I express my most joyous congratulations upon the occasion of your marriage!"

She did glance up to him then, and within those fine eyes flickered a spark of… something… but it was quickly dampened by a deep shadow of humiliation. Crimson stained those soft cheeks he had only an hour ago caressed as his own, and he could see her desperately trying to swallow. He had no right to speak to her, for she had not yet responded to Lady Catherine. Angels above, could anyone else see the inferno threatening to consume him if he did not go to her at once?

"Miss Bennet," Lady Catherine repeated, as if the young lady were deaf, "you are either exquisitely modest, as Mr Collins claims, or unfavourably reticent."

She blinked, slowly, and with deliberate lassitude, lifted her eyes to his aunt. "I believe you might be the first person to ever think me reticent, My Lady."

"That is well. Anne," Lady Catherine gestured to his silent cousin, "does her appearance please you?"

Darcy had scarcely even noticed Anne's arrival, and as he glanced in her direction now, he could not miss the faint narrowing of her eyes as she acknowledged him. Well, let her be displeased with him! She was party to all this fallacy, let her suffer some of his disdain. But why was Anne to pass any approval on his Elizabeth? Could not everyone else see the contrast between the two? One vibrant and healthy, the very angles of her face formed by every expression of feminine goodness and cheer; the other sallow, ill-disposed toward civility, weak, and pale. They were not even of the same class!

Anne glanced over Elizabeth's dress, the very one she had worn all day, and appeared unimpressed. "She is respectable enough, I suppose," was her diffident reply.

"It is fitting that you have some sort of attendant," Lady Catherine decided. "That is the very reason I insisted that Mr Collins present his betrothed this evening, for she will be coming to Hunsford after her marriage. You may retire to dress, Anne, and Miss Bennet may assist you."

And that was the moment that Darcy, with his carefully schooled detachment and his barely restrained sense of decorum, ceased to care what anyone else thought.

Thirty

If she had been humiliated before, she wished to die a thousand deaths now. What right had *he* to be the one to witness her mortification at the hands of Collins? There had been some sense of foreboding when that sweating, beady-eyed fool had dragged her into the veritable mansion on Grosvenor Street.

Then, when he had fairly pushed her before him into the drawing room, and the fine, distinctive figure which had been her refuge this day had been the first to greet her eyes, it had demanded all her willpower not to turn the other way and flee like a small child. What cruel destiny had made *his* aunt one and the same as Mr Collins' own Lady Catherine de Bourgh?

Darcy. That was his name. Fitz*william* Darcy, a name which must have cost ten thousand pounds just to hire someone to inscribe all its characters. A fine specimen, indeed! What a fool she was! One needed only glance at the thick Indian rug—which was all she found the courage to stare at—to know that he was as far beyond her as the Prince Regent himself.

He was gazing at her now, drawing her attention to one safe corner of the room as that horrible woman was issuing her invectives and decrees. His chest was heaving with a torment which, intimately as she understood him, could have been no less than her own. There was fury sparking in his face, ire curling his fists, but there was something more; something meant only for her. Regret. Sorrow.

So, this was how it was to be. Neither of them had any choice in the matter; he would marry the heiress, she the parson, and they would be thus perversely connected for life. Her own gaze faltered, but not before reflecting back to him the same frustration and remorse. She had been right to refuse his offer—she knew it, and her family's security would forever be her assurance of that—but for just a moment, she wished there had been some way she could have accepted.

He had turned back to his relation now as if he could no longer bear to look at her. "Aunt Catherine," he thundered, shaking even the other young woman and nearly causing Collins to faint, "you will desist at once! Is it not sufficient that you abuse my hospitality to such a degree that you have insinuated yourself into my private affairs, and now you think you have enough power over me to force a marriage where there was no misconduct on my part? Must you also degrade this young lady by issuing orders to a guest?"

"Guest?" scoffed his aunt. "If she is a guest, it is because *I* have had her brought here. She must and should be flattered by the honour of my condescension."

She could see him coiling with rage in her defence but could no longer remain silent herself. "I beg your pardon," Elizabeth interrupted just as Darcy was preparing a counter-attack, "but I am here against my wishes and find this an honour I can easily forego. I do not know if it is your usual custom, Lady Catherine, to browbeat your company into waiting upon you, but if it is, I believe I perfectly understand the reason. It must be difficult to procure guests for your amusement if such is their first experience with your hospitality. If it is quite the same to you, your ladyship, I should like to return to my uncle Gardiner's home at the earliest opportunity." She finished this little speech with a hesitant glance his way, then again fastened an impertinent gaze on his aunt.

He smiled as if he wanted to cheer and applaud, but he was the only one. Collins nearly dropped dead of horror—a pity he did not, for that would have been one problem solved. An older gentleman, whom Collins had informed her would be Mr Darcy's uncle, the Earl of Matlock, was shaking his head in grave disapproval of her saucy tongue. The bride's mouth had dropped open in indignation, but Lady Catherine… oh, that lady's reaction was opposite in equal measure to Mr Darcy's own. She purpled in an instant, her eyes wild with insensible fury.

"I have never… you, Miss Bennet, are a wicked, disgraceful woman! Collins, is this typical behaviour for the young lady you would make your wife?"

The parson's waxen face had lost all colour. "In-indeed not, My Lady! Perhaps she is fatigued. Yes, I do believe that must be it, for she is not quite herself!"

"In fact, I am not at all weary," Elizabeth replied serenely. "I have had a most refreshing day, until approximately an hour ago. If I have little patience with your arts, My Lady, it is because I had the pleasure of enjoying companionship of a far more restful and genuine sort and am in no humour at present to tolerate anything less agreeable." She rewarded Darcy then with one more glance, a lowering of lashes, and then was quiet.

That glance proved to be a mistake. Darcy's eyes had warmly touched hers, and when he looked away again to his aunt, her icy gaze was fixed upon her nephew.

"I see it all now," she murmured, her tones low and menacing. "Miss Bennet, did you name your guardian as a Mr Gardiner? Of Cheapside?"

"Indeed," she answered without reserve.

"Then *you* are the very strumpet my nephew took for his amusement. I have it in a note, and not so much of it was illegible that I cannot make out such a similarity in the name. You are a disgraceful harlot, Miss Bennet, and I shall see that your marriage to my parson will never come to pass!"

Collins was glancing helplessly between the patroness he adored and herself—the woman he had claimed as his reward for his merits. "But… your ladyship!"

"I am no harlot!" Elizabeth retorted hotly, but Darcy was protesting with equal vehemence and in nearly the same breath.

"Lady Catherine! I will not tolerate a word against this lady. If her presence displeases you, you may feel free to leave the house."

"I have heard enough!" roared a new voice. All eyes turned to the earl, who strode now to his sister's side.

"Darcy, this foolishness shall cease at once. Were you or were you not in the company of this… woman all day?"

His eyes were lingering on her—she could feel them, and he could not seem to tear them away. By the time he found the words of truth, they were unnecessary. "I was."

"And who is she? How is she known to you? I presume she is your mistress?"

Elizabeth's face flushed, and she realised he had still been looking only upon her, until he rounded on the older man.

"Uncle!" he objected. "Miss Bennet is a lady! How dare you make such an accusation?"

"I am still waiting for you to explain to me how a lady, such as you describe, would have been your entertainment for the day. Anne, my dear, if you do not wish to remain for the answer, you may go."

Elizabeth surged forward with a heedless urge to defend herself from this brutish aristocrat's accusations, but three voices raised at that moment against her own. Collins was waving his hands in excitement, the fair-haired "Anne" was whining to her mother and spinning as if she would faint, and Darcy himself stalked toward his uncle. Elizabeth tried to make herself heard above the din, but one voice—Darcy's—checked her. He held up a staying hand as he passed her and closed upon his aunt and uncle, demanding the floor.

"You seek a scandal? Very well, I shall tell you all, but prepare yourself for something dreadful, for what I have to say will not portray our own family in a favourable light. When I discovered myself to have been drugged, and my own staff unreliable," he levelled a searing glance at both his aunt and cousin, "I left the house at once for Richard's apartment. I overestimated my abilities, and Miss Bennet and her family discovered me and very kindly brought me to safety. They had no notion of my identity, only that I was in some distress, and their own goodness exhorted them to act. It was in their house that I passed the night. After I left it, I found it necessary to return to find out if Mr Gardiner would offer his support of my testimony. Miss Elizabeth has been nothing but a helpful friend, and I will hear no abuse of her character."

"And where is this Mr Gardiner? What of his testimony? If you have it, I would see it in writing or hear it from himself. I still think this tale of yours utter lunacy, Darcy."

"Unfortunately, we were unable to procure it. Miss Elizabeth had offered an introduction at his place of business, but—"

"This woman has pulled the wool over your eyes, Darcy!" Lady Catherine sneered at her, then summoned Mr Collins with a crook of her finger. "You know not whom you have chosen to champion, but I am familiar with this woman's family. They are a brood of vixens all, and though Mr Collins had most generously offered redemption for the one who appeared the most worthy, she has today proved that she is little better than the worst. Nay, more wretched even than that, for the others only entangled themselves with passing tradesmen. This wicked Jezebel would ensnare what belongs to another, against all claims of nature and decency! Collins, you will have nothing further to do with this woman, and let her family's disgrace be complete. You will have the satisfaction of seeing her fall, as is her nature, but it shall not be my own nephew she lures to his demise!"

Elizabeth felt ill. Collins and that homely blonde woman were smirking in triumph at her shame, the proud uncle curling his lip in disgust as he looked down upon her, but William... she cast one imploring glance his way. Surely, he could not believe or condone the lies spoken, the slander used as a cane over her back! Yet he would not look at her. His face was heated, but he stared at the floor, his fist clenched behind him.

"Aunt Catherine," he growled, "whatever Miss Bennet is or is not, it can be no concern of yours. And Mr Collins," he shifted his menacing glare, "I am certain your bishop would be interested to hear how willingly you almost desecrated the sacrament of marriage by validating a falsified marriage license. The document Lady Catherine claims to have was not applied for by myself, and therefore cannot be authentic. Shall I send a letter regarding the oversight of your responsibilities as a clergyman?"

Collins paled, but before he could speak, there was a commotion outside the door. Several voices could be heard at once—one of them Elizabeth thought she recognised as Darcy's cousin from earlier in the day. Another… she nearly sagged with relief as she identified her uncle's tones.

A moment later, Colonel Fitzwilliam crowded through the door without ceremony, and behind him thronged more men she did not recognise… but Edward Gardiner was among them. He found her almost at once, and the look of anger and fear melted into something harder, more determined.

"See here, what is this?" demanded the earl. "Richard, what the devil?"

"It is not I who have the right to speak first," the colonel bowed in Elizabeth's direction. "Father, I was just introduced outside to Mr Edward Gardiner, and he has some rather choice words for the assembled party."

Elizabeth felt her uncle's heavy stare once more and flinched. It was not her reasonable, good-natured uncle who had come to collect her, but the exhausted, irritated, affronted businessman who had only now been assured of her safety. The conversation he would demand of her later was certain to be unpleasant.

"By your present attire, I presume you must be Mr Darcy," Mr Gardiner bowed shortly. "I understand we have some manner of business."

"Indeed, sir." Elizabeth studied Darcy—he looked relieved, humiliated, doubtful, but he glanced once to her and seemed to collect himself. "I regret the inconvenience—"

"Sir, if you please, I am weary, and I am not certain how well disposed I am toward you at present. I should like nothing better than to secure my niece, satisfy your request, since she seemed to think your mission one of import, and retire. Colonel Fitzwilliam here tells me that you were seeking an alibi from me and that you are the man my wife and nieces scraped from the paving stones at half past eleven last evening, dressed as a servant and looking full of drink. Elizabeth, is this he?"

She nodded, too embarrassed to look anyone in the eye.

"Very well. I shall swear to it in the presence of any witness you desire."

"And are we to believe this?" interjected Lady Catherine. "Upon the avowals of a known seductress, with a besmirched reputation, we are to relinquish our own claims at the pleasure of a tradesman? Collins! Tell of this harlot's family!"

"Ah, your ladyship is wise," he bowed, raising an index finger. "I—"

"Mr Collins," Uncle Gardiner pronounced, "I have heard something of your own conduct. Is it or is it not true that you were free to invent some facts of your own, as you were in a position to offer aid to my youngest niece and declined to do it? And did you stand on my own street and discredit Elizabeth's name in public? I will tolerate no further attempts to slight my family's honour to satisfy your own ends."

"I was only seeking the safety of my betrothed—"

"Mr Collins, your belongings should be ready for your departure at your earliest convenience. I would advise you not to linger before collecting them, for my staff have been instructed to burn anything that remains by morning. The constable has heard my complaints, and I have no doubt there are others in this company who could make use of his services. Elizabeth! Let us take our leave."

She could not bear to look at him. He started to follow as her uncle turned away, drawing close enough to murmur for her alone, "Elizabeth, forgive me."

She glanced to the floor at his feet... those horrid shoes... the too-short breeches, but her eyes travelled no farther. "Goodbye," she whispered. Her uncle took her by the arm, and she did not look back.

Thirty-one

She was gone. The one gambling piece and the one prize he might have dreamed, in his wildest fancies, to claim at the end of it all, and she was gone. Darcy started after the closing door for one moment of soul-splitting agony, his heart numb as the family eruption ensued at his back.

"And what had you to do with all this, Richard?" his uncle was demanding. Darcy sighed and turned to face them all.

"I?" Richard answered innocently. "I knew nothing of it until Darcy appeared at my apartment this morning; barefoot, unshaven, and dressed like a table ornament. I did nothing more than my family duty—I mocked him, gave him a pair of shoes, and attempted to pry whatever entertainment I could from him. He is devilish sober, as he always is, but I did learn an interesting titbit or two."

"Richard..." Darcy shook his head.

"Indeed, the fool has spoken enough!" Lady Catherine spat. "What manner of falsehood he means to tell now, I care not. We return to the present matter, which—"

"Catherine, you may save your breath to cool your porridge," the earl grumbled. "Darcy has proof of where he was, and this... costume... he wears.... Nothing but madness or desperation would have found him in public so attired."

"Then madness it is! It matters not what occurred last night. I am determined to see him do his duty, for he has delayed for years!" She whirled next on him. "Think you that I have no other means of seeing this done?"

Darcy felt a cold stab of fear in his stomach. Had they, after all, uncovered some knowledge of Georgiana's error? Was there some leverage his aunt and cousin were prepared to wield against him? He spared a short glance at Richard, who was shaking his head in some denial, but it was little comfort.

"And how is it, Nephew," her ladyship expounded, "that you abandoned all thought for what was proper and went instead to Vauxhall Gardens? This is all a fabrication to escape your duty to Anne. Miss Bennet a lady, you claim! Was your intent to bind your honour up to another so that this Mr Gardiner's demands might be heard over my own? Who is he, that his sentiments bear any consideration?"

"Aunt Catherine," Darcy's tones were hard as ice, "leave my house at once."

"Darcy, you cannot order your own aunt, a peeress by birth and my own sister, to do anything."

"I can, and I have. She has insulted me in every possible way, and I do not desire to speak with her again."

All in the room fell silent before his cold, bitter pronouncement. And well they might! Had he not always kept the peace, sought to please his mother's relations and made concessions even at the expense of his own wishes? But this betrayal, this was the fracture that would sever the genial fellowship the Fitzwilliams and Darcys had long enjoyed. He glanced at his uncle, for the earl alone possessed the sense and the capacity to extend an olive branch.

The silence was broken, however, not by the earl but by a high, keening wail. He raised a brow and cynically appraised Anne. She had been weeping for some minutes, but now her sensibilities overcame her, and she was heaving and snivelling into a handkerchief.

"F-Fitzw-williamm!" she gasped, fanning herself and stumbling as if she would faint. "Y-you cannot b-b-blame m-m-meeee! It was all Mama's idea—"

"How dare!" hissed Lady Catherine. "Wicked, treacherous girl! You would turn upon me when it was I who attempted to save you?"

Darcy looked curiously at his uncle, then to Richard, but found no help there.

"I told you he would not cooperate, Mama," Anne whimpered. "He is too cruel and stubborn, he has never cared what should become of me!"

"If you had not been such a manipulative little fool, you could have secured him properly!" snapped Lady Catherine.

"I beg your pardon," Darcy interrupted, "but I have been clear for years that I had no intentions toward Anne. I am offended and astonished that not only would you persist in this scheme, but that the pair of you would stoop to such deceitful means to achieve your ends. Anne, could you expect to have merited my respect, had you succeeded in ensnaring me for life? Would you truly have wished to spend an entire marriage hearing my honest opinions of your actions? And Aunt Catherine," he turned a withering glance upon that lady, "I can but think you motivated by something truly horrendous if you could justify betraying me in such a devious manner."

"You forced my hand, Darcy!" she scowled. "Had you only done your duty in the first, *years ago*, Anne would never have been permitted—"

"*Mother!*"

Lady Catherine narrowed her eyes. "It was not *my* doing, after all."

"*One* of you two," interrupted the earl, "explain at once!"

"I believe I might be able to offer something of an explanation," Richard broke in. "Darcy, there is a most interesting fellow just in the hall who wishes to speak with you. He had just arrived almost at the same moment as Mr Gardiner and myself, and I believe he ought to be heard." He flicked his head toward the door, and Wilson, who had been among the horde of followers when Mr Gardiner arrived, opened it.

The man who entered was short, with a thinning pate of hair, a wiry, athletic frame, and quick movements. He glanced once to Lady Catherine, whose eyes flared in rage, and then paused more lingeringly on Anne. Before either lady could speak to discredit their visitor, the earl himself had gestured, unequivocally, for silence. This appeared to set the man at some ease. He quickly identified Darcy as the master of the house and presented himself in due course.

"Sir, my name is George Barrett. You may well be familiar with my name, as I am one of the principal owners of Vauxhall Gardens."

Darcy looked quizzically to Richard, then back again to Mr Barrett. "That is a singular coincidence."

"Indeed, sir. I understand you have just come from there. I do hope the venue pleased."

"I think it the most enjoyable day there… or anywhere… in my memory," he answered quietly. "But what brings you here, sir?"

"Mr Darcy, you will think me decidedly forward, but I had rather suspected that you would be reluctant to provide the means which were sought by Lady Catherine and Miss de Bourgh. I am well acquainted with the ladies, and last summer I enjoyed the company of Miss de Bourgh, particularly, when we were both taking the waters at Bath for our health.

"Before you rush to any conclusions," Barrett held up a hand, "I have no improper relationship with Miss de Bourgh. Through a series of rather unfortunate encounters with the landlord—I was a guest in the same hotel and more than once found myself in the midst of the affair—I learned something of the ladies' circumstances."

At this juncture, Lady Catherine emitted a loud cry of outrage. "Lies! You would slander and impugn a daughter of nobility—"

"Catherine! I will hear the man," the earl warned.

Barrett smiled tightly and turned back to Darcy. "I presume you are aware that the de Bourgh coffers are all but bankrupt?"

"I… was not, in fact." Darcy watched his uncle for his response, but only discerned a faint tightening to his cheek. "I advise on many matters at Rosings, but I am not privy to my aunt's personal financial affairs." He paused, allowing his aunt the dignity of making some response, but her only answer was to cross her arms and look pointedly at her daughter.

Anne sighed and shrugged. "I follow the horse racing. I have for years, as there is little given to me for amusement. I have never seen a race, for Mama says my health would not withstand the exposure to the weather, but I did buy some rather fine horses."

Darcy shook his head in confusion. "How is this pertinent to the matter at hand? We all own fine horses. How many did you purchase?"

Anne puckered her lips and rolled her eyes toward the ceiling. Lady Catherine merely continued to glower at her, but Barrett gently cleared his throat.

"I understand there were at least seventy horses, all totalled, from the beginning," he answered quietly. "One less conservative estimate is more than double that figure, but the numbers are not reliable. Miss de Bourgh broke down one evening at the pump rooms and shared the entire tale. It seems she had brought on a dishonest racing steward."

"Anne?" the earl asked. "Does he speak the truth?"

She huffed and sniffled, her hands gesticulating helplessly. "He said he loved me! He was always saying nice things to me. He said the horses I bought were not selling for fair prices or winning good purses because they were no good or needed better feed. Fool, I! I bought him everything he asked for, and he sold it all and pocketed the money. And then when I discovered it and confronted him, his solution was to offer marriage, for he claimed that an invalid and a lady such as I could never expose him without publicly ruining myself. What was I to do? I had reached the bottom of Rosings' reserves!"

Darcy could not have been more astounded if Anne had casually announced that she was, in fact, with child as he had originally feared. He cocked an eyebrow toward Richard, who merely shrugged back in open-mouthed astonishment.

If this came to light! Not only Anne would be humiliated, but with her all her male relations who had the place of advising her and preserving her from ruin—most particularly himself, the presumed betrothed who did nothing in the eyes of the world to stop the charlatan from taking her for all she had. Little wonder his aunt had claimed some further leverage upon his pride!

"Sir," Barrett interjected, "I have offered a sensible solution, one which would see the ladies safely into financial security and would answer for my own wish to seek an establishment. I fancy the weather and the setting in Kent and have offered to lease Rosings for a rather handsome sum. The ladies might preserve their annuities and retrench, and I would assume the responsibility of the estate.

"I am not a married man, sir, but I hope one day to alter that circumstance, and I have resources enough to take my leisure at present. A sensible man would have given in at the first refusal, but one who is perfectly aware of the advantages on all sides and determined to prevail, may, I confess, seem rather foolish in his quest. I presume, sir, that it is not your pleasure to marry Miss de Bourgh? If I trespass, then I shall beg your forgiveness and withdraw at once, but as I believed I might yet be the best means of recovery for the ladies...."

"You are correct." Darcy glared across the room at his aunt, then his cousin, and received back a look which could have scalded water. "Barrett, if you will be so good as to call tomorrow, we can discuss terms. Lady Catherine and Miss de Bourgh *will* be receptive of your offer," he informed them all.

"Thank you, Mr Darcy," Barrett bowed. He paused just before Anne, offered a half smile which was not returned with quite so much grace, and then took his leave.

Darcy merely stared at his cousin. For her part, she bore it without flinching, and in fact gazed serenely back as if waiting for some sort of apology. There were all manner of questions he must now ask, but the why, the when, and the how of the de Bourgh ladies' reversal of fortune was not entirely a matter for his interference. Nor, thought he bitterly, was he in any humour at present to perform the service. Let the constable hear the rest of that tale! There was one thing, however, that he would make clear.

"Aunt Catherine, Anne," he glared between them, "I will not be so discourteous as to turn you out without friend or help. Take care—my patience has already been tried, so what I offer is not to be negotiated. I shall provide a modest allowance for you to live on. Five hundred per year should be more than sufficient for two ladies even with your accustomed manner of living, particularly if you should remove to Bath. I will actively promote marriage prospects for my cousin, but you are both to understand that the groom shall never be myself. My help is not unconditional, for if so much as a whisper of suspicion against my character *or* Miss Bennet's honour ever reaches other ears, my support shall undergo an immediate and very embarrassing seizure. Am I quite understood?"

Cowed at last, both Lady Catherine and Anne now stared at one another. "Your terms," Lady Catherine's voice wavered, "are... generous... nephew." She looked as if she wished to cleanse herself of his acquaintance, but it was enough, and he drew back, satisfied.

"Catherine, Anne," the earl intoned gravely, "my carriage is waiting outside. I would advise you both to take advantage of the countess' hospitality this evening. Darcy and I have some matters to discuss regarding your circumstances and the disposition of Rosings, and I fancy it will require you to remain as our guests at least a few days."

Darcy nodded his thanks to his uncle, but the sight of Wilson, standing patiently behind Richard, recalled him to one more detail he must attend in his aunt's presence before any of his house could begin to function again. "Wilson," he gestured to the man, "recount, if you please, your discovery of last evening."

Darcy had the dubious pleasure of again watching the colour rise in his aunt's face as Wilson, with humble simplicity, laid before them his discovery of the drug in his master's drink and the subsequent plans for his ruination.

"Lies!" the lady spat, "Outright slander! And you would believe the word of this intoxicated servant, one who is not fit to clean the fire grate, over that of your own aunt? He has taken advantage of my fall from grace for his own aggrandisement!"

Darcy was not required to answer, for at this moment, Dawson entered with Mrs White, the housekeeper, and Mrs Fuller, the head cook. He evaluated each coolly, but not a hint of embarrassment shone on either woman's face until he began to speak.

"Mr Dawson, have you ever received gratuities or gifts from anyone besides myself?"

The butler appeared to be holding his breath. He spared a reluctant glance toward Lady Catherine, whose eyes narrowed threateningly, but then his gaze faltered, and his courage broke. "Yes, sir," he confessed. "Christmas and Easter gifts, and a few other occasions. Many times over the years, in honour of Lady Anne Darcy, of course."

At this, the accused began to sputter. "Is it not my right to be kind to those who served my beloved sister? She was always excessively fond of everyone here at the townhouse, far more so than anywhere else, and expressed to me on her deathbed her wish that they be rewarded by our family for all their kindnesses to her. Should such a burden fall on her son, newly master of the household at such a young age? Indeed, such a thing would be most unfitting, and so I determined to see it done with as little trouble to yourself as possible. You see, Darcy, the obligations undertaken on your behalf!"

"And Mrs White," Darcy continued as if he had not heard, "how long have you been employed in this house?"

The woman paled. "Twenty-three years next April, sir."

He smiled kindly. "Then you are nearing the age for receiving your pension. I believe we have spoken of this before, have we not? And had you any cause to be dissatisfied with what was offered?"

She looked down. "No, sir."

"But am I correct in my assumption that you have accepted a second offering from another quarter?"

She visibly swallowed, casting another guilty glance toward Lady Catherine. "You are, sir."

"Mrs Fuller, is there any need to ask these same questions of you?"

The cook had refused to raise her sullen eyes, and Darcy could see that her cheeks were quite red. "No, sir," was the unhappy reply.

"I will expect resignation letters from all three of you on my desk this very evening. Mr Hodges and Mrs Reynolds will arrive from Pemberley by the end of next week, and you may continue in your duties and receive your pay until they relieve you. Thank you, that will be all. Wilson, you may retire, and take tomorrow as a holiday."

"Excellent advice," his uncle clapped him on the shoulder as the rest of the party began to withdraw. "Forgive me for not believing you before, Darcy. A devil of a day you must have had! You look as if you could use a holiday yourself."

Darcy felt his shoulders sag, the tension of battle draining away and leaving only a hollow ache behind. "I have already had a holiday, Uncle. I could not survive another."

Thirty-two

"Uncle, please, say *something*!" Elizabeth pressed her back against the squab of her uncle's carriage and cringed, waiting for the accusations she deserved.

Mr Gardiner sighed, stretching his tall frame in the very seat where drugged, helpless Fitzwilliam Darcy had been crammed only the night before. "Lizzy, what shall I say? Dare I congratulate you on losing Collins as a suitor? On having the grand adventure in Town you longed for? What have you gained for your wantonness?"

She shifted her toes on the floor. "It was not what it must seem, Uncle."

"Then pray, tell me, Elizabeth, what am I to think? Did you go with this man willingly and alone? Do you truly think that simply because he was not dressed as a gentleman, no one will ever speak of it? That it will not become the tittle-tattle of London?"

"I know you doubt me, but I believe my reputation is safe. Even Mr Collins will be too intimidated to speak, for what you and Mr Darcy both threatened him with was sufficient to inspire a mortal terror in him."

"He is certainly not the only person who could testify to your foolishness. I mean to call on this Mr Darcy again to see what must be done to ensure that nothing more is said."

"Oh, Uncle, please do not! It would be more harmful to his interests even than ours, if anything comes of it, and what more unavoidable way than to intrude upon his notice again? Would that not generate intrigue, if someone is indeed seeking to create a scandal? Better to let the matter rest and have nothing more to do with him, for good or ill."

"You seem to place a great deal of faith in your understanding of the man. How do you have such confidence in his discretion?"

Her lip curved, her shoulder tipped, and she shook her head. "I spent more hours learning his character than I have with any other man outside of you or Papa. I saw him at his lowest. He was not always agreeable, which I took as evidence of his truthfulness. I should not have trusted him so, had he flattered my vanity from the outset, but he never did. I believe him to be genuine, Uncle."

"A wealthy gentleman masquerading as a servant! You think him free of deceit and guile?"

"More so than anyone I have ever known. You are perhaps right to doubt, Uncle, but I believe my faith in him will not be unjustified. If there is any threat to my reputation or his, it will not be because he did not guard it."

Mr Gardiner shook his head. "I still cannot understand why you would undertake such chicanery. You will claim it was all done out of charity, to help some poor soul who was put upon by his wicked relations, or perhaps excuse yourself by saying you wished to avoid Collins at home, but Lizzy, think of what might have happened!"

"Nothing did happen, Uncle. I never had any fear that anything would, either."

He kneaded his eyes, and she felt a stab of pity. Her poor, weary uncle, and after his terrible day, he had been forced to reckon with her crisis! "Tell me what you were thinking, Lizzy. You are a sensible girl, or I always thought you to be. How hard is it for a cad to work upon an intelligent young lady?"

"He is no cad. Perhaps that is where one must begin. I do not pretend that I am infallible, Uncle, but in nearly every way, he was the perfect gentleman and guardian."

"'Nearly' every way? What was this chink in his shining livery?"

Every remembrance of pleasure fled. Before her, she could still drink in his tender look, see his loving eyes half closed, feel the soft brush of his mouth, and hear the ardent plea in his voice. And then, that insulting offer, that dash of salt on her exposed heart, and that proof that he was not, after all, the complete fulfilment of the image she had crafted for him.

"Lizzy? What sort of face is that? He must have offended you in *some* way or another."

She shook her head. "Nothing of import, Uncle. A gentleman is still a man, after all, and I suppose none of them are perfect."

"Knaves and wretches, to a man. Remember that, Lizzy, when you do marry, and give the poor soul the same generosity of spirit you seem to have bestowed on this Darcy fellow. By the by, you must still inform your father of this on Friday when you go home. When he learns of it, I doubt you shall be permitted out of Longbourn's drawing room until the day your parents find you a husband, and God help you all in that search. I hope it all comes right, Lizzy. I am sorry to say that we shall have to curtail any further plans you had for amusement while here in Town."

She leaned her head against the glass as the city rolled by. "I have seen enough of London for a lifetime, Uncle. It was a holiday I shall never forget."

~

The house on Gracechurch street looked the same as it had two days earlier. For no reason he could describe, this struck Darcy as novel. Why should everything not be different? He was admitted with little ceremony and duly presented his card for Mr Gardiner.

As he waited, he would have been a cur not to confess that his ears strained for any sound from the family rooms or the stair. Was *she* still a resident of the house? Or had she already made her return to Hertfordshire, where she must be once again lodged in the apartment above some humble Meryton shop? Perhaps her father was the local bookseller—that would account for her great literacy and intelligence. Or perhaps a curate, or a steward for some generous landowner—either would have taught her that consideration for others and her understanding and sense.

No sound was forthcoming, save the scraping of a door behind him, where Mr Gardiner himself stood to welcome him into the study. "Mr Darcy," he offered a slight, but respectful bow. "Please, do come in."

"Thank you for seeing me, Mr Gardiner." Darcy followed the man and was shown to a perfectly suitable study, lined with various sorts of books and furnished with understated quality. Darcy glanced about with approval and accepted the seat which was offered.

"Mr Darcy," Gardiner began, "I must say, I remain curious about the events of two days ago. How was it that when I was not to be found, you and my niece took it upon yourselves to wait elsewhere and without any sort of chaperon? Why should her safety and her reputation have been jeopardised as they were?"

Darcy's toes curled within his boots. "These are fair questions, sir. Miss Elizabeth must already have informed you of her desire to avoid the house and the reason for it."

"Indeed, and while I can hardly blame her, I cannot condone either her actions or yours. If she was so desirous of avoiding Collins, she could have remained within her room rather than taking up with a stranger."

"Mr Gardiner, I understand and accept your accusations of ungentlemanly conduct. Allow me to assure you that Miss Elizabeth has earned my highest respect, and I sought to protect her, and her reputation, as vigilantly as I do my own sister's."

Gardiner studied him gravely. "Why did you come to speak to me today, Mr Darcy? I have already sent a signed statement to the earl, concurring with your account of having passed the night in this house rather than your own. What more would you request?"

"I came to offer my gratitude," he answered in a quiet voice. "Both to yourself and to Miss Elizabeth, if I may."

"Lizzy is upstairs even now, preparing for her departure. She leaves for Hertfordshire within the hour, and when I asked if she would receive company, she declined."

Darcy felt as if all the air had rushed from his lungs and could not understand why. Had he really counted so desperately upon seeing her one last time? "I am sorry to hear that," he managed, a little roughly. He looked down to his hands, uncertain what he was next to say.

"Lizzy will naturally inform her family of her... high jinks. However, from all I can see, her reputation has been spared. I understand you protected her adequately both while in Town and in the presence of your own relations. For that, I must owe you something of my own gratitude, though I have not forgotten that you were the man to have placed her at risk. I presume your own circumstances have been brought to order?"

He released a low sigh. "Not so thoroughly as I would wish. My character has been cleared, with much gratitude to yourself, but there remain certain unavoidable matters which demand the exercise of duty."

Gardiner frowned. "May I wish you the very best in your endeavours, sir." He rose, signalling that the interview was over.

"If I may ask one thing, sir," Darcy interjected as he stood. "Miss Elizabeth—her prospects are not in any way damaged?"

Gardiner permitted a twitch of his cheek. "I daresay no more than they already were by matters which were beyond her control. You may be easy, sir, for my niece assured me that she would not seek any sort of recompense from you for the risks she undertook. You are free to concern yourself only with your duty to your own family."

Darcy drew a slow breath of freedom... and it stabbed him like an arrow. "I... I understand."

"Good day, Mr Darcy."

Darcy bowed his farewell and moved toward the door. His feet were numb, even more so than when they had been pinched and blistered by the wrong shoes. It was as if they simply refused to carry him away from *her*, but his mind had decreed that he was to go, and so his body shuffled on without them. Could he not have at least bade her farewell?

A noise sounded on the stair, and he turned in that direction full of hope. It was only two men, carrying a travelling trunk down the steps. He closed his eyes, then one last desperate attempt turned him back.

"Mr Gardiner, sir, Miss Elizabeth informed me that you take pleasure in the Lake District. When next you journey North, I hope you will consider stopping in Derbyshire."

The man's face warmed. "We always spend a day or two, at least. Mrs Gardiner lived many years in Lambton, sir, and she frequently toured Pemberley as a girl. She took me back there last year, and a fine estate it is."

"Indeed! Lambton? I hope you shall someday visit again. I understand you are a proficient angler, and I would be honoured to provide you with tackle and bait if you should like to try my trout stream or the lake."

"I thank you, Mr Darcy, perhaps I shall."

Gardiner offered no more than this cautious acceptance, and there was nothing else he could think to say to delay his departure. With one more conscious sweep of the doors and corridors of the house, Darcy surrendered. "I hope so, sir. Good day."

~

"He asked after me?" Elizabeth sat down heavily in the padded chair opposite her uncle. "I am surprised."

"Why should you be? Mr Darcy is known to be a gentleman, and I believe he took an interest in your welfare. It was no less than one would expect, after all."

She shook her head, slightly dazed. "I simply did not expect to hear of him ever again. I thought your business was complete, and he had sent that handsome box of cigars and brandy in a show of his appreciation."

"Those were for me. Ladies do not often value a good smoke or drink so well as they do a kind word, and he came to offer it. Altogether, Lizzy, I suppose it could have been far worse. You could have been found with a rake."

"I knew he was not a rake from the first, Uncle," she tried to smile. "But I cannot decide whether I am pleased that he called or not. It is at an end, is it not? Nothing more can come, and I always did hate farewells. They seem the end of everything pleasant and hopeful. I am glad I did not come down before when he was here."

"It was for the best," her uncle agreed. "A dreadful risk you took, Lizzy, but I suppose when you were already facing Collins as your best prospect, the fanciful mind of a young lady feels there is no farther to sink."

"I was wrong. I know that, Uncle. You and my aunt have been gentler than I deserve."

"Perhaps that is because your foolishness was in the service of another, or perhaps because your aunt has a touch of sentiment for Mr Darcy's family.

They've a good reputation in Derbyshire, you know, and though she would die before confessing it, I believe she was flattered that one of our family did a good turn for they who have always been so good to others."

"I see." Elizabeth twined her fingers and hesitated. "And Mr Darcy... has it all come right for him? Did he speak on that at all?"

"He said that he still had a duty to his family and did not seem best pleased to be fulfilling that obligation."

"Oh." Elizabeth's fingers clenched one another until the knuckles were white. At that moment, she resolved not to look at her father's papers for at least six months, or as long as it would take for all the gossip and marriage announcements to die away. Poor Mr Darcy, after all his dread and proven innocence, to be bound by the one who had entrapped him! That such a good and noble man must be sentenced to a life with one who respected him so little seemed to her nothing less than a statement of the general unfairness of the world.

"Excuse me, Uncle," she whispered, "I think I must finish my preparations for departure."

"Of course, Lizzy. I am sorry I cannot go with you, but your aunt will offer whatever support or counsel you might require when you return home."

She nodded, sensing a blockade of tears threatening to spill from her eyes if she tried to blink. "Thank you, Uncle."

~

The streets of London were grey as she looked out upon them. No character remained to be experienced that she had not already savoured, no prospect illuminated her way that she had not previously shared with better company. She suspected it would always be so, for once a light is kindled, then extinguished, the observer is forever after aware of the present darkness of their surroundings. Would that she could remain in that vibrant place, full of colour and life! There had been a way; he had spoken of it, asked her if she would—

But no... to do so would be to sacrifice her character, her integrity—all she had left. She could not do it, even for him, and he would not love her for it, even if he thought himself satisfied. She would not remain herself, and he would have been the cause.

Even then, she had sensed the notion was as shocking to him as it was to herself. He did not *seem* the sort of man to ask for *carte blanche*, and he had even defended her from that accusation before his family. However, his desires had been obvious, and had clearly shaken him so, that when he acknowledged that he could not have her by honourable means, any alternative might have presented itself in the moment as eligible. Surely, he had already thought better of it, and she had made up her mind to forgive him for it... so long as she never had to look on him again.

He would be married, and likely very soon. Another woman would be his comfort, would hold her babe and see *his* eyes gazing back… Elizabeth stifled a gasp and hoped her aunt and sister did not notice that she would only look out the window as the carriage rolled through the city.

Yes, she could live without Fitzwilliam Darcy. So long as she never had to face him again.

Thirty-three

"Lizzy, dear, I am so glad you are home!" Jane Bennet was the only family member to greet the travellers at the door, but her sincere pleasure at receiving her sisters and her aunt made up for whatever might have been lacking from their parents and other sister.

Elizabeth kissed her elder sister on the cheek and offered a wan smile. "Jane, have you been keeping well? Has it been very trying here? I am so sorry you could not have come with us!"

Jane gave a dismissive little wave of her hand, but her tone was not nearly so light as it might have been. "Mama has been keeping to her room, and Papa only emerges from the library to remind Mary that her governess is to arrive soon. Mary has not ceased crying in a fortnight."

At this, Kitty emitted a loud groan and began to pout. "And I suppose I shall have to be under her authority as well! It is not as if *I* have done anything wrong. I shall have to spend my days playing the pianoforte with Mary and never attending another ball for two more years!"

Mrs Gardiner turned to speak some low words of remonstrance to her younger niece, but they went unheeded. Kitty gave her coat and bonnet into Mr Hill's hands, then lumbered off with a petulant sigh to her own room.

Elizabeth was quickly divesting herself of her own outerwear and leading Jane aside to the sitting room for a private interview. "And Lydia? Have you had word of her?"

"Only once. I understand she is not permitted to write often, but the last letter sounded as if that place is perfectly horrid."

Elizabeth sighed and shook her head. "I wish she did not have to go there! Perhaps... well, I hope someday she might come home again."

"Do you mean after one or two of us are securely married? Perhaps then Papa will suffer her to come back?"

Elizabeth tried to smile, but it looked more like a grimace. "Perhaps, yes, that is what I mean."

"Mama was simply determined that you would come home engaged, or at least with one or two fine prospects. Did you meet any gentleman while you were out with Aunt? I hear that uncle has a number of acquaintances—a few promising young clerks and solicitors, he says. They are not gentlemen, of course," Jane patted her sister's shoulder, "but must a man be a gentleman to be agreeable?"

Elizabeth felt her aunt's eyes on her, and she shook her head. "No. I did not meet anyone, gentleman or otherwise."

"Oh, well," Jane dismissed her fears, with perhaps more philosophy than confidence. "Our new neighbour, Mr Bingley, is settled in now. I am sure you must have heard all about it. Mama is quite dispirited though, for Papa simply refuses to visit him, but I am in hopes that it is not too late to meet him one day. There is an Assembly next week, and anyone can be introduced in a ballroom. And surely a young single gentleman might have some friends, so we are not without hope."

"Jane," chided Elizabeth, "I cannot abide such talk! Is the seeking of a husband to be the only conversation worth having? Are we to speak of nothing else now but single men and assemblies? Are we to forget entirely that we are rational creatures, capable of thinking and feeling and forming attachments that have nothing to do with fortunes or connections?"

Jane cast a doubtful look to Mrs Gardiner, who shook her head very subtly. If Elizabeth noticed this gesture, she chose to ignore it.

"I am sick to death of the whole business, Jane," she continued. "It is all a sham, and happiness is not for those who desire it, nor even deserve it, but for those who can afford to extort it from others. And who is to know what lies beneath the appearance of goodness? Nay, it is too much, Jane, and I cannot bear speaking of it just now."

"Dearest," Jane ventured hesitantly, "you sound very tired. Perhaps you want to lie down and rest."

"No, Jane, I am not tired. I am weary."

Jane bit her lip, her porcelain brow wrinkling very slightly. "Are they not one and the same?"

"I am afraid not, for one can be cured by slumber, and the other only by some magical ambrosia." Elizabeth turned and accidentally met her aunt's eye. Conviction cast her gaze to the floor, and she spared them each one more forced smile before asking of Jane, "Is Papa in his study?"

"Yes, just as he always is."

"Thank you, Jane. I believe I must speak with him." Elizabeth began to walk away, her eyes still low, but turned back in a moment to fondly touch her sister's cheek. "Dearest Jane, what a relief it is to see you! I wish I had some measure of your goodness. Then, perhaps, I might deserve the happiness I wish for you." She turned away again before Jane could respond, her shoulders stooped in apparent sorrow, and disappeared in the direction of their father's study.

Jane was left to watch after her with an astonished gasp. "What was that all about? Has Lizzy been suffering low spirits all this time over Lydia and Mary?"

Mrs Gardiner sighed and shook her head. "Elizabeth had a rather… unique holiday in London. Perhaps I might say that her experience in Town is one that she is likely to recall with equal measures of sentiment and regret for many years."

"Oh, dear!" Jane cried. "That sounds serious. I hope she has done nothing too shocking."

"That," Mrs Gardiner raised a brow, "would be a mild description."

~

"What do you mean, Lizzy? I cannot understand these words you are saying to me. I think rather they are Lydia's words, but they are coming from your mouth. You do not mean to tell me that *you* have shocked half the *ton*. Indeed, would that I could have seen it! And this great lady Collins admires to the point of folly, did you truly prove such a frustration to her designs? My dearest girl, I cannot think whether I should congratulate you or confine you to your bedroom until you turn eighty. Had this gentleman any notion of the hornet's nest into which he had stepped? Did he presume you would cause him no trouble if he sported with you for the day?"

"Papa it was nothing like that. Well, at least it did not begin like that."

"Elizabeth Marie Bennet, I had thought better of you! At the least, you could have made your mother happy by being seen embracing the man in public. That is how it is done, or so I am told. Think of the jewels and pin money! By the by, is the air balloon ride worth the full shilling?"

"Papa, please do not tease me! The matter is far too grave. I know I have done wrong—I have dashed my chances at respectability when my position was already fragile. Do not, I pray, cast more guilt upon me with these jests!"

"Then I shall perform the requisite rites of fatherhood and demand an accounting of your actions. Will that suit? And, indeed, I am curious. How is it that my one intelligent daughter, the one who is capable of discerning what the others cannot and more determined than any to never fall for empty charm; how is it you are as easily smitten by a bicorn hat and a set of shiny brass buttons as my most foolish child?"

Elizabeth bit her lower lip. "He was not wearing a bicorn hat. It was a rather humble sort, in fact."

Her father rolled his eyes. "Would you care to explain to me how you think you could have escaped such a caper unscathed? And your virtue! Shall I be doubting that?"

"Papa!"

"Well, the question had to be asked. Tell me the plain truth, Lizzy. How many will be speaking of this, and is there some detail that must be covered up, so that the Bennet name does not become a byword for loose females?"

"Only my aunt and uncle are familiar with the details. Kitty does not even know the full tale. Mr Collins is far too ashamed of his own behaviour to breathe a word—and the... the gentleman threatened him, on pain of divestiture, should he in any way betray his knowledge of the affair."

"You are lucky then. Elizabeth, I never thought I would have to say something like this to you, but I am afraid I must insist you marry almost immediately. You are too old for Mary and Kitty's schoolroom, and I cannot afford to send another daughter off to join Lydia, even if I wished it. But you *must* wed, and straightaway. If word of this should spread—"

"I know, Papa. Please do not remind me! I shall do my duty and marry the first man to approach me, if any such man should exist."

"I fear it shall be a come down in the world for you to secure someone quickly... at least you are spared Collins, but I do not know who can be brought up to scratch. The one we find might well be more insufferable than he! I will speak to your Uncle Philips, perhaps he knows of a shopkeeper in need of a clever wife. Good heavens, Lizzy, it pains me to do this, but you leave me no option!"

"I know it is all my own doing, and I freely accept the consequences. Make whatever arrangements you wish, and I will abide by your choice. Pray, seek the most respectable match you can. It is not for myself, but I would not see Jane suffer, nor Kitty and Mary."

Her father snorted. "Mary shall be facing a similar choice to yourself, most likely."

"You know that nonsense with Lydia was not her fault, Papa. Is there not some redemption for her?"

He frowned. "Mary is only seventeen. I have yet a little time before I must decide what is to be done with her, and perhaps by that time you and Jane will have secured respectable matches, and some of it will be forgotten."

Elizabeth stared at the floor. "I understand, Papa. May I go to my room now?"

"Aye, and do not show your face again for a month."

"Yes, Papa," she muttered in dejection, moving slowly toward the door.

"But you must come out again to sit with your mother in the drawing room every morning, in case any should call on us. And be certain that you are ready for next Thursday's assembly! Your mother will not tolerate your absence from that occasion."

Elizabeth groaned.

Thirty-four

"Wish me farewell for these three weeks," Colonel Fitzwilliam announced himself at the door to Darcy's study. "I am off to Bath to set up Aunt Catherine and Anne in their new establishment."

Darcy looked up from the letter he was writing to Georgiana. "The duty fell to you? I had thought your father was to escort them."

"He made the initial inquiries, but I am to be the whipping boy. It is the price I must pay to keep in Mother's good graces, for my own prospects depend upon her skill at morning calls—and, of course, the allowance from her fortune which is one day to become mine."

"I hope you survive the journey unscathed, then. Be certain not to drink any brandy you are offered, or you may wake up to a different sort of prospect altogether."

"I shall heed your advice! And what of you, Darcy? There is still some talk, but it is largely dying away, and more quickly than I might have expected. Are you feeling the consequences of the debacle?"

"In some measure, but the momentary discomfort of the exposure does not begin to compare to a lifetime with a wife I could not respect."

Richard dropped into a chair. "Is there such a woman, Darcy? I have never enquired about your women—"

"There has never been any cause to."

"Quite so. But now there is, and a rather fetching one at that. Do you intend to keep up your acquaintance with Miss Bennet?"

Darcy sighed and dropped his pen. "She is from trade. Surely, the question does not bear asking."

"Fitzwilliam Darcy of Pemberley might agree with you, but I see another man before me—a man who was rather smitten by a pair of fine eyes and an honest heart. Can you deny that you took pleasure in the time you spent with her?"

Darcy rose and began to pace. "I have never understood it possible to enjoy a woman's company so. She is one I could call a friend, and more than that, even. I respect her, as I do very few others."

"Are you certain that is all? She blushed rather hotly in your presence during that fracas the other evening. Can you truly tell me you have done nothing to entrap yourself?"

He shifted his shoulders inside his tight coat and looked anywhere but at Richard's face. "I cannot. Viewed in a prudential light, her uncle has every right to make demands of me for even a fraction of the day's events. But I called on him again, and I was calmly assured that the family intends nothing of the kind. She would not impose, which is yet another example of her goodness. Do not lecture me, as I see you are prepared to do. Every feeling of justice and honour objects, but she is correct. It would not work, it could not work!"

"Yet you enjoyed her company, and as more than a friend. Perhaps something else could be worked out? There are many ways in which a man may choose to enjoy female companionship. You desire her, do you not?"

"How could I not? Though it took me some while to confess it, even to myself, I could easily call her the handsomest woman of my acquaintance."

"Then you must contrive some way to keep her near! Set her up with a pretty little cottage in the country, or better yet, an apartment in Marylebone. It would be just the thing."

"I have never kept a mistress, as you well know. It did not seem fitting while my father lived, for in his tender sentiments, every woman was to be compared to my mother, faults and virtues alike. I could not... there would have been none worthy of notice, and certainly none so appealing as to make me wish to see his disappointment in me. It was even less fitting when Father died, and I became guardian to a young girl. It was necessary that I might have shown my face to her as a figure she could respect, a man of honour. I could not set such an example for her."

"Poppycock! Blame your father and Georgiana, will you? You never had a mistress because you are a sentimental prude."

"I would not term myself so."

"Father has accused you of it for years. You always talked of marriage, when you could be induced to talk about it at all, as placing some special importance on adoration for your mate."

"I had said it was important that one be able to regard and admire his prospective mate. I most certainly did not use the word 'adore.'"

"It is the same thing in your mind. Come now, what are you going to do about this young lady of inferior birth, of whom you cannot cease thinking? I cannot see why you do not simply make her your mistress."

"For Miss Bennet…" he mused, stroking his chin and staring at the floor, "I could almost be persuaded to the arrangement. But no, it would never do. It would shame her, I know this very well. It would kill that unpretentious honour and genuine integrity which I love about her character."

"So, you do love her!"

"I did not say that. I said I admire her character.'

"No, you very clearly used the word 'love.' I have never heard you use that word, even to describe your feelings for Georgina."

"What matters the verb? I esteem her highly, and I am concerned for her situation. If her family truly is in disgrace, and with little means or standing to recommend them, there will be great difficulty in securing a respectable marriage for her or any of her sisters. I would not see her sunk to a low match, or even to become the mistress of another man. Perhaps I could persuade a gentleman of honour to consider her as his bride. Would you?"

"Indeed not, for I have just come from Miss Wakeford's father and asked permission to call on his daughter more frequently when I am returned from Bath. With Mother also working on my side of the affair, I am not without hope. Eight thousand pounds, Darcy, and a pleasant face to match! I would be a fool to cry off."

Darcy ceased his pacing to choose a chair opposite Richard, all the better to divert his energies from walking to thinking. "Well… perhaps Bingley might be brought up to scratch. He is fixed to settle in Hertfordshire already, and an introduction might not be difficult to arrange. Yes, now that I think of it, he would do very nicely for her. Certainly, he could do better in terms of fortune, but his position is not so delicate as mine, and he cannot object so strongly to her station. For himself, he is amiable and respectable, he would never treat her ill, and he is easily enough persuaded that I can make him see her virtues."

"And why would he do that? Why should Bingley oblige you so that he would let you have the choosing of his bride?"

"Indeed," replied Darcy testily, "he must see it! He is no fool, but he is perfectly eager to marry. He will no doubt be induced to it by some country girl or another once he is settled in Hertfordshire. Why should it not be Miss Bennet? Once he meets her, talks to her as I have, he cannot help but acknowledge for himself that she is without her equal among women."

"Why don't you just admit it, Darcy? You are head over ears for her, and you will never be content seeing her in the arms of another man."

Darcy lurched back to his feet, for his efforts at avoiding eye contact with his cousin were failing at every one of Richard's shocking insistences. "I would be content to see her well off," he retorted. "And I would be doing a service for a friend! How many women are so genuine, so unaffectedly transparent, yet possess her quality of poise and dignity? I can count them on one hand. Nay, less than that! She is the sort of woman who would make a man proud of his own manhood by her regard."

"Oh! She is a passionate sort of woman, is she?"

Darcy made a sour face and would have slapped his cousin, had he not been quite so far across the room. "That is not at all what I meant."

"Then what did you mean? Does she pander to your rather inflated sense of self? Compliment you excessively?"

Darcy resumed pacing, desiring to sort his impressions and to express them in words. "Quite the opposite, in fact. I have never met another woman with her quiet sort of confidence. She did not feel the need to praise herself before me, nor me to myself. She is intelligent enough to know her own mind, as well as her own place in the world, and she treated me with the respectful sort of amity that one might grant to... I cannot think of any near comparison. Perhaps she treated me as a friend, rather than a prize. Yes, perhaps that is it. When we spoke, she was speaking to me, not my position, though I am quite certain she knew something of my true situation almost from the beginning.

"And she was kind, in a way I have rarely seen. Never for a moment did she give the sense that she would submit to another out of weakness, but the way she so gently permitted me to be her protector for the day, deferring to me when she could manage perfectly well on her own... it was as if she were according me an honour, and such it became, to be chosen as the man graced with her companionship. It was a heady experience. How could any man not crave the regard of such a woman?" He turned to face his cousin, a challenge in his voice.

Richard had crossed his legs in his chair and leaned forward now, his elbow upon his knee and his hand brushing his chin. "Indeed," he mused. "How could any not? And this treasure of a woman, you would pass into the keeping of another man?"

"Do not think it my preference. Were matters different—even slightly!—I would not struggle so. I care nothing for a fortune, and even some sort of family embarrassment might be hushed up and forgotten in time with the right resources and prestige to countermand it. But you know well her position, as does she! She comes from a family in trade, and that, the *ton* will never forgive. I think not only of myself, but of the cuts she would face in society. No, she was perfectly right when she bade her farewell. She knows her place in the world, and it is not in mine."

"Mmm," Richard nodded thoughtfully. "Yes, I see your point. Well, you have thought it all out, and I congratulate you, Darcy. Matters will be settled according to everyone's benefit, and you do not have the trouble of offending your relations or society. We must keep them happy at all costs, eh? One never knows when their interference in your private affairs might be beneficial, and they certainly deserve your unmitigated accommodation. Cannot have anyone about to rumple feathers, you know! And since you have this sorted without my help..." he trailed off and grunted, shifting himself out of his chair and to his feet.

Darcy frowned. "Where are you going?"

"Back to my own bed, of course. I must face our aunt in the morning and try to persuade her not to tuck Anne into my arms at some point during our travels. For that, I will need at least a little sleep. Did I hear something about some very fine brandy you had about here to help a man rest?"

"You would never make it home," Darcy snorted derisively.

"I would borrow your carriage, of course," Richard winked. "Sleep well, Darcy, and do not forget your own place in the world." He touched his forehead in an irreverent salute and was gone.

His own place in the world! Yes, that was precisely the trouble, was it not? And men of his station did not marry the nieces of Cheapside merchants. At least, not usually. Surely, not more than one or two. Three, perhaps. He rubbed his eyes.

And whom among his family was he trying to please? Certainly not Lady Catherine. Perhaps not the earl and countess, for though he did not prefer to be at odds with them, their motives were not his own.

But Georgiana… she would need a steady sister, one who could counsel her and encourage her, one who could navigate Society and charm the mothers of sons, one who could mentor her as she prepared to make her curtsy. And naturally, such a woman could not have come from trade! How many such women were accepted at court? Certainly, not more than one had been presented. Two perhaps. Three at the utmost.

Darcy tried to return to his letter, but if he had struggled to express himself before, it was impossible now. He had been thinking to ask Georgiana to come to London, for he could not easily depart for Pemberley until his private affairs were sorted. How long that would be, he could not be certain, but at the very least there was the financial bother with Anne and his aunt and their retrenching.

There were also a new butler and housekeeper to bring on. Mrs Reynolds and Hodges should be arriving from Pemberley soon to oversee the process of replacing the remaining staff, but he would insist on meeting each new hire they recommended. He meant to be the master once again, and this time, he would take care to know each person who worked for him as well as his own friends. After all, it did not take so very long to know someone intimately… one day, to be exact. His head fell between his hands.

Egad, how he wanted her! His cool detachment when speaking with Fitzwilliam was nothing but a sham, for if he had shown even a glimmer of his true preference, he would be on a horse to Hertfordshire within half an hour of the confession. Everything about her, from her easy wit and vivacity to her gentle compassion, her honesty and her resolve… could there be a woman better formed for him? And how easily she had seemed to adapt herself to his peculiarities! Surely, she cared for him. Yet, when he had spoken, she had refused, and when he had called again on her uncle, she would not see him.

Perhaps it had been his address. Something in his manner which bespoke uncertainty, or insincerity. What was it he had said?

"*Some way… I could protect you,*" he had mumbled. Perhaps he was not articulate, but how could that have given offence? "*I know that the relative position of our families would render it disgraceful, but there must be some manner in which we can… perhaps something can be arranged. You would not need to wed that fool.*"

Darcy dropped his hands from his face. Had he truly said *that*? By heaven, she must have thought him to be asking something utterly the reverse of his true intentions! Casually as he had tried to speak when discussing the very subject with Fitzwilliam, every feeling of attachment and civility recoiled at the notion. Make Elizabeth a Cyprian! 'Twould be more loathsome than desecrating the great sculpture of Venus herself, and the man guilty of such a crime, a hundred times more wretched.

How she must have despised him! And again, his single-minded focus on only his own desires, without considering how he must have appeared to her, had dashed him. No man of feeling and consideration could so insult a woman of such integrity, whose happiness and welfare had become as dear to him as his own, by suggesting that she become a Paphian to suit his whims.

And yet, that was what she had understood. Darcy tried to stand, to walk to the fire and stare into it, but he was too nauseated. Weak with self-loathing and reproach, he clutched his eyes and tried to claw from them the vision of her: laughing eyes gazing up to him, full of trust and affection. In one ill-judged blurt of his cursed tongue, he had done away with her regard.

"Elizabeth," he wept into his palm, "forgive me!" Oh! What he would give to have that moment back, to once again cradle her in his embrace for even one of her sweet kisses—long enough to assure her that she was a woman worthy of being pleased, worthy of any man… even himself. No, rather the reverse. He wished he might be worthy of her.

Trade daughter or no, there was no help for it. He loved Elizabeth Bennet— loved her with a devotion that defied all understanding, that could not be accounted for by the single day from which it had sprung. How could he ever accept a substitute? She was, as the old hermit in the Gardens had declared, more than she appeared, and anyone else who failed to recognise her qualities could go hang. "*Lift up thine head; never lookest thee down,*" he had counselled her. Indeed, she ought never have cause to do so!

And what of himself? He was a fool, with a missing heart. It was gone, given freely to an impertinent miss who became ill from too much motion. Perhaps that was one of the things he loved best about her! Perfectly imperfect, and at peace with her flaws. He clutched his head, all the glories and agonies of that one exquisite day flooding back.

"*Hard it is,*" the raving old fool had pronounced over him, "*when cast down thou art from artifice and pride! Seekest not thou pleasing lips and hands that lie. Woe upon thee, if thou learnest not, for verily the price is thine love and life!*"

Darcy blinked, his chest pounding and his ears ringing with comprehension. He had been such a blind, stupid fool! And he would be cursed to be a lonely one if he did not act.

He snatched another sheet of paper, his letter to Georgiana temporarily forgotten. Hertfordshire was near enough to London that he could be in Meryton in four hours, and back again for any need within a day. As soon as Mrs Reynolds set up command of the house, he could be free.

His resolve fixed, his heart set, he bent his head to his letter.

Dear Bingley…

Thirty-five

"Darcy! I cannot tell you what pleasure it gives me to see you. Why, you have come a full two days before I expected you!"

"Bingley," Darcy nodded to his friend as he entered the house, "forgive me for not arriving last week as I had first intended. I am afraid the delay was unavoidable."

"Think nothing of it! I am only delighted that you have come. You must know how eager I have been to ask your opinion of the house. What do you think of it?"

Darcy looked up at the ceiling, then cast a cursory glance about the room. "The grounds are perfectly acceptable, and the house seems suitable. Have you been satisfied thus far?"

"Darcy, I cannot express how pleased I am with the situation! This is the friendliest county in all England. I simply must have you meet all my neighbours."

Darcy nodded held up a hand. "In time, perhaps, but I am in no humour for meeting all the country gentlemen just now."

"Oh, but they are quite amiable. Why, I have never met so many pleasant gentlemen in all my life. And a few of them had deuced handsome daughters!"

"Naturally. Bingley, I hope you have not attached yourself already to some country tart."

"Darcy!" Bingley laughed, "Fastidious as ever. But I assure you, I have not yet met any angels in Hertfordshire. You know, you do have the most wondrous timing, old boy. I have been invited to an assembly tomorrow, and I am assured that some of my new neighbours will be in attendance. It is a public ball, so of course, it is not quite so private and therefore less to your tastes, but you simply must accompany me."

"And spend the evening dancing with milk-faced farmers' daughters and being stared at by their mercenary mothers? That is not why I came to Hertfordshire."

"Naturally, Mr Darcy! Indeed, you have expressed my sentiments exactly." Caroline Bingley had walked in upon their conversation and proceeded to draw close to his side, laughing immoderately at his ill-humoured remark. "And so I have told Charles, that the company here is terribly backward and uncivilised. Why, I simply do not know how I can endure a rowdy evening of country jigs and drunken boors. I could not even dare wear my fine gown to such a venue! I certainly hope none of our friends ever learn of it. We shall be laughed from all the better drawing rooms in London!"

"I doubt the stain of attending a public ball lingers as an odour about one's person," he assured her dryly. "But I have other reasons for preferring not to attend, if it is all the same to you, Bingley."

"Oh, come, Darcy, you must not be such a stick! I have already informed some of my neighbours that I am expecting a friend, and you would not stay away when word is had that you have arrived. They will feel slighted, and justly so. I say, did you mention in your letter that you had other business in the area? I'd no notion that you had any connections whatsoever in Hertfordshire."

"It is nothing of import. I had simply wished to encounter a friend who hails from the area, and I am to understand has returned here."

"Oh, well certainly he will be at the assembly. Even the tradesmen from Meryton come, I understand. I had met one rather amiable fellow, an attorney I believe he was, and he assured me that the company at the local Assembly is made up of everyone who is anyone in the area. You simply must go!"

Caroline emitted a dismal groan. "Charles! You did not tell me that tradesmen will be at the Assembly!"

"And what shall we call ourselves, Caroline? Children of a tradesman?"

"I will thank you not to use such a term again." She turned to Darcy with a long-suffering gesture of exasperation. "He simply *will* not see what you and I must both understand. Pray, Mr Darcy, enlighten my dear brother regarding the need for keeping proper company!"

Darcy narrowed his eyes. "I have found the company of tradesmen and their families more agreeable than some of the Gentry of my acquaintance, Miss Bingley."

She touched her décolletage, her lashes fluttering and her looks doubtful. Clearly, she could not discern whether he meant it as a compliment or an indictment and sought to find pleasure in his words where she could.

Bingley chanced to have dismissed the entire exchange and thought only of settling his guest in comforts. "I say, Darcy, the road is dusty at this time of year, and your throat must be dry. Shall I send for something from the cellars?

I had a very fine brandy sent down last week. I believe even you could not object."

"Brandy?" Darcy's brow pinched. "Thank you, but no. I do not think I wish for another brandy for some while. The last I had unsettled me rather badly."

"Then you must sample my French wine, and I even have some Scotch. Both smuggled, of course, which can only improve their flavour. There is something about partaking of the forbidden, is there not?"

"I cannot deny that. However," he shook his head, "tea will suit me well enough. I think I must keep my wits about me."

Caroline Bingley was always a gracious and flattering hostess, or at least she was when he was present. She offered every civility and saw matters settled very prettily, but Darcy could hardly exert himself to take note of her overt attentions. His mind conjured images only of another, one who would have spoken *with* him rather than *at* him, and he proved a rather absentminded guest.

After some while, he recognised his own dullness and challenged Bingley to billiards. There, Miss Bingley would not follow, and he might have a private word or two with his friend. It was his turn to set the balls, and when he had done, he lowered his cue and slowly studied the table.

"What is this about some friend in the area?" Bingley asked. "Is it someone you know from school? Perhaps I might know him as well."

"No," Darcy answered shortly and took his shot. He missed and stood back for Bingley.

"A business contact? I understand there are some very respectable shops in town."

"No, nothing like that." Then, desiring to change the subject, he asked, "What of the area? Have you ridden far yet? How was the shooting?"

"Capital! Netherfield itself boasts some very fine coveys, but there is another estate not far from here called Longbourn. I have not met the master, but I have been given to understand that they have the best shooting in the area. I am quite looking forward to making his acquaintance, but he has not yet called. I heard some things whispered about town hinting that the family are keeping to themselves of late. Indeed, I wish I knew why, for they are among my nearest neighbours. I cannot simply call on the man unless he should first visit me."

"You had better leave it, then. If the man does not desire to make himself agreeable, you shall not befriend him by presuming the liberty of introducing yourself."

"I see how it is. You think the man to be like yourself, one who would be offended by informality?"

"You think me so readily affronted that I would be put off by a visiting neighbour?"

"It suits with your history to at least receive such a visitor less warmly."

Darcy frowned and was slow in settling into his turn at the table. "If such has been my reputation, I shall take measures toward a remedy. However, I would have done my duty in the first and welcomed a new neighbour before he found it necessary to intrude upon my notice. This master of Longbourn must be an uncivil sort."

"Well, perhaps he is, but then I had heard something of his eccentricities before. I believe he simply enjoys being contrary and is just as likely to turn up when he is least expected. I have met many others, however. I tell you, Darcy, everyone else has been positively welcoming."

"I daresay they have. Most probably have daughters to settle somewhere or another."

"Darcy, you are in a fine way this evening! But, naturally, there have been a few fathers and uncles who were full of praise for their young ladies. Why, I met the most agreeable fellow, Sir William Lucas was his name, with two daughters. And there was that attorney I mentioned in town who claimed some dashed fine nieces—four of them, as if one were not sufficient to invoke pride!"

"An attorney in Meryton with four unmarried nieces?" Darcy's brow furrowed, and he made another shot. Could it be *her* family? But they were five daughters, not four… unless one was not accounted for because she was betrothed elsewhere. "What was the fellow's name?"

"Philips."

Darcy's cue shot to the side of the ball, and he straightened to find Bingley regarding him curiously. He cleared his throat and nonchalantly tended to his cue, as if the blame for his missed shot could be assigned to the equipment.

Bingley stared for another second, then lined up his own shot. "There is also a Mr Long, who claims two nieces as his wards, and a Miss King, a Miss Jones, two Miss Smiths… oh, come, Darcy, even you cannot think with pleasure on the bountiful feminine population in this country! How can you not be eager for a ball?"

"Hertfordshire seems to be overrun with single young ladies," Darcy retorted testily. "I should not wonder that ten have already claimed you for their own."

"One would suffice!" Bingley laughed. "I confess, Darcy, I am quite in raptures with Hertfordshire, and I would be well pleased to meet with an agreeable young lady and settle here. How fine it would be to secure myself family in the area! I have not so many relations as you, of course, so perhaps you may not sympathise, but I tell you, it is dashed lonely to have such a large house and only my sisters and Hurst to liven it."

"An extended family can be as distressing as it is supportive," muttered Darcy as he lined up his cue.

"Yes, you mentioned something of that in your letter. I hope that business is settled. How ever did you escape the unhappy arrangement? You must have had the friendship of an angel!"

Darcy felt a distant smile growing but concealed it as he bent over the table. "I met with just the very sort. Pray, I am in no mood to speak of it. However, I shall be satisfied to meet with my acquaintance again when I can discover the address. I would like to set about it promptly."

"Very well, perhaps in two or three days, you shall seek him. Tomorrow, Darcy, let us ride out together and survey my field, and then you simply must attend the Assembly with me in the evening. He may very well be in attendance, and you will be spared the trouble of searching further."

Darcy deliberated, his fingers drumming on the billiards stick. "If you insist. I will accompany you to the Assembly and then seek my friend."

Thirty-six

E lizabeth would much rather have stayed home. Nothing could repay her
for the discomfort of sitting on the edge of the room all evening, shunned
by all the gentlemen and openly ridiculed by the other ladies. "Jane," she
whispered, "I am going to experience a headache in a moment."

"Lizzy," cautioned her sister, "everyone will know it is a fraud. You would
do better to smile and pretend that you prefer sitting out to dancing."

"If we are not asked to dance for the next set, Mama is going to find some
poor waiter or musician and drag him over to us by his ear. Do you truly think
that could be less mortifying than pretending to have a headache?"

Jane said nothing, but the artificial smile on her face appeared wooden as
she nodded in the direction of Maria Lucas. The Lucas family was one of the
few who still addressed them freely, but this evening, Charlotte and Maria had
been much in demand as dance partners, while the formerly favoured Bennet
girls sat in Charlotte's usual place.

"I do not mind being passed over tonight, Lizzy," Jane decided with hollow
optimism, "for look how happy Charlotte is! I think the new rector has taken a
fancy to her. He has asked for a second set." There was a softening around
Jane's eyes, and she continued to smile out on the dancing populace of
Meryton. It seemed everyone, simply *everyone* was in attendance, and all having
a merry time of it… save for themselves.

"Where is this mythical new neighbour of ours?" Elizabeth wondered. "I
thought we had depended upon his vaunted good humour and his ignorance
of our family's circumstances, not to mention your great beauty, to purchase us
at least one dance this evening."

"When I called on Charlotte earlier today, Sir William assured us all that he is planning to come and that he is bringing a guest. This friend is only lately arrived, I understand—a passing wealthy gentleman, but no one seems to know much of him yet. There is great hope in general that he also might prove to be unmarried. You must imagine Lady Lucas' delight at hearing of him."

"And Mama's, if she has heard. Her nerves will not withstand the evening."

Jane cast a watchful eye over to their mother, whose fluttering fan concealed excited whispers traded with that very neighbour. "I believe she already knows."

Little more was said on the subject of Mrs Bennet and her nerves, however vexing the topic might be to the conversants, for shortly there arose from the general assembly a low murmur of expectation and curiosity. Some new arrivals had graced the entrance, and it required no great powers of discernment to conclude that the newcomers must, indeed, be this very Mr Bingley's party.

"Lizzy, can you see his face?"

Elizabeth shook her head, leaning slightly to peer through a parting in the line of dancers. Indeed, there was some disturbance near the door, but from their seats at the back of the room, only Sir William's broad shoulders could be seen as he made the first general introductions. Elizabeth felt her sister drawing a shaky breath and sitting slightly taller beside her, her trembling hands smoothing the front of her gown.

Dearest Jane! It was not for their mother's sake alone that she wished to please this gentleman, but also that she had heard it said what an affable and pleasant young man he was. Jane had confided to her sister that her dearest wish was to meet an amiable gentleman who might find her worthy of notice and whose regard she could return. She could then, she hoped, give happiness to all her family, and not least to her favourite sister.

Elizabeth watched her with some sadness. Sweet, sensible Jane deserved so much better than the disappointment which was to be theirs this evening! There seemed no way to tell her that their family was beyond recovery.

~

Darcy tugged surreptitiously at the inseams of his formal jacket and strained his stiffening neck. What the devil was he doing here? *She* would not be here, surely! Bingley had assured him that this assembly would be well attended by all in Meryton, but the price of the tickets alone could be prohibitive for his Elizabeth's family, with five daughters to dress.

Far better that he should have started in the morning by casually paying his custom to the various shops in town, perhaps beginning with Mr Philips, the attorney, and learning which business might be under the management of Mr

Bennet. Yet how was he to do that, if he was expected to spend half the night prancing about a dilapidated Hall with the unpedigreed gentry of the county? There was no help for it. Nearly as soon as they entered the door, a portly older gentleman, who seemed to think a great deal of the brass medal upon his chest, stopped their party and bowed most humbly.

"Mr Bingley, it is an honour and a pleasure to see you attending our humble assembly. I do hope our little event adheres to your expectations and you find nothing which does not please."

Bingley seemed to be floating three inches above the ground as he took in the atmosphere. Nothing would dampen his spirits on such an occasion, and Darcy had the mortification of seeing a grown man's eyes sparkle when they met pale muslin and coiled tresses everywhere they turned. He was a man ready to be charmed, and he had found a willing market. Darcy nearly left the building, but Bingley was already answering.

"Splendid, Sir William, splendid! Oh, Sir William Lucas, you have met my sister Mrs Hurst and her husband Mr Hurst, as well as my younger sister, Miss Caroline Bingley. Allow me also to present my good friend Mr Darcy from Pemberley, in Derbyshire."

Though he had probably never heard of the place, Sir William's eyes widened in appreciation for the impressive introduction, and he bowed deeply. "Mr Darcy, what a great honour it is, sir! May I present my daughters; Miss Maria here, and my eldest, Charlotte, is dancing over there."

Bingley smiled at the younger girl and dutifully offered her his arm for the present set. Darcy, however, found himself staring across the room at the elder. *Charlotte?* Had Elizabeth not mentioned that was the name of her dear friend? How many Charlottes could live in such a village as Meryton? He watched the young lady and her plain-faced partner with interest.

"Indeed," Caroline Bingley sniffed in disdain after leaving her wrap at the door, "I am abominably sorry we came. Why, look at the gowns of these third-rate ladies, and the attire of the 'gentlemen!' Pray assure me I must not stand up with any farmers with soiled fingernails." She stood beside Darcy now, her lip curled in fashionable distaste as she surveyed the room.

"Even the cloak room was a disgrace," she sniffed. "Why, it is full of nothing but rumour and ill-bred gossip! I have no doubts of rodents as well."

Darcy's eyes still roved the room, as he paid Miss Bingley as little notice as possible. "Cloakrooms in London are rife with malicious talk. I daresay, perhaps they have set the example."

"Oh, but you have never heard the like of this backward country set! It must prove what a simple, unsophisticated little village this is. Why, the whole talk is of how some young chit, a Miss Bennet was her name, went off one evening for amusement and was found the next morning at a public-house, playing cards. They say she had been at it all night and had a pile of shillings and three impoverished companions to her credit."

Darcy jerked to face her. "A Miss Bennet, did you say?"

"Oh! You must have heard the same report, I see. She is perfectly ruined, of course, and her sisters with her."

"Her sisters?" Darcy's chest was quaking in agitation, and his fists clenched.

"Oh, indeed! Do you remember what I said of rodents, Mr Darcy? Apparently they breed in Hertfordshire. Five daughters, and no sons at all! I have heard even that one of this strumpet's elder sisters was later found in some disgrace of her own, but of course, I could not dignify the report by feigning interest enough to enquire further. But really, playing cards at a public house, all night with strange men! Can you fancy it?"

An elder sister disgraced? His head shook in denial. Had some report of Elizabeth already been spread about her home village? He must find her, and rapidly! Darcy gazed mutely about the room until he found a face which might answer for his present wants. Ladies dancing, ladies sitting on the edge of the room with fans over their faces, matrons chattering in the corner... and Miss Charlotte Lucas, just being led from the floor.

"I declare, they might have hired an orchestra that could play in harmony," Miss Bingley sneered. "We are a long way from Grosvenor Square, are we not, Mr Darcy? I fancy you did not relish coming here this evening to watch the swineherds stomp some milkmaid's toes with their muddy boots."

"No," he answered with forced steadiness. "Much to my relief, we are nowhere near Grosvenor Square, and that is not the reason I came here this evening." He gave her a brisk nod and walked in the direction of Sir William, and it was with some wicked delight that he heard her indignant huff.

"Sir William," he bowed upon reaching that gentleman, "may I importune you for an introduction to your elder daughter?"

The gentleman looked as if he would fall over from delight, but he collected himself tolerably well and made the honourable presentation. Charlotte Lucas was a plain girl, and that was a generous assessment. Her girlhood looked to be long gone, and she had the aspect of one who was looking down the long shadow of spinsterhood with resignation. She smiled and performed her curtsy, but unlike her father, there was no mercenary twinkle in her eyes when she heard his name. She seemed a sensible young woman... exactly the sort his Elizabeth might befriend.

"May I offer you some refreshment, Miss Lucas?"

She sighed in obvious relief. "I thank you, Mr Darcy, for I am much in need of it. I have seldom danced so much in my life as I have tonight!"

"Then I shall spare you the exercise. Perhaps, as I am a stranger to the region, I might impose upon you to tell me something of the neighbourhood."

"This is your first visit to Hertfordshire, Mr Darcy?"

"It is. However, I have been longing to visit, for I recently made an acquaintance who lives in the area. I was hoping to meet with my friend again, while in residence."

"Indeed? Is your friend here this evening?"

He smiled. "I have only just entered the room, but I find it doubtful."

"Perhaps it is someone I know, in which case I would be pleased to give you what information I may."

"I think it likely."

"Well, sir," she pursed her lips, a mannerism so like his Elizabeth that it might have been learnt from her. "If you will but give me the name of the gentleman—or lady—I may tell you whether or not they are to be found here."

He was silent a moment, amused at the coy tease and the sensible, easy tone in which it was delivered. Yes, surely this must be *the* Charlotte, friend of Elizabeth! He swallowed and dared to confess the fateful name. "The *lady's* name is Miss Elizabeth Bennet."

Miss Lucas raised her eyebrows, and a little puckering of her lips betrayed her as an interested party. "Lizzy? You say you met her in Town?"

Darcy felt his palms begin to ache and sweat, and anyone looking on would surely have noted the burning flush he felt spreading across his face. "Indeed, last week," he managed. His voice did not crack, did it?

"Oh, how very interesting," she mused. "My poor friend has been most unfortunate."

"Unfortunate? How is this?" he asked, altogether a bit too sharply. "Have there been ill tidings of her, or unfavourable talk? There was an uncharitable relation, I am to understand."

"Poor Lizzy! It has been a dreadful affair, with her family and Mr Collins and all that. She never did wish to marry him, but recent days have been worse even than she feared."

"Mr Collins! You do not mean that there is still some connection there?" His heart began a series of turns, flipping incautiously against his breastbone until he was certain Miss Lucas would perceive a fluttering of his cravat. He had thought her safe from that tyrannical buffoon! Had he followed her from London, exposed her, and made demands? Was she publicly betrothed, after all?

"Of course, there is still a connection," Miss Lucas was tilting her head in puzzlement. "He is her cousin, after all, and heir to Longbourn estate."

"I do not see why it should signify what he is to inherit. He ought not to have claim upon her hand if she does not wish to bestow it."

Miss Lucas stared. "It signifies because when Mr Bennet dies, the family shall be turned out of Longbourn and Mr Collins shall claim his inheritance."

"Mr... Mr Bennet... he is the master of Longbourn..." Darcy could scarcely breathe well enough to form the words. Her father owned an estate rather than some shop? She... she was a gentlewoman? A modest one, but... but...*but!*

"But she is not betrothed to Mr Collins," he insisted. He opened his mouth to beseech her for every assurance, then closed it again and simply waited in dreadful suspense.

"Oh, goodness no, I can assure you of that. I understand he has been most offensive, and Mr Bennet let Lizzy off the engagement, but you know, matters are far from well, what with Lydia and Mary."

He could breathe again. The stars ceased spinning in his vision, and he fought to steady his voice. "Lydia and Mary? And who are they?"

"Her sisters, of course."

"Ah! She mentioned something of them."

"Poor Elizabeth! Lydia's folly is beyond help, but Lizzy and Jane tried defending Mary. Public talk prevailed, as it always does, and Mr Bennet was obliged to keep her home."

"Miss Mary was... the sister who was disgraced?"

"There was no help for it. They were all searching, but it was Mary who found Lydia, escorted by Mr Collins and his manservant."

Darcy was leaning intently close, so closely that if Miss Lucas' mother were watching, she might already be sending for a dressmaker. He forced himself to straighten. "Found her... at the public house?" he blurted out.

"It was a bad business! It might all have been settled quietly, but for Mr Collins. I see that you are sympathetic to my friend, sir, and so you must know something of that man's crimes against civility."

"In—" Darcy cleared his throat. "Indeed. He is an unscrupulous, indecent sort of man."

"I almost cannot blame Lydia for refusing to go home under Mr Collins' escort. They say he promised such doom upon silly Lydia that she refused to be trapped in the same carriage with the man. Not that he offered to take her at any rate, of course, for it would have been a shame upon his office, so he said, and so he and his manservant simply left. Poor Mary waited in a corner all night—she would not leave her sister, do you see—but they were both ruined in the affair when it all came out."

"And this... this sister... no, the other—Miss Jane, I believe her name was, that she praised so highly—?"

"Who could not feel pity for Jane? Lizzy is my particular friend, of course, but Jane is nearly as dear. She deserves none of the scorn she has received."

"Then she is still at home?"

"Well, not at present. Do you see? She is sitting over there with Lizzy just now."

Struck with awe, he jerked his head about, and there, just as the line of dancers moved in the right way, he found a dark head bowed before the world. Her beautiful face was cast down, the sparkling eyes fastened on the floor. Was she aware of his presence? Had she seen him already?

His neck reached its limit, and careless that it caused him to turn his back on Miss Lucas, he impatiently turned his body the other way, and then he saw. Her eyes lifted bashfully, she blushed, and then addressed a blonde girl beside her. She raised her fan to shield her face as if she hoped she had not been noticed, and he was forced to look instead at the blonde. She was as stunning as Elizabeth had declared her to be, but as sad and dejected-looking as her sister.

A sudden urge seized him. It was not enough merely to go to Elizabeth. He must procure Bingley's company as well! She could not be easy while her sister looked on in pain and solitude, and if all that was said of Jane Bennet were true, he would be securing for his friend the finest treasure in the room—besides the one he meant to win for himself.

"Sir," Miss Lucas interrupted his reverie, "you may think me vulgar, but I have little of prospects to lose, and I do not mind appearing unladylike. May I ask the nature of your interest in Elizabeth? Are you truly a friend?"

He looked back down to the lady who had been so accommodating. "What manner of question is that? Did I not consider her a friend, would I have enquired after her welfare?"

"I would not see my friend injured," she explained shortly. "But if you do indeed hold good intentions, pray, do not be discouraged. Elizabeth is not usually how she appears tonight. Any other friend of hers would already know this, but I am surprised at how much has been new information to you. May I ask, sir, precisely how did you meet Lizzy and claim friendship with her if you truly know so little about her circumstances?"

The smile on his face must have been ridiculous, but he cared nothing for it. "I was her servant for the day."

Thirty-seven

Elizabeth tried fanning her face and looking in the other direction, but it was no good. *He* was Mr Bingley's wealthy friend, and he had seen her! There was no escape. He was casually walking toward her now, Mr Bingley at his side, and pausing here and there as if he might have been only taking in the room from its various aspects… but that gait, that set to his jaw, were too familiar. He was bound for her and only wished to appear to others as if he had no aim.

A rebellious thought seized her, to take herself to the ladies' retiring room and wait out the whole of the evening there, but she dismissed it quickly. That was cowardice, and though Elizabeth Bennet might take issue with boats and air balloons, she was no coward. At any rate, Mama would be certain to find her out. Her mother was in another corner now, speaking energetically to Lady Lucas, and thus had no notion as yet that the long-desired acquaintance of Mr Bingley was at the point of being made. Well, let the formidable introduction take place without her notice for the first few moments. It would be easier.

"Jane," she whispered, grasping her sister's hand, "stay close to me."

"I have no choice at present," Jane whispered back. "I think no one will ask us to stand up at all this evening, Lizzy. Oh, how mortifying this is! If it were not deceit, I should feign illness and ask to return home."

Elizabeth said nothing, only watched him… them… approach. They had collected Sir William Lucas, and now their object was perfectly clear. The elder gentleman smiled his pleasure at being useful, then, glancing at them, looked doubtful when Darcy made some request. Good Sir William tried, it appeared, to dissuade Netherfield's new tenant and his wealthy friend from any embarrassment, but their resolve appeared to be fixed, and in a moment, the three gentlemen walked directly toward them. Jane stiffened beside her.

"Miss Jane Bennet, and Miss Eliza Bennet," Sir William bowed, "may I have the pleasure of introducing Mr Charles Bingley, our new neighbour at Netherfield, and his very good friend, Mr Fitzwilliam Darcy of Derbyshire."

Jane lowered her lashes modestly as both gentlemen bowed first to her, as the eldest, and then to Elizabeth. Sir William turned back to the gentlemen with an air of confidence, as if he were imparting some secret in his full speaking voice. "The elder Miss Bennets of Longbourn are considered quite the beauties, and I think you must agree they are fine looking young ladies, eh, Mr Darcy? And such dancers they both are! Why, a more graceful young lady was never born than Miss Bennet, and Miss Eliza's enthusiasm is always a delight."

Elizabeth was looking steadily at Sir William, but Darcy was not. She felt the heat of his gaze on her and knew very well that every symptom of discomfort rose from her décolletage up to her cheeks.

"A delight, indeed," she heard Darcy reply, and from the corner of her eye, she could see that dry teasing warmth tugging at his mouth. "Your recommendation has not fallen ill, Sir William, for I find I am curiously tempted to dance, and certainly hope the ladies do not object." But he did not offer for her... not yet. That honour should go first to Jane, but he would not even look at her sister.

"Miss Bennet," Mr Bingley bowed, his manner ebullient and his face awash with every expectation of pleasure, "Would you do me the very great honour of granting me the next set?"

Jane accepted at once, and as the music from the previous dance was just ending, they were away before Darcy could make his obligatory request. Elizabeth had no alternative but to look at him now.

"Miss Elizabeth," he bowed and offered his hand, just as he had done to help her into the carriage... and the balloon... and the waltz. "May I have the pleasure?"

There was no possible way to refuse, even if her treacherous heart had not desired it. She rose and gave him her hand, and he smiled down at her as he led her away.

Once Sir William could no longer have heard, she murmured, "I believe I must thank you for the condescension, sir, in introducing your friend to my sister. I fear there are... more ladies than gentlemen present this evening, and the sweetest girl in the room has been passed over. You may suppose, after what you must have heard, that you have done the most deserving person in the world a very great service. However, it is not necessary for you to follow form and dance with me. I assure you, sir, you must not exert yourself out of any perceived sense of obligation."

He looked down in surprise. "You mistake me, Miss Elizabeth. While I was pleased to introduce a very good man, one whose happiness is of particular importance to me, to a woman whose character has been made known to me as exemplary, that was not my first object. I wished to speak with you."

"But what remains to be said between us? You must not deny yourself the pleasure of a more cheerful partner for the half hour."

"You may not have guessed as much, Miss Elizabeth, but I am not fond of dancing. The most pleasurable instance of the exercise in my memory was last week's indulgence. That incident stands out as the exception, but I would hope it to become the rule. Thus, I prefer the company of the woman who partnered me for that memorable encounter."

"I think we would be very likely to quarrel, and would you then engage yourself to suffer through an entire set with such a partner? A few moments at the punch bowl would surely suffice, for is not your new…" she bit her lip. "I am given to understand that newly engaged gentlemen are not expected to dance with every young lady who must be sitting down in want of a partner. Would it not displease your bride?"

A low laugh rumbled beside her. "I have the pleasure of disabusing you of one misapprehension. Allow me to assure you that I am not unhappily betrothed."

"I thought…" she felt herself faltering as the floor beneath her feet seemed to tilt and the figures before her blurred. "That is… I had heard there remained some obligation…."

"Indeed, I have pledged myself to my aunt and cousin's support, but not in such a way that I had once feared. Your assumption is natural, of course—when you left me that evening, I grant you that my circumstances looked rather bleak. However, certain developments followed which, I hope, I shall one day have the liberty to disclose in full."

Elizabeth felt as if a great fist had been closed round her heart, and then suddenly withdrawn, but the heat remained in her face. "That must have pleased you, sir."

"More than you can imagine."

The couples were forming now, and they parted to stand opposite one another in the line. She could feel the weight of his gaze, the admiration he scarcely troubled himself to conceal, and she felt conspicuous. Oh, if anyone around her could see that flame kindled in his eye, could understand what he meant by it!

Who was she to attract his notice? One of five disgraced daughters of an impoverished private gentleman? Of what virtues could she boast which might make her worthy of an honourable offer? No, surely, he, stubborn man that he was, meant to renew that conversation from which she had once fled. The humiliation of what he had certainly come to ask of her would be hers for the rest of her days, even if she refused—which she must! Elizabeth glanced nervously down the line, and while one or two had taken note of the fine-looking gentleman, there were no gloved titters as they appraised him, nor knowing smirks as they identified his partner.

Elizabeth dared to raise her eyes to his face. He certainly was fine. If he had been imposing and powerful-looking in livery, he was now resplendent in his own dress attire. His look was grave and steady, his eyes never stirring from her face, but perhaps one who knew him less well, did not know his habitual aspect, would miss that slight twitching of his mouth, or the softening around his eyes. She swallowed, and the music began.

His hands were as warm and strong as she remembered. She tried to look away, her eyes on his shoulders as they passed one another, but this only recalled to her the memory of another dance, when her hands had rested there….

"Miss Elizabeth, is my company distressing to you?" she heard him murmur lowly as they passed one another again.

"Not at all, sir," she stared directly at his chest, and thought somehow that she rather missed the brass buttons and gold braid of the livery.

"Yet your eyes tell another story. Do you fear that I have come to expose you, Miss Elizabeth? I assure you, nothing could be farther from my intentions. Why this obvious discomfort when I have been previously acquainted with your ways? Think you that I do not well remember your characteristic impertinence?"

She bit her inner lip and parried with a question of her own. "You did not say before that you were on intimate terms with our new neighbour at Netherfield and intended a visit to the area. Surely you might have, for I recall clearly that we spoke of it."

He bent low as he turned her in the dance. "And you failed to mention that your father is a private gentleman with a respectable estate. You might have made note of that rather pertinent detail, though it matters little to me now. You were rather vague, as I recall."

Elizabeth was forced to wait until they had been brought back together by the dance before she could reply. "Sir, you know well enough my family's circumstances. What is more damning in the eyes of society? That I have an uncle whom I adore who makes his living in trade, or that my own family of gentleman's daughters are presently shunned for the disgrace of a sister?

"If you have not been told more, I shall spare you the asking—my youngest sister was unaccountably foolish. Her fondness for spending money and bonnets and favour among the gentlemen led her on to do something abominably stupid, something which has injured us all. She has now been sent away to a boarding school for fallen girls. My middle sister, who is righteous as the day is long, bears the taint of association in the affair, and her prospects are similarly ruined. I do not pretend that my own appeal is such that a man of your station could possibly—"

They parted again, and Elizabeth was prepared to speak once more when they came together, but he pre-empted her. "Miss Elizabeth, I believe I understand you. When last we spoke in the Gardens, and I so inelegantly made you an offer, it was not the sort of offer you must have supposed."

She turned sharply, as the dance required, and looked him full in the face. "It was not?"

He lifted his hands to take hers and turn her about. "Indeed, I could never disgrace you so. Unfortunately, you had quite overcome my senses, and I was without rational thought and words. I am afraid I expressed myself rather poorly."

He turned around, and she did as well, then a moment later the scripted steps brought them back together. "I have not the talent of expressing myself easily," he confessed, taking the liberty granted by the dance and leaning low to her ear. "You may have noticed that I became practised in your company throughout the day, and I hope I became perfectly amiable to you. However, there was a moment there, when a new prospect opened before me, and I understood something I had not done before. I had not the words to express it then, but I have now."

Elizabeth did not trust her voice and managed only a whisper. "And that is?" How he heard her in the crowded ballroom, she could not know, but he answered.

"You had informed me eloquently enough that your expectations had been somehow damaged. I wished to find some way to materially aid your family's respectability. It must be something more than mere domestic felicity—a public recognition of sorts, so that you would not feel the sting of the world's scorn. I would never wish for the woman I love to bear such pain."

She blinked. "Love?" She heard her voice break, but he could not attend her this time, for he had turned to another partner. A different gentleman faced her and led her to another part of the line. It was two frustrating minutes before they came together once more, and for the whole of it, she was forced to look on as he drew the admiration of others, all while leaving her with the agitation of heart which such a confession must inspire.

When they were brought together again, he clasped her hands and seemed undesirous of letting them go. "Miss Elizabeth, you look a bit breathless. Shall we sit out the remainder of this set? Allow me to find you some refreshment."

She followed as he withdrew her from the line and could not miss the rabid elation writ across her mother's face when they passed. Mrs Bennet was winking and clapping her hands together at Elizabeth's great conquest, for if nothing else, the notice of such a man as Mr Darcy for even a single set could not permit her to sit out another dance the whole evening. Elizabeth looked away.

Mr Darcy procured glasses for them both and invited her to stand with him in a corner which was little occupied. "Pray, Miss Elizabeth, permit me to speak first, for I fear the words shall fail me if I do not express them at once."

She nodded her acquiescence, her eyes on her glass, and he continued.

"I have been a selfish being all my life. I was given good principles but left to follow them in conceit. The price for this ignorance and disdain for the feelings of others, you well know—I lost the loyalty of even those whose own prospects were dependent upon myself. So thoroughly had I rested in my assumptions that when all came to light, I discovered how dismally I had failed in my duties. I would not have you think me an indolent master, Miss Elizabeth, nor that the Darcy family are habitually negligent.

"Without attempting to flatter myself, I shall relate to you one episode two years ago when I received word that the spring flooding in Derbyshire was threatening many of my tenants' houses. My sister and I both rode the distance from London on horseback and worked in the fields beside our tenants for many long days until the danger was over. She was but thirteen, but her care and devotion to the task were the same as I inherited from our parents. Such are the expectations for one who would bear the Darcy name.

"I tell you this, Miss Elizabeth, because while I have been rightly accused of pride, occasionally of too much reserve, and quite frequently of ignorance of another's sentiments, I could not generally be called careless. Indeed, the loss of my household's loyalty pained me far more than the inconvenience of broken trust and violated privacy. I ought to have done better, and I shall make reparations for my vanity all the rest of my days. If you should choose to hear what I have next to say, I would have you understand my flaws as well as my virtues."

Elizabeth had stared at her glass all this long while, but she raised her eyes when he ceased. "Sir, before you speak another word, I would beg you to cast your eyes to the far side of the room."

His brow puckered in curiosity, but he obliged her.

"You cannot fail to see the lady who is pointing at us and speaking loudly to all her acquaintance. I daresay she has already appraised your fortune and enquired after your family, given that you have spent more than two minutes in my company."

His eyes narrowed in faint distress. "I am to understand that lady is your mother?"

She winced. "She is not known for her discretion, sir. Nor would she find your consequence sufficiently imposing that her behaviour might be curtailed at the risk of displeasing so august an acquaintance. Now, would you and your friend Mr Bingley not be better suited by dancing with the Miss Lucases, or Miss King?"

He turned back to her. "I am not a man to be easily diverted, nor have I grounds to cast aspersions on the peculiarities of anyone's relations. My own are vexing enough to keep me humble in that regard."

"And what of Mr Bingley? Are you quite secure on his account?"

"My friend, Miss Elizabeth, tends to follow the most natural path, and that is to seek amiable young ladies with handsome faces. He is not a rake, nor is he inconstant, but on occasion, he has unwittingly caused himself disappointment. I knew from your account that Miss Bennet must be a rare creature, and I was pleased to introduce my friend to a beautiful young woman of good character. As for myself," he drew half a step closer, and his voice lowered, "I am bewitched."

She drew a shaken breath, her lashes fluttering. "It was unconsciously done, sir. You must not assume any debt owed to me—"

"Do you know, Miss Elizabeth, we spoke far more freely when I was attired as a servant. Perhaps it was fitting, for your servant I have become. A wiser man might perhaps reprimand me and think me a fool for rushing in where circumspection would be more prudent, but I cannot help it. My feelings will not be repressed, and I must tell you at once before the dance ends, and another comes to take you from me, how ardently I admire and love you. Perhaps for you, one day was insufficient proof of how perfectly suited we are for one another, or how devotedly I would serve only your happiness, but my own resolve is formed. From this moment, I would surrender my heart into your keeping and beg you, most urgently, to agree to become my wife."

Elizabeth coloured, breathless and silent. He took her glass, as her hand was shaking, and set it on the tray of a passing waiter, then seemed to catch his own breath in earnest attendance. His look, so tender and patient, so full of pleading and hope, gave her all the encouragement she could have wished for.

"I... I know not what to say, sir," she stammered as he leaned a little lower. "I am... I am pleased, but... oh, one who felt less might find it possible to speak more!"

His expression upon hearing her was all that could be expected of a sensible man, violently in love and constrained to make that confession in a public venue. His voice, the tone and pitch of it, carried all the warmth that his body could not express. "Then I shall call you *my* Elizabeth and note with immense satisfaction that for perhaps the only time in our long lives together, I have the advantage of fluency. Say nothing more, Elizabeth, until I have been introduced to your father, but if you will have me, take my hand, and with it, my life."

She blinked the flood of joyous tears from her eyes and laughed, a full and abundant exultation such as she had never known. His hand closed round her fingers, and she clasped it as her security, her strong comfort. "Come, William," she coaxed, "there is still another set to dance."

Thirty-eight

His interview with Mr Bennet was everything surreal and confusing. Darcy had expected a protective father, one who instantly discerned his true history with Elizabeth and accepted his suit as little more than some resolution to the obligation owed the family, but Mr Bennet had baffled him. Clever, the man was, and undeceived from the moment of Darcy's introduction when he had mentioned that he had first met Elizabeth in London. However, rather than sensing himself thoroughly grilled and chastised, he felt rather like a mouse, battered around by a cat before escaping to safety.

"I hope he did not shock you very much," Elizabeth apologised when they had an opportunity to speak of it. "Papa can be a touch querulous."

"He seemed rather fixated on my attire and asked me what I thought of the back of his carriage," Darcy grunted. "I told him that it looked to be death on wheels for any required to ride on the back, but that I would happily risk such a dare to prove the earnestness of my suit, if a challenge was his intention. He seemed contented with that and granted his blessing."

"Oh, Papa! He was sporting with you, I am afraid."

"So I gathered. However, the conversation became more serious a moment later, for we began to speak of libraries. I think I have found one subject upon which your father will speak with unwavering gravity. I believe," here, he smiled shyly, "that you also will approve of the Darcy family collection, for it has been the work of many generations."

"Shall I be flattered that you consider my pleasure, or shall I accuse you of excessive pride, sir?"

"Whatever pride I had was dashed the moment I took up your parasol and committed to a day in your service, madam," he bowed. "You have mended my character, Elizabeth, but I fear it shall want frequent patches."

"I am to understand that it is my turn to indulge you with the improvements to myself which you have wrought."

"There can be no alterations," he squeezed the hand resting in his elbow. "No one admitted to the pleasure of your company could think anything wanting."

"Oh, you pay your compliments very prettily, sir, which I shall presume as evidence of your improved address, but it will not do. I have long been guilty of judging by first impressions, believing my instincts and feelings to be sound and untainted by the undue oversight of reason. Will you laugh, sir? I thought you the handsomest, rudest, most hopelessly inept footman in all London before I took the time to look again and saw the gentleman beneath the livery."

"But you *did* think me handsome," he grinned. "Your insight did not fail you."

"Mr Darcy!" she laughed, her cheeks crimson. "Perhaps your lesson in humility has not been so well learned as you profess."

"Indeed, it has. By you, I was properly humbled, but you must permit me to inspire some feminine chagrin from time to time. Your countenance colours and your eyes sparkle most becomingly, my dearest loveliest Elizabeth."

Her colour did deepen, but for this, she had no saucy retort. She merely tightened her arm through his, and they walked on together through the early autumn woods, the stillness broken only by the occasional rustling of leaves beneath their feet.

"Elizabeth," he ventured at last, "I spoke with your father about Miss Lydia and Miss Mary, and he has given his permission for me to raise the question with you. Do you believe their situations might be improved if they were to come to Pemberley? I would place Miss Lydia at a nearby school for the daughters of gentlemen, or bring on a private tutor if you prefer. Miss Mary may have her choice of situations, for she seems fond of learning. However, she might profit from the company of my sister and Mrs Annesley, and perhaps the benefit will be mutual. Would that suit? It would require more of you, but I felt perhaps it would please you better."

Elizabeth was biting her lip. "You are kind, William, but you have not met Lydia. You may regret the arrangement."

He tilted his head to survey her in bemusement. "Your mother I have withstood, and you well know that I have no sources of pride in my own family's decorous conduct. I believe I will survive. Your father gave his approval of the scheme."

"For the very compelling reason that he will avail himself of your library while you see to the management of his daughters!"

"A price I am more than willing to pay," he smiled, catching her eye until she blushed again. "I had also shown him the arrangements I intended to make for your own provision. Has he spoken to you of them?"

Her face became an even deeper shade of precious rose, and she smiled her embarrassment. "He said you were exceedingly generous."

"It is far less than you deserve," he replied warmly. "My only regret is that we must wait out a prolonged engagement. I would not taint our marriage with a quick ceremony, and I believe your mother was gratified to make all her arrangements. Moreover, the Countess of Matlock intends to call on you next week. Her support will be exceedingly helpful to you later."

"You did not mention the additional benefit of the time secured for Mr Bingley and Jane while they act as our chaperons," Elizabeth smiled and glanced over her shoulder to the oblivious pair walking behind them. "Do you suppose they would even notice if we were to step behind that tree?"

"Elizabeth," he warned, "the last time I stepped behind a tree with you, I nearly kept you there."

"Indeed? A pity you did not speak of your difficulty, for I might have comforted you."

"If you had, my conversation with your father would have gone rather differently."

She laughed, that artless, joyful music which had first won his heart. "I must ask you, sir, at what point during the day did you first begin to suffer in your affections for me? Was it perhaps during the Italian Walk or as we admired the fountain?"

"I cannot say that it was, although a certain charade of yours stands out in my memory."

"Which charade was that?"

"When you played the scarlet, drawing the eye and desire of every man including myself. I hope one day you will repeat the performance, but only in the privacy of our own home."

"I thought you had promised never to speak of that moment again?"

"Before another living being, yes. Recall, if you will, that was also before I was assured of your hand. Now that I have won it, I would like to revisit that most delightful incident as frequently as possible. But you had asked when you were first secure of my admiration, which was long before that. As you have first put the question, I shall ask you. When did you begin to think of me as more than a troublesome intruder upon your day?"

She paused in the road and smiled up at him. "I cannot pinpoint the spot or the hour, but perhaps I might say that I knew I was forever lost when you rescued me from myself."

"The balloon," he smiled. "A moment I shall forever treasure in my fondest memories. For myself, I believe it was when I first opened my eyes." Darcy kissed her hand and resumed walking, his best friend and the lover of his heart close at his side.

~

It may easily be guessed that in short order, Elizabeth was not the only Bennet sister with happy news to share with her family. All Mrs Bennet's predictions of hedgerows and starvation were now supplanted by visions of carriages, jewels, and other wealthy men for her remaining daughters. When the happy mother, at last, prevailed on her husband to send her with her two eldest daughters to London to shop for their wedding trousseaux, Elizabeth had the pleasure of meeting her future sister, Miss Georgiana, at Darcy House. The girl was everything her brother had represented, and within a very few moments, a hesitant alliance was forged between the two which was only to strengthen through the years.

Among the others she met in the house, Elizabeth also made the acquaintance of one Mr Henry Wilson, who was presently studying under a Mr Hodges from Pemberley to take over the duties of a butler. Darcy's sly smile when he introduced them, she returned with an equally conspiratorial expression as she wished Mr Wilson well in his new post of polishing silver rather than boots.

On the third day of the Bennet family's stay in London, the party were all invited to the home of Mrs Jennings for dinner. Mr Darcy and Mr Bingley were pleased to escort them, and that good lady was full of effusions when she found proof with her own eyes that two girls in whom she had taken an interest had already secured, without her assistance, two exceedingly eligible matches. There was, however, a bit of disquiet in her eye whenever she looked upon Elizabeth seated beside Mr Darcy.

The whole of the evening, her gaze flicked in their direction until Mrs Bennet became convinced that Mrs Jennings nursed something of a matron's fascination with her future son-in-law. This much was, of course, untrue, but the usually ebullient Mrs Jennings was rendered discreet.

There was one point near the end of the evening when she approached the engaged couple with a question about whether Mr Darcy liked thinly sliced ham and punch, but his response was so perfectly civil, so absent of any hint of suspicion, that she let the matter drop. In future years, never once did the typically garrulous woman imply any impropriety in the courtship of Mr and Mrs Darcy.

Happy for all Mrs Bennet's maternal feelings was the day she saw her two eldest daughters sign the registry and mount lavish carriages for their new homes. Elizabeth kissed both her parents, her aunt and remaining sisters, then joyously consigned herself into the keeping of her new husband. As he settled her inside with warm rugs and hot bricks for her feet, she nestled close under his arm and knew, at last, real comfort.

"So," she murmured after a few moments of sweet distraction, "*this* is how you behave when you ride *inside* the carriage with a lady. Upon my word, sir, it is a very good thing you did not do so three months ago."

"Indeed," he agreed, "for we would have missed all the sights." Then he pulled her close and proceeded to divert her most pleasurably for the whole of the distance to London.

~

Darcy retired early to his chambers. No book was necessary on this, the most auspicious of nights, but he had asked Wilson to unlock the cabinets and send up a brandy. The drink, for him, was rather more sentimental than desired, but he carried it with him when he knocked on the door to his new bride's chambers. She had just sent her maid away and answered it herself... and it was a very good thing she was alone in the room, for Darcy would not have wished for his reaction to be witnessed by others.

Her silken hair tumbled round her shoulders, thick and dark and luxuriant. Those sparkling eyes lit and roved freely over his informal attire, and he felt flushed from head to foot. Her figure... by heaven, she was perfection; the lines of her body fell precisely where he had imagined they might, and he could not find the words even to bid her a good evening, or tell her how lovely she was, or how delighted he was that she was his own.

"Is that a brandy? I thought you had sworn off drinking that."

He held it aloft. "I confess, it has a propensity to leave me defenceless and heedless of the rest of the world. Since you so obligingly rescued me on the last occasion, I felt secure in your comfort, should I choose to surrender myself to your power. However," he smiled and set it aside, "I believe the only fine wine I shall ever desire is here."

"I do hope so, William. Oh! I have a gift for you."

She turned from him, and he was left to mourn his empty hands, which had a moment ago caressed satin hips. "Is my beautiful wife not gift enough?"

"I think when you open it, you will understand. I thought first of purchasing you a copy of *As You Like It*, but you already own several. This was my next best idea."

He lifted the lid of a dark parcel and chuckled. "Shoes?"

"They are specifically made for dancing, or so I am told, and are guaranteed not to injure your toes. I am rather hoping you will give me a few more lessons in the waltz."

"I am not certain which of us was the master and which was the pupil, but I shall endeavour to please. Since you are in the mood for giving gifts, I have a small little trifle that I had intended to give you later. Do you see that box on the mantel?"

He brought it to her, and she very carefully opened it. A moment later, she dangled a silver tag from one fingertip. "My own pass to Vauxhall?"

"It holds no value. It was one of the remnants from this last summer, and the park officials sold it to me for a pittance. The tags for '12 have not yet been minted. The true worth is on the back."

She turned it over and read the engraving.

Elizabeth Darcy
A day I will cherish
As long as I live

She clasped it in her hand, and her eyes glistened. "Thank you, William."

He took it from her hand and laid it gently on the mantel again, and as he did so, he felt her warm arms slide round him. He turned and drew her head to his shoulder, then simply remained there, at peace and at one with her.

"In truth, I pray we shall have many more such days to cherish. I would have you at my side for all life's adventures, and I hope they shall be many," he whispered into her hair.

She tipped back her head, offered him a languid smile, and then her hands caressed up his shoulders to his face. Her thumbs softly stroked his cheeks, but when he bent to kiss her, she gently lifted his head away. Her eyes wandered over his face as if memorising every groove, every angle, with the newfound freedom of ownership and belonging. "William?"

"Elizabeth?"

"Teach me to dance."

His brow furrowed. "Now?"

Her eyes dropped to the opened collar of his shirt, then fluttered shyly back to his. "Help me to fly."

"I do not understand."

She stood on her toes and a shiver of desire coursed through him when her lips grazed his throat. "Show me everything there is to see, hold me safe, and give me courage when mine fails."

"Ah," he whispered. His very being now quivered at her touch, and his hands began to learn each dip and curve of her form. "I shall ask something of you in return."

"Yes, my William?" Her reply was indistinct, for she had now worked two more of his buttons free and was brushing her lips against his chest.

He took her hand and began to gently lead her. "Teach me to take my leisure with you, each and every day."

Epilogue

25 July, 1859
Closing Day at Vauxhall Gardens

"Hold my hand, Elizabeth." Fitzwilliam Darcy, still robust at seventy-five years of age, visibly braced himself for the iron grip of his wife's fingers when the initial shock of her blinding panic overtook her. In nearly fifty years of marriage, she had never fully overcome her troubles with motion or her fear of heights, but for this, she always exerted herself.

"Are you certain of this, Grandfather?" Twenty-one-year-old Fitzwilliam Darcy stood beside his father, Bennet Darcy, and eyed the ageing vehicle with open scepticism. "It looks hardly stable."

"You will not deter Mother," Bennet informed his son. "And woe to him who tries."

"Indeed, saucy boy," Elizabeth Darcy took her husband's hand and stepped up to the basket with a tart little smile. "Such you shall discover for yourself well enough, if you persuade Miss Bingley to have you."

"Miss Bingley! Pray, do not tease me, Grandmother. There is nothing in it. Are you certain you are well? Father or I could attend you, if you insist on this venture. How will you manage?"

At this, the elder Fitzwilliam Darcy turned and very firmly closed the gate with his own hand, levelling a stern look of command to both his heir and heir-apparent. "We have all we need."

The balloon master was given the order, and father and son stood back, helpless to protest as the basket began to lift from the ground. From there, they could see the thrill of terror when it first shook Mrs Darcy, but then the nearly instantaneous peace when her husband bent low to speak words of encouragement in her ear. The last sight the younger men would have of the couple's faces was of cheeks nearly touching, heads turned together, and fingers laced as one.

"Father, I still do not understand," protested the son. "Why should they have been so eager to grace this tumbling ruin with their patronage? Why, the crowds later will be monstrous, and it is not as if there is anything left of mystery to see. It is all to close down, and I hear the new owners plan on building houses. It makes no sense that they were so adamant to come. And why were they so insistent upon a balloon ride, of all things, that Grandfather would have paid such an exorbitant sum for a private tour? He hates throngs of people, and this," he gestured to their surroundings with marked distaste, "is disgraceful."

Bennet Darcy chuckled as he watched the balloon lift his parents away. "Have you never heard how they first met?"

"Grandmother always promised to tell me one day when I was older. She claims it some shocking tale, but do you know, I believe she was simply teasing. You know how she is, and Grandfather only encourages her."

"And well he might. They saved one another, you could say."

"And it had something to do with…" another sneer of disdain, "this place?"

Bennet laughed. "Have you never seen that silver admission tag that your grandmother keeps in her reticule? It was from the summer of '11, and she never stirs from the house without it. Yes, they spent a day together here, a tradesman's niece and a footman. It ought to have ruined them both, but instead, it was the making of them."

~

The shivers had subsided, and Elizabeth's fingers now rested easily in Darcy's. His cheek brushed hers, his breath was soft and warm in her ear. She turned enough to catch his eye. "One last time, my love."

"What will everyone think?" his voice rumbled low in his chest.

"What they have thought for years—that Mr and Mrs Darcy have a most improper marriage. That is only fitting, after how we began."

His hands, still clasping hers, lifted from her sides to wrap tightly round her, and he drew her close enough to nuzzle the back of her neck. "I miss the simpler gowns of former days. This is a beastly contraption, and I do not understand how you can move in it," he groused.

"And requires much assistance in its removal," Elizabeth reminded him. "But so far, I can make do with only a footman."

"If you do not take care," he warned her, "I shall be forced to shock even our good balloon master here."

"I doubt he will object, after what you have paid for the privilege."

Darcy turned her in his embrace; slowly, so that she might not be unsettled. Her hands now slid up his chest, and she shamelessly kissed his chin. "Do you know, Fitzwilliam is certain we shall fall to our deaths, and the family shall forever bear the stain of its patriarch meeting his end in such an ignoble way. He reminds me a good deal of his namesake."

"Like all Darcy firstborns, he was named for his mother—who happened to have been Richard's daughter. It was not for myself, if that is your implication."

"You know very well that none who have any memory at all can look at him without seeing you all over again, full of yourself and certain of your own importance. I fear it shall be a dreadful shock for him!"

"What shall, my love?"

"Have you not guessed it? He is head over ears for my grand-niece, but he is too proud to confess it. That is why I take care to tease him regularly on the topic."

"She scarcely knows he exists, save as a nuisance."

"And that, my love, is what makes it so delicious! She will bruise his vanity rather badly, but he has your stubbornness—"

"And yours."

"Precisely. I think he will make a go of it once he has sufficiently blundered and then made his recovery."

"See here, Elizabeth, I did not pay so much for you to tell me of my own grandson's resemblance to myself. I can see that very well from the ground. Look there."

Still with his arms round her, she turned her head to the northwest. They were well clear of the trees now, and she had nearly forgotten the shifting of the floor beneath her feet as the ageing basket squeaked in the gentle summer breeze. Beyond the borders of the park, they could see the Vauxhall bridge, built some years after their first visit, while Westminster, untouched by the fingers of time, stood on the opposite side of the river and more to the north. Far beyond she could see toward Hyde Park, where Prince Albert's dazzling Crystal Palace had been first raised, then removed in less time that it had taken their youngest grandchild to learn to read. The wheat fields across the river had fallen under cobblestone, and old wooded areas had become houses.

"So much has gone away," she lamented. "And we shall nevermore see what was so dear to us!"

"Do you think? I see it every day."

She looked back to the man she had loved for nearly half a century. His face was lined, his thick black hair now a strikingly handsome silver, but his eyes had never changed. They were those which had wept with her, rejoiced with her, which had seen all that was good and wicked within her, and yet still gazed with adoration each morning when they found her. She traced his cheek. "And do you have no regrets, William?"

"Only one."

"And that is?"

"Something I ought to have told you long ago. Prepare yourself, for you shall be astonished."

She raised her brows and waited. He always seemed to enjoy watching the suspense build within her, so she simply smiled back with serene patience. There was nothing here but sweet, warm air, brilliant sheets of colour filling the sky, and him. She was in no hurry to look elsewhere.

He bent low and whispered in her ear. "I am terrified of this contraption. I always have been, though I refused to let you see it. Each time we have set foot aboard, I have feared it would be the last. The only thing which lends me courage is you, and the certain knowledge that if I fall, it shall be in your arms. My greatest regret is that I never told you how you have freed me from the fear of what may come."

She raised up and kissed him, glorying in the strong arms which still bound her to his heart. His lips caressed hers with the abandon of youth, his hands still cradled her as tenderly and ardently as if she were a new bride, and neither gave a second thought for the poor balloon master, who was likely covering his eyes.

She drew back and brushed a hint of sentiment from those dark, expressive eyes she knew so well. "Let us live this day, William, just as we did the first, as if it might be our last. Hold me, and do not let me fall."

He kissed her forehead, her cheek, then her neck as he pulled her tightly against him. "At your service, madam."

Printed in Great Britain
by Amazon